BROKEN BAY

By the same author

CUTTERS END
STONE TOWN

BROKEN BAY

MARGARET HICKEY

BANTAM
SYDNEY AUCKLAND TORONTO NEW YORK LONDON

BANTAM

UK | USA | Canada | Ireland | Australia
India | New Zealand | South Africa | China

Bantam is part of the Penguin Random House group of companies
whose addresses can be found at global.penguinrandomhouse.com

Penguin
Random House
Australia

First published by Bantam in 2023

Cover photography by Jarrod Andrews
Cover design by Christabella Designs
Author photograph © Charlotte Guest
Typeset in 12.5/17.5 pt Adobe Garamond Pro by Midland Typesetters, Australia

Printed and bound in Australia by Griffin Press, an accredited
ISO AS/NZS 14001 Environmental Management Systems printer

A catalogue record for this
book is available from the
NATIONAL LIBRARY OF AUSTRALIA
National Library of Australia

ISBN 978 0 14377 726 7

penguin.com.au

MIX
Paper | Supporting
responsible forestry
FSC® C018684

We at Penguin Random House Australia acknowledge that Aboriginal and Torres Strait Islander
peoples are the Traditional Custodians and the first storytellers of the lands on
which we live and work. We honour Aboriginal and Torres Strait Islander peoples'
continuous connection to Country, waters, skies and communities. We celebrate
Aboriginal and Torres Strait Islander stories, traditions and living cultures;
and we pay our respects to Elders past and present.

For Mrs Reynolds, Miss Richardson, Mrs Cavigan,
Mr Hickey, Mr Quillinan and Mr Bourke

Adelaide Advertiser, 1 September 2022

CAVE DIVING EXCITEMENT AT LATEST SINKHOLE OFFERING

In a historic first, Australia's leading cave diver, Mya Rennik, will tomorrow afternoon enter the pristine waters of a Limestone Coast sinkhole that has until now been unmapped. The owner of the land on which the sinkhole sits has reached a deal with Cave Diving Australia for limited use of the cave below his property.

'We've always known about the sinkholes,' Mr Frank Doyle stated. 'Back in the day, people used to throw old tractor parts and carcasses down them. Now we've discovered this one here, well, what with all the interest in the area, might as well find out what's down there.'

Ms Rennik estimates the initial underwater cavern to be roughly 200 metres wide and 30–40 metres deep, with numerous tunnels leading to other as yet unexplored caves. 'Given the extensive network of the Limestone caves, we hope to begin mapping the tunnels and laying out lines so that cave divers from all over the world can appreciate the beauty that lies beneath this unassuming land,' she said yesterday.

PROLOGUE

Away from all the cameras and the spectators, Mya does what she knows best, what she longs to do, and that's be underwater by herself. For all her accolades and recognition in the field, it comes down to this: the sense of beauty and wonder she feels in the subterranean world. It's an honour, of course, to be chosen to be the one to lay line in an undiscovered cave, and there's even talk of naming the chamber after her. People go on and on about her supposed fearlessness and competitive nature but all that stuff fades away when she's down here, in the blue.

Through the small hole up on the surface, she can still make out the rounded shadows of heads peering down. They'll be taking note of her time, checking the equipment, side-eyeing the press and onlookers who've come to gawk at her achievement. Most of them are open water divers; they don't understand the attraction of what she's doing. She gives them a thumbs up before returning to focus on her shimmering surrounds. The white limestone, the water, clear as air. She holds the reel below and beside her, then tugs on it gently, feeling its tightness. Her first tie-up is to a jutting rock, tinged with green. Divers that come after her will appreciate its visibility and distance from the cavern walls.

Down, down another thirty metres and she's almost at the bottom. She chooses a white rock shaped like a wizard's hat to make a second tie. Now she scans the surroundings, the stalactites, the cave coral, and the waving emerald fronds, and there – *there!* A gap in the cavern wall.

Mya slows her breathing. She knows to do this when she feels an adrenaline surge and, using small ridges in the limestone, she glides over to the gap. Her torch highlights a definite hole and, tantalisingly, another dim light in the distance beyond it. It's narrow – cave divers don't refer to such places as 'squeezes' for nothing – but she's been through tighter. She can do this. Timing is good, oxygen levels good, breathing good. Her tank is side-mounted for this reason, as she'll need to be as flat as she can to get through.

She ties off a sideline to take with her and moves into position, angling into the space, the tank scraping the wall, disturbing a small amount of silt. She waits a few seconds for it to settle. The squeeze continues for half a metre. The floor of the tunnel grazes her face as she edges forward. Calm. Slow, slow. The space is too tight for her to look at her watch, but she knows she needs to get a move on, and besides, she couldn't turn around in this space if she tried. Slow. She can do this.

There's a small rock in front of her; she moves it and continues. Another touch to the right side of the tunnel and this time she waits only a second before gliding through the silt that billows as a result, to where the space becomes a tunnel, around one metre high and two metres wide. Light in front, that's good. Timing is fine, though she'll have to think about returning soon.

She's nearly at one third of her oxygen and that's the rule to head home: a third to get down, a third to return and a third for emergencies. The tunnel opens and she's through, she's through!

The space is enormous. It's a cathedral, glittering dark blue and silver. She makes a sound in her mask, a muffled whoop. As big as a football stadium – bigger. *This is why we do it*, she thinks, as she twirls around. This feeling: you're the first human ever to set eyes on a place.

Prickles of light glisten on the walls around her, more tunnels. There are years of exploring to do here, years, and the thought gives Mya immense pleasure. She takes a minute to soak it in and just marvel at the space. But practicalities remain; this was only meant to be an observation dive. She has to get moving.

First, she must tie off the sideline – it will make it easier for divers after her – and she looks around for a suitable place. There's a ledge nearby and she glides over to it, quicker now. In her haste she swipes the side with her flipper and silt fills her vision, thicker than before. She swears, but manages to find a protruding rock on the ledge and begins to work the rope, tying quickly in the torchlight fastened to her head. The silt clears slightly and just for an instant she sees a dark shape on the rock shelf. A moment of confusion. The silt grows thick again and she blinks. It's gone. But even so, she glides down towards the shelf, and as she does so, the silt begins to clear.

The oval shape is there. Can it be? A stab of confusion. *Keep calm*, she thinks. She reaches out to touch the object and when it rolls towards her, she feels a deep dread. Her breath is becoming heavier and she takes out her hand-held torch, the strong one, and rests it on the ledge for further clarity, peering at the thing once more.

It's an old oxygen tank, covered in thick silt. A tank. Here? No time to ponder its presence. Get moving. Her flipper scrapes the wall.

More silt and – no! Now the torch is caught in her sideline. In the beam of her headlight, she attempts to untangle the rope from the torch, tries to slow her breathing. One loop over the torch, it should be easy, but the rope is a snarl of blue string and, looking at her watch with a start, she decides to leave. The tangled rope and torch will have to stay.

It's time to go, it's really time to go.

Mya glides for half a metre before she's jolted to a stop. Looking behind her, she sees something impossible – another line? Her sideline is blue and now this, an orange line which is tangled up with her flipper. She bends down, grabs onto the rope and yanks it. The effort takes too much energy. *Breathe.* She's trapped in the rope. *Breathe.* Oxygen levels now into the last third.

Leave. Now.

Mya takes out her knife, flicks it open and moves to cut the orange line. It's become entangled with her sideline now, a snarl of orange and blue. *Cut the rope!* Her hands are deliberate and then frantic as she fails to free herself. She's breathing too fast. Silt rises again in a cloud. *Too much movement.*

Her hands are shaky, panicky, but she does not stop. She tugs the rope, and there are more tangles now and maybe she's cut her finger and her knife is making strange slicing movements – and yet, it is only when she becomes aware of the looming figure rising up in the silt and sees the ghostly mask, inches from her own, that Mya understands she won't be going home.

CHAPTER 1

Arctic wind lashed the boat. Judy and Phil, in silent communication, began pulling the nets back in. Big orange cylinders, soaking and heavy. Their daughter Georgia, sure-footed on the unsteady deck, checked all twenty as they landed on the hull. Empty, every single one.

'I'll tell you what's not human,' Phil was saying. 'Diving underground. What nutcases do that nowadays?'

'This nutcase.' Judy retrieved a newspaper from her back pocket and stabbed her finger at the photo on the front page. 'Says here she was the female world record holder for deep cave diving.'

'Rocks in her head.'

'Well, it's still a tragedy.'

'*You* both dive,' Georgia pointed out. '*You're* divers.'

'In the ocean. Not in some bloody pit in the ground.'

The family packed the nets away in silence. Above their heads, the painted red sign reading *Sinclair Lobsters, finest in SA!* hung like a speech bubble from a bad cartoon.

The old boat strove against the wind and rain until landmarks on the shore became visible. There was the old whaling factory, there was the Catholic church, there was the outline of Coles.

'You all right now, love?' Judy turned her attention to him.

Mark Ariti nodded, white knuckles tight on the rail, his back to the callous sea. After all the vomiting, he'd broken into a cold sweat, head thumping, dizzy with nausea. Concentrating on what the family was saying and doing had helped. A little.

'Things will look up, Phil,' Judy said to her husband. 'Come summer, our fishing trips will be booked out!'

Phil looked at her, glum.

'So, what happened?' Georgia asked. 'If that Mya person was so great at diving, how come she died?'

Her father looked at the deck almost angrily. 'We don't know how. What they're saying on the radio is that when she didn't resurface, other divers went down the sinkhole to look for her and saw that she'd gone through a squeeze. None of them were qualified enough to go through, so they're waiting on experts to retrieve her body.'

Georgia frowned. 'She can't have been that good if she couldn't make it back out.'

'Oh, she'd have been good all right,' Phil said, nodding at the sea as if it was agreeing with him. 'But being good isn't enough in cave diving. You have to be outstanding, and lucky. And stupid.'

The young teenager shrugged. Stepping into the cabin, she shut the door hard behind her.

'There'll be an inquiry,' Judy mused. 'More people in town.'

Phil shook his head and held his hand up to ward off a sharp ray of sunshine cutting through the grey. 'Should just leave the body there and cover the hole up. No point endangering others.'

'The family will want to bury her.' Judy rolled up the newspaper and stuck it in her bag. 'If it was Georgia down there, I'd want her back.'

'Georgia would never be that stupid,' Phil said, although on that note he looked doubtful.

'*We* should get into the cave diving industry,' Georgia called from inside the cabin, her little face poking through the window. 'Forget about the daytrippers and the fishing charters. We could cater to the divers of the world.'

'Not on your nelly,' her dad shouted back. 'Lobsters at least have got a bit of sense.'

Judy gave Mark a gentle pat on the shoulder, handed him some water. 'You're looking green again, love. Take some small sips.'

'Perfect day for it,' Phil commented. 'Five knots, sea's not quite half a metre, count yourself lucky. Cold, choppy, but yesterday the swell was up to three metres.'

God, I hate the ocean, Mark thought.

'Still,' Judy said, chirpy, 'you caught a nice flathead, Mark. I'll gut it for you so you can have it for dinner.'

Mark only liked fish that was battered and covered in tartare sauce. He didn't want the fish, tried to reject the offer with a weak wave.

'Squeeze of lemon, pinch of pepper and you'll have the best meal of your life.' Judy hauled the fish out of an esky and slapped it onto a bench in the centre of the deck. 'Bit of lettuce on the side, slice of tomato and bob's your uncle.' She slid a knife into the belly of the fish and its guts fell out. 'You've had a bit of sea sickness,' she continued, her skilful knife moving through the flesh, 'but it's been a good day, hasn't it? You're one of our first charter customers – we'll want a true assessment, the good and the bad.'

A small piece of curled innards fell on Mark's shoe. He croaked something.

'What's that, love?'

'I said, it's—'

The boat caught the bottom of a wave, dipped low and then heaved up again. Mark turned, leaned over the side and retched. Long strings of saliva blew about in the wind like spiderwebs. He burped, then spewed again. After a wretched minute, he slumped back onto the bench, wiping his hand across his mouth. 'It's probably the best day of my life.'

What else could he say? That he hated every moment, hated his sister Prue for giving him the voucher for an ocean fishing trip in Broken Bay, hated the unpredictable weather, hated the diesel fumes and the relentless waves?

Judy gave a short laugh. 'You'll survive,' she said. 'I remember when I first went out with Phil years ago – thought I was dying when we left the heads.'

Mark peered up at the woman as he tried a sip of water. Like her husband, Judy's face was a synoptic weather chart, etched hard with swirled wrinkles and dark freckles, deep lines rushing from chin to neck in a strong current. Clear blue eyes, the exact colour of the sea, and a wiry body. But while Phil had the same weathered look, they differed greatly in build. He was a burly giant – a sea captain character from a children's book. *He should have a pipe out the side of his mouth and a parrot on his shoulder*, Mark thought. Only the bird would be blown to Antarctica in half a second.

At the start of the voyage – because that's how Mark liked to think of it, *a voyage* – Phil had told him not to fight the rocking of the boat. Stand legs apart, move with it, like it's a horse. And only now, returning into the bay, was Mark game to try it, getting up from the bench. The waves were smaller, choppy, and foam smacked hard into his face, but his new stance made him feel less weak. For the second time in three hours, he took stock of the empty cray nets, sodden ropes and faded sign.

'Not a good season?' Mark asked.

'Something's off with the crays.' Phil shrugged. 'Water's too warm or too hot – can't tell these days, probably both.'

'Nowadays trout's rare in the river where I'm from. Used to catch them easy. It's the droughts, or the floods.'

'Or the fires,' Judy piped up.

The three grew silent. They knew what it was. Felt the slow dread each time the temperature edged into the thirties in winter, or when creeks overflowed in February. There had been two mass fish kills in the past three years in Mark's hometown of Booralama, the sight of them a horror: massive cods, floating dead on the surface, others panting in the shallows.

'From up north, aren't you?' Phil asked, and Mark nodded. 'Nice country, but I couldn't live there. Start to feel antsy if I'm more than three days away from it.' The big man threw his arm out towards the ocean.

'I'm more of a river man,' Mark said.

'You don't say,' Judy quipped, and they all smiled.

Judy slowed the boat and steered them into the mouth of the river where the jetties were now lined with old fishing vessels and tinnies and the odd yacht. Golden light on the water shimmered, peaceful. Deceitful.

'Come with us for a beer,' Phil suggested. 'You're one of our first customers on Sinclair Tours and we owe you one after this trip.'

Mark needed a Panadol and a lie-down, but the beaming couple looked so pleased by the idea that he agreed. They arranged to meet in an hour at the Royal.

After stumbling weak-kneed onto the jetty and then into his car, Mark drove back to the Hibernian Motel, his home for the next two nights. The streets were wide and bare, bluestone gutters gleamed hard in the afternoon light and, out of all the shops, only Coles and the bottle-o were open. Broken Bay was a small town, tough, full of ugly buildings and squat houses. Perhaps it was on the verge of discovery by sea changers, but the wave of city cash seemed a while off yet. An old whaling station and Catholic church on the main street were the only grand structures, and what that signified required a clearer head. *The body and the blood.*

He pulled into the car park of the motel and waved to Ian Bickon, the mule-faced owner. Ian was hosing a dying camellia with serious intent, staring into the dirt, the stream at full pressure. Was Ian *waterboarding* the plant?

Once inside his room, Mark pulled off his shoes and lay on one of the single beds, looking up at the salmon-coloured ceiling. It reminded him of the curled piece of guts on the boat and, with some relief, he realised he'd forgotten to bring the flathead home.

It was 5.30 pm. A stiff breeze blew through the open window, the lace curtains rising up in a bad burlesque. An arm's length away, the second bed lay frigid and cold. Ian had placed him in a room with two singles rather than a queen because, he explained, Mark had come to Broken Bay on his own. Mark had been tempted to tell Ian about Rose, maybe even show him a photo, boast to Ian that his beautiful girlfriend was a doctor. But then he'd have to admit the reality of their looming split.

Mark reached for the bedside lamp and flicked it on. It was all decided – after months of deliberation and lengthy discussion, Rose was off to Tanzania for a year working as a medic in a town south of Dar es Salaam. Visa sorted and flights booked, Rose was due to leave in a week. She'd asked him to go with her, and he had said no. A no-man's-land had expanded between them, memories curdling like photos in the heat. Mark had his boys, he'd built a life in his hometown, had his friends, the house. Rose knew all that, Rose liked all that – but still Rose was going. She held a dim view of long-distance relationships. Dim. As someone who'd previously lived in Broome while her ex-partner was in Hobart, she said she knew how it was likely to go. Mark got the message. He could have explained to mule-faced Ian that perhaps he and Rose weren't meant to make it. She didn't have children and, while she liked his, clearly preferred it when his two sons were not around. She found Booralama dull on weekends – it mostly was – and she liked to go to yoga retreats and camp at music festivals; he did not. She was funny and smart and good-looking . . . but he and Rose were over. She was already talking about a move to Kenya after Tanzania.

Mark closed his eyes and thought about the women he knew. If he really pressed Ian, held him down and forced him to listen to his relationship woes, he might have told the man about his ex-wife, Kelly, mother of his two boys, and how they had built an amicable relationship. Or even about his friend and colleague Jagdeep, steadfast in loyalty and grit. If after that Ian still showed signs of life, Mark could tell tales about his sister, Prue, his friend Donna and his mother, Helen, dead now for over a year.

But Ian wouldn't care. And who could blame him? Ian only liked to inflict torture on plants. And good on him. *Good on you, Ian.*

Mark had a shower, then stood side-on in front of the mirror while he towelled himself, noting the puff of grey chest hair and gut. A whole lifestyle away from a six-pack, but running three times a week helped to stave off elastic waists and man boobs. He moved to face the mirror, sucked in his stomach and wondered at the years since he was a teenager, when stripping off his T-shirt at the local pool had been a kind of joy.

Mark flicked on the small TV and caught the tail end of a story about the cave diver Mya Rennik. Local farmer Frank Doyle was meeting with Australian cave diving experts to discuss the prospect of diving there after Mya failed to surface from the sinkhole on his property. 'With increased safety measures, the ever-growing sport could offer substantial tourism funding for the area, now that the lobster and dairy industries are in freefall,' the young journalist concluded, sober faced.

Mark's phone rang: Prue.

'How was your time with Sinclair Tours?' she asked.

'Like *The Poseidon Adventure*.' Mark began putting on his clothes. 'Only worse.'

'*That* bad?'

Once he'd done up his shirt buttons with one hand, he sat on the bed to put on his shoes. 'Prue, you know how much I hate the sea.'

His sister put her hand over the phone, calling out to someone in the background. 'Yes, yes,' she said. 'But really, you've only been in a boat on the ocean, what – twice, three times? Twice in a tinny with Dad and me, and the other on a boat off Hamilton Island. You've got to give these things a chance! Be more adventurous!'

Mark considered: the boat off Hamilton Island with his friend Dennis was on relatively calm waters and the main reason for his vomiting was the bourbon and prawns. The tinny, though, that was a distant memory, infused with a strange anxiety. 'Where were we in that tinny?' he asked.

'Port Fairy in Victoria one time and the other, Broken Bay! Where you are now. Don't you remember? It was just you and Dad. You went down there for a boys' weekend.'

'I was a kid, Prue. I can barely remember.'

'You both had the best time!'

Mark made a doubtful humph.

His sister began telling him about all the times she'd been sailing with her husband in English Bay, Vancouver. How they'd take their three sons and go fishing for salmon and halibut and how sometimes they'd dock their boat at some bay, crack open some nice beers and—

'What's it like being rich, Prue?' Mark asked, staring at the painting of leaping dolphins on the wall opposite. One dolphin was smiling and a ray of sunshine bore down on the beaming creature. 'Like, really rich?'

'It's good.' Prue was always honest. 'Less to worry about. Rich people don't stoop, ever noticed that? You should bring the boys here for a holiday.'

'Yeah.' He should.

'And what's your accommodation like? You book somewhere nice?'

'Sheer luxury.'

'How's Rose?'

'She's great, just great.'

They chatted for a few more minutes; Prue asking the questions, Mark answering, before he checked his watch and said he had to go.

It was close to six o'clock. Outside, the wind made a high keening sound and somewhere nearby a door banged on its hinges. So he and his father came to Broken Bay on holiday when he was a kid. Why? Mostly they went to Queensland to visit cousins, long trips in a hot car with his parents smoking the entire time. Why had they come on a father–son holiday to the far east of South Australia? His parents hated the cold. Vague memories of grey water and a brittle wind hovered in his mind. The memory lingered, then died.

CHAPTER 2

The Royal smelled of warm booze and old carpet. Low ceilings, wooden beams and a huge fireplace gave the impression of an English pub. Only the massive television, spewing out betting ads for the AFL, gave it away. Mark spotted the Sinclairs on high stools around a table near the window – a view of the grey sea behind them like the backdrop in a Scandinavian film.

Mark walked over, greeted the couple, and Phil moved to buy him a beer. Other patrons, mostly old, nodded at the big man as he stepped up to the bar. He paused to chat with a woman wearing a bright pastel dress, leaning in, listening to what she had to say.

'All talk's of that cave diver,' Judy told Mark. 'People coming into the town, press and whatnot, wanting to be there when she's brought back up. Police haven't let on when it's going to happen, so it's all a bit of a mystery.'

Normally, Mark knew, police divers would retrieve a body. But cave diving required a different set of skills. Police divers would still be called in, but all cameras would be on the experts sent down to rescue a mate. There wasn't a full-time police presence in Broken Bay – as in most small country towns, the old police station was largely unmanned – so cops from Adelaide would have travelled the four-and-a-half hours down to be on guard. Mark didn't envy the city cops having to leave their homes for an investigation. In two more nights, he'd be back in Booralama and working in his own station, staffed by him full time, and another cop two days a week.

'So, when's your best bet, Judy?' Mark asked, mainly out of politeness. 'When do you reckon they'll bring the diver up?'

'I'm not sure,' she mused. 'But it'd have to be soon.'

Phil returned, placing two pints and a white wine on their table. 'Police are keeping a tight lid on it, but Cherie reckons it's happening tomorrow morning. Divers are already camped at Doyle's, planning the retrieval. Because no one's ever been down there before, they've called in the big guns.'

'Who's that?'

'Man by the name of David Furneaux. Another world champion. Good friend of the one who didn't come up.'

The cave diving community would be relatively small, and it was a good bet that all the serious cave divers would know one another. How many people would want to put themselves through that?

'Cherie's the fount of all knowledge.' Judy spoke to Mark out of the side of her mouth while she waved to the woman at the bar. 'Cherie Swinson. Used to be an actress. There was a time she'd put on little plays in her living room, called them the "Sunday Soirees". Quite good too, though her Eva Peron wasn't much.'

'That's not all Cherie said,' Phil continued. 'Gerri Doyle's selling up, apparently.'

'*What?*'

Mark sat bemused between the gossipy couple. He drank his beer, felt his shoulders relax, and looked out to where the sea was now a calm silver, glistening in the moonlight. Or was it streetlight?

'Yep, put her house on the market.' Phil took a large swig of beer. 'Says she's out of here. Shouldn't come as a surprise.'

'But there's another term to go! What about her teaching?'

Phil shrugged. 'Probably got sick of living in the same town as her father. That can't be easy. To be honest, I never understood why she's stuck around this long.'

'Yes, but . . .' Judy shook her head, picked up her wineglass, then placed it down again. She turned to Mark, explaining, 'Gerri's the daughter of Frank Doyle, the man whose farm has that sinkhole that's got all these divers excited. She's lovely. Our daughter's favourite teacher, been here since she was born.'

'Doesn't mean she has to stay forever,' Phil added.

'No, but . . .' Judy looked upset. 'She's always been so close to the family.'

Mark stared into his beer, then finished it in one glug. He stood and tipped his glass to Phil. 'Another?' The man nodded, asked for a mid-strength. 'Judy?' She shook her head and Mark made his way to the bar.

The woman named Cherie gave him a deliberate once-over. 'Hellooo there,' she said, lowering her fake eyelashes and shifting about on her stool.

'Hi.' Mark ordered the beers, trying not to look at the squirming woman.

'You friends with the Sinclairs?' Cherie, who looked to be in her late sixties, reeked of cigarette butts. She raised her hand to flick away a curled lock. Bangles up and down her wrinkled arm rang in tinny unison.

'Just been on one of their tours. Can't recommend it enough.'

'Well, good for you.' The woman wriggled closer. 'They're doing it tough, and Phil hasn't had an easy life. So sad.' Cherie sniffed and dabbed at her nose daintily, Southern Belle style.

The beers arrived and Mark thanked the barman.

'You know,' Cherie said with a coy smile, 'I think I recognise you. Are you an actor?'

It happened sometimes. People recalled his name, had a vague memory of his face from when he'd been, for a short time, a celebrated cop after a number of high-profile cases. His profession meant that he didn't enjoy the brief adulation; it was best to keep a low profile in case disgruntled ex-crims or those associated with them took note.

'Let's take a selfie!' Cherie's voice rose in excitement. 'Here!' Without asking for permission, Cherie whipped out a phone. 'Say rhubarb!'

Annoyed but not enough to protest, Mark said 'rhubarb' as the flash went off. He was aware of Cherie's damp hand on his arm and felt a sliver of distaste. 'Well, I'll be off to Phil and Judy,' he said, moving away and grabbing the beers.

Cherie stared mournfully into her wineglass. 'Those poor women . . .' She trailed off.

Mark paused, conflicted between wanting to know more and wanting to get away – but Cherie had turned on her stool and was talking to someone else. He made his way back across the room to the Sinclairs. They'd been joined by a red-haired man, maybe early forties, in a neat, checked shirt and jeans.

'This is James Doyle,' Judy said. 'It's his farm the sinkhole's on. His father, Frank, is the one that's been on the news, and his twin sister is Gerri – the teacher we were talking about. James is just telling us about the search for the diver.'

Mark reached out his hand and introduced himself. The two men shook.

'We're still trying to work out when the retrieval's happening,' Judy said.

'Judy writes a piece for the local paper,' Phil explained. 'She's not usually this much of a stickybeak.'

'It's not just me!' Judy said. 'The whole country is interested.'

Judy and Phil turned expectantly to James. 'So?' Judy asked, and James smiled.

'I really don't know, Judy,' he said. 'But there's a group of divers camped in the back paddock. Dad's sent me to buy beers for everyone.'

'That's a turn-up for the books,' Phil said, and the man gave a half-laugh.

'I know. I think he wants to keep in sweet with them – hopes they'll return and keep spending money. He's already charging them rent, you know.'

'The bugger!' Judy exclaimed.

'Well, you know what he's like, once he gets his mind stuck on something . . .'

Phil shook his head. 'I can just see it. Frank's new project: Cave diving capital of the world!'

'What do you reckon about it all?' Mark asked James, curious. 'Do you want people diving on your father's land?'

'It's his land too,' Phil pointed out, and Judy put a hand on her husband's forearm.

'I don't know.' James spoke carefully. 'We know how danger-ous the sinkholes are and I don't want anyone else dying. I still remember hearing about the Franklin Three – scared the life out of me as a kid.'

Mark sensed a collective shudder, racked his brain and couldn't recall anything on the subject. The Franklin Three: the title held gravity.

'But then again,' James continued, 'cave diving's become so popular, maybe Dad's right and we should capitalise on it. Dairy's not going anywhere.'

The pub door opened, and a group of men walked in, noisy.

'And we've just heard the news about your sister selling up!' Judy's voice rose. 'Where's she going?'

James shrugged. 'She says she'll go and see Teddy in Lincoln, maybe end up buying near there. You know what Gerri's like, always making plans.'

'Teddy is Gerri's son,' Judy explained to Mark. 'I still can't believe she's selling up!'

'She should get a good price for her house.' Phil turned to Mark. 'It's right in town.'

'Yeah, well, better get going,' James said, facing the door. 'Dad wanted these drinks pronto.'

Phil rolled his eyes. 'Can't hold the old man up.'

The group farewelled James and went back to their drinks. It was harder to hear in the bar now; the men who'd arrived were shouting across the room to each other and the TV volume was turned right up. Two Melbourne teams were playing, so not many were glued to the box. *They should turn it off,* Mark thought. *Get some music going.*

As if on cue, a tune started up. He strained to listen over the noise and there it was: drums, upbeat, a catchy rhythm and the vocals of Amy Winehouse. 'Valerie'. It made him happy and sad, this song. The beat was buoyant, but the words reminded him of Rose.

The Sinclairs stood and beckoned for him to follow. They walked out of the bar area into a dining room, old tables set with lace cloths and fake flowers, a sign that read *Live, Laugh, Love* on the wall. Mark imagined what it would be like if the entire population of the world was living, laughing and loving. Some sort of crazed music festival probably, where everyone was on Es and no one was watching the kids.

'So,' Mark said, leaning on the rounded bar. 'What is this Franklin Three?'

It was so quiet in the dining room, Mark missed the bustle of the bar. An old couple sat at a far table, both staring at their phones.

'It was a tragic accident,' Judy said.

'Happened years ago – what, '71?' Phil said, draining his glass. 'A year or so before I was born. The sinkholes had always been around here, we knew that, but no one made a big deal of them. They were used as dumping grounds, or to pump water from.'

'There's a whole aquifer under here, just below the surface,' Judy added. 'Fresh water, clear as gin.'

'Land's basically a giant pav,' Phil said. 'Cracks at the slightest.'

The Limestone Coast stretched from the Victorian border all the way to Kingston and northwards to Franklin. It was a strange land to Mark, all big sea and wetlands and wind. Booralama, with its dry northerlies and big river reds, was another world.

'When we were kids, our parents used to tell us, "Never go into the underwater caves, remember the Franklin Three?" It was like a ghost story. Everyone around here got told it.'

Mark felt as if he knew the story, a vague and frightening memory, in the same vein as the legendary tale of the girl trapped in her car and the tap-tap sound, which turns out to be the head of her boyfriend wielded by an axe murderer. He could feel himself adding the Franklin Three to childhood nightmares already fixed hard in his brain, along with drowning in quicksand, being hunted by Russians, and getting your shoelaces stuck in an escalator. 'What happened?' he asked.

'Geologists identified a sinkhole not too far from here, along Discovery Bay, in the mid-sixties I think,' Phil said. 'Locals called it "the Tomb". Two experienced divers went down there, only one came back. It was big news. Sinkhole got fenced off, danger signs erected, parents issued strong warnings.'

Judy joined in the story seamlessly. There was something heartening in it, Mark thought; a couple who knew each other's speech rhythms, the way they told a tale.

'But you know what kids are like,' she said, putting down her glass. 'They want to break the rules. And when they live out here, on farms or in the town, bored, with nothing to do – well the Tomb must have held this fascination. It certainly did for the Franklin Three. I know I was always drawn to it because of the story. Never went down it though.'

Drawn to it. An invisible thread pulling you in, leading you below.

'And a good thing too. Deathtraps, they are.' Phil stood, indicating their now empty glasses. 'One more? Then we'll have to go and pick up Georgia.'

Mark said yes. Judy put her hand over her glass and shook her head. 'I won't be right to drive if I have another.'

As Phil moved back out to the bar, his big head bent low at the rafters across the doorway, a group of three walked into the dining room, looked at the specials board, conferred, then walked out again. Mark had a quick glance at the meals on offer: the battered flathead held no appeal. If pressed, he'd choose the steak and chips.

He turned back to Judy as she continued the story. 'Three young locals from Franklin, a brother and a sister and one of their friends, broke in through the fenced-off area around the Tomb after a party. It was late. They'd been drinking – bottles of beer were found on the surface, along with a cassette recorder and smokes. That's what alerted authorities to them the next day. Their parents reported it when they didn't come home that night. Can you imagine?' Judy shivered. 'Phil's dad, Murray, was one of the divers who were sent to retrieve the bodies. He never got over it. And although Phil's one of the best ocean divers around here, you would never, ever get him in a cave as a result of the stories Murray used to tell. The three boys learned to scuba dive but it was always *no caves*.'

Mark took a sip of his beer, thought about the warnings people give to their kids. No underwater caves seemed a pretty sensible rule, even for ocean people.

'God, that sounds awful.'

Judy put down her wine. 'It was horrible, just horrible what the divers reported back.'

'What's that?' Mark asked, dread in his guts.

In the dim surroundings of the dining room, Judy's low voice was that of a professional raconteur. Mark leaned in.

'The divers found one of the kids in a tunnel leading down from the main entrance. He was the deepest of the three and facing the wrong way – theory is that he was suffering from narcosis and got confused which was the way out. He panicked and drowned.'

'Narcosis?' Mark wasn't hungry anymore.

'Nitrogen narcosis. Divers become confused, show poor judgement, have trouble focusing. It's like being drunk. Divers call it "the Martini effect". Every ten metres you go down, it's the same feeling as drinking one Martini. Poor kid was found at around forty metres.'

Phil returned, plonked the two beers on the table and sat, listening to his wife.

'The siblings were harder to find. It took Murray and Greg, the other retrieval diver, half the day to bring them both to the surface.'

Mark took a long sip of beer.

'The brother and sister had exited the main chamber and gone through a narrow passageway. Murray was the only one who was experienced enough to go through it.'

Phil looked deep into his pint and took up the story. 'By the time Dad worked out where the tunnel was and entered it, the silt had subsided. The siblings were found on the roof of a dome space further along, with no entrance to the surface. It was thought they'd disturbed the silt and then got lost – ascended straight up rather than going back along the tunnel they came through.'

Mark jumped as a door opened at the far end of the room. A man in an apron gave them a brief wave before turning to the specials board and wiping the words 'Steak and Chips' off with his sleeve. In its place, he wrote 'Fish of the Day' and then left.

'Greg said there were scratch marks all along the top of the dome. They were scrambling, desperate to find a way out.' Judy made scratching motions in the air with her fingers.

'So, you can see why we're not overly happy with Frank Doyle opening up this sinkhole to the public,' Phil said.

Mark could have added that today the dives would be regulated, safeguards put in place. Dive licences, proper fencing. But Judy's scratching in the air – he didn't say a thing.

'One thing's for sure,' Phil continued, and Mark noted the quiet pride in his voice. 'Dad was a hero that day. Hardly anyone else could have done what he did, bringing up the bodies of those kids.'

'Their families were so grateful.' Judy smiled sadly. 'They all wrote letters to him, didn't they, love? Murray allowed them to bury their children.'

'Sounds like one hell of a man,' Mark said.

Phil nodded into his empty beer. 'He really was.'

A lady walked past, said hello to Judy and Phil, asked them whether they were going to the working bee at the school. They were, but only for an hour because they had work to do on the boat. Mark's eye wandered over to the specials board again, he thought about ordering some chips.

'Anyway, must go, love.' Judy tapped her husband's arm. 'Georgia will be waiting.'

'Hope we haven't scared you off the place completely,' Phil said, rising. 'It's a great spot.'

'I came here on holidays when I was a kid, actually.'

'Really? Never know, I might have given you a dunking.' Phil was shaking his hand. 'Not many holidaymakers around here when I was growing up. We treated them pretty bad.'

Mark didn't remember that. He hardly remembered anything about the trip.

They walked out to the bar. Phil and Judy waved as they opened the big front door and a gust of sea wind swept in, making everyone in the bar gasp. *Impossible to hide from the elements here*, Mark thought. On the surface, bracing wind and savage seas; below, more danger still.

CHAPTER 3

Mark bought another beer and felt himself loosen with the effects. He looked at his watch. Dinner time, and he was alone. The beer went down his throat with no joy. Young blokes were now glued to the footy game, North Melbourne up by one point. Mark barracked for Port. His team was past its glory days but on the up, the pundits claimed. On. The. Up.

He should eat; thought about Fish of the Day and was instantly reminded of his catch on the boat, its pulsing body, its slimy guts. *Maybe not.*

At the bar, Cherie Swinson was laughing loud, head thrown back, bleached blonde hair like some aged popstar from the eighties. She caught him looking, gave a brazen wink. Mark stared into his beer. As a teenager, he'd kissed girls at blue light discos after they'd spewed from drinking too much Moselle. In his twenties, he'd slept with women because they were there. But now, he couldn't do it. Cherie's simpering gaze, her overt gestures, her outrageous flirting: she was an attractive woman, but she wasn't his type.

It's not you, Cherie, it's me.

Mark turned his gaze away from the crowd and onto the photographs lining the wall: rows and rows of black-and-white images, mostly fishing and football memorabilia. The winning teams of '85, '87 – blokes grinning, arms crossed in the traditional pose, fists pressed into biceps trying to make them bigger, hairdos modelled on *Miami Vice.* No netball photos. Women didn't exist then. In the early nineties there was another win, and there, in the triumphant Sharks line-up was Phil Sinclair – Captain – sitting proud in the middle of the front row. A big unit, his grin sending out wattage, making Mark smile back at the man even thirty years on. Another win for the Sharks eight years later – and this time, Phil was out, but two other Phil-lookalikes stood tall in the back row. Mark checked the names: Nic and Mat Sinclair. Marginally less built, but the same white hair as their older brother, the same strong features that drew you in. *Well,* Mark thought standing back, *the three Sinclair brothers from Broken Bay.*

Mark didn't have a brother. Only Prue. As a kid he'd pined for a sibling, an identical twin preferably, so they could fool teachers and classmates like in *The Parent Trap*, only way better and with no divorce. Prue and Mark didn't look alike. He was apparently the spit of his father, dark hair and hazel eyes, while Prue was fair like Helen, their mother. The Sinclair boys were startlingly similar.

Mark moved across the wall to earlier times. Black-and-white images of great whale carcasses on the beach, men standing on top of them in suits. A dead shark – huge mouth being held open by grinning blokes. A newspaper cutting from 1974 stuck in a frame – *Monster attack off Broken Bay*! and a young man showing a gnarled stump of an arm, beaming as if he'd won the lottery. Shark attack. Mark shuddered. Why all the smiling?

Was the man proud to have had his arm ripped off by a great white?

Back to the seventies now, another row of champions. It didn't take him long to find Murray Sinclair, father to Phil, Nic and Mat, and the man who'd helped recover the bodies of the Franklin Three. Like his eldest son, Murray was captain. Mark was about to turn his gaze away when he caught sight of another familiar name: Frank Doyle. Mark leaned in. Yes, the man looked like his son James, skinny and pale. A terry towelling hat pulled low. Frank Doyle's look was distracted, one side of the mouth pulled downward. What was he thinking? Mark narrowed his eyes; yet again, he'd forgotten to bring along his new glasses. He moved closer to the frame and looked again: it was the light, perhaps, but Frank Doyle's smile seemed more like a sneer.

A glance at his watch told him an hour had passed since the Sinclairs left, and Mark felt he should go. He wasn't at the stage yet of being the last in the pub, pushed out the door by some weary barman. Not yet. But still, he wasn't ready to head back to his hotel room with only the dolphins and mini bar for company. He decided on a walk.

Outside the Royal, Broken Bay was deserted save a lone car inching up the main drag. An aching wind gnawed at Mark's bones as he walked along, his shadow looming in the streetlight, broken glass treacherous on the path. He wasn't fit to drive. The Hilux could wait in the Royal car park until tomorrow.

The ocean was dark and choppy, no lights on the horizon. Next stop: Antarctica, the most isolated landmass on earth. In his mind, Mark saw ice mountains loom in pointy brilliance. Was it luminosity that sent early explorers that way? Why travel to a place where death came as easy as stepping out of your tent?

Shackleton et al were welcome to it, he thought. Antarctica's cadaverous beauty held no appeal for Mark.

An orange and yellow light in the distance hinted at a takeaway shop and Mark was suddenly ravenous. With hunger came a new sense of purpose and he quickened his steps along the damp street. A car slowed down, parked out the front of the shop and a tall man got out and walked in. Closer now, Mark read the name of the shop, King of Souva. There really is a higher force, he thought, his mood lightening considerably. A souvlaki was just what he needed. Something warm and familiar to soothe the drunk and lonely soul. *Praise be to Zeus.*

Inside, the tall, rangy man he'd seen walk into the shop was now on his way out and, with a sharp pang of recognition, Mark saw that he was without doubt one of the Sinclair brothers.

'Froggie!' the old man behind the counter called. 'You forgot your potato cakes!'

The lean man almost barged into Mark on his way back to collect a second package. 'Sorry, mate!' he said. 'Can't forget the essentials.'

'No, you cannot,' Mark agreed, standing by to let him pass. He scanned the menu before ordering his usual – lamb, garlic sauce, no tomato – and the old man got to work.

It was hot inside the shop. Mark got a Coke from the fridge and took a gulp. 'Was that one of the Sinclair brothers just now?' he asked, for no good reason.

The old man nodded. 'That was the youngest one, Mat.'

'Why'd you call him Froggie?'

The man took a knife from the bench, turned away and began carving the meat from the spinning cone. 'Everyone calls them that.' He shrugged.

'Froggie,' Mark pondered. Nothing about the Sinclair men looked reptilian to him. Were their eyes spaced far apart? He knew a bloke called Gecko for that reason – but no, not the white-haired football-star brothers and sons of Murray.

'I think it's because they're French. Philippe, Nicolas, Mathieu.' The old man turned back around, a plate of steaming meat in front of him. 'You know what Aussies are like. They don't call people by their proper names.'

Mark was taken aback. 'Yeah,' he said. 'I do know that. *I'm* Aussie.'

'And something else too though.'

'My father was Greek.'

'Thought so.' The old man sniffed in triumph. 'I can tell.'

'How?'

'It's just your look. There's something about you.'

No one had ever, ever said that to him. After his vasectomy, his ex-wife had commented that his balls made her think of the Elgin Marbles – but apart from that, nothing Greek at all in his features. 'What's the look?'

'It's just a look. Others like you can tell.'

'Where are *you* from then?'

'Here now. In the past, Livadia.'

'Right.' Mark had no idea where that was.

'Greece,' the old man added.

Mark nodded. Half-ashamed, though he hardly knew why.

'What's your name?' the old man asked as he poured garlic sauce over the meat and wrapped the souva.

'Mark.'

The old man gave him a look.

'Marcos.'

Another look.

'Marcos Ariti.'

'Aha.'

Mark cleared his throat, changed the subject. 'I was just at the pub with that bloke's' – he gestured outside – 'older brother, Phil. Nothing about him seemed French to me.'

The old man handed him his food. 'Their mother was Parisian. French enough for you, Marcos?'

Oui. He took a bite. Delicious. The UN should have a department devoted to them, emissaries could be sent across the world spreading souva joy. Mark took another bite, wondered what next to talk about. He didn't want to leave.

'They seem like a nice family, the Sinclairs.'

'They are.'

'Good at footy.'

The man made a noncommittal sound and began wiping the bench.

'You said "*was* Parisian". Did she pass away?'

'Killed herself.' The man stared hard into the drinks fridge, his wrinkled features sharp in the downlights, like an actor in a play. 'Jumped off the cape here, left Murray with four small children.'

Mark put down his souva and stared into the drinks fridge too, trying to see what it was the old man was looking for. Glass bottles glinted. A fly was caught on the inside, buzzing against the door. He frowned, trying to recall something. The sound of the fly was like a troubled idea beginning to thrum.

Another customer, a woman with a bandaid across her nose, entered the shop. Cancer scare? Mark touched the bridge of his own nose. At fifty-three, he was seeing more and more of them around: the after-fifty plaster. He hadn't noticed them when he was in his forties. *Sunspots, they'd be a good way to identify middle-aged white Australians in a police line-up*, he thought. Weird-shaped freckles, Coco Pop moles and melanoma scars. Mark felt his nose again, rubbed at the dry spot there. *Don't put it off*, he said to himself. *Join the after-fifty plaster party, it's where all the fun kids hang out.*

The old man turned to serve the woman and Mark, holding his unfinished souva, waved thanks before stepping out into the dark once more.

That night, lying on his single bed in the Hibernian, Mark wondered about names. He'd always been known as Mark. Only called Marcos when in trouble, or when his father had had too many drinks. Half Greek, half Australian.

Like the Sinclair boys: half Australian, half French. Names could be switched to suit the circumstances. They meant different things to different people.

At 3 am Mark woke with a hangover. Gulping water from the tap and dreading the day, he worked out what had been nagging him. The Sinclairs. There was the father, Murray, and the three sons. Why then had the old man in the Greek takeaway said that Murray's wife left four children when she died?

Mark stared into the mirror, face barely visible in the dim light, not sure why it bothered him so.

But it did. He'd seen photos of three Sinclair offspring.

Who was the fourth?

CHAPTER 4

When he woke again three hours later, it took Mark a few seconds to remember where he was. His legs dangling uncomfortably over the edge of the narrow single bed brought him back.

Aha, he thought, the dolphin picture confirming it, *I'm in purgatory.*

Back when he'd first booked this stay, and before she'd made her decision on Tanzania, Mark had planned on Rose being with him in Broken Bay. He thought that today they'd be driving up to the coast, having a picnic somewhere, checking out the beaches. There was a petrified forest up the road that sounded frightening yet cool. But now, Rose wasn't with him, and you never enter a petrified forest on your own.

He kicked off the floral doona and lay for a moment, staring up at the ceiling. His boys were with Kelly on a week's holiday in Noosa, the highlight going to the movies to see *Batman*. Kelly would probably buy them outfits to wear for the occasion, capes and stuff. How could he compete with her holidays? He should really up the stakes, take the boys to Disneyland. Wear Mickey Mouse ears, eat corn dogs. The thought made Mark shudder.

For the Christmas holidays, he'd promised camping in the Flinders Ranges. *Take that, Donald Duck.*

With a heavy sigh, Mark dressed in running gear and stepped into a brittle morning. Early Saturday, and Broken Bay was deathly quiet. He checked the map and headed towards the sea. One kilometre across town and there it was, grey and restless under a low sky. A few walkers with dogs were striding down the main street, puffer jackets tight, green bags held piously aloft, while a stiff breeze was bending the coastal trees low. Everything was in supplication to the wind.

Picking up his pace, Mark jogged west, past the King of Souva and Coles. In the supermarket car park, a pale-faced girl was rounding up trolleys with a scowl. Mark didn't blame her, he'd seen one near the jetty and another in the middle of a roundabout.

Fifteen minutes in, and Mark began to ease into the run. This was usually how it went: agony, then the settling and later, the aches. For now, he was in the good part and, breathing in the sharp sea air, he could see for the first time the appeal of the place.

The vast bay curved like a crescent moon and hugged the foot of the town, bordered by sand dunes covered in tough grass and shrubs. Mark panted as the path began a sharp incline, weaving up towards what he gathered was the head of the cape. The water from this angle was a deep blue, and the waves formed long, clear lines to shore. What a contrast to the day before! In the sunlight it looked like an extended silver rope sat at the tip of each crest, and he followed its progress as it rose and fell.

Mark sweated and goaded himself up to the top – *Move it, Ariti, you fat bastard* – where he turned around. There it was, the whole of the bay and the world beyond, the Limestone Coast, a jagged blue edge that clung to the shore from Victoria to the Coorong. Sinkholes all over it, Phil had said. The surface a pav. Underneath: another world.

To the right the ocean spread out wide, the beach rocky and dangerous. He narrowed his eyes, blinked. What he'd thought were floating black dots were in fact surfers, a whole group of them. Needing a moment to catch his breath, Mark sat down on a wooden bench conveniently placed at the top of the cape, and eyed the small stick figures. He marvelled at the surfers and their communion with the water. Each wave caught must be like a gasp.

For a few minutes, he was at peace. Anxiety about his boys, his relationships and work seemed distant as the ocean moved, alive and bursting.

Thirst broke his reverie. He needed water; beauty only sustained a man for so long. Moving from the seat, Mark turned to see a small square plaque nailed to the wood.

In memory of Juliette Sinclair, who loved this place.
Beloved wife and mother
May she rest in peace
1950–1985
Broken Bay Council and the Sinclair family.

Mark peered out to the land in front. There was no fence, but he knew that barely metres away there must be cliffs. He edged forward. Clinging to the branch of a low tree, he bent, peering out. In three more steps, he'd be standing on a ledge of smooth granite, and then over the edge – soaring for a short moment before landing either in the ocean or on the rocks. It was beautiful and terrible, as most popular suicide spots are. It had been this spot, around thirty-seven years ago, where Juliette Sinclair had thrown herself to certain death.

Mark backed up, clinging to the tree for as long as he could. On the footpath once more, he did a few stretches and then slowly began jogging down the hill. The Sinclairs – what a family. At the pub, Phil Sinclair had shown no sign of trauma in his pleasantly rugged features. His mother gone when he was only a boy, his celebrated father dead too. And yet, Phil was as genial as could be. *The face can hide so much*, Mark thought. Beneath: all is a mystery.

Broken Bay came into full view. There were no boats in the bay, but he could make out the movement of a fishing trawler edging out of the river. Was it Sinclair Lobsters? He strained his eyes, sweat making it difficult to see. Something about the boat and the bay jogged his memory: yes, he'd been in a boat here, a dinghy with his father. His father was yelling something at him . . . It didn't bring up feelings of joy.

He looked at his watch: almost 8.30 am. Time to go and shower, walk into town and pick up his car from the pub car park. To hell with another night here; he could drive back to Booralama, the river, the redgums, his garden with the drooping wattle.

At the foot of the hill, Mark was surprised to hear a siren and, just as he whipped his head around, a police car went flying by. He frowned. It must have come from Waldara, another station that was unmanned most of the time. Police senses tingling, he hastened his pace, moving to cross the road, when an ambulance flew past, lights flashing. Alert and now alarmed, Mark broke into a jog and was startled by the blast of a car horn, and the rumble of a vehicle slowing down beside him.

'You want a lift?' It was Phil Sinclair. 'Judy's got wind of something going on at the sinkhole. We're heading out there. I'm guessing it's the retrieval.'

Mark hesitated a moment before hopping in. Beside him, their daughter nodded gravely at him.

'You were so sick yesterday.'

'I was.'

'You spewed, like, five times.'

'It felt like fifty.'

Another car sped past them as they drove out of town, flat paddocks now, cows.

Judy twisted around from the front seat. 'Got a phone call ten minutes ago from one of the locals telling me to get down to the Doyles' for the paper. Retrieval of Mya's body is happening – but I'm thinking it's something else too. There's so much activity!'

'Judy's got a good imagination,' Phil said, changing gears. 'She probably thinks Elvis will rise up out of the hole.'

'Mum's got a "Suspicious Mind".' Georgia grinned at him. 'Get it?'

'Good one.' Mark grinned back.

'Those bloody sinkholes!' Phil rapped a hand on the steering wheel. 'What's the bet someone's died trying to retrieve the body?'

'Might be a *murder*,' Georgia said, rubbing her hands together in excitement.

'Stop that,' her mother snapped, and Georgia stifled a laugh.

'Do you like murders?' Mark asked the girl.

'Very much.' She held up a book titled *Killer Cold Cases: Murder & Mayhem*.

'Each to their own,' Mark said. 'I like jogging.'

A P-plater drove past, and Phil gave the horn another workout as they sped past him dangerously.

'Calm down!' Judy said. 'You'll give yourself an aneurysm.'

'I'll give them an aneurysm.'

The single lane road was clogged now, with cars banked up for at least 200 metres. Mark saw a policewoman up ahead directing cars away from a private driveway.

'Have you solved any murders?' Georgia leaned in towards him, spoke under her breath. 'I know you're a policeman.'

Mark paused. Had he solved any murders? He'd investigated murder cases. Solved? Resolved, perhaps.

'That's difficult to say,' he answered.

The girl opened her mouth to respond, but he broke in, leaning between the two front seats. 'Phil, can you drive up past these cars on the side of the road? I'll tell the cop who I am, get us through that way.'

'Will you show them your badge?' Georgia asked, as her father pulled left onto the dirt beside the road and began moving ahead.

'No need.' He winked at her. 'I'll just give my name and we'll sail through.'

At the farm gates, the young police officer held up her hand, took her time while she checked, then rang for confirmation that this was indeed Detective Senior Sergeant Mark Ariti from Booralama. Beside him, Georgia smirked.

Once through, they snaked their way up a muddy track, originally made for a tractor, not a convoy of emergency services and onlookers, Mark thought. Police tape and a tent had been set up, warning off the gawkers, and beyond were an ambulance and police car, plus a handful of uniformed types. With unease building, Mark got out and walked towards the police cordon. Behind the tent stood a clothes rack, lined with wetsuits. Oxygen tanks littered the ground. The expected police divers from Adelaide.

'Have to ask you to move back.' A young policeman blocked him from ducking under the blue tape.

'I'm a cop,' Mark said. 'Booralama.'

'Doesn't mean I can let you in,' the fresh-faced officer replied. 'You could be anyone.'

'We're all anyone, mate. Just that I'm the cop sort.'

The policeman hesitated. Shook his head.

'Give it a rest, for Chrissake. Let him through!'

Mark looked up with surprise to see his old friend Angelo Conti, Assistant Commissioner, exit the tent. 'Angelo!' Mark said, baffled, as the young policeman shuffled away. 'What are you doing here?'

'On my way to Melbourne for a conference. Got the call, a body – and the old copper instinct in me just can't let go. Took a detour through cow country to get here, two hours.'

Mark considered Angelo for a moment. His decision to make the detour was why people in the force liked him. The man never forgot where he came from, what it was about the job that hooked him from the start, what the regular officers went through. But the man was wily too – he knew where the big cases lay. 'Come on, Angelo, we all knew there was a body,' Mark said. 'The retrieval of the cave diver.'

'Yeah, but Mark, this is—'

A shout came from the barrier behind them and a furious old man burst in. 'My own land!' he yelled. 'Won't let me in!'

Frank Doyle, Mark thought.

Angelo muttered something to the officious young policeman, who trotted over to Doyle, touched him on the arm and said something about waiting for a bit longer. Across the barrier, Mark saw Phil, Judy and Georgia looking on with interest.

Mark was on the verge of asking what exactly Angelo was up to, when a sudden flurry of activity near the tent sent the police hurrying in that direction.

A round sinkhole, roughly a metre in diameter, was embedded in the muddy grass, and out of the dark blue water a diver emerged, holding out a rope, which was collected by one of the surface crew. Others reached down to relieve the diver of their oxygen tank before helping to lift them from the water. The first crew began pulling on the rope.

'David's twenty metres below me,' the diver said, muffled beneath the wetsuit mask, and now surrounded by others. Mark was vaguely surprised to hear it was a female voice.

He bent over the sinkhole and watched, first as bubbles, and then a dark shape slowly emerged. The other diver, who Mark assumed to be David Furneaux, surfaced and ripped off his mask. 'She's coming up now,' he declared, breathing heavily. 'Be careful.'

Other staff had tied the rope to a turning wheel and were slowly winding it up. 'Really slow,' David repeated, and a hush descended over the group.

Mark heard the female diver's voice from the tent. 'We need to tell the . . .' she hesitated, and Mark frowned. He was unable to see her, yet the voice was definitely familiar.

But now the body of Mya Rennik was being lifted to the surface and, save the gentle sobbing of an onlooker, who Mark could only guess was family, the Doyle farm was quiet. A black wetsuited figure emerged, floppy, head bowed to the chest.

Two members of the surface crew bent to lift her up, and Mark was repulsed to hear a sloshing sound as they tried to gain purchase under the arms.

Something was wrong. Something was horribly wrong.

Mustard-coloured matter began leaking out of the part of the wetsuit where Mya's face should have been. As she was laid onto a stretcher, David leaned over to move the head up and touch the mask.

'This isn't Mya,' he said.

He was right; the body was far too decomposed. A woman rushed forward, too quickly for others to hold her back, and wrenched off the mask. 'What have you done?! This isn't Mya!' she screamed. 'Where's Mya? *Where's Mya!*'

In horror, Mark looked down at the rotting skull. Only the facial bones and long hair, white-blonde, remained intact.

'Where's my daughter?' the woman shouted at the two divers. 'Go back in and get her!' As her anguished cries reached the onlookers at the barrier, alarm broke out.

There were sounds of scuffling. Mark stepped back from the body and turned to see the young policeman and James Doyle grappling with Phil Sinclair. Mark held up his hand for calm and began walking over as, with supreme effort, Phil Sinclair broke through the lines.

'Cover the body up,' Angelo growled, and someone placed a cloth over the distorted face.

Phil raced over; looked hard at the greasy mask lying on the grass and the body, now covered. Only the hair, as white as his own, crept out from beneath the sheet.

'It's not Mya!' The cave diver's mother was being comforted now as someone led her away. All eyes turned towards Phil Sinclair.

The big man collapsed to his knees. 'My sister,' he said. 'You've found Eloise.'

CHAPTER 5

The wails from Mya's mother faded and ragged weeping from Phil Sinclair filled the space. Judy walked past Mark to place a hand on her husband's shoulder. Together the couple looked at the long tendrils of hair, now beginning to dry on the grass in the morning sun.

Mark's head spun, he felt cold. *A sister?*

Angelo cleared his throat. 'We won't be able to formally identify the body till the experts confirm it.'

'Sinclair DNA is all on file,' Judy said, voice flat. She was still looking at the body. 'When Eloise went missing, and in the years after, the police collected DNA from family members. You'll have everything you need.'

Of course the police would hold their DNA. Family members were the first suspects in a missing persons case or a homicide. *Blood is always thicker than water*, Mark thought, *till someone kills a household member.*

'It's her,' Phil said, looking at the hair. 'It's my sister. And'— he pointed to the diamond-shaped mask on the ground—'that mask was ours. See the way it's tied up at the back? We didn't have the best equipment, so we just shared. My brothers and Eloise, they had to tie their masks up like that. Smaller heads.'

The mask was covered in a grey slime, reminding Mark of the ghastly skull, the oozing flesh and dank smell. Vomit rose in his throat.

'God.' A strained voice behind him made him jump. 'Eloise. It's been, what, twenty years?' It was James Doyle, pale-faced and shaking. 'She was *here*, on our farm?'

The body was now being loaded into an ambulance, where it would be taken to the nearest morgue for further examination. In the background, the divers were conferring, taking notes.

Phil rose from his knees and put his face in his hands, rubbing at it. 'All this time,' he said, almost child-like, 'she was next door.'

Judy put her arms around his large frame and Mark had to look away.

'But she couldn't dive,' Phil was mumbling. 'She didn't know how to.'

'We need to clear this scene,' Angelo said, not unkindly. 'I'll have to ask you all to move on. The sergeant will give you further instructions on where we'll go from here.'

Did Angelo mean him? Mark stared pointedly at his friend, who offered nothing in return.

'Mark?' Judy turned to him. 'What do you want us to do?' Husband and wife looked to him for direction. They were both stooped, holding each other for support, faces etched in shock and grief. Georgia stood beside them, pale and unsure.

'Go home,' Mark said. 'Get some rest and I'll call you later. It won't be me investigating, but I'll find out as much as I can and get back to you.'

They nodded and turned, stumbling across the paddock in frail, uncertain steps.

Mark was left standing near James Doyle, who was staring at his phone. 'Gerri will want to hear this,' he said. 'She and Eloise were best friends.'

In the beat that followed, a cow bellowed, deep and low.

'It's been twenty years since she went missing,' James explained, running a hand through his thinning hair. 'We all grew up together, Eloise was our age. Then one day she disappeared. She would have been eighteen. Some people thought she ran away, others thought she'd been murdered or something, by a stranger in town. But here she is . . .' He spoke slowly, raising his hands up and then down again. 'I never thought I'd see her again.'

'We'll need you to hang around for some questions later too,' Mark said, and James looked up. 'It's your land, and a body's been found on it.'

'It's Eloise – you heard Phil.'

'We don't know that yet.' Although Mark felt certain it *was* the young Sinclair girl. Phil had seemed so sure. 'Just a few questions, it's procedure.'

James nodded, grim-faced. 'I won't be going anywhere, and neither will Dad.' A short distance away, Frank Doyle was having words with Angelo. 'God, the sight of him,' he said bitterly. 'He's probably looking for some way to make this into a tourist story.'

'He won't get far with that bloke,' Mark replied and as if he'd heard them, Frank Doyle came barrelling over to his son.

'Could be anyone!' the old man said to them. 'Could be some random thrillseeker – doesn't have to be the Sinclair girl.'

'Let's go, Dad.'

'You heard Phil and Judy, the girl couldn't dive – it's not her!'

'Dad.'

46

'This is my land!'

'It's the scene of an investigation now,' Mark said. 'Unidentified body. We'll take over from here.'

'What about this lot?' Frank gestured wildly to the cave divers and the rest of the police.

'They'll be moving on too.'

Frank Doyle stormed off, apoplectic, his son following, offering words of appeasement. The pair looked like something from a bad Hollywood comedy, the father behaving like the child, the child placating him.

'Mark Ariti. I thought it was you.'

Mark turned to see Detective Senior Sergeant Jane Southern peeling off a wetsuit, her long, lean body a marvel, always a marvel. 'Jane,' he said, shaking his head. 'I recognised your voice. What are you doing here?'

Sometimes Jane came to Mark in his dreams. Their fleeting moments, the rushing about, the unfamiliar rooms they met in. Always her lithe limbs, the way her body looked in the light shed by gaps in the curtain, wavering, never fixed.

Jane was now fully out of her wetsuit and standing before him in her bathers. 'I could ask the same of you.' She picked up a towel and began drying her hair. 'I'm working.'

'I'm here on a holiday, a long weekend. My sister organised me a boat trip and—'

'A boat trip! I thought you hated boats.'

The drying of the hair continued. One hand rubbing, her head bent sideways, hair shaking droplets all about. The scene felt illicit.

'Yes,' he said, daze-like. 'Yes, I do.'

'Well, I'm freezing.' Jane threw the towel over one shoulder and began walking back into the police tent.

'Hey, Jane!' he called after her, not wanting to be left behind. 'What's going on here?'

'Give me ten minutes,' she called back. 'I'll give you a lift into town if you like, and we can chat.'

He realised rather late that he *would* need a lift back into Broken Bay now that the Sinclairs, and in fact all the onlookers, had departed. Only the police and Angelo, now conferring with the cave divers, were still there. Mark watched his old friend reading charts held out to him, nodding, looking at his watch, asking a question, nodding again. The man was presidential.

The green paddock he stood in was damp and littered in sludgy cow pats, their sweet, earthy smell a reminder that this was a place of work and not a tourist attraction. Not yet anyway. In the corner of the field, the cows huddled, heads down. Mark felt the dry patch on the side of his nose, gave it a thoughtful rub. Yes, he reminded himself, he should book in next week, have it seen to. Rose had said a few times that he should, that she could freeze it off for him. But he never had the time. Rose said a lot of things: things about travel and books she'd read, even the lovers she'd had, who'd either bored her to death or were too fancy for their own good.

Did I *bore her to death?* Mark wondered for the first time. Were there one too many discussions about mince? Or which bird he'd seen that morning by the river? He had no strong views on pronouns or carbon taxes or Johnny Depp. He liked Port Adelaide and watching Westerns. He looked forward to *Landline* each week. Had he bored her?

'Mark!' Angelo was walking towards him. 'I'll be off now. Can't keep the Melbournians waiting. You right here?'

'I'm not sticking around here, Angelo.' There was a warning in Mark's voice. 'I've got to get home.'

'You've got another person there you can call on, haven't you?' Angelo placed a meaty hand on his shoulder. 'Can't you stay a few more days? Could do with a steady presence here.'

The hand on his shoulder was both light and heavy. Mark knew what that hand could do. In the early days, he'd seen it pressed hard into the throats of violent men, heard the crack when it struck the face of a man who made child porn and who wouldn't reveal his accomplices. Nowadays, Angelo's hand was made for confident shakes and pertinent reminders of quid pro quo.

Mark didn't answer.

'Rose good? Boys good?' Already Angelo was moving off towards his car, an assistant racing to keep up.

'All good.'

And Angelo, with a final nod, was off.

Was Angelo a friend or foe? It wasn't the first time the question passed through Mark's mind. In the early days at the police training academy, their friendship had been firm. They'd played football in the same team, lived in the same share house, drunk in the same pub. He'd been a groomsman at Angelo's wedding, and a few years later Angelo had been his. But their career trajectories were like a gold medal tally where Angelo was the USA and he was Bangladesh. It made things difficult.

Now Jane was striding towards him. In her jeans, boots and big jumper, she looked like an advert from one of those *Country Living* magazines. Behind her, a diver was getting out a thermos and retreating to the white tent.

'I can only be an hour or so,' she said. 'We'll be working here the whole day.'

'Do you know where the other diver, Mya, is?' Mark asked.

'Yes.' Jane was his height; he'd forgotten that. 'David said he saw her in the same chamber as the other body. It's at the end of a squeeze.'

Mark shuddered. The term coupled with cave diving could only mean great danger, dark and cold. He was still in his running gear, footy shorts and Booralama tennis shirt, and his legs, growing blue in the brittle wind, were like fresh rabbit meat.

'You're freezing,' Jane said. 'Get in the car.'

Rubbing his arms, Mark hurried to Jane's police car and climbed in the passenger seat, grateful for its warmth. 'Get something to eat?' he asked as she buckled her seatbelt. 'You can leave me in town, my car's there.'

Jane nodded, pulling out of the muddy track and onto the single lane road towards Broken Bay. There was a brief silence, bordering on awkward.

Mark racked his brain for something to say. 'Weird seeing Angelo there. You reckon there's something more going on?'

Jane paused, eyes on the road. 'I don't know,' she said slowly. 'It was a bit strange. He said he had a conference to go to.'

Mark snorted. There was always a conference with Angelo. 'So, you're a police diver now?' The last time he'd seen her, Jane was back in Forensics after a brief stint in Fraud with him.

'I'm a qualified water operations officer. Help out with marine search-and-rescue. This is the first underwater recovery job I've been involved with. Usually, it's looking for weapons at the bottom of a dam or in a river.'

'When did you learn to dive?'

Jane turned to him briefly. 'I've known how to dive for years. I grew up about forty kilometres from here, near the Victorian border. My parents were abalone farmers and prawn trawlers. You don't remember?'

Once again, he did not. Those were not the things Mark remembered about Jane Southern, the woman who male officers called 'Ten' behind her back. A wave of shame came over him.

Jane turned the radio on. Maroon 5 was playing, and in the silence that followed, Mark felt vaguely responsible.

'That body,' he said eventually. 'If what the family's saying is correct, it's been down there for twenty years.'

Jane changed gears, turned left and then right again – the sea was beside him, grey and fleeting silver in the bleak morning sun.

'The state of the body fits that time frame.'

The squishy sound as they lifted it out of the water, the floppiness. The facial bones beneath the old mask.

'A body underwater goes to mush,' Jane continued. 'Rigor mortis doesn't set in and the body in a wetsuit is more like a soap composition. Except for the exposed areas, of course.'

The oozing yellow liquid. The skull.

'So, what happened? Why did the divers pull up that body instead of Mya's?'

'Not one hundred per cent sure, but it seems that the older body was lying on a ledge face down in a large cavern beyond the first squeeze. The rescue diver, David, assumed of course that it was Mya and tied a line to it. On the way out, he noticed the second body, on the ceiling of the cavern, the headtorch still faintly on, tie ropes all around it.'

'Mya.'

'We think so. David surfaced, told us about the two bodies and we called for more police, then he went back under.'

'So, Mya got lost down there?'

'No, we don't think so. The initial theory is that Mya found the first body, got caught up in the lines, managed to cut herself free and then narcosis set in and she couldn't find her way out – became disorientated and went straight up rather than back through the squeeze.'

The two were lost in thought for a minute. Ghastly to think of both women's final moments in the dark labyrinth. They passed the Royal and Mark remembered his car. 'Turn in here, please,' he said. 'My car's in the pub car park and we can walk from there.'

Jane raised her eyebrows but said nothing. She was like that, a woman of few words.

There were two cars and a supermarket trolley in the parking area at the back of the Royal. Both were Toyotas, but his was the one with the windscreen smashed in, damaging cracks in circular, dartboard formations.

Mark swore, got out of Jane's car and walked around his own destroyed one. Jane joined him, examining the vehicle with a forensic eye.

'Looks like it was hit twice,' she said.

'Yeah.' It was Saturday morning in a country town. Chances of getting a repair done today were nil. Still, he punched questions into his phone, hoping Google would come up with something.

'Anyone here know you're a cop?' Jane was peering closely at the car, looking from the driver's side into the interior.

Mark considered this. The Sinclairs knew. He'd first told them on the boat and then reminded them this morning at the entrance of the Doyles' farm. He hadn't told anyone else, but that didn't mean they weren't aware of it. Someone in the pub might have recognised him as the copper who booked their cousin in Booralama for drink driving. The Sinclairs could have told someone. If Broken Bay was like home, Pass It On wasn't a kid's game, it was a local pastime.

'Doesn't have to be a cop-hate thing,' he said. 'Could be a bored-local thing.'

'What, there's no skate park?' She said it dryly and Mark had to smile. Every town had a skate park; councillors thought they were the ultimate in crime reduction. Because, you know, every kid likes to skate.

There appeared to be nothing stolen. The glove box was firmly closed and there was no sign of forced entry. Only the windscreen was damaged.

Google told him there was one auto mechanic who did windscreen repairs in Broken Bay, but the business was permanently closed. Mark shut his eyes, tried to remember what his insurance said about smashed stuff, about towing. Whatever the details, he thought: *It's a good bet I'm trapped here till Monday at least.*

Jane held her hands above her eyes and pointed up. 'CCTV on the pub roof.' Sure enough, a video camera, perched on the side of the double-storey building, pointed down at the parking area.

'Yeah? What's the odds they're not working?' Mark felt glum. And cold. And hungry.

'Come on,' Jane said. 'Not much you can do right now. Let's get you something to eat and I'll grab a coffee.'

In the main street, two doors down from the King of Souva, they found a little cafe, The Collective. Warm inside, a cheery buzz, and the smell of comfort food. Mark felt better once they sat at a table, which looked out to the sea. Jane ordered a takeaway coffee, Mark a big breakfast and a flat white.

'Why throw something at the windscreen twice?' Mark wondered aloud. 'Were there two of them?'

'Could be. Or someone picked up a rock, tried it, didn't do enough damage and tried again.'

'Arsehole.'

'Yep. I'd report it soon if I were you.'

Who to? Myself?

'And check out those cameras.'

'Yeah.'

Outside, the sun was making a break for it and shining bright through dark clouds. Far out to sea, little boats bobbed up and down like toys.

Jane's coffee arrived, and she wrapped her hands around the takeaway cup. 'I've got to get going,' she said, not leaving. 'It was good to see you, Mark.'

Mark shook himself, not quite believing that Jane Southern was sitting before him. It had been three-and-a-half years since they'd put a stop to their messy, destructive affair. 'Everything okay, Jane?'

She smiled. 'Yeah. Work's good, been busy.'

'You with someone?' he asked, hoping she was. Her marriage to Rod, a fellow cop, had ended once their affair came to light. His own hadn't lasted much longer.

Jane shrugged. In the light of the window, her features appeared more defined, sharper. Her black hair gleamed, though surely it must be dyed now. She was what, fifty-six? Fifty-seven? Whatever – Jane Southern was a stunner. She reminded him of an Australian actress, but he couldn't remember which one.

'It's complicated,' she answered. 'You?'

Mark thought about Rose, their arguments in the weeks leading up to Tanzania, no fixed date of return. He missed her already. 'Same,' he said.

Jane moved to go and he stopped her, holding up his phone. 'What's your number? Looks like I might be around for a few more days now. Maybe if you're here we could catch up for a drink or something.'

Or something. He cringed, hating himself.

Jane hesitated before taking his phone and entering her number. 'I'd say I'll be gone tomorrow afternoon. Let me know what you're doing later on and I'll see where we're up to.'

He nodded, something warm bubbling in him, despite the day's events. Jane left with a wave and his breakfast arrived, the waitress a young girl with a shiny moon face. Eggs, bacon, sourdough, sausages and a hash brown. What was not to like?

'You want salt and pepper?' the girl asked.

'Yes, please.'

She brought back two wooden shakers. Mark was glad. He hated those little sachet things, which exploded everywhere when his big hands tried to rip them open.

'You here about the dead divers?'

Honestly, who needs Twitter when you live in a small Australian town? 'Not really.' He paused. 'But I might be.'

The waitress nodded, her round face pleasant. 'I didn't even *know* there was a sister!' she said, eager to talk.

'You know the Sinclairs?'

'Everyone does.' She made an exaggerated gesture with her hands. 'They're like, *really old*, but they're so good-looking. Nic is married to Cath – she's my friend's aunt – and Mat's wife is this, like, *supermodel* from Franklin.'

By Mark's calculations, the brothers Mat and Nic would be in their late thirties, early forties. *Like, really old.* If Eloise was alive today, that would make her around thirty-seven.

'I've met Phil,' Mark said. 'Their older brother.'

'Yeah, like, everyone knew there were three sons – but a daughter, *who went missing* . . . It's wild.'

Mark wished the girl would go away. He looked pointedly at his eggs.

'My friend says there's this photo of the sister in the pub. She says she's like *so gorgeous,* and that no one ever twigs that it's like, *the sister.* Everyone probably thought it was like, *some random* come to town.'

Mark felt a twist of interest despite himself. A photo at the pub? He hadn't noticed it the other night. 'Is that right?'

'Yeah, and my friend told me that our teacher, Ms Doyle, was like *best friends* with her. Can you believe it? It's *so sad.* If my best friend went missing, I'd be, like, *totally* a mess.'

It was exhausting listening to her. Mark needed a lie-down. Like, *really.*

The door of the cafe opened and a couple walked in, pram in tow, young kid grizzling. The waitress turned her attention to them, and Mark looked at his breakfast with pleasure. Got stuck right in. Just as he was finishing up, his phone buzzed. A text from Angelo:

Special investigations team heading to Broken Bay on Monday. Any chance you could liaise with them re: family, local connections?

Smashed windscreen, Mark texted back. *I'm not going anywhere.*

Mark thought about Angelo, how he always seemed to get what he wanted.

Thanks mate, his friend wrote.

It's all as you foresaw, Mark might have added.

CHAPTER 6

Mark walked back to his motel, cars whizzing by – families, probably, returning from sport in the nearby town. There'd be one kid in the back crying, another whingeing – he knew the drill. A car tooted at him. Why toot at a middle-aged bloke in footy shorts walking up the road? People tooted at anything.

At the motel, he booked in for an extra night. Ian didn't look delighted at the extra business. He was staring at a computer screen, transfixed, but even so, the man did look up for Mark the number of a local named Stabber, who towed cars. Mark didn't ask about the origin of 'Stabber'. It could be because he had a 'stab at anything', that he once stabbed himself with a fork, that he looked how a stabber should look, that he actually *had* stabbed someone, or that no one knew what to refer to him as, so they called him Stabber. Mark had friends named Spadger, Squirrel, Leisure, Oxy, Pommy, Pot Hole and Spewk. It was at Spewk's wedding that Mark first learned his friend's name was Tom.

While Ian was searching for the number, Mark pocketed a free notepad from the counter advertising 'Broken Tyre & Brakes'. He liked notepads.

'I've got hundreds of those,' Ian said without looking at him. 'Stupid bugger who owns the business didn't think to add "Bay" on the end of "Broken", did he?'

'Easy mistake,' Mark said. *Not.*

In his room, Mark gave the dolphins in the picture a dirty look, threw off his clothes and stepped into the shower, turning the hot water on full blast, using nearly all of the coin-sized soap and trying not to feel guilty about wasting water. Afterward, he lay on his bed and called his ex-wife Kelly. He wanted to talk to his boys.

Steve, Kelly's new husband, answered the phone. Kelly was swimming, he said. The men chatted about nothing. It was as awkward as ever. Mark didn't mind Steve – he seemed like a nice bloke – but there was a nervousness between them that no amount of small talk could hide.

'Boys there?' Mark asked at last.

'Get them for you now,' Steve answered, relieved. He held a hand over the phone and called out for Sam and Charlie. 'Is it true you're down at the retrieval site for the diver Mya Rennik?'

'I'm in the same town,' Mark answered. 'How did you know that?'

'Kelly mentioned that you were there this weekend and I read something about it online this morning, that they'd found a missing girl.'

Mark could hear the boys running down a long hallway.

'Kelly saw the missing girl's friend speak about the case once. She said it was quite interesting. No doubt it'd be on YouTube or something.'

'The name of the other woman retrieved hasn't been released yet.' Mark sounded more harsh than he intended. Steve was trying to be friendly, he reminded himself.

'Oh, sorry!' Steve was at pains to make amends. 'It's just that, I mean, it was online. "Speculation grows that the body is that of Eloise Sinclair, who vanished in 2003", and all that. Sorry, Mark.'

It was hard to fault a man so good. Steve was Jesus in chinos. 'That's okay. And I'll look up that video. Thanks.'

And suddenly Mark's boys were fighting for the phone. He told them to put it on the bed and turn on the speaker. Their voices made his heart constrict – he was too far away from them. He shouldn't have left Adelaide. Maybe he should have stayed with Kelly.

Taking turns, he asked each of them how Noosa was. Asked them whether they were going to have a pie or a sausage roll for lunch, and what sort of waves there were. Often Mark's mind wandered when they chatted and sometimes he made excuses to hang up early, but this time he was all ears. What *did* Charlie say to the kid who called him an idiot down the street? Was Sam *really* going on a camp to the Flinders Ranges in term four? *Is* bloody hell a swearword? Mark considered Sam's question carefully. 'Technically yes,' he answered. 'Maybe don't say it at school.'

Mark wanted to see his boys. He longed to grab them, to mock wrestle and hug them tight. But that opportunity was weekends away. A lifetime. He reminded them that they were going bike riding with him when they got back from their Queensland trip, fully aware the equivalence in fun was shaky.

'Will Rose be there?' Charlie's voice was like a little bird's. Mark wanted to capture that sound sometime, listen to it when the chips were down.

'No,' he said. 'She's going to live in another country, remember? Tanzania. It's in Africa.'

There was a pause. 'Will she be coming back?' Charlie asked.

Mark looked at the wall. 'Course she will.'

'She's better than you at Uno.'

'Not always.' It was true though, she was. Wild cards, Rose always got them – they sought her out.

The boys rambled on about what they were up to that afternoon and Mark wound up the call, telling them he'd speak with their mum the following day to organise the weekend.

It was unexpected, he thought, that the boys missed Rose. He'd always assumed they'd behave like the children from divorced families on television, forever running to their rooms in acts of overripe petulance. But perhaps kids weren't always like that. He considered: Rose never tried to act like a mother. If she seemed bored or distracted at times, it was probably because she was. She never tried to pretend to love his boys, she never bribed them with treats or gave them undue attention. And yet, they liked her.

But then everyone liked Rose. His friend Dennis said more than once that he was a lucky man. Squirrel and Donna were equally effusive. When Prue was drunk one night, she'd admitted over Zoom that she liked Rose better than Kelly. Jagdeep, a fellow cop, said he'd done well for himself. Even Kelly viewed Rose with faint admiration.

Rose, Mark knew, was good at compartmentalising herself. Despite her sense of fun, her spontaneous acts of adventure, her regular moments of regret, she wasn't some hot mess like Bridget Jones. At the hospital, in her role as doctor, she was firm and measured. As a friend, she was loyal, and in her free time she was always seeking out something new for them to do: rock climbing lessons, paddleboarding on the river, camping in the Flinders Ranges, a quick visit to see a friend in Broken Hill, an exhibition in Adelaide. Rose sometimes exhausted him, but with her he was never, ever bored.

Mark looked at the alarm clock beside his convent-like bed. Its beady little face told him it was almost 2 pm. What the hell was he to do about the car? He punched in the number Ian had given him for Stabber.

'Hello there!' The voice on the other end was jovial. Nothing stabby about it. Mark explained what he needed and the man said he'd be along to collect the car on Monday, advising Mark to leave the keys at the pub for easy pick-up. He'd tow it to the nearest repair shop and have it back to him with a new windscreen by Wednesday at the latest.

Mark hung up, pleased. He then rang his colleague in Booralama with the news. Marni usually worked two days a week, but the extra days covering him weren't a problem. 'There's nothing much going on here,' she said. 'Half your luck, I'd love a break by the beach.'

Some break.

Mark then interrupted Ian's screentime by ringing reception and booking two more nights at the Hibernian. Next, the car insurance. He was put on hold for twenty minutes. Someone gave him a website, which would tell him all his insurance details. He was asked for a passcode, which he didn't have or couldn't remember. Much conferring. He managed to create a new code and was forwarded on to another person. Someone from another department looked up his details and said that his current insurance policy held no cover for towing or windscreen repairs. Mark was asked to complete a survey, which he declined.

A wave of tiredness came over him. A snooze would do him good, but he remembered the cameras on the Royal and, above all, Judy Sinclair asking him what they should do next. What they should do was wait. The investigation involved a second body, in all likelihood that of her sister-in-law. Other departments would now be involved – somewhere in Adelaide, phones were ringing, people were sorting out overnight bags, explaining to their partners that they'd be away again. An investigative team were arriving on Monday – they would take care of things, and yet. And yet. Phil's big face, his kind features ravaged with grief and shock. 'What should we do now, Mark?' they had asked him and Mark couldn't forget it.

He rang the phone number for Sinclair Tours and was unsurprised to get no response. He left a message, as reassuring as he could be, letting them know he'd be around for a little longer, that the force would be in contact. He hung up, dissatisfied. It would never be enough. What could you offer a family like the Sinclairs now?

Changing into jeans and a jumper, jacket over the top, Mark began walking back into town. With no car he was getting a workout; his hip would soon give him hell. He rubbed at it, then remembered the patch on his nose, gave that a rub too. *Middle age is such fun.* The tagline wouldn't sell as a romance.

A hoon sped by in a car, music thumping, the whole vehicle reverberating with the sound. In his early twenties Mark sometimes liked to do circle work in his friend Stitcher's ute. The tight turns took skill and Mark was good at it. It was daring and methodical at the same time. Stitcher was on a disability pension now: car accident on the Nullarbor, acquired brain injury. He'd fallen asleep and driven straight into a truck. Thankfully his wife and kids had been back in Perth with Heidi's family. A year later, it still shocked Mark that the old Stitcher was gone. Dennis practised meditation to help him come to terms with it, Mark had never tried. He hadn't visited

Stitcher yet. Guilt ate at him when he thought about it. He was planning to go, he was.

Mark smelled the ocean before he saw it. Briny. The memories of being here with his father were starting to come back to him, mist-like, through a fog of half-remembered events. They'd gone out in a tinny. He recalled now a bad feeling in the little boat, like he'd lost something. There had been other boats in the bay too. And yelling? Mark strained at the memory. Nothing.

The Royal was surprisingly still closed when he arrived, but Mark knocked on the door anyway.

'Hello!' he called. No one answered. He knocked again, pushing gently at the big front door. It was open. Mark stepped inside and the door closed behind him. The front bar room smelled of stale beer and the deep red carpet was yet to be swept. Chips were ground into swirling patterns of roses, a cigarette butt squished into a petal, there were hardened patches where something not nice had been scrubbed at and forgotten. The carpet was an optical overload and made him feel ill, like the time he saw *Moulin Rouge*. God, that was an awful show. He'd been hungover and Kelly had made him go. Mark felt around his collar, breathing in the fetid air. At the end of the bar, a beige towel dangled limp, like an arm over a hot bath.

'Hello!' Mark called, walking about slowly, looking at the photos again. 'Anyone there?'

He saw once more the grinning man by the shark, the Sinclair brothers in the football team and their father. And there was Frank Doyle, Murray's age, always standing slightly apart, the grin or smirk marking his pale features, the hat pulled low.

Another photo, one he hadn't looked at before, caught his eye. This one was of a lobster trawler with a massive haul, *2001* written in the bottom left-hand corner. The same type of nets he'd seen on the Sinclair boat, big ropey cages tied together with orange twine. A bumper trip out to sea by the looks of it; lobsters filled the nets, kids held live creatures up for show, the muscular tails and claws caught by camera in mid movement. With a jolt, Mark recognised a teenage James Doyle holding a lobster aloft, his red hair distinctive among the blondes and brunettes. Leaning in closer, Mark realised it wasn't James at all – it was a girl. With her hair tied back and flannelette shirt, he'd assumed it was a male. The flame-haired lobster-holder could only be Gerri Doyle, James's twin sister, teacher and former best friend of the missing girl.

To the right of Gerri, standing further back, was a girl with long white hair. *Eloise.* Tall like her brothers, with slender limbs and a dreamy smile, unfocused on the camera lens. She must have been around sixteen. She was beautiful, Mark could see that, youthful and unadorned with make-up or fancy clothes. Her hair, reaching halfway down her arms, contrasted sharply with Gerri's flame locks: the girls made a striking pair.

Two young men stood behind the women. One cocky looking, with sandy-coloured hair, an arm draped loosely over Eloise's shoulder. The other, a grinning man with dark features, beside Gerri, their shoulders touching, both laughing at the lobster Gerri held outstretched. Mark took a moment to look at the four of them. They reminded him of something. What was it? Yes – the soap *Neighbours*, when Scott and Charlene and Anne and Mike were in it. Four wholesome young people on the cusp of life. The nation had gone wild for that show. But the foursome in the photo on the wall were younger than him – by at least a dozen years. They'd probably never heard of Charlene and Scott. It was a mistake Mark commonly made, thinking he was the same age as everyone else.

He took a photo of the image, and as he was putting his phone back in his pocket, it rang. A shaky voice greeted him. 'Mark?' It was Judy Sinclair. 'Thanks for your call. We wanted to know if you could come over soon – everyone's here and we'd just like you to, you know, run through for everyone what happens next.'

Mark hesitated. 'I'm not sure if I'll be much help, Judy. There should be a team arriving from Adelaide on Monday, and in between then there'll be lots going on behind the scenes: the formal identification, autopsy, checking the old police files and—'

'It's just that,' Judy interrupted, 'we feel we know you a little bit. Phil likes you and we're all in a kind of shock and a familiar face and . . .' She trailed off.

Mark found himself agreeing to meet them, asked for the address, then at the last moment remembered he didn't have a car. He was telling her that when a booming male voice from the pub toilets cut in.

'Is that Judy? I'll drive you there. Just give me five.'

Mark paused, then let Judy know he had a lift. While he waited for his mysterious driver, he tapped out a text to Jane. *What time are investigative team arriving on Mon? Family anxious.*

In the quiet of the pub, the flush of the toilet seemed impossibly loud. The door opened and an old man appeared, face like a beetroot, a limp in his gait. 'Prostate,' he said thickly, pointing at his groin. 'Makes taking a leak longer than a trip up the Hume.'

Mark made an interested sound.

'Like a creek in drought, some piss-weak dribble you wouldn't pay to see.'

Moving on . . . 'You the owner? I did call out, sorry – didn't hear you.'

'I was focused on my useless dick, that's why. And yeah, I'm the owner. I'll take you there. Good family. Real shame.'

Ten minutes later, in the man's car, Mark explained about his windscreen and Stabber's suggestion with the keys before asking about video cameras on the roof.

The publican held his hand out for the keys, put them in the glove box and then shrugged. 'Why d'you want to look at the cameras? What's it gonna do? Take some kid to court who can't pay proceedings?'

Mark told him he was a cop. 'Vandalism's against the law, no matter what it is.'

The man looked at him askance, then shrugged again. 'Whatever floats your boat. I'm Barry Coffey, by the way.'

'Mark.' He waited. 'So, you got security cameras?'

'Yeah – brand new. Got them installed six or so weeks ago.'

'Yeah?'

'Yeah.'

'Customer complaining about some bloke,' Barry said eventually. 'Nothing in it from what we could tell, but you know, got to make the ladies feel safe.'

Mark straightened. 'Yeah? What was she saying?'

'Not much. Said someone followed her home from the pub a few times, waited out the front of her house.'

'She call the police?'

'She called everyone. Probably called the prime minister. That's Cherie for you.'

The wriggling woman in the bar. *Those poor women*, she'd said. Who had she been referring to?

His driver continued. 'Police came down, looked into it. Nothing. Hate to say it, but as fond of her as I am, the woman's got form in the fib department. Reckons she went out with Mel Gibson.'

'It could be true, you never know.' Mark's friend Dennis once had a drink with Natalie Imbruglia.

'And Hugh Jackman.'

There was a pause.

'Doesn't mean she's not telling the truth about this one,' Mark added, less confident.

'Well, we got the camera installed so we could see whoever comes in and out, who might be following her and, bang, it's all stopped. Mind you, she's a good bird.' He nodded. Repeated himself. 'A really good bird.'

They were driving towards the Doyles' again. Cows raised their heavy heads to look at him; he looked back. Seagulls perched on stone fences. No fish 'n' chips here – what were they waiting for?

They turned right, down a dirt driveway and the Sinclairs' house, bordered by cypress pines, came into view. A hodgepodge of buildings, a massive shed, the main house run down but neat, a sleep-out. The garden needed pruning; shiny leaf almost covered the front fence. Dogs barked, and he heard someone tell them to shut up. They did.

'Let you go here,' the publican said. 'Pay my respects later.'

'There's been no identification of the body as yet.'

'If Phil reckons it's his little sister, then it's his little sister.'

Mark thanked him and turned towards the house.

'Hey Mark. Go easy on them, eh?' Barry said as he pulled out of the driveway. 'No family around here has been through more.'

CHAPTER 7

Mark knocked on the Sinclairs' door. No answer. He knocked again. *It's like the Three Little Pigs around here*, he thought. He knocked again and then, tentatively, stepped inside to chaos – a child crying, television blaring, teens lounging on the couch, staring at their phones. The dogs started up again.

He raised his voice above the din. 'Could someone point me to Phil or Judy?'

A girl and boy, entwined on an easy chair, looked up guiltily. *Young love! The world grieves, the world moves on.*

'Auntie Judy's in the front room with Uncle Phil.' The girl, flush-faced, pointed through to the next room.

'Got all the family here, have they?'

'Yeah,' she said. 'If you've brought something, there's room in the freezer, I think. The fridge is full.'

Mark knew what she meant. This was the longstanding tradition in rural towns. When someone dies, when something bad happens to someone in your town, you better bring something. A casserole, a cake, a lasagne, a pav. You mow their lawns, you put the sheep out, you bring the cows in, you collect their mail.

In other countries, mourners lay flowers down in front of homes. In rural Australia, they bring shepherd's pie.

Mark walked through the kitchen to see a steady line of women at work, washing, drying, sweeping the floor, Glad-wrapping leftovers, making sandwiches, putting dishes in the overstuffed fridge. CWA, he guessed. 'Judy?' he asked, and a big woman with a handsome face pointed him to the next room.

There the atmosphere was different. Fewer people, mostly Sinclairs judging by the mass of white hair and attractive, sporty looks. The younger brothers Mat and Nic stood talking by a window, Mat jiggling a toddler on his hip. He recognised Mark from the souva shop and gave him a grave nod. Judy was gathering cups. Two well-dressed women – he assumed the brothers' partners – sat on a couch, whispering. Georgia was there, cross-legged on the floor with another child, playing a silent game of Snap. And then, to his mild surprise, he saw James and Gerri Doyle standing huddled by the empty fireplace, sorrowful and pale.

Phil Sinclair sat in the middle of the room, head bowed in sorrow, big arms on his knees. He looked like a giant marionette, broken and discarded among all the other bright things.

'Mark!' Judy called out, and at once all eyes were on him. Expectant. Mark gave an uncertain smile.

'You'll help us, Mark, won't you?' It was Phil, desperation in his voice. 'We want to know what happened.'

'There're so many questions,' Judy murmured. Heads bobbed up and down in agreement.

You'll help us, Mark, won't you? It was a question with strings attached – or ropes. Big thick cords that wound and wound themselves around his chest. It meant more time in Broken Bay, it meant getting to know these people, it meant becoming attached. But there was something about the Sinclairs, their failing fishing business, the ageing photos on the pub wall, the women in the kitchen working. Mark felt he knew them.

'Yes,' he said simply. 'I'll do my best to help.'

A collective sigh, a small shift in the air.

'Our little sister!' Phil said in dismay. 'I'll never forget the . . .' He stopped, looking down.

The skull, the yellow leaking, the damp hair, the mask with green on it. The body in the wetsuit, lying there on the cold ground.

No one else had seen her body besides Phil. For them, Eloise was preserved as she had been, youthful and fair.

'Was she wearing her bracelet?' Phil's eyes were pleading. Mark wanted to say yes, yes, to whatever the big brother asked.

'I'm not sure,' he said. He hadn't seen an arm.

'Eloise always wore it. It was a silver thing with the letters J and E on it. She never took it off.'

'It was our mother's,' Nic broke in. 'J for Juliette. When she was a baby, Dad got an E for it. Eloise wore it every day.'

'I don't know.' Mark felt hopeless. 'I'm sorry, I'll check for you.'

There was another long pause, the only sound the flicking of the Snap cards.

'What was she even doing there? That's what I don't get.' It was Mat, holding the now sleeping toddler. 'She couldn't dive.'

'Did anyone know that sinkhole even existed?' one of the women on the couch asked. The question hovered in the air.

'I didn't,' James said. 'I mean, it was our land – but we didn't know it was there.'

'Not till Dad found it,' his sister added, 'and that wasn't that long ago – what, three weeks? A cow almost fell through the hole.' Gerri looked at her twin for confirmation and he nodded.

The Sinclair brothers introduced themselves. Nic was married to Cath, who was sitting on the couch talking with April, Mat's partner. With her flowing locks and long legs, April must be the supermodel lookalike the waitress in the cafe had referred to. Nic had two children, Mat just the toddler. Mark listened, taking it in. There was an anguish about the men, he thought. For all their friendly overtures and grateful thanks, they were hungry for answers.

'When can we head out there?' Mat asked. 'See the site where El was found?'

'I'm not sure. It'll be secured for now, at least until the investigative team has had a chance to go over it.'

'But what'll they find?' Nic jumped in, voice raised. 'After twenty years – cows trampling through the place, tractors and utes driving over it . . . I mean, really, the police have got Buckley's.'

There was a general murmur of consent.

'Brett should be here,' Mat said tersely. 'Even if he's a complete arse, he should be here.'

'Mat.' Judy's voice was stern. 'No need for . . .'

'Apparently he's in the Philippines,' Gerri said from her place near the fire. 'I emailed him about Eloise and the sinkhole, but he already knew. Social media is all over it.'

Of course it was. All those onlookers at the dive site, Phil calling out his sister's name: impossible to contain the news when everyone owned a camera.

'Hopefully when he gets back he'll come here for a chat,' Gerri added.

Mat laughed. 'Oh yeah, Gerri, I'd like Brett to come down for a chat. Just give me five minutes with him. Alone.'

Mark shifted on his feet.

'You'll want to talk with Brett,' Nic said quickly to Mark. 'He was Eloise's ex.'

Mark's phone buzzed. Jane.

Investigative team of three arriving Monday early morn. One of the divers and I will stay on to hand over. Dinner tonight?

Despite the situation, something flipped in Mark's stomach. He typed back the thumbs up emoji, then deleted it fast. *Sounds good*, he wrote.

Suggestions?

He had none; he had one. *The Royal*, he typed.

The little dots appeared. *See you at 7.*

'You on the phone to your girlfriend?' It was Georgia, her scowling face looking up at him.

'Work colleague.' Mark put his phone away.

'Anything to report?' Judy was beside him, her hands still full of teacups.

Mark cleared his throat and told her about the team arriving early Monday.

'That's good.' Judy nodded to herself. 'Good.'

'So, what's this about Brett?' Mark asked. 'What's the story there?'

'He was Eloise's boyfriend. For about two or three years?' she asked Cath. 'He was from a neighbouring family,' Judy continued, 'now in Adelaide. Works in marketing or something. Still right into surfing, the outdoors and all that. He was always very fit.'

'I heard his wife is a psychologist,' Cath said.

'He'd like that.' Mat huffed. 'Lots of time on the couch.'

No one laughed.

'Were he and Eloise an item at the time of her disappearance?' Mark asked.

'Yep, you could say that,' Gerri piped up. 'Brett was devastated when Eloise went missing.'

'He was questioned in the days after, his whole family – we all were,' Phil said, tiredness etched in his voice. 'There'd be records of it. Police came down from Adelaide, searched all round this house and beyond. Helicopters, news on the telly, you name it.'

Mark thought of the old reports fading in some filing cabinet. Ten years ago, an effort was made to digitise all investigative reports from that point onward. But two decades ago, the search would have been old-school, in hard copy. Reviewing old case files was long work, hard on the eyes and back. Mark wondered if he would be tasked with the job and hoped not.

'Remember the sighting in Port Douglas?' Nic looked at Gerri, almost defiant. 'Some crank rang the radio to say they'd seen Eloise up there, in a servo buying a pie.'

'Press went mad for it,' Judy added. 'Headlines were all, "Missing beauty found alive and well in North Queensland".'

'Only,' Nic added, 'Eloise was vegetarian. We knew it wasn't her.'

Still, Mark thought, *it wouldn't have stopped them from thinking it* might *be her.* Maybe she started eating meat, maybe she was buying it for someone else, maybe she was sending them messages, had joined a cult, had amnesia, was kidnapped, was in witness protection. Knowing wasn't the same as believing. It didn't stop the hope.

'There was that time you thought you saw her, Gerri,' Mat said sadly.

'Yeah – on an island off Bali. I really believed it was her getting on a ferry. I called out, tried to get her attention, but whoever it was didn't see me. Just false hope, I guess.'

'Well, whatever it was, it made us feel a bit better, didn't it?' Phil said. 'At least we could imagine she was happy somewhere, travelling.'

'Eloise would have loved Bali,' Judy murmured.

'The beach, the people and the warm weather,' Phil agreed, clasping his wife's hand. 'She really would have. I should have let her go that time – remember she wanted to?'

Judy looked down at him. 'You can't beat yourself up about what you should or would have done differently, Phil. Eloise loved you.'

'I used to see Eloise too.' Nic gave a half-smile to Mark. 'In shopping centres or on trains. It was never her.'

'And all this time,' Cath said, 'she wasn't that far from the house she grew up in.'

'On *your* land.' Mat glared at James and Gerri Doyle.

All eyes turned to the red-headed twins. Gerri started crying softly. No one moved, save her brother, who made a helpless gesture with his arms. *Blood*, thought Mark, *the ultimate tie that binds. When it comes down to it, family's the thing. You could be friends with people your whole life, see them every day, love them even – but when the chips are down, it's blood that sticks.*

'We know just as much as you do,' James said. 'I don't know how she got there, I don't.'

Gerri sniffed and wiped at her face. 'All this time I've been missing her and she's been . . .'

A waiting pause.

'. . . she's been in the cold water, underground. She used to hate cold water, remember? She never went for a swim unless it was above thirty degrees at least. Remember the pool? She hardly ever went in. And in your boat, Phil? You'd all be spearfishing and she'd be on the deck, pretending to work but really . . .'

'Reading,' Phil finished for her. 'Eloise was always reading. Never had her head out of a book. When she was little, she loved those Enid Blyton books. *The Famous Five*. She read them all.'

'It's why I'm called Georgia,' Georgia said, looking up at Mark. 'Eloise liked George the best.'

'Who didn't?' Mark asked, and the young girl allowed herself a grin.

'It's funny,' Phil continued as if he hadn't heard. 'She loved those adventure books, but she wasn't adventurous at all herself.'

'She told me once she was going to build a raft and sail to Peru,' Nic said, and they smiled. 'She would have been eight.'

'And when she read *Tomorrow When the War Began*, she wanted to move out and start her own colony.'

'I remember that.' Gerri's voice was bleary through the tears. 'We were all going to live out there by the ponds, catch fish and hunt for rabbits. No school, no telly or jobs, just this whole other life out there by ourselves.'

'As if!' Nic shook his head, eyes wide in mock exasperation. 'Without her comfy bed and those twenty-hour showers she used to have, El wouldn't have lasted a day.'

'She was a real homebody.' Fat tears were running unchecked down Phil's cheeks.

'I don't know,' James Doyle spoke up. 'El was tough. Maybe we're not giving her the credit she deserves.'

Mat scoffed at that and a deep flush spread across James's face, right down to his neck and shirt.

Gerri, sniffing, placed a hand on her brother's arm. Reassuring him? Or pressuring him to stop? Mark couldn't tell.

'Eloise was like a, like a . . .' James continued, stumbling over the words. 'Like a sister to us. She was always at our house. We're just so . . .'

'No one's accusing you of anything,' Judy said firmly. 'We all know how much she meant to you, and you two to her.'

There was nodding from everyone, even a reluctant Mat.

'Eloise loved your family, mate,' Nic said, looking annoyed at his brother. 'Your mother was so good to us after Mum died.'

Another tragedy. Mark felt the weight of the room press in. Everyone seemed to hold their breath.

'Well, they're together now,' Judy said to the brothers. 'Your mum and Eloise. Mother and daughter.'

There was an extended pause, respectful, until a young voice rang out in fury. 'That's bullshit, Mum!' Georgia rose to her feet. 'Why are you trying to make it all sound better? Grandma killed herself and now her daughter's been found in a sinkhole. They're not together! One's in a morgue and one's six feet under!'

'Stop that now, Georgia!' her father said, sharply. 'We're just trying to find ways to cope.'

'Cope! Who wants to cope?'

There was something magnificent about her rage, Mark thought. She was impressive, as young female leaders often are. A modern-day Joan of Arc, resplendent in her Broken Bay football–netball hoodie.

'I'm over all this "rest in peace" stuff!'

Bet she plays wing attack.

'We need action!'

If she cried 'To Battle' right now, I'd take up arms.

'And that's why we've got Mark here,' Phil said, voice cracking.

'Extra police are on their way,' Judy added, 'and we'll find out more in the next few days. But really'—there was a warning in her voice—'it just goes to show how dangerous this area can be, you have to be so careful. Sinkholes and potholes and the ocean – it's perilous.'

Judy thinks it's an accident, Mark realised. *Judy thinks that Eloise fell down the sinkhole somehow, that there was some sort of mishap.*

Sure, there were plenty of places to have an accident around here. But Eloise was pulled out of the water in a full mask and wetsuit, kitted up with oxygen tank, a torch and guidelines. She was prepared.

She had meant to go down that sinkhole.

CHAPTER 8

Mark looked at his watch. It was time to go. He had a quick chat to Judy, promised Phil he'd let them know if he heard anything, and gave a small wave to the room. Georgia waved back, and the others nodded, turning once more to each other. Mark headed through the kitchen again. A plate of egg sandwiches cut into triangles sat on a platter and as he walked past, he reached out to grab one, only to be given a deft smack on the hand by a small woman, neat in jeans, shirt and pearls.

'They're for family,' she said, sternly.

Mark coloured, blinked. What was it with these women? He'd known their type all his life. 'It's just an egg sandwich, not the collection plate,' he grumbled, as she shooed him out the door.

On the front verandah, Mark was surprised to find Gerri fishing about in a bag, a plate of food dangerously balanced in the other hand.

'Oh hello,' she said, hitching her bag back over her shoulder, car keys in her fist. 'Sorry, we weren't properly introduced inside. I'm Gerri Doyle. I sneaked out the back. It's too much for me in there.'

'I'd shake your hand, but you're a bit loaded up there.' Mark nodded to her neatly Glad-wrapped plate of sandwiches, party pies and slices.

Gerri made a face of helplessness and gave a short laugh.

'How'd you manage to get all that?' he asked. 'I got told off for trying to take one egg sandwich.'

'Oh, have this plate – please! They've loaded James and me up with enough to last a lifetime.'

'Really? No, that's fine.' He half thought of marching back into the kitchen – *Why did she get one?*

Gerri walked down the porch steps and Mark followed.

'It's because we knew Eloise so well. Nic and Mat don't like to admit it, but she was mostly at our house growing up. Everyone knew it. Locals around here are treating us as if we were her family too. They're giving us food, offering to mow the lawn or whatever.'

'I'm really sorry,' Mark said. He knew how wide grief spread in country towns.

Gerri tilted her head; she would have heard the words a hundred times already. Her pale face looked out to the driveway, where the line of battered cypress stood. Mark followed her gaze. 'Eloise and I used to play in those trees,' she said. 'We'd try to make it all the way up to the road, falling down through the branches, clinging on, leaping across gaps, scrambling back up again.'

Mark waited.

'We'd take a whole afternoon to do it. Can you imagine? They were high even then.'

They *were* high. It would take guts to leap from limb to limb. But they were sturdy things, the cypress trees: planted as windbreaks and to offer shade to stock. Not many of them where he grew up. In Booralama it was all river red gums, the native trees that dropped branches, exploded in fire and were tricky to climb.

'The thing is,' Gerri spoke almost in wonder, 'James was right. Eloise *was* more adventurous than her brothers thought. She used to leap over those branches without a care. I'd be almost crying in some high spot up there with the wind blasting away, and there'd be Eloise – flying over the branches, arms outstretched, jumping the gap into the foliage of the next tree.'

The two were quiet for a moment.

'Do you need a lift?' Gerri said finally. They were in the paddock near the house, where all the cars were parked. 'I can drop you in town.'

In the car, Mark looked across at Gerri. She and James would be around thirty-seven, thirty-eight, the same age Eloise would be if she were alive. Gerri's face, now concentrating on the potholed driveway, was pleasant to look at. Lightly freckled, brown eyes, red hair escaping a low ponytail. Eloise and Gerri must have been the talk of the town in their late teens. All the boys in the district would know the two best friends – distinctive not only for their beauty, but for their well-known family names: the lobster-fishing Sinclairs and the dairy-farming Doyles. Growing up, Mark's older sister Prue had a best friend with dark hair named Maggie. In Booralama, he'd heard one old man remark that they were better looking than the girls in ABBA, which made Mark kind of sick, but proud at the same time.

'So, what was it like growing up here?' Mark asked. 'Were you always friends with the Sinclairs?'

'Yes. I was born around the same time as Eloise. When Juliette died, my mum helped out a lot with the kids. Phil was only thirteen, Mat and Nic were two and three. Eloise, like us, was just a baby. She pretty much grew up with me and James. Before she went missing, I couldn't remember a time when she wasn't there.'

'So, their father – Murray – he raised the four kids largely on his own?'

'Yep, he never had another partner. Pined for Juliette till he died of a heart attack, seven, maybe eight years later. He always drank, but it was worse when Juliette was gone. Murray and my dad were similar ages, although they weren't friends. Dad is, well – how do I put it? – much less gregarious than Murray was.' She gave a small laugh. 'Still, Dad says it was such a shame to see how Murray descended after his wife's death. I think Phil, who would have been around twenty, ended up taking over a lot of the responsibility.'

They were on the main road now, passing a truck loaded with cattle, their heads pressed against the railings, tongues out, calling for escape. The truck smelled like shit and death. Mark looked away.

'So, tell me about Brett.'

Gerri gave a short laugh. 'Growing up, Brett was the hottest boy around.'

'A spunk.'

'Yeah.' Gerri looked at him sideways. 'I suppose.'

Spunks, that's what they called good-looking boys when he was growing up. Dennis was always being called a spunk by hoards of giggling girls from Waldara Tech, and by older women, who glowered dangerously through made-up eyes. No one said 'spunks' anymore.

'Brett was tall with sandy hair, a surfer, funny, and loads of charm. Eloise and he were like this perfect couple, they went out together for years.'

'Yeah?'

'We had this sort of gang as we were growing up,' Gerri said, her voice a little dreamy. 'There was Brett and Eloise, James, and me and Scott. Nic and Mat too.'

A tractor in front pulled over to let them pass. Mark gave the driver a nod. 'Who's Scott?'

'Scott Boxhall. He was Brett's friend, and my boyfriend. We were always together – and James.'

The 'and James' made Mark wonder how much Gerri's brother enjoyed being part of the gang. 'Where's Scott now?'

Gerri slowed down as she passed the Broken Bay sign and the ocean came into view, vast and skittish. 'Dead. Car accident – two weeks after Eloise went missing.'

'God, I'm sorry.' The suicides, the car accidents, the brutality. In that regard, Broken Bay was no different from a million others. But even so: two weeks after the disappearance of a local girl? Mark's cop brain registered it, filed it away.

Gerri moved forward in her seat so that she was peering over the steering wheel like an old woman. The sun was setting, fierce in its decline, making the road appear fuzzy and unfixed. It could have been this road that Scott died on. A young man, perhaps a few beers in him, loud radio on – some song he liked. Or, something else entirely.

'It was awful,' Gerri admitted. 'We all lost it there for a bit. Eloise going missing and then Scott dying two weeks later – it's a blur. Things were never the same after that.'

They passed an old shearing shed, falling apart in a paddock near the sea. Mark wondered what held it all together; any moment now, with a great tearing sound, it would surely topple down.

'So, you have children?' Gerri attempted to lighten the conversation, though her face was still set hard against the fading sun, her outline like a Grecian bust.

'Two boys, Sam and Charlie.' He'd see them in three weeks. 'They live in Adelaide with their mum.' Mark didn't know why he added that; it was the tiredness, the falling rays, the warmth in the car.

'Oh.' Gerri looked vaguely surprised. 'Well, I've got a son too, Teddy. He's at an agricultural college in Lincoln. He's almost twenty! They grow up so fast.' There was a pause, then she added – perhaps in the general spirit of sharing – 'I had him very young. Scott was his father.'

Mark's eyes widened and he shook his head. 'I'm sorry.'

'Well, I've made sure that Ted knows all about his father, and about Eloise too. All the old stories. Now there's just James and me left here, and Nic and Mat. And I'm planning to leave. I've actually put my house in town on the market. I should have left years ago, I know.'

Mark shrugged. He knew how difficult it was to leave the town you'd grown up in.

'At one time in my late twenties,' Gerri continued, 'I moved to Adelaide and stayed there three years, met this nice man, thought I'd settle down with him. But I couldn't. Dad, James and all my memories of Eloise – they've held me here fast.'

A reflective silence filled the car. Mark thought again of his childhood friend Stitcher, decided he'd fly to Perth the next chance he could. *Old friends*, he thought, *they're channels to our former selves. How else can we recognise what we once were, what we've become?*

'It must have been so hard for you,' Mark said.

Gerri gave him a brief glance. 'Yeah, it was. I went off to uni in Adelaide, did teaching and then just fell in a heap. Volunteered with the Families of Missing Persons charity, wrote a really terrible book and, basically, wished myself back in the past. Having Teddy

83

during all that time was hard, but it probably saved me too. He's a great kid.'

'I bet he is.'

They were in town now. Mark told her the name of his motel. Out the front of the Hibernian, owner Ian was pulling weeds out of the nature strip, yanking at them like he hated their guts.

'Something's really pissed that man off,' Mark commented. 'Every time I see him, he's attacking something.'

The two watched Ian hacking at the capeweed like Rambo in Nam.

'That's Ian for you,' Gerri said. 'His first wife died and the second left him ten years ago. He says she took all his money *and* the dog.'

Ian was on his knees now, pulling at the roots of a gum tree, scarlet-faced, teeth gritted.

'Well, anyway, he seems nice.' They both laughed and Mark got out of the car. 'Police'll be speaking to you all at some stage probably,' he said. 'Don't go anywhere for the next few days.'

'It won't be you?' Gerri looked up at him, her face slightly flushed.

'I don't think so. Have to see.'

She nodded, gave a half-wave, and sped off back down the road.

CHAPTER 9

Mark's room had been aggressively cleaned and was thick with a Glen 20 fug. In the bathroom he washed his face and took a close look at the rough patch on his nose. He reminded himself to make an appointment with the doctor. *Just make it!* One phone call. Have it frozen off, chopped out, scooped with a doctor's steady hand. But that thought led him, as so many of his thoughts did, to his favourite medic, his most lovely doctor. Rose, soon to be in Tanzania, thousands of kilometres away.

He slumped on the low armchair, flicked on the telly. Rugby. He didn't play, didn't know the sport well, but watched it anyway – thick-necked blokes going for broke at the leather, straining for it, chasing it like it was the answer to all their thick-necked prayers. The score was 12–10, a close one. He turned the volume up.

There was beer in the mini bar. As kids, one of the golden rules – on the same level of importance as not sticking knives in the toaster – was, don't take anything from the mini bar. Feeling reckless, Mark reached in and cracked a beer open. It was, he reflected as he took deep gulps, possibly the most adventurous thing he'd done in twenty years. His own image was reflected in the little telly: either the monster in *Frankenstein* or Norm from *Life Be in It*. *What's it all for?* he thought. *What's it for?*

The thick necks chased the ball. Mark drank.

The phone rang: Kelly.

He ignored it.

His phone buzzed: Kelly. *How are you Mark? What are you up to?*

Watching rugby, he replied.

Just emailed you that video on the talk Steve told you about. It's in regards to your new case.

My case? Is that how it's being referred to?

THX.

It was the first time he'd ever written *Thanks* in that way. It looked abrupt but did the job. Maybe he could change, be a new person, drink out of mini bars, write THX and move to Tanzania. Maybe he could.

Mark had another beer while checking his emails. The link was to a video recorded five or six years ago during Missing Persons Week. Geraldine Doyle had presented at a conference in Perth that Kelly was at. In her previous role as a family lawyer, his ex-wife had specialised in domestic violence cases, AVOs, custody battles. 'Too high on the pathos for my liking,' she'd written, referring to Gerri's performance. Mark grinned into his beer. Kelly was more of your logos, logic type.

'I think she wrote a book about it too,' Kelly had written. '*My Best Friend* or something terrible like that. Maybe you should read it.'

Mark had no intention of reading it. He enjoyed reading, but didn't do it much. He fell asleep to Clive Cussler, lulled by the familiar, but could read and re-read passages of *Henry V* or *Macbeth* and be astounded, think about the words for days.

There was comfort in the lack of rancour in Kelly's email, but a certain hollowness too. He didn't love her anymore. She'd moved on and that was okay. But what was left between them, after all that time together? There were the boys, of course – but every memory he had of her now was overlaid with a bitter tinge.

6.30 pm, time to get ready for the Royal and for Jane Southern. He'd have to walk there. Not for the first time, Mark cursed the person who'd shattered his windscreen. Stuck in Broken Bay till at least Wednesday, and at the mercy of a man named Stabber, tower of cars.

The Royal was busy. The football–netball crowd – a home game, and Broken Bay Seniors were the winners. A spot in the granny loomed, and Mark knew what that meant for a town: excitement and parties and good will. It also meant more DV callouts, more people pissing up against the walls.

A girl with a red face and a loud voice was singing with her arm wrapped around a beaming woman in her seventies. Mark paused by the door to watch. It was warming, the obvious affection between the two. The young woman's voice was clear and strong: the Pogues' 'Fairytale of New York'. It took a moment for Mark to realise she had changed the words 'Christmas Day' to 'Broken Bay'. There was something about bells ringing out, and the NYPD choir, and Galway Bay. But the swapped words resonated the most with Mark, and the people in the bar.

The old lady and the young singer swayed together, joined in happiness. Mark appreciated that about country towns – the line between generations faded. With small populations, you couldn't afford to only be friends with people your own age. You played sport, you worked, you sang with others decades older or younger than you.

Mark waded his way through to the bar. No sign of Jane. He checked his phone: bang on 7 pm. She was probably in the dining room. Barry, who'd driven him to the Sinclairs', gave him a nod, served up a beer and said something Mark couldn't hear. Mark smiled vaguely, and Barry moved on. Mark turned again to the singer before realising that the older woman was the one who'd smacked his hand when he attempted an egg and lettuce grab. Ahh, the joy of small towns! A couple of days in and he was beginning to make connections; in a day, he'd no doubt meet someone who knew his cousins from Hay.

There were people everywhere in the pub, young and old. Mark spotted James talking to his father, who was staring deep into his beer. A group of teenage girls took one nervous step inside the pub door and were roared at by Barry to go home and come back when they were eighteen. A raffle was called out, Black 38. There was a whoop and a woman in double denim came forward to collect a generous meat tray.

'Hello, handsome.' To his left, Cherie was perched on a stool, looking up at him with juicy eyes.

'Cherie.' Mark looked around for Jane. Where was she? *Where was she?!*

'Been out to the Sinclairs, I hear.' Cherie was tossing her head, aiming for seductive. Masses of stiff yellow hair whipped around like macrame curtains in a breeze.

'Yep, just for a visit.'

'So, are you in Broken on business then?' Cherie's voice was coy, but there was an edge to it. 'Because I've got something to report, detective.'

Mark remembered Hugh Jackman. He remembered Mel Gibson. He took a long sip of beer.

'For a start, a stolen phone.'

'You need to file a report at the station, Cherie. There're cops here now. They can take your report, or you could always ring it in.'

'It was taken from here last night.'

'It's not lost?'

'I've asked Barry. No one handed a phone in.'

'Report it,' Mark said. *Are you there, God? It's me, Mark.* 'Police investigate all thefts.'

'And there's more.'

Mark waited.

'Someone's watching me!' Cherie said suddenly in a hoarse whisper, leaning so far forward on her stool that she almost toppled into him.

'You've told the police?'

'Oh yes. But nothing ever gets done. Everyone thinks I'm making it up. It's been happening for well over a month now.'

The singing started up again, Peter Garrett.

'But I'm not, I'm really not.'

Mark looked more closely at Cherie. Her hand shook as she brought her straw to her lips; the corner of her mouth trembled as she sipped. A year before, Mark had spent hours watching police surveillance tapes of a woman who was being investigated by authorities. It was only when Jagdeep pointed it out that he saw it: the woman was afraid. The trembling, the shallow breathing, the thin sheen of sweat – Cherie had all those symptoms.

'When do you think they are watching you?' Mark asked, more attentive. 'And where?' He had to lean in; the loud singer was really giving Pete a run for his money.

'At night. When I'm down the street,' Cherie whispered. 'And . . .' She motioned for him to bend lower. 'And *here*,' she said. 'In *here*.'

Mark felt a coldness in his guts. He resisted the urge to look behind him. 'Do you know who this person is, Cherie? Can you point them out now? You don't have to say a thing.'

A pause.

'No,' she answered. 'But I can feel it.'

Mark couldn't arrest everyone in the bar on a feeling. Still, there was something so nervous about her that he persisted. He cleared his throat. 'Would you like to talk about it now?'

The woman sniffed, ran a hand absentmindedly over her arm. 'No, I've done all that. And I'm used to it. I'm always being watched – it's the life of an actor.'

'Not in your private life. It's not something you should get used to. Why don't you come in and we'll write up a new report?'

'Let's do it on Monday,' she said, nodding, her mouth twisting into a smile. 'I can drop by the station then.'

'Good.'

'Do you like theatre, detective?'

Mark had rarely been to the theatre. He'd rather watch films, or a good TV show. 'I can't really say.'

'I've almost finished writing a play. You'll have to come and see it.'

'Yeah? What's it about?'

'Oh, this and that.' Cherie was back to full flirtatious mode. 'But I think you'd like it. It's got everything: drama, fear, rivalry, heroism . . .'

The bar was hot. People were crowding in.

'Sounds like a winner,' Mark said.

'I've been doing my research,' she said, taking a long sip of her drink. 'And what I'm discovering could even be of interest to the law.'

'I hope you're not hiding information of a criminal nature, Cherie.'

Cherie looked up at him from her straw with her big, blue and slightly bloodshot eyes. 'Why no, detective.'

'Monday then,' he said. 'I'll be expecting you.'

Cherie's straw made a loud slurping sound as she came to the end of her drink. 'Yes, sir!' she said, with real pleasure.

The door opened and Jane Southern walked in. Heads turned, they turned all right.

'Bye then, Cherie.' Mark sculled the rest of his beer and put it to rest on the bar. 'And *I* believe you.' He wasn't sure he did, not entirely, but he wasn't dismissing it either.

Cherie placed her hand on his sleeve. 'Thank you,' she said. 'You're a good man.' Then added playfully, 'I'll catch you on Monday – *it's a date!*'

Someone else crowded in front of him and he took the opportunity to move away from the bar. He waved at Jane, pointing above the heads towards the dining room. She smiled and followed. Nudging past the crowd of drinkers, he was mildly surprised to see Ian, the Hibernian owner, drinking with another man by the bar. He nodded g'day to them. Ian nodded back, still unfriendly. Inside the dining room, there were the same little round tables with their single rose in jars, the lace tablecloths and white serviettes folded neatly on top. The specials board loomed. He moved closer to it, read 'Zucchini Soup and Fritters'.

Zucchini, he thought with a sigh. *The carp of the veggie garden.*

Jane stepped in front of him, a man with her. 'David, Mark. Mark, David.' The men shook hands. 'David's the cave diver leading the body retrieval,' Jane explained.

'You've been busy.'

'Yes, we've been at it all afternoon.'

Was Jane being funny? An awkward beat followed.

They found a table and Mark looked across at David as they sat down. Shorter than Mark, rather stocky and wearing a shirt with three pens neatly placed in the chest pocket, David didn't look like the world champion of anything.

'Did you manage to recover Mya?'

'No, not yet, but we know where she is. We'll be able to get to her tomorrow.'

'That's good,' Mark said.

'We tried to get her, but it's difficult,' David continued. 'She's become lodged into the ceiling of a chamber. Silt posed a real problem today. The surface is so flaky. We had to make a different plan.'

Lodged into the ceiling. Silt. *God.*

'David will bring her to the restriction, then we'll have another diver help bring her through,' Jane added. 'I'll be on the other side, in the entrance chamber. It'll take three of us, plus at least two more divers on top with the equipment and for standby. We couldn't have got it done today. It's too much.'

Mark tried to imagine it: the breathing, the lack of visibility, another dead body passing between them.

'Jane will be at the final stage in the entrance chamber,' David said, 'bringing Mya up to the surface.' There was a pause. David was repeating Jane's words. Now the man was fiddling with his napkin, twisting it into a rope. 'Jane's been great. She's organised the whole thing.'

Mark nodded. He knew this about her. Jane cleared her throat and looked at the menu before declaring she needed a drink. What did they want? Mark asked for beer, David for lemon squash.

The moment she left, David started talking again. 'We did think about drilling through twenty metres of earth above Mya, but this land is so unstable, we'd risk creating a massive sinkhole. Could be a disaster. So, we gave up on that idea.'

Mark listened, knowing how grief and shock could sometimes make people want to vent, explain themselves aloud. Around them, more people filed into the dining room, choosing tables, taking seats. Each time the door to the bar opened, he heard the happy noise and wished himself among it – not here, listening to David talk about underwater caves and restrictions.

'Drilling sometimes works, but the land has to be stable. I've heard of it being done to rescue people trapped in concrete drains. But that's concrete! If we drilled here, it could create cracks right through to the coastline. So yes, in the end, we decided a three-team retrieval was best. Despite the silt . . . it's so thick down there.'

'The silt sounds terrible.' Mark drifted off, let the man speak further.

'Well, it can be. More people, more chance of disturbing the sides of the chamber – then you get silt and visibility is gone. Just one flick of your fins will do it. It is possible to dive with no visibility, but you have to be one hundred per cent reliant on your guidelines, and no diver wants to be one hundred per cent reliant on just one thing.'

'Were you good friends with Mya?'

The man's face dropped. 'Yes. Cave diving in Australia is a small community. The CDAA – that's the national cave divers association – requires divers to have an advanced scuba-diving qualification, as well as at least fifty logged dives, including two night dives and five dives deeper than twenty-five metres. Only then can they take part in basic cave-diving programs. There's not many of us that have done all that – well, officially I mean. In the old days, of course, people just did whatever they wanted. There are some real horror stories.'

Like the Franklin Three.

'So, we all know each other. I'd dived with Mya in Mexico and South Africa – the Nullarbor too. She wasn't exactly like family, but we were friends, definitely. And I had the most immense respect for her, as a diver and a person. I still do.' David raised his chin. 'She was incredibly daring, always pushing to go further, seek out new caves. She's left a girlfriend and parents who are devastated. From what I heard, none of them liked her diving, but they couldn't stop her from doing it.'

'I'm sorry.'

'It's just something we have to do.' David shrugged. 'It's part of us. Diving's what I live for. And we all know the risks. Every time we dive, we know that death is a real possibility. There's no room for errors, none. Mya knew that as well as anybody.'

'Probably doesn't make it easier.'

'But you see, in a way it *does* make it easier.' David leaned forward. 'Mya was a professional. She died doing what she loved best. We all say it, the risks are worth it.'

Are they?

'Do we know the cause of death?' It seemed like a stupid question to ask about someone who'd died metres underground, in a water-filled cave.

David rubbed his forehead, looking tired. 'We think it was the guidelines. She must have got mixed up in them when she found the other body. It happens. The lines always have to be clear. If they're not, it's dangerous. Add silt, add the Martini effect, then they're a death knell.'

Jane arrived back with the drinks. 'Better order food now,' she said. 'Place is filling up.'

David ignored Jane's suggestion and kept talking. 'Mya had her own guideline and the sideline she'd taken into the second chamber, but she got caught up in Eloise's rope. She had a knife out – it looks like she'd managed to cut it, but with the effort and the time it took, she ran out of oxygen and drowned.'

Mark stared hard at his beer coaster and then looked up at David, who was rubbing his forehead, elbow on the table. 'I'm sorry, mate,' he said.

The man nodded.

'Let's order,' Jane said, and they walked to the bar.

Mark asked for the fish of the day from a man who looked like a John Dory and whose name tag, pinned to his grey-green top, indicated his name was indeed John.

'Thanks, John,' Mark said, pressing his bankcard to the little machine. 'What fish have we got with the chips?' *Your brothers? Your sister?*

'Grenadier,' John said, his thin spiky hair unmoving. 'Fresh.' This was the type of story he'd like to share with Rose. She'd enjoy it, probably have one to tell of her own. Maybe about a grey-haired nurse who looked like a shark, or a sunburned Englishman named Bernie. What was Rose up to right now? Jane Southern was beautiful tonight, as Mark knew she would be. 'Striking' was the word generally used about her. There were other words too – muttered by men in lines behind her, by male colleagues when she gave them instruction. He'd once been in something like love with her. But on this evening, he was surprised at how little he felt for Jane Southern. It was Rose, all Rose.

On his way back to his table, Mark was mildly surprised to see one of the Sinclair wives sitting by the fireplace. With her was the well-dressed woman who'd smacked his hand and was earlier singing with the girl. He went over to them, said hello. They said hello back.

'Is that the other police you're with?' the wife asked. Cath, he thought, married to Nic.

'One of them is. The other is a professional cave diver.'

Both women shuddered. 'Why, why was Eloise down there?' the older lady said. 'Murray was always strict about it – no cave diving. Not after what he'd seen down the Tomb.'

'Did you know Murray well?'

'I knew them all.' She sniffed. 'Murray, beautiful Juliette and all the children. It's tragedy after tragedy.'

There was a brief silence. Jane and David had already returned to their seats and were sharing a plate of chips.

'Margery and I were just discussing how perhaps it's time Judy and Phil move back into town,' Cath said. 'They've been in that place for years and, really, with Nic and Mat gone, there's no point in them being there. Plus, the farm's a dud. It's too much for them – all those old buildings, probably drenched in asbestos. Georgia would much prefer to be in town.'

The older woman was nodding. 'They could get a nice little apartment, overlooking the bay. That's what I did when Gordon died. Best thing that ever happened.'

Gordon dying, or leaving the farm?

'It's hard,' Mark said, 'to move from a place you've lived all your life, where you've grown up, raised your family.' He knew these things. It was what made him reluctant to sell his mother's house, where he now lived. The memories, the shared history of place and people.

Margery gave a short laugh. 'They had a much nicer house to begin with. They only moved when Murray's business went bust after Eloise was born.' The woman rubbed at the pearls about her neck. 'The original house was just lovely.'

'Right in town, as you turn up the hill – the double storey overlooking the bay.' Cath had a wistful expression her face. 'Just beautiful!'

'Murray made a decision to buy three more boats, expand his business – just when the bottom fell out of the fishing industry. It does that, has peaks and troughs, but in the mid-eighties, there was a bad patch, and Murray had to sell the bay house. Fortunately, he had enough to buy the fifty acres out of town, near the Doyles. So now they live this kind of semi-farming, semi-fishing life.'

'Their old house has a balcony from the main bedroom,' Cath said, still dreaming of her sliding doors moment. 'You can see the whole bay and all the lights of town.'

'It was soon after Juliette died when they moved. She would have hated it out there in the mud.'

'*I* hate it out there!' Cath muttered, ripping bread off her plate and shoving it into her mouth. 'Nothing grows – it's like a desert. People told them not to buy it, but apparently Murray thought he could make it work and Frank Doyle sold it to them for such a good price.'

'Juliette loved that house by the bay,' the old woman mused, her head tipped to one side. 'She used to stand on the balcony and look out in the evenings, like some sort of romantic character from a film. What a beauty she was!' The woman sighed. 'But yes, the family moved out of town after she died.'

'Such a shame!' Cath said mournfully.

'In the end, I guess, it was a good thing the Sinclairs moved there. Gerri and James had Eloise and the boys to play with as they were growing up. It was lovely to see them all trooping out and about.'

Mark thought about Eloise flying like a bird from branch to branch on the cypress trees, Gerri waiting underneath. Where was James at those times?

Jane was waving at him, pointing to his meal, which had just arrived. He went to say his goodbyes to the women, but they were still carrying on the conversation.

'. . . but the house still looks good, doesn't it? I think of Juliette sometimes when I look across at it at night and see Cherie standing there.'

'Does Cherie live in the old Sinclair house now?' Mark was faintly surprised. 'The one by the bay?'

'Oh yes.' The woman played with the pearls at her neck absentmindedly. 'It's next to mine. She bought it from Murray when he moved, and has been there ever since.'

'Lots of people wanted to buy it, didn't they?' Cath said. 'It is the best one around. There were some big farming families from up north who were interested in it, but Cherie got in first.'

Mark paused. He couldn't reconcile the Cherie from the bar with that impressive house.

'She used to be an actress, and a costume designer – quite well known too.'

Mark blinked. Was the old woman reading his thoughts? He wouldn't put it past her.

'She even went out with Mel Gibson.'

Cath gave a smirk. 'And Hugh Jackman too, wasn't it, Margery?'

'Yes.' The older woman was matter of fact. 'Him too. Cherie was very pretty in her younger days, really beautiful to look at.'

Mark finally said his farewells and turned for his own table.

'Did you order an egg and lettuce sandwich, dear?' Margery called to him, laughter in her voice. 'I hope you got something substantial. I don't want you taking food from anyone else's plates.'

He had to laugh. Margery reminded him of his mother's friends.

His plate of fish'n'chips looked inviting. Big and unfussy, more batter than fish and more chips than salad. Good, it was what he felt like.

It wasn't long before David pushed the conversation back to the topic of cave diving, of other retrievals he'd been involved in, of the time he'd dived in Norway, under layers of ice, to almost one hundred and thirty metres, where at such depths and temperatures any tear in a suit could result in agonising death.

'It's this feeling though, there in the deep cold – hardly anyone has ever dived there, you're one of the first, you're in a place never seen by humans and although death is a distinct possibility, it's worth it. It's worth it!' Keyed up on adrenaline and made anxious by his ordeal, the man's voice was loud enough to make other diners stop and stare.

Jane put down her knife and fork. 'I think it's time we went back to the hotel, David,' she said. 'You need to rest. We've got a big day ahead of us.'

There was a long pause. David stared into his gnocchi, largely uneaten. 'I'm sorry,' he said. 'Today has been difficult. There's so many things to process.'

'Will you be right to go back down there tomorrow?' Jane asked. 'If you're feeling shaky or anxious, then we'll change the date or get someone else.'

'I'm okay,' David said. 'I really am. But you're right. I need to get some sleep so I'm sharp tomorrow.'

Jane turned to Mark. 'I'll be in touch about both divers,' she said.

Mark remembered Phil's question. Had hoped to ask it in more official circumstances, but plunged in now before David and Jane left. 'Was Eloise by any chance wearing a charm bracelet?' he asked. 'Her brothers said she never went anywhere without it.'

'No bracelet on the body.' Jane was refusing to state it was Eloise till she had forensic confirmation, even though social media had been naming her since the beginning. 'I'm sorry.' She folded her serviette, put it neatly on the plate. 'The pathologist took swabs today, dental photos. With a bit of luck, we should have confirmation of whether or not it is Eloise Sinclair by early next week.'

'Can you get them to hurry it up? The family are distraught.'

'I'll see what I can do. But I can't promise anything, you know that.'

People did things for Jane. Men did things. When she asked a favour, they relented. He'd relented.

'The thing that's really puzzling,' David said, shaking his head, 'is that the unidentified body was tangled up in unfixed rope. I mean, I get that one rope was Mya's blue sideline – and that was tied to her guideline in the main chamber, but there was that other rope she was caught up in . . .'

Jane discreetly nodded to her phone, flat on the table. On it was a photo from the dive site of the round entrance to the sinkhole. Sodden rope lay in a tangled mess on the grass. A dark shape in the corner of the frame looked at first like a thumb on the lens, but Mark soon realised it was Eloise's wetsuited foot. He moved forward, studied the whole photo closely. Leaned back, considered it again from afar.

'We're keeping the detail about the rope from the press,' Jane said to Mark, pocketing her phone.

'Why would anyone have unfixed rope on them in a chamber?' David mused aloud. 'Was she hoping to tie it to something?'

'The family says she didn't know how to dive,' Mark said.

The three fell silent.

'Okay, there was no guide rope, so maybe she thought she needed the rope for something else, as the first tie-off or something.' Jane sounded doubtful. 'But why wasn't it tied to something in the first chamber then?'

Mark nodded. 'She was down there by herself, clearly told no one she was going. She probably had no clue as to the safety rules.'

'Pretty stupid not to think of a guideline.' David shook his head.

'Unless,' Jane said, voice low, 'unless it *was* a fixed guideline that somehow came free.'

David and Jane stared at each other. Mark looked on, questioning.

'Guide ropes are generally tied to a secure place in the initial chamber,' David explained. 'Usually a few metres below the surface to prevent thrillseekers and amateurs having a go. If they can't see a rope – they're less likely to attempt a dive. But in this case, the rope was loose, it had been pulled all the way through the chamber, then the restriction and then the second chamber, so that Eloise was tangled up in it.'

A beat followed, tense. David went to say more but Jane put up her hand.

'Speculation,' she said. 'That's all this is. The police will work out what happened, leave it to us.'

Mark knew what David was going to say – the thing that had crossed all their minds the moment Jane said, 'Unless . . .'

Unless there had been people in the cavern diving before her. Unless there was someone else present on the day of her dive. Unless someone else untied the guideline. Unless someone else left Eloise in that dark, underwater cavern, deliberately. Left her there to die.

On his walk back to the motel, Mark felt the first warm breeze of spring. After all the rain and mud, the endless dreary days and biting cold of a bitter winter, the light air felt like a release. The sea and the saltbush, fresh smells, alive. He walked. There was no one about, despite it being a Saturday night. The drunks, the drug-affected, the homeless, the disaffected – they'd be out later, in the early hours of morning, when anonymity is easier to achieve and the dark makes light of unsavoury things.

Mark thought about Rose. It was the breeze that did it, the hint of new beginnings. His step lightened at the thought of calling her, apologising for his part in their conversation a few days earlier. But as he turned into his dour accommodation, he remembered the other thing. The thing that had stuck in the back of his mind as he ate his dinner. The photo of the crime scene Jane had showed him, the rope that entangled Eloise. Thick, orange rope, tied with trusty knots. Mark had seen rope exactly like it before – on board the boat of Phil and Judy Sinclair.

CHAPTER 10

Mark woke with a slight hangover, the smell of beer on him, mouth like sandpaper. He definitely should not have drunk that third beer from the mini bar when he got home from the pub. Yawning, Mark looked at the ceiling. Little cracks spread outward, random, artistic. It was probably asbestos, but it did look good. He closed his eyes.

If he was at home in Booralama now, he'd head to the Fat Bean for breakfast, the cafe Dennis owned. Rose usually joined him, even if she'd worked a late shift. They liked a late breakfast. It was nice sitting there, just together, eating breakfast and reading the papers. Sometimes Dennis would sit down, have a chat about the week, ask what they were up to. He was single, despite being widely known as the best-looking man over fifty this side of the Goyder line. Rose thought that one of her cousins would be a good match for him. Her name was Hilary, but don't hold that against her, Rose said. Hil's a real cracker.

Rose's parents were putting on a going-away dinner for her at their swanky house in Unley Park on Wednesday night, the evening before she was due to fly out. He had been invited, of course, as were Dennis, Squirrel and Donna and some of Rose's mates from the hospital. Mark liked Rose's family, loaded as they were. They were warm, interested, intelligent people – slightly confused at the path their third child had taken, but supportive nonetheless. It would be a good party, if he was still invited after their last conversation.

Call Rose, he told himself. *Call her.*

There were tea- and coffee-making facilities in his room. He made himself a tea – in the mug, not the tiny cup and saucer – and turned on the telly. Sitting on the edge of his bed, he drank, balancing the mug on his pillow while he thought about the local people he'd met. He tapped on his phone, pulling up the YouTube video of Gerri delivering the speech during Missing Persons Week and her relationship with Eloise Sinclair to a room packed full of lawyers and their lackeys.

Mark took a sip of tea and wished he'd chosen the cup and saucer as a bit of it spilled on his pillow. *Being a little risky resting it on the pillow, Mark. What's next? Downhill skiing?* He wiped at the stain with his forearm. It didn't do much. The tea was good. Hot. Milk just right.

Gerri was introduced as a person who *knew what it felt like to have her world yanked out beneath her*, to have her best friend gone and *nothing to show for it but anguish*. There was steady applause, not over the top. The audience was lawyers after all, not life coaches.

Gerri took to the stage smiling in a sad way. Her younger self was more lean, face free of lines, but in Mark's mind she was no more attractive than the woman he saw a day ago. At the lectern Gerri paused, then drooped her mouth comically. 'Does anyone have a pair of glasses? I've forgotten mine! Middle-aged moment!'

Cue quiet warm laughter; it was relatable.

Glasses borrowed, Gerri looked at her notes briefly. 'I just really miss my friend,' she said plainly. 'I think about Eloise every day. I have a son – he'd like to meet her. At night, I can't help myself, I think the worst. Not that she's been raped and murdered, but that she's being held somewhere, by someone who treats her badly and won't let her go. This is what it means to have a loved one missing. Your mind goes through all the darkest tunnels – you can't stop yourself. Other times, I think that maybe she's had an accident somewhere. She's fallen off a cliff, or she's been hit by a truck and the driver didn't know and she's in some deep ditch somewhere still.' There was a pause in the crowd; this brutal honesty was unexpected. Gerri took her glasses off. Looked at them, put them on again. 'I just really miss my friend,' she said. 'Sorry.' An audible sniffle from some-where in the back row.

Mark felt it himself: Gerri's grief was plainly written on her face. What else was there to say? Oh, but Gerri did have things to say. Collecting herself, she glanced at her notes and launched into tales of her and Eloise as young girls growing up in the country. The usual things: riding horses, riding bikes across the paddocks – one day even trying to ride the cows! Swimming, playing around on boats, helping each other with homework. Sleepovers with other girlfriends, whispering secrets into the night. The camera panned to the crowd, most were being atten-tive, while some were discreetly looking at their phones.

Mark checked his own phone. Time for breakfast: eggs, good heavy bread and a coffee. He shifted a little on the bed and his mug of tea wavered, almost spilled again. He placed the drink on the side table.

Gerri was now talking about the day Eloise went missing. Mark turned up the volume as the lawyers on the screen leaned in.

'It was just an ordinary Saturday. We'd been hanging out the day before – my brother, Eloise and me – but she wasn't feeling well, so she went home. She said she was maybe planning on going snorkelling with her boyfriend, Brett, the next day, but she'd see how she was feeling. On the morning she went missing, her eldest brother, Philippe, saw her briefly and they had a chat. Later on, she went into town with one of her other brothers. When they came home, she went to her bedroom, everyone else went out and that's the last time she was ever seen.'

Mark turned off the clip, put his phone on the bed and began to dress for the day. So many questions to consider about the case, past interviews to scour. Which brother was the one she went down the street with? What did she do there? It was all very vague.

His jeans felt a little looser today; it was all the walking. He shifted the pillow so that the tea stain faced the window and had a quick scan of the room, patting his pocket for his wallet. A leaf blower started up outside his door. Ian. There were no leaves on the concrete outside; the man just liked doing angry things. That sound! It had a maddening hammer to it, a disconnect from the job at hand.

His mother, Helen, had favoured the rake. What a joy, she often said, to rake the leaves in your garden and spread them for compost. Mark pictured his mother now, in the garden, leaves clogging up the rake spears, dirt on her face and in her silver hair. She'd married his father, a serious man of Greek heritage who tended only to growing food, not flowers or shrubs. *What was the attraction between them?* Mark wondered, not for the first time. Had his mother's face once launched a thousand ships? He tried to remember what she'd looked like in the wedding photos he'd packed up months ago, and couldn't recall. To him, she'd always be Helen in the garden, cheerful and sprightly as a wren.

It grew quiet outside. Mark tentatively poked his head out the door – Ian was nowhere to be seen. He stepped outside, gently locking the door behind him.

'Off somewhere, are you?'

Save me. 'Yep, breakfast. Any recommendations?'

Ian stood for a moment in contemplation, the leaf blower at his side like an axe. 'No,' he said. 'I've never been one for eating out, especially not for breakfast.'

'Did you have a good night at the pub?'

Ian grunted. Mark caught something about it being better than the Friday night, but still just okay.

Mark started to walk backwards. 'Well, have a good day. I'll be off then.'

'You going to talk to Brett Twymann?'

Ah, Mark thought. That was why Ian had started the blower outside his door. Gossip. 'No doubt someone will, or already has,' Mark said deliberately.

'A real piece of work that bloke. Slippery.'

'He used to go out with Eloise Sinclair, didn't he?' Mark feigned innocence.

'Her and every other girl in the town,' Ian said bitterly. 'The girls liked him – you know how they go for the daredevil types.'

Mark shrugged. *Do they?*

'My eldest, Liz, had a thing for him for a while there, but despite a bit of attention, it was always Eloise he went back to.' Ian shook his head. 'I said to her, "Lizzie, don't go for the slippery ones. It's the nice guys you should be aiming for."' Ian revved up the leaf blower again. The sound was deafening. 'But they always finish last,' he yelled. 'We always finish last.'

Wind roared as Mark walked into town, head bowed. He didn't like being 'we' with Ian, and he didn't like the suggestion that blokes like him always finished last. It wasn't true. Surely it wasn't true. He tried to think and no, blokes like him were at least in the top three, top five.

A horn tooted and Mark looked up to see the publican Barry. 'Need a lift, mate?'

Mark nodded, climbed inside Barry's ute. 'You on your way to the pub?'

'Yeah – bit of cleaning. Got Cherie to come and help me, she does sometimes.'

'Saw her last night. Had a little chat about the person she thinks is watching her.'

'Yeah?' Barry changed gears, waved at a couple pushing a pram on the footpath beside them. 'She have any more to add?'

'She said that she could sense him, "*in here*".'

Barry turned his mouth into a grimace, gave a shudder. 'She can put the wind up you, can't she? Mind you, we've checked the cameras every time she's said it. Nothing.'

'You don't believe her?'

Barry looked sideways at him. 'Do you?'

Did he? 'I think so.'

'Yeah, well.' Barry pulled right into the main road. 'Let us know if there's anything we can do to help. Cherie may be a bit slippery, but she's a good bird. Great actor too, generous. Heart's in the right place.'

Slippery again. Tricky, evasive.

Barry dropped him off opposite the bay. Mark wandered into The Collective cafe and sat at the same table near the window. Dramatic music played. Was it the theme track to *Phantom of the Opera*? Strange.

He took a brief look at the plastic menu, then got out his Broken Tyre & Brakes notepad and drew up a rough family tree for the Doyles and the Sinclairs, adding in some notes about Brett and Scott below it:

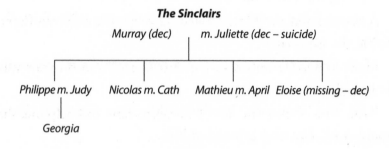

The Sinclairs

Murray (dec) — m. Juliette (dec – suicide)

Philippe m. Judy   Nicolas m. Cath   Mathieu m. April   Eloise (missing – dec)

Georgia

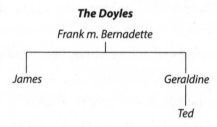

The Doyles

Frank m. Bernadette

James   Geraldine

Ted

Brett Twymann: Boyfriend of Eloise.
Scott Boxhall: dec. Car accident two weeks after Eloise went missing.
Boyfriend of Gerri. Father of Ted.

After a thought, he added:

Cherie: Local. Thinks someone is watching her. Actress/Costume designer
Barry Coffey: Likes Cherie, but thinks she may be lying?

Lastly, he wrote after a pause:

The Franklin Three.

Satisfied at last, Mark sat back. A sulky waiter arrived. Mark ordered eggs, toast, coffee and a tea. Did they have salt and pepper shakers? Could he have those too?

'*And* a tea?' the waiter asked.

'Yes, please. Breakfast isn't breakfast without a good cup of tea.'

'I'm guessing it's not chai you want then.'

'You're a good guesser.'

Turning on his heels, the man headed into the kitchen.

A young father nodded at Mark from the next table. Friendly. 'You're the cop, right?'

Mark gave a silent groan. 'I'm a cop, yeah – not necessarily *the* cop.'

'Cos, that would be, like, John McClane from *Die Hard*, wouldn't it?' The man grinned at him.

'Or Axel Foley, *Beverly Hills Cop*?'

'I always liked Clarice Starling. That last scene in *The Silence of the Lambs* with Buffalo Bill watching her through night-vision glasses? That was some serious shit.'

'Yeah,' Mark agreed. 'It really was. Now you say it, I think she's *the* cop.'

The baby on the man's knee started whingeing and the man gave her a bit of banana. Mark remembered doing that with his boys.

'I used to be friends with Brett Twymann,' the father said, after a pause. 'It's funny what people say about him.'

Mark waited as the man handed his baby some more banana and watched as the child squashed it between her chubby fingers. He knew that the public liked to be involved in cases, particularly the gruesome ones. Public intervention was mostly a hindrance; there were those who liked to insert themselves in a sad story, who found energy in the drama, but sometimes, sometimes there were gems.

'There's this whole thing being built up against Brett, like he had something to do with Eloise's death. Not that he murdered her or anything, but how he was this awful bloke who everyone was glad to see the back of. People are going on about how he treated girls, how he was a bully and was arrogant and all that.'

'Yeah?'

'He's a little older than me, but when I knew him, Brett was a good bloke. Had it all, of course – the looks, the best girlfriend, could surf like nobody's business. But he was okay. Not up himself like they're making out. I missed him when he left town. With him and Scottie Boxhall gone, it just wasn't the same.'

So, according to this affable father, Brett Twymann was a good bloke. Mark wondered, and not for the first time, what that entailed. The spectrum was broad: someone big and male from the country, someone who could take a joke, someone who had a go, a prime minister who could drink a yard glass in world record time. A decent man. In time, Brett Twymann could be them all.

The baby spat out the banana and the man scooped the yellow goo in his hand. 'Not like those Sinclair boys,' he said.

'Eh?' Mark was looking at the man's hand.

'Nic and Mat – they could be a pair of cocky shits. Used to play tricks on us younger kids, then call us pussies if we didn't laugh. You know, "Aww, don't be like that, it's just a joke" kind of thing. Yeah, right. Like being locked in the teachers' toilets after school is a real joke. Ha ha.'

This didn't marry with what Mark had heard about the Sinclairs. He felt a vague disappointment in them. *I thought you boys were better than this.* 'Phil seems like a good bloke.'

'Phil's great,' the father said, the regurgitated banana still in his fist. 'And you know what? We all grow up, don't we? Mat and Nic are fine now, as far as I can tell.' The man stood to leave, hoisting the little one on his hip.

Mark looked at his list again. 'Do you know much about the Doyles?'

'Can't say I know Frank or Bernadette well. My older sister nursed Bernadette when she first got diagnosed with dementia. From what I hear, she's in some flash care home for the elderly in Unley. Fullarton Home – they have an open garden day that my wife likes to go to. James keeps to himself, bit of a loner, but Gerri's all right. Top teacher. Back in the day, she and Eloise Sinclair were the two hottest girls around here.' The man looked dreamily into space. 'Life's a bit different now, eh?' He nodded towards his baby, who was beaming at Mark.

Mark beamed back. It was hard not to. 'Why did Gerri stay in town all these years, do you reckon?'

Father and baby moved towards the door. 'She moved once, I think, but came back. She's got her family here, she's protective of James and, well, it happens. People move back. Small town, you know everyone, it's comfortable, houses cheaper, life is never a surprise. Sometimes that's all you want, isn't it? Plus, it's pretty nice here – look what we've got!' He gestured to the windows and the view beyond. The sea, the sky.

Both men stared at it for a few moments, till the baby started to grizzle.

'Having said that'—the baby placed her chubby hand over her father's mouth and the man moved his head from side to side trying to speak—'my wife's sick of this joint. She says she'll give it two more months, max.'

'Where's she want to go?'

The man flicked the banana expertly into a bin, picked up a serviette and wiped his hand. 'Where they all want to go, mate, northern New South Wales. The weather, the lifestyle, the Instagram. But more importantly – anywhere but bloody Broken Bay.'

CHAPTER 11

The ocean was calm. Just a light wind now, high enough to make the tips of the tall banksias sway, but not low enough to touch the waves. The surface of the sea was deep blue, a silk sheet, barely ruffled. It amazed Mark how often the ocean changed colours. It could appear greenish, grey and every shade of blue. The river of his hometown was changeable too, but more subtle. Mostly light caramel, and after a rain it turned a deep chocolate brown. Quicksilver in the morning sun, and yellow under a blooming wattle. In drought, the river took on a sickly green hue, and everything about it was cast in depressing light.

But the ocean, the ocean was everywhere. Its magnificence could not be sullied by drought, or so it seemed. It was too powerful, too vast. It would swallow you up in an instant with no tree branch to cling to, no shallows a few steps away.

The father in the cafe had said his wife wanted to go to northern New South Wales, to the place where lifestyle meant something more than living. But looking at the bay now, at the white beach, the small town on the edge of it and the soaring cape, Mark thought that perhaps his wife should reconsider the move. Because they would come, he thought; the Instagrammers and the casually rich. They would come, one moody photo at a time, natural fibres pressed tight against slim frames and hashtagging van life. Byron Bay and its like were too crowded now, the search was on for towns like this, and cool people were hungry for change.

Mark finished his breakfast, paid, and thought about what needed to be done before the investigations team arrived in the morning. He texted Jane to ask her about the recovery, received no reply. Possibly the dive to recover Mya's body was occurring right now. Mark wondered at David Furneaux's task: the recovery through silt-filled underwater tunnels of his former diving companion.

The thought of going back to the Hibernian and listening to Ian take it out on machinery didn't appeal. He walked the other way, looking at his phone. Rose would be up by now, well and truly. He should call her. He didn't want to. He really should.

Mark dialled her number.

'Mark,' Rose said.

'Rose.' Suddenly he was tongue-tied.

There was a pause. 'I've been wanting to ring you,' Rose said. 'I've thought about it since the day you left – well, not the day you left, I was too angry, but today and yesterday and the day before that.'

'Me too. I'm sorry. I was a real dickhead.'

Isn't it time you settled down? he'd said to her. *You're not twenty-four anymore.* It was a stupid thing to say, the sort of thing a father said to a child.

'And I know I don't have any right to tell you what to do with your life. You can do what you want, it's all up to you. I wish I hadn't said it.'

Rose was quiet.

'It's because I'll miss you so much, that's why I was such an idiot.'

'I know.'

Neither of them spoke. Mark watched a little boat out on the bay, straining against its moorings. The tide was coming in.

'I know you can't leave the boys,' Rose said. 'But isn't there another way? Surely there's not just one path from here on in.'

He knew what she meant: marriage, mortgage, paying off the house, kids leaving, retirement, weddings of children, nieces and nephews, Metamucil, checking seniors cards for discounts, sore knees, reading the obituaries and SmoothFM. The path from full-time to part-time, then retirement. Younger workmates pretending to be sad when your desk is cleared. Farewell cards with names you've never heard. A trip around Australia in the Jayco, wine with other campers at dusk. A hip replacement, a cancer scare, All-Bran for breakfast.

But there were other things too: reading every Shakespeare play, bushwalking, trips up north when it wasn't school holidays, going to wineries, visiting old friends, only talking to people who you really wanted to.

'It's not all bad, Rose.' And it wasn't, it wasn't! Mark had old friends in Booralama, a steady job, his mother's house. He liked the idea of a Jayco. There was comfort in stability, in the familiar. *Rose doesn't like it because most people do*, he thought.

'I know.'

They'd said it all before: Rose didn't want kids, she wanted a big life, adventure and possibility. Hundreds of years ago, Rose would have been one of those people who set out on ships in search of new lands. She would have said goodbye to friends and lovers at the docks and then stood out on the front of the boat – eyes fixed on the horizon, not the shore.

'My ticket's booked for Thursday at midday now. They had to change the flight.'

Mark felt a pang. He'd hoped for a day together after the party. 'I'm stuck in Broken Bay with no windscreen – plus Angelo wants me to help out with work here. There's been that cave diver's body we had to retrieve.'

'Cave diving! I met someone who did that in Mexico.' Rose was intrigued. 'Imagine!'

That word 'Imagine!' highlighted the difference between them. Where she saw wide open caverns with beams of light, he saw only darkness and confinement. Perhaps the only real difference between them was the ability to form a positive mental concept. When John Lennon sung about imagining no possessions, all Mark could think of was his house and car. Rose would see a glittering world.

'Yeah, imagine.' Mark didn't want to imagine an underwater cave right now. He wanted to imagine Rose and him together in five years, in ten. But he couldn't.

'Charlie called me the other day.' Rose changed the subject.

'He did?' Mark had never heard of one of his sons speaking to Rose without him present.

'Yeah, he wanted to know about the large intestine. Some project for school.'

'Right.'

'He's such a smart kid. I can see him as a doctor, you know. Kelly and Steve agree.'

Mark was stunned. Here was this whole other life going on without him: relationships, knowledge-sharing, talks of careers. He felt ashamed. Not for the first time, he had pictured himself at the centre of things: Kelly, the boys, Rose, his friends as planets orbiting around him. Whereas he was just another ball of gas in the unruly universe.

'You'll still be able to come to the party, won't you? Mum would love to see you, and Grandma of course.'

'Yes, I'll be there.'

'And we can talk then? Can we?' A female voice was calling in the background – one of Rose's sisters, or a niece. She'd been in Adelaide for a few days, getting ready for the move.

Mark felt a prickle at the back of his eyes. 'Course.'

But really, there was nothing more to say.

The wind died down, the bay was blue and sun speared hot through the clouds. If this was a movie, Mark thought, the wind would blow against his face and he'd stare at a choppy sea, grim-faced and stoic. With his chest out, hair pushed back by the wind, he'd look full of manly sorrow. But what did the ocean ever care about broken hearts? It wasn't there to make him look noble, and besides, his hair now wasn't the sort to flow backwards. Only Keith Urban had hair like that.

Mark began walking along the bay path. A group of middle-aged men on expensive bikes rode past him in a pack of bright logos. Their little bums rose in chorus from their seats as they pedalled up the hill, and with their jostling and brightness, the sleek clacking of gears and cleats, they were like a mass of Christmas beetles rushing home.

There were birds on the shore now, tiny ones, running over the sand with cartoonish speed. Dotterels? Sand pipers? Mark wished he'd bought his bird book and binoculars with him. He watched them for a while, running back and forth, always together and never alone. Further along, on the Victorian coast, were the short-tailed shearwaters. They travelled each year from Alaska, back to their same nests on an island off Port Fairy, only to have most of them be eaten by foxes and cats. No one admitted their cat was a bird killer. Not *their* cat. But give Kitty half an hour and see the feathers pile up. Those little birds, Mark thought as he walked. If only he could channel some of their grit. Maybe his life was too easy, too settled.

A car drove by, a BMW, the couple inside like plastic people, looking out. It slowed and stopped ahead of him. As he drew level the passenger said, 'Pardon me?' The woman had the sort of shiny, understated hair only achieved with lots of money. Mark knew that because his wealthy sister had such hair. 'We'd like to know—'

'We've just spent the night here on our way through.' The driver leaned in beside her, cutting in. 'It's quite charming, this place, isn't it? I mean, the beach is marvellous and the real estate is so cheap. You could have ocean views here for less than a mill. Do you know a decent place where we can have some lunch? We'd love some wholesome country food.'

'I'm not a local,' Mark said, bending down towards the car window. 'But I ate at the Royal last night, and it was fine.'

'We're not fussy,' the man said. 'We can rough it, can't we, Daaa? We love all the country things.'

'Daaa'? *Di* – Diana. When the Queen spoke about Princess Diana's death on television, that was the thing he got most from it. Rich people can't say 'Di'.

Daaa nodded, a graceful hand to her ear. Maybe she *was* royalty.

Mark gave them directions and as they drove off, he bowed deeply before tying up a shoelace.

It took him a while to notice the double-storey brick house half hidden behind the she-oak and moonah trees. Banksia, native grasses, rocks and shrubs lined the front yard. Dark wood, large windows, discreet. There was a front fence, thin palings in the same wood as the house. A balcony on the second floor. Mark turned the other way – if you stood on it and looked out, the view would be unparalleled, across the whole bay and town. It had to be Cherie's place, the best house in town, according to Cath.

It was also the former home of Murray and Juliette Sinclair. What a loss to have to move from there to the muddy shambles that was their place five kilometres inland. Mark stood before the trees, pondering the house and the garden. A figure, half obscured in the shade, stood in one of the rooms, and Mark moved quickly on. He could easily imagine Cherie spotting him and calling for him to come inside for a drink. The house next door was dark wood, equally tasteful but only one storey. In the front garden, deep in cuttings and debris, was the guardian of egg sandwiches, karaoke singer and friend of the family: Margery.

Mark said good morning and she stood up. For a brief moment, his heart constricted; with her sunhat and gardening gloves, surrounded by garden detritus, Margery looked just like his mother.

'Would you like a cup of tea?' she asked. 'I was just about to put the kettle on.'

There was no reason to decline. Mark followed her inside to her kitchen. There, she made the tea and bustled about looking for biscuits, while they chatted. It was pleasant just to talk to someone about the good things in life: gardens, sunshine and English Breakfast versus Earl Grey. Once he'd helped her locate a tray, she laid it with a teapot, cups and saucers and slices of fruit-cake and carried it outside. They sat down on chairs overlooking the garden and the sea beyond. Their general chat turned to the Doyles and the Sinclairs.

'The families have always been competitive,' Margery gave a wry smile. 'Fortune has struck each of them at different times. Years ago, the Sinclairs were wealthy, lobster fishing was lucrative and they owned a large boat, plus the house next door. At that time, the Doyles were poor dairy farmers, scrabbling about for a decent living. Murray Sinclair, doing so well, thought he'd expand his business and went into debt buying up a small fleet of boats. But the next three lobster seasons were disastrous. At the same time, land prices were rising and the Doyle family was on the up. The Sinclairs went broke, Juliette died and Murray had to sell his house in town. It was the Doyles who sold them the land and the old farmhouse, so Murray and the children could at least have somewhere to live. Murray was a good man and he tried – but he had a problem with the drink, got depressed and died of a heart attack. Phil was twenty at the time, Eloise would have been seven, I guess. Phil took on the family business and the parenting of his siblings, and despite all the help from the community, he had his hands full. Then the Doyles renovated, bought new equipment, modernised their farming. Now, Phil and Judy can barely make a living. Strange how it all works.'

Honeyeaters hung from the callistemon, like kids drunk on fairy floss. Bees buzzed, the she-oaks swished about. *Shhh. Shhh.* The Sinclairs had put their hopes into the sea, and the Doyles into the soil. For the time being, land was winning – but watching the ocean roll in, Mark had no doubt of its power to reign again.

'Did you know Juliette very well?'

'Oh, we were great friends.' Margery brushed crumbs off her chest. 'When she arrived here with her backpack, we had so much fun together. She got together with Murray in the first few days! There weren't many people my age in Broken Bay. I'd just married Gordon, so I was a little lonely.'

A common story, Mark knew. The landowner goes to the city for business, meets a young woman. They have the time of their lives, he brings her back to the town, and she's entranced by the romanticism of rural life. They move permanently. Winter settles in, the rain and the mud. The farm doesn't go so well, there's repairs on the house to be made, but the land comes first. Bats in the roof, a dead possum in the tank water. There's For Lease signs on every second shop, and the town doesn't seem so quaint anymore.

'She was interested in everything – and so funny,' Margery continued. 'She'd buy hideous paintings in op shops because she felt sorry for them. In their ugliness, there was something beautiful, she said. That was Juliette: a Brigitte Bardot beauty herself, but it was the little things that interested her, pulled at her heartstrings.'

Mark picked a leaf off a banksia and rubbed at it.

'And clothes! She'd buy these awful jumpers from the op shops too, all holes and smelling of mothballs, but somehow when Juliette wore them, they were beautiful again. I told this to the children of course, the boys and Eloise. They loved hearing about their mother.'

The bay was filled with boats now, all sizes, like a kids' bath. Thick clouds sat low in the sky, awaiting instruction.

Mark could understand Juliette's sentimentality about ugly and discarded clothes. He felt anxious when he saw self-published books with cheap covers sitting on the front desk at the post office. He sometimes bought them out of pity, rarely read a word, but never threw them away. Someone had taken the time to write a book. It could be a classic.

'Juliette had four kids and a husband who loved her,' Mark reflected. 'And yet with all that, she must have felt terrible enough to take her own life.'

Margery's head whipped around, sharp. He remembered the slap on his hand, felt it tingle now. 'Don't believe that rot. Juliette didn't kill herself. She had a husband who adored her, three gorgeous sons and a new baby. She might have been homesick, terribly so, but depressed? No. Not Juliette.'

The ferocity of her response surprised him. 'I've been told it was suicide.'

Margery gave a humph. 'Murray was broken after Juliette died. He completely lost it. I wouldn't have trusted what he said to police at all. He loved her, but really, him going on about her being homesick, stressed and tired didn't help. He showed them a letter she was writing to her mother, which detailed all the things and people she missed. The police looked at it, listened to Murray and concluded suicide straight away.'

Mark was silent. Suicide was so common, he could see how the cops – faced with a grieving husband and family, who gave evidence of sadness and the letters to prove it – would come to that conclusion.

'Juliette told me the things she was pining for. Good bread, her sisters, shops, fashion, art galleries and bookshops. She missed the short distances in Europe, and her little dog who had grown old and couldn't walk. She was homesick for France.' A pause. 'Don't you see?' Margery said. 'They're all normal things! And when she'd written in her diary about not being able to sleep? About seeing things when her eyes were closed? She had young children. There was a gap after Phil, then suddenly she had three kids under three! The woman was exhausted! And no wonder she'd begun pining for home, the lobster fishing was going through a hard patch, they were worried about keeping the business, Murray was hardly ever there.' Margery shook her head, cross. 'I marched in there and told the police straight out:

Juliette wouldn't have killed herself, she wasn't the type. Oh, but they didn't listen to me.'

They wouldn't have. Country cops in the early eighties, the husband telling everyone how tired and sad she was, her own diary letting on how exhausted she'd become – they would have concluded *poor young foreigner girl couldn't cope.*

'The thing was, everyone misjudged her as some sort of dreamy nut. Well, she was dreamy – but she was fierce too, and free, and very funny. I still miss her after all these years.'

Mark looked more closely at the old lady, her blue eyes rockpool sharp. She would have made a wonderful witness. She still would. 'What *do* you think happened then?'

Margery sniffed, patted her thighs in a matter-of-fact gesture. 'Nowadays, I think she fell off the cliff. It would be like her to stand right on the edge, looking out – she had no fear of heights. And it was such a starry, starry night. There were meteor showers. I remember because my husband had just returned home after six weeks in the mines and we stayed up for hours, watching stars from the front room. There were telescopes set up along the bay for people to watch and a little band. All the locals were out, but we were lucky enough to be right in our home.'

Not suicide then: a fall. A tired mother goes for an evening walk, stands on the edge of the cliff, feels the fresh air awaken her, marvels at the stars. And then, what – she stumbles? She hears something, turns around and slips. A chunk of loose rock beneath her collapses and she loses balance. She sees something down below in the ocean, strains to look, and in the next second she's falling through the air.

Accidents happen in country such as this. Falls, breaks, snakes, sharks, caves, extreme weather – there didn't need to be a malicious reason for everything. Even so . . .

'You said that "nowadays" you think it was a fall. What did you think at the time?' Mark asked.

Frowning slightly, Margery reached into the pocket of her cardigan, pulled out a handkerchief and wiped it on her hand, where, Mark noticed, droplets of blood had formed. The perils of gardening – his mother always had grazes across her hands and forearms. 'I thought,' Margery said with some bravado, 'that Juliette had been pushed!'

Mark felt a jolt. 'What made you think that?'

'Juliette mentioned that she'd felt someone was watching her. I told her to report it, but really, why should she? It's just a *feeling* she had – you know the one, when you're being observed.'

Yes, Mark knew. He sometimes had it when he was walking in the bush near his home. Once, when he was hanging the clothes out on his line, he felt it so strongly he called out for the person to show themselves. But he attributed this to his last case, where he'd become involved with a group of birdwatchers whose core business was surveillance.

However, it couldn't be ignored that Juliette, like Cherie, had expressed – albeit in less dramatic terms – the feeling of being watched. Real or imagined? Not much to go on, but he'd ask around.

'Did Juliette give any details about her concerns?'

'No, just that sometimes she felt uncomfortable when she was out walking. No one ever said or did anything to her directly. I told the police this, but really, what could they do? And, as one of the late officers said, it's no wonder people were watching Juliette – she was a stunner. After a while, I began to see that that's all it was. I convinced myself it was nothing. Who around here would harm Juliette, the woman who never hurt a fly? No, I came to understand that her death was most likely an accident.

Her body was found out in the bay the morning after Murray reported her missing. She'd gone out for a walk after dinner and never returned home.' The woman gazed out to the bay, remembering. 'It was a day like this when they found her, changeable; sunny one minute, then grey and chilly the next. A local brought her in. So many on the beach that morning. It was just under thirty-seven years ago, but sometimes it feels like yesterday.'

Mark would have been around sixteen. Something stirred within him, an old memory, the dinghy, yelling in the background. His father forgetting him in the deep gloom that followed. Their trip to Broken Bay, his troubled recollection.

A bolt of memory. 'I think I might have been here when Juliette was found!'

'Really?' Margery leaned forward, interested.

'I can't be sure, but I think I was in a boat with my father that day. I've only just realised it. Someone in another boat found her body floating. I didn't see it.' Mark felt an eerie numbness, confusion. 'There was all this shouting, and then for ages it was just cold and quiet.'

'You could be right.' Margery nodded. 'It was the school holidays. We had a lot of visitors.'

The two sat in silence, watching the water from across the road. With the blue expanse of the ocean and cheerful colours of the boats, it was hard to imagine a body suspended there. Had his father seen Juliette being lifted out of the water? Mark racked his brains, mined his memory: nothing. But something made him feel as if his father caught a glimpse of swollen blue limbs and straggled hair as Juliette was pulled from the ocean.

He changed tack. 'Did you know Bernadette Doyle?'

'Of course. She was older than us, but we all knew her.' Margery's lips pursed shut.

'Were you friends with her, Margery?'

The old woman cocked her head to one side and fingered her pearls as she spoke more deliberately. 'It was hard to get to know Bernadette. She seemed to me to be a private lady, but she was always very nice when I spoke to her.' Margery smoothed the sleeve of her shirt. 'She was different to Juliette and me. In age, but in manner too. She was . . . old-fashioned, rather religious. You'd describe her as *stoic*. When we were younger, I thought she was boring.'

Mark thought about the Doyle twins: Gerri the well-regarded teacher, on a speaking tour; James the quiet farmer, on the edge of things. He wondered how much the twins resembled their parents.

'And of course, Bernadette was very good with Eloise when Juliette died. Eloise was only a baby, but as she grew, she was always at their place. I would have liked her to come here more often, but without children I suppose our house was not as much fun.'

'I heard Bernadette's in Adelaide now.'

'Yes, her family moved her up there not long ago. She has Alzheimer's, poor old thing. We don't have the right facilities for such patients here. I've thought about visiting her next time I'm up. It must be lonely, to be away from home.'

'But her family visit her?'

'Oh, I'm sure they do. The twins are lovely. Always very good to their mother.'

No mention of their father. 'And Frank?'

Margery's lips tightened again. She may as well have said, *I'm not a gossip, I don't speak ill of people.* An admirable trait, but frustrating for a cop. 'Frank and Bernadette have been married a long time. I'm sure he's missing his wife.'

'You don't sound too convinced, Margery.'

A steady breeze rattled the she-oaks. A northerly. Change was coming. He could feel it – the wind gathering pace, collecting debris and dust on its way to the coast. Beginning life as a whirly wind, the northerly would make its long trek over the central desert, past the Coongie Lakes, up over the red dunes and sweeping plains, then down past the town of Keith and onto here, the Limestone Coast. He could feel its approach, with all the tease of a quick spring and dread of a blistering summer to come.

'Frank has been lucky in life,' Margery stated. 'A devoted wife, lovely children and a farm that's now extremely valuable. He may not be the most personable of men, but that doesn't make him bad.'

It didn't. But even so, Mark wanted to find out more about the Doyles, about the Sinclairs and about this woman, too, who so reminded him of his mother.

Sensing she wouldn't be pressed on the topic he rose and, ignoring her protests, carried the tray inside and washed the cups out in the sink. When he'd helped her put the tray back on top of the cupboard they stepped outside again and said goodbye.

'I couldn't have children,' Margery said, putting her gardening gloves back on, 'and it rarely worried me. But sometimes I do think it would have been lovely to have a son.'

Mark took a few seconds, cleared his throat. 'Hopefully see you around, Margery.'

But Margery was already on her knees, head bent in westringia, hands in the fertile dirt.

CHAPTER 12

It was only mid-morning and Mark was at a loose end. He was at the mercy of police bureaucracy, of analysts, of coroners, of men who towed cars. Even so, there were things he could do. Sitting on the rock wall beside the beach, he googled oxygen tanks – in particular, the type of tanks cave and scuba divers used two decades ago. He read a long thread about steel versus aluminium tanks and then another on the most popular type used for spearfishing and cave diving. After a moment's thought, he texted Jane Southern, asking her to qualify what tanks both Mya and Eloise had carried on their last, fatal dives.

Next, with Margery's words on his mind, he looked up the public coroner's report on Juliette Sinclair's death. The concluding evidence did, as he'd heard from police and locals, state suicide as the cause of death.

Juliette Monique Clement Sinclair died on 4 June 1985, aged 35 years. On that morning, her body was found by fishermen in the bay of Broken Bay, South Australia. Cause of death was blunt force on impact from the fall from the nearby cliffs and subsequent drowning.

*Before her death, Mrs Sinclair showed signs of postnatal depression
and exhaustion. There was no alcohol or drugs present in her
system and, despite her depression, the autopsy showed that she
was in excellent health.*

The phone rang and Mark scrambled to save the report before
answering.

'Detective Senior Sergeant Reynolds here. Adelaide police,
records department.'

Mark knew Reynolds from way back. 'How are you? How's
the family?'

'Assistant Commissioner Conti has asked me to send you all
records on the missing persons file: Eloise Sinclair, aged eighteen,
Broken Bay, last seen on November fifteenth, two thousand and
three.' Reynolds was a man of few words who'd never learned
the art of small talk. The weather, a polite interest in family –
Reynolds didn't get the memo.

'It's a Sunday.' Mark only said it for show.

'Sunday or Monday, Angelo asked me to send these through.'

'Thank you, really nice of you.'

'Posting now to your secure work email address.'

The phone went dead. You had to respect someone like that,
all business. No fun at parties, but the man got things done.

Mark continued back along the bay path to the cafe where
he'd eaten breakfast. Almost immediately, his phone began
dinging – the files were being sent through. Photos, newspaper
articles, the lot. He accelerated, excusing his way past a young
couple and their tiny dog, watching as his emails piled up.
A man was running, staring at his watch as he sped along, seemingly obsessed with heart rate and pace. Mark felt his own pulse
quicken at the thought of something to do, a purpose.

At the cafe, he found the same spot he'd been in just over an hour ago and got out his notepad and pen.

He opened the first file: a transcript of an interview:

Police report, 17 November 2003
Senior Constable Jason Mullard

On the morning of 16 November 2003, at approximately 9.30 am, I responded to a call from Philippe Sinclair of 120 Bay Road, Broken Bay. Philippe said that his younger sister, Eloise, aged 18, had not come home and was unable to be found. On the day prior, Philippe said hello to Eloise in the morning and she'd indicated she wasn't feeling well. Philippe drove to his boat and prepared for the day's fishing with his younger brothers, Nicolas and Mathieu. They did not return till about 10.00 pm. Philippe said prior to joining him in his boat, his brother Mathieu had taken Eloise into town in the morning for some shopping, while his other brother, Nicolas, was fencing in a nearby paddock. Philippe's wife, Judy, was in Adelaide with friends for the weekend. At around 9.30 am the next day, Philippe, Nicolas and Mathieu realised that Eloise was not in her bedroom. After calling her friends and hearing that none of them had seen her, Phil immediately notified the police and I drove to the Sinclair house to file a report.

Mark paused. The slip from Philippe to Phil indicated that the police officer knew the family. This wasn't surprising given the size of Broken Bay, but it would have raised the eyebrows of a few city cops. Most adults, after all, turned up safe and sound. It was the benefit of knowing everyone in a country town: Eloise's disappearance must have set off alarm bells in the local cop too. He must have known, either firsthand or from friends in the family, that she wasn't the type to wander off.

Mark rubbed his eyes, he didn't have his glasses on him. The report continued:

I then went to the home of Eloise's boyfriend, Brett Twymann, only to find that he was out. There was no one else at his home. Given there was an onshore wind and that Brett is a known surfer, I drove to the cape beach and caught him as he was returning from the water. He said he'd seen Eloise in the morning of the day prior, down the street, and then not at all after that. He had spent the day fishing with his friend Scott Boxhall and his father Greg Boxhall, and then attended a BBQ in Broken Bay. Mack Johnston, Kate Dixson and Andrew Thornly (friends who attended the BBQ) were able to corroborate this. I then contacted Adelaide police station, where I spoke to Senior Sergeant Tony Harris and requested that an investigative team from Missing Persons become involved in the Sinclair case.

The report was well written. Concise. The next file was the transcript of an interview. Mark brought the phone close up to his eyes to read.

17 November 2003, Broken Bay police station. Time: 1.00 pm
Transcript of interview with Brett Twymann and Senior Sergeant Michelle Bamford

MB: We're taping now.
BT: Yes.
MB: Brett Twymann, can you say for the records your full name, age and address, please?
BT: (sound of chair scraping) Brett Twymann, aged 19, 33 Moyne Lane, Broken Bay.
MB: And can you please state for the recording that you have not requested a lawyer at this stage?

BT: *I have not requested a lawyer.*

MB: *Thank you.*

BT: *But should I have a lawyer?*

MB: *That's up to you, Brett. Please let me know if you would like to stop this interview. As you know, you are not under any sort of compulsion to be here. We're just trying to get a full picture of what happened the day Eloise was last seen.*

BT: *Oh yeah, sure.*

MB: *Thanks for coming in.*

BT: *No worries.*

MB: *You're fine to keep going?*

BT: *Yeah, fine, cool.*

MB: *Drink of water, or . . .*

BT: *No, no, I'm right.*

(Indistinct murmuring)

MB: *So, in your own time, can you please give us an account of your relationship with Eloise Sinclair.*

BT: *She's been my girlfriend for what, nearly three years?*

MB: *You're happy in your relationship?*

BT: *Yeah. What should we be doing? What's the next steps to look for her?*

MB: *First we just have to ascertain her last movements before she went missing.*

BT: *Yeah, right. Cool. Well, I saw her what, on Saturday the 15th? I caught up with her in town, the morning before I went for a surf. She said she wasn't feeling all that well. I was going to the salmon holes, spearfishing with Scott Boxhall and his dad. I said she could come if she wanted, have a snorkel or whatever. I was going to go back home after surfing to get changed, have something to eat, so she could meet me then. After spearfishing, me and Scott were going to go to a barbecue. I invited her to that too, but she said no. She was going home as she wasn't feeling good. So I said see ya and I haven't seen her since.*

MB: You left on good terms?

BT: Yeah, normal.

MB: What does that mean, 'normal'?

BT: Just normal. She'd been moody, but nothing to write home about.

MB: What was she moody about, do you think?

BT: Maybe because I'd been in Indonesia surfing, Roti. She didn't come, she didn't have any money, and she wouldn't have been allowed anyway. She was a bit pissed off at me going. Also, it's my birthday next week and I was planning on going out with the boys.

MB: Was she mad at you for that, do you think?

BT: Maybe. It could have been either of those things, but to be honest, I didn't think about it that much.

MB: So, you said goodbye to her down the street and then you left to go surfing?

BT: Yeah. Surf was good. It was a good day.

MB: And then you went spearfishing and, later on, to a barbecue?

BT: Yep. I didn't end up going home in between, surf was too good.

MB: You didn't try to contact her during the day, see how she was feeling?

BT: No. I should've. I wish I did.

MB: Was Eloise with anyone when you saw her down the street?

BT: One of her brothers, Mat. I told you all this yesterday.

MB: This is to formalise it, Brett. So, then what did you do?

BT: I went to the salmon holes with Scott and his dad, then the barbecue and didn't get back till late. Then, yeah, I went to bed. In the morning I went for a surf and next minute there's the police at the beach asking if I'd seen her and it just went wild from there.

MB: *Were you worried?*

BT: *Yeah. Eloise doesn't normally go far. Her brothers keep a tight rein, so it was weird when no one said they had seen her. Everyone started looking. I went straight to Gerri's, started calling people, her friends and that. But no one had seen her.*

(Murmuring, indecipherable)

MB: *Are you okay, Brett? Would you like a break? We're finishing up soon anyway.*

BT: *Yeah, I'm just, like, shocked, right? Where do you reckon she is? Has she, like, had an accident? What happens now? Shouldn't we be out searching? We could make posters or something – get them out everywhere.*

MB: *As I said, we just need to ascertain where Eloise was on the day she went missing. We're trying to piece it all together so we can begin looking in the right places.*

BT: *Yeah.*

MB: *Was Eloise troubled by anything, Brett? Anything at all?*

(A long pause)

MB: *Was she upset about anything in your relationship?*

BT: *Not that I know of.*

MB: *No fights or anything?*

BT: *Not really. Eloise was Eloise, she didn't really go in for fights.*

MB: *What does that mean, 'Eloise was Eloise'?*

BT: *I don't know, she was her own person. She wasn't interested in all the normal stuff. She liked books. And looking at the sea and clouds and stuff. Op shopping. Can we go now? Can we? This is a waste of time, isn't it? When are you going to look more, maybe she's been in an accident or . . .*

MB: *We will, Brett. So, can you think of anywhere Eloise would head off to? Some place she'd like to get away to?*

BT: *No. I've told you this before. No.*

MB: None at all?

BT: Well, she liked to go to that spot where her mum jumped off.

At the top of the cape?

(Indistinct murmuring)

BT: You don't think she's jumped, do you? Because she wouldn't do that.

MB: We're keeping all options on the table. We just want all the information we can find, so that we can locate her.

(Sound of a chair scraping)

BT: She wouldn't kill herself.

MB: We're just . . .

BT: And while we sit in here talking, she's out there somewhere! This is a waste of time. I'm going to have a look.

(Indistinct chat)

MB: Brett, you can't just leave, this is a police matter and . . .

(Door closing)

MB: Interview with Brett Twymann has concluded.

Interview suspended.

'Can I get you anything?' A waiter in full tweed appeared before him, Wonka-like.

'Just a coffee, please. Maybe a slice if you've got it.'

Now jazz hands and a sing-song voice. 'We have p-p-peppermint and even iced vovo-vo-vo!'

Mark nodded, unsure of his place in the world. 'Is this the same cafe I was in just an hour ago?'

'Unfortunately for you, yeah.'

'Well, a coffee, please. And a slice. You choose, whatever.' Mark wanted to get on with reading the files again.

The waiter clicked his heels, saluted and left. Mark raised his eyebrows, looked again at his phone.

A news article:

Adelaide Times, 22 November 2003
Search for missing Broken Bay woman continues

Eloise Sinclair was last seen by her older brother at their family home on the outskirts of the small town of Broken Bay, close to the Victorian border. Police across the two states are continuing their search for the 18-year-old, in the hope that she may be found alive and well.

Inspector Doug Herbert said an initial search in the area did not find any more evidence or an explanation of where Ms Sinclair could be.

'We've scoured the area,' he told ABC radio. 'There's been search-and-rescue boats in the bay, with local fishermen joining the search. A number of police have been out on foot, assisted by the SES and local volunteers, but we haven't been able to find anything.'

According to locals, Ms Sinclair is a friendly person and trusting of others. Her family are reported to be devastated by her absence. Ms Sinclair's boyfriend, Brett Twymann, has spent the last few days assisting police in their enquiries. No charges have been laid and all lines of enquiry are open.

The search continues.

Mark thought the article was sly. Either that or he'd become cynical over the years. What after all did 'friendly and trusting of others' mean? He pictured Eloise as readers then might have: a Miranda from *Picnic at Hanging Rock* type, smiling and dreamily distracted, getting into a van because the driver said he'd give her a lift, he knew the way. 'Friendly and trusting' was journo shorthand for 'kind of stupid'.

Interesting, too, that in the article there was mention of Brett helping out with the investigation. Nothing at all on Mat, the brother who'd last seen her.

Mark read the interview with Brett again. He goes out surfing, then spearfishing, then to a barbecue while she stays home? It read like an episode of *Puberty Blues*.

Mark flicked through the files from Reynolds – photos, so many of them, of Eloise smiling at a birthday party, her arm flung around a grinning Brett. The two did look happy together. Despite their obvious differences in the things they liked to do: 'Watch clouds, read books. Op shop.' Mark knew all about ties formed in small towns. When you were familiar with people from an early age, it was easy to grow comfortable in each other's company, accepting flaws and differences. Mark's friend Squirrel liked greyhound racing and car rallies. Squirrel left school after Year Ten and never moved towns. Squirrel knew where you could pick up eighty-five-inch tellies on the cheap. If Mark met Squirrel now, they wouldn't be friends. But Mark had known the man since he was four. It meant something.

There was a police note:

Initial search of the Sinclair home, and Eloise Sinclair's room in particular, revealed little of interest. Phil Sinclair, older brother to Eloise, reported that a wetsuit, usually worn by his sister, and a snorkel and mask were missing. All three brothers could not say definitively whether or not the missing items could have been lost, discarded or given away previously, but all agreed that they could not be found.

Mark looked out the window. If Eloise had taken the items, where was she planning to go? Was it just for a swim or a snorkel? There had been searches of the bay too. How would she get there from her house? No one had reported seeing her at the beach, or hitchhiking along Bay Road. Perhaps she knew about the sinkhole on the Doyle property – even though everyone said they'd only found it weeks ago. But what then? She swims around the top of it? Somehow gets pulled into a squeeze and then into another chamber? It lacked plausibility.

Mark rubbed his eyes. There were too many questions.

Finally, he came to the police report on Mathieu Sinclair's version of events.

Report on Mathieu Sinclair's statement, 20 November 2003, Time: 10.00 am
Senior Constable Jason Mullard

Mathieu Sinclair was spoken to first at his home on the day after Eloise was last seen, on 16 November and then on the Wednesday following (19 Nov). Mathieu came to the station voluntarily, accompanied by his eldest brother, Philippe Sinclair. Mathieu presented as nervous and tired, but eager to help. He'd been searching with volunteers in the surrounding areas since the alert was raised. Mathieu said on the morning prior to her being reported missing, he'd been with Eloise in Broken Bay, buying bread and milk and paracetamol. His older brother Nicolas was fencing in a paddock close by. In town, Mat and Eloise met Brett Twymann, Eloise's boyfriend, and the three had a brief chat. Brett asked Eloise to go to a BBQ with him that evening, but she declined as she was feeling unwell. Mat then drove himself and Eloise home. Mat said they had a brief argument on the drive home about her choice of boyfriend, but nothing serious. On returning to their house on Bay Road, Eloise went to her room. Shortly after, Mat joined his brothers for lobster fishing on their family boat. When they got home that evening it was around 10.00 pm and they all went straight to bed.

The next morning, Philippe checked in to see how Eloise was feeling and discovered that she was not there. It appeared that, according

*to him, she had not slept there the night. Philippe and his brothers
began calling her friends and once they had established that she
was nowhere to be found, they called the police. The brothers began
searching the area for their younger sister.*

*At this point in the interview, Mathieu became upset and asked if
he could go. He left the Broken Bay Police station at 10.40 am.*

That slip from Mathieu to Mat again. The interview was
adequate for an initial conversation, but Mark could find no
more on Mathieu Sinclair in the files.

A mug of coffee and a biscuit were placed before him.

'I got you an Anzac,' the young man said. 'You kind of look
like an Anzac, you know, from Gallipolli and that. Our Australian
son, that kind of thing.'

'Well, I don't know about that.' Mark took a hurried gulp of
his coffee.

'David Williamson the playwright wrote *Gallipoli*, did you
know that?'

'Yes.' Mark loved that film.

'He also wrote *The Removalists*, which is so brilliant – it's really
violent, but the violence means something, you know?'

Mark didn't know how to answer that. 'Are you a playwright?'
he asked.

'Nope, an actor. I'm actually preparing for auditions at the
moment.'

'Yeah?'

'Reading through monologues, trying to get a feel for different characters.'

'Right.'

'I've just finished *Chicago* with my theatre group in Adelaide.
It was a blast, but now I need to focus.'

Mark ate his Anzac. 'So you're doing the whole actor-slash-waiter thing until something comes up?'

'No, parents own this place, they roped me in when one of the waitresses quit. There are no staff around, literally no staff – so here I am. I was meant to be having a break before I left, and now I'm serving skinny flat whites.'

'That's show business.' Mark didn't know why he said it. He finished his biscuit, wished he'd asked for two.

The young man slapped a hand against his forehead. 'That reminds me! I forgot to pick up my wig from Cherie's house last night!'

'Do you mean Cherie Swi—'

'Yeah, Cherie Swinson. She's an actor and a costume designer, lives just up the road. She had all these, like, famous boyfriends when she was young.'

Mark listened as the man waxed lyrical about Cherie's past life, her amazing costumes for *Annie Get Your Gun*. They'd even done a few little performances together in Broken Bay. Had Mark ever seen *Oliver!*? It was so good.

Mark couldn't understand the enthusiasm. In the few musicals he'd sat through, he felt only a hot embarrassment for all involved. A memory of seeing Cats made him shudder.

'Cherie's writing her own play.' She's designing costumes for it and I've been helping with ideas. You've got to make an impact, you know? Really highlight the character.'

'You really do.'

The waiter smiled kindly at him. 'Well, anyway, Mum might have to send me the wig. I'm flying to New York tonight. Auditions! Broadway! Bring it on!'

'Well, hats off, mate. Good on you.'

'Do you want anything else?'

'No thanks.'

The showman bowed and Mark returned to his notes and phone, but thought instead about the young man's ambition and confidence. '*I can't wait!*' What a chance he was taking, from Broken Bay to New York to pursue his wildest dreams. Mark imagined him on the plane, looking out at the vast expanse of the Pacific, no fear, only anticipation and a steady beat in his chest for what was to come. He would take it all on, the boy from Broken Bay. He'd fly there already thinking he'd made it, that the world was his. And because he thought that way, it probably was.

The front door of the cafe opened, and three young women piled in. Mark snapped back to his notes. The search for Eloise had been extensive. Police and volunteers had scoured the surrounding area. A pit on the farm used for dispensing of dead animals had been thoroughly investigated by authorities, forensics checking for human remains, clothing, anything related to Eloise. Nothing of interest was recovered: besides the remains of dead cows, there was a Kelvinator fridge, an old bike and three worn tyres.

Those pits, they gave Mark the creeps. Farmers usually either dumped dead animals in a pit or chose to burn them. Disposing of dead cows and sheep had to be done fast: risk of disease, soil contamination and scavengers to the site all posed serious threats to a healthy farm. Best to move the dead bodies with tractors, no touching the carcasses, or as little contact as possible. Bad farmers let their animals rot, and everyone knew it. Mark could remember the smell of decomposing bodies drifting over Booralama from the Malthorp property whenever a westerly hit. It was only when authorities took Trevor to court that he was forced to act appropriately. No one liked to drink with the

Malthorps. Their kids left town as soon as they were old enough to drive.

Back to the notes. There was a coloured overhead map of the Sinclair farm and surrounds, as well as photographs. The Doyles' animal disposal pit was over five hundred metres from their own house and twice that from the Sinclairs. Dams and a dried seasonal creek were a good distance from it: the Doyles managed their dead well. Mark wondered briefly at the depth of the pit – it looked wide. You couldn't dig too far down in a place like this; water was everywhere, metres below the surface. He wandered his eyes over the map, noted the proximity of the Sinclair house to the Doyle and the Twymann farms. It would be just a short trip over the paddocks for all of them to see each other.

Mark scanned the road that ran alongside the Sinclair and Doyle properties, the paddock outlines, and made a mental note of the sinkhole's approximate location. Nothing to indicate the entrance to a subterranean world was there. He could see only cows, a round concrete trough further along the paddock and fence lines. Twenty years ago, the land was drier, the paddocks were brown, the tracks were dirt rather than mud. Two dams appeared worryingly low. This land, this wide brown land, was a moody, changeable thing. One moment barren, the next floods and storms.

Mark continued reading, increasingly impressed by the thoroughness of the investigation. The public loved to knock police work, find fault wherever they could. It was rare that a judge or a newspaper editor admitted, 'That was well done. Good work.'

Mat's car had been gone over by forensics: evidence all through it of his sister and other members of his family. No surprise there, but nothing of a suspect nature. There'd been considerable news about the case at the time. Eloise was photogenic – images of her with white hair whipping about her face adorned the national papers for days. The tragic tale of her mother was brought up regularly – sometimes hinting Eloise might have followed in her footsteps. Local fishermen were asked to keep an eye out on the bay for a body, farmers were told to check their land. Nothing. After a few days, interest in the case began to die off. After two weeks, Broken Bay and the Sinclairs may well have never existed at all.

Except they did, of course, and the trauma of Eloise's disappearance ricocheted like shrapnel through the people of the town.

Mark put down his phone and rubbed his eyes again. His notes were haphazard and scrawled in red pen, they looked like the kind a serial killer might write:

Thorough search

Mat Sinclair and Brett interviewed

Brett chief suspect – but alibis

Sinclairs known to police as 'Phil'/'Mat'

Town divided on Brett

Overhead images of the Sinclair, Doyle and Tywmann farms. Animal pit, dry paddocks, fences and troughs

On a whim, he brought up images of the Sinclair family, the ones from the newspapers in the days following Eloise's disappearance. A photo of her as a young child with her family accompanied a particularly saccharine piece. A good-looking lot, the Sinclairs. White hair, tall and blue-eyed. There was baby Eloise on her mother's lap, and the three boys hanging about her. Of the three, Phil looked the most serious. Responsible already, at around thirteen years old. This photo must have been taken not long before Juliette's suicide – or accidental death, as Margery claimed. There was nothing in the image to indicate sadness or impending doom, but then again, there never was. Mark recalled a photo of a family in America, five children and their parents grinning widely into the lens as they stood in front of the Disneyland sign. The following day, the mother had drowned all the children, one after the other, claiming that the devil told her to.

His eyes turned to Murray Sinclair – a huge man, bigger than his son Phil would grow to be, all handsome and rugged brawn. The man who'd helped retrieve the Franklin Three.

Mark googled 'Franklin Three' and found an old article from the seventies.

Adelaide Advertiser, 9 February 1971

In a tragic turn of events, the bodies of three young locals have been retrieved from a sinkhole close to the town of Franklin. Siblings Rachel Heaghney (18) and Edward Heaghney (22) and their friend Adam Robine (22) were reported missing early morning on Saturday, 6 February. Local farmer Bobby Donnell found their clothes and belongings, including evidence of alcohol, beside the sinkhole. It is thought that the trio drowned while attempting to dive the sinkhole known locally as the Tomb. All three victims were open divers, however none had experience in caves and did not appear to use any sort of guideline.

Locals were the first on the scene to assist. Lobster fisherman and experienced diver Murray Sinclair later claimed that Robine still had a full tank of oxygen and was found with the breathing apparatus out of his mouth. Robine appeared to be diving downward instead of towards the surface, indicating severe disorientation. The siblings, after becoming lost on their ascent, had managed to find an air pocket in a small cave not far from the main chamber. The second retrieval diver suggested that the two suffocated when the oxygen ran out. When asked what was the main cause of death for the three, Murray Sinclair said, 'What it always is: panic.'

Mark felt a deep dread. Scratch marks on the ceiling. Dying in a water-filled cave was the stuff of nightmares. Whatever beauty lay down there, the dark subterranean world held no attraction for him. He took a big gulp of water.

A photo accompanied the article: the sinkhole where the three had vanished. Unlike the cave entrance at the Doyles', this one showed a much lower water level. He looked at the year again, February 1971. The country was deep in drought then, unlike now. The three teenagers would have had to climb down the limestone walls to reach the surface. That, or jump straight in. He reflected: three young adults, high on life and alcohol. Someone suggests a dive down the Tomb, and the others agree. Perhaps one is reluctant, maybe feels a creeping anxiety at the idea, but the enthusiasm of the group, the beauty of the night and the confidence of youth all conspire to form a *Yes*.

Mark wondered briefly why the second diver wasn't named in the article. Could be many reasons; the person didn't want their name in the press, the journo forgot to ask.

He finished off the coffee. It was cold. There was a loud crash as the door to the cafe burst open. The publican from the Royal stood there, wild-eyed and out of breath.

'What's up, Barry?' Mark jumped up, sending his chair screeching backward. 'What's happened?'

'I think she's dead.'

'What? Who?'

'Ambos on the way, but she's not . . . there's blood . . .'

'Who, Barry? Tell me.'

The man's arms flapped in the air, his mouth agape. 'Cherie! Someone's killed her.'

CHAPTER 13

Mark's phone dinged, and dinged again as he was running out the door and up the road, a deep dread in his guts. Barry was beside him, heaving, their footsteps in tandem. His phone then rang, and he answered as he ran. In the far distance, an ambulance siren keened.

'Detective Ariti, we've had a triple zero call to the following address in Broken Bay . . .' It was the central police station, Adelaide.

'I'm almost there,' Mark said. 'What's happened?'

'A Barry Coffey rang to say a local woman was found unresponsive in her front yard. Ambulance should be arriving soon.'

'On my way.'

'Secure the area. Investigative crew will arrive as soon as possible.'

Mark hung up as he and Barry turned into the front yard of Cherie's house. Next door, Margery gave him a frightened look as he passed by.

'I put her on her side,' Barry was saying, 'felt her pulse, but nothing. I put my jacket on her, but I don't know. I don't know.'

Cherie was curled up underneath the low canopy of moonah trees, lying on ground that was soft with dirt and sweet-smelling foliage. She looked like a child. If not for the violent gash on the side of her head, she'd be almost peaceful. Blood ran in a dried stream down her scalp and past her ear, creating a congealing pool of deep red. The white in her wound was smashed bone and dirt was thick at her neck.

Barry vomited, long and loud into the bush. Did Barry have blood on his hands when he'd burst into the cafe? Mark tried to remember. He didn't think so. Something like that would stick in your mind.

A police car pulled up and the young officer from the dive site hurried over. Mark held up his hand to show where he was, and then turned to the body once more.

He looked closer. There were ants climbing over Cherie's face. Tiny flies hovered around the wounds. Nature wasn't sentimental, it didn't stop.

The ambulance siren grew louder, then stopped abruptly as it pulled up. Someone was talking to Margery; Mark could hear them as he crouched beside Cherie, feeling in vain for a pulse. There was something else. On her right forearm, in crude writing, there was a series of letters, or numbers. Mark's eyes swam as he tried to read it. But even as the rational side of his brain was computing '81EU' or '8LFU' or '8LFV', his creative, more emotional side was registering that the word, or whatever it was, was written in blood. The fingertips of Cherie's left hand were covered in the stuff, dried now, clinging to her nails in a gruesome parody of a manicure.

Mark took photos from every angle as the paramedics moved in. Then, backing out of the moonah, he went to stand beside Barry. Over the fence, Margery looked on.

'Will she be all right?' she was asking. 'Is that blood on her head?'

The ambos were writing notes and moving away from the scene, conferring. Nothing they could do now for Cherie Swinson.

'There was blood on her arm,' Barry said. 'Was it writing?'

'Will she be okay?' Margery kept asking, to no one in particular. Their questions made Mark's head thump.

His phone started ringing again. 'No,' he said to her before answering it. 'Cherie is dead. Don't go anywhere – I'll need to speak with you.'

He took the call. 'Mark, can you confirm that the victim is deceased?' This time, the caller was his colleague and friend Sergeant Jagdeep Kaur. He didn't have time to be surprised.

'Yes.' Before the paramedics said it aloud, he knew it. The tiny insects swarming, the cold skin, already a blue tinge to it.

'The man who called it in said she had a gash on her head. You can confirm that?'

'Yes, I took photos, will send through.'

'We'll be there as soon as we can.'

'Jag,' he said. 'What are you doing on this?'

'I'm in training with Investigative,' she said. 'New horizons and that.'

Across the road, he couldn't see the horizon. Clouds were racing, a capricious northerly made low waves erratic. Impossible to tell where the sea ended and sky began.

'Okay, see you then,' he said. But she'd already hung up.

Mark talked with the ambulance officers. He needed them to guard the scene while he checked the house, then he'd take over and wait till Jagdeep and the team arrived. The paramedics, no strangers to waiting over the dead, agreed.

Mark walked over to Barry, still talking with the police officer and Margery. 'Barry, how did you come to find Cherie's body? What were you doing here?'

Barry trembled, took deep breaths. 'I was at the pub, cleaning and whatnot. Cherie said she'd pop in to help but she didn't show up. I gave her a ring, left a few messages. Nothing. I drove here, knocked. Called out – no one at home. I went to leave but saw her there, under the trees. Is she really dead?'

Mark didn't answer. He remembered the dark figure he'd seen in the upstairs room, just before he'd had tea with Margery. With a chill, he pondered the idea that Cherie's killer could still be in the house, or hiding somewhere close by.

'Barry, go into Margery's house and wait there. We'll be back soon. Don't go anywhere, you'll both need to be questioned.'

Margery nodded bravely and turned, leading Barry into her home.

Mark beckoned the other officer to follow him. 'We're going to have to go into the house. You okay with that?'

The younger officer was visibly nervous, his shaking hand hovering over his chest where the taser was. He gave a reluctant nod.

'What's your name?'

'Sean. I mean, Constable Sean Cleary. I met you at the dive site.'

'That's right. Now, we're going to check out the place. I want you to follow me, Sean.'

Mark was unarmed. His heart thumped, breath quickened. They walked up a series of steep steps to a deck at the side of an expansive living room. Metal wind chimes hanging from a wooden beam spun wildly, giving off a ghostly tune. The glass door to the house was open. Mark took a few photos.

'You all right, Sean?' Mark asked.

'I'm good.'

Sean didn't sound good. He sounded young, unsure. Mark took a deep breath and stepped inside. On first glance, nothing was out of order. The shell of the house oozed wealth, but inside the furnishings were cheap and cluttered. Cherie wouldn't win a prize for her art collection: a standard print of *Footprints in the Sand*, a framed copy of The Irish Blessing, two Clydesdales grazing in a meadow.

He told Sean to stay in the hall before moving to the bedroom. The walls were lined with film and theatre posters: *Annie Get Your Gun, Chicago* and, unnervingly, *Cats* – the movie version with Taylor Swift in canine, alien form. He checked behind the door, in the wardrobe, under the bed. There were framed photos: mostly of Cherie in the seventies and early eighties, looking like a Charlie's Angel with wavy brown hair, white teeth and tight, tight jeans. Cherie, as Margery had remarked, had been very beautiful.

'You still there, Sean?' he called.

The other man answered in the affirmative.

Mark peered at another shot – a house party perhaps, Cherie lounging on an old couch – and was that good-looking rooster with his arm around her shoulders really Mel Gibson? Mark didn't have time to ponder. There was a square spa in the bathroom. A long mirror had lights above it and the words 'Hello Sunshine!' written in gold.

Mark felt a heaviness come over him. The chipped gold, the fading letters. The house was too big for one person. With four bedrooms and a small study, it was perfect for the Sinclairs and their family of six – not a woman on her own. A sign above a bookcase read 'Dare to Dream!' What had Cherie been dreaming of? The cosy mottos like 'Destiny gives you the tools, you make the decisions' and inspirational wall art suggested she needed to convince herself that her life was as fabulous as it had ever been, that the halcyon days of mixing it up with the stars were nothing to compare with her happy life here in Broken Bay.

He took photos of every room, searched carefully, not touching a thing. There was nothing to suggest anything untoward had happened – no visible signs of disturbance or the common ransacking that occurred in robberies. Forensics would, of course, take a more detailed look.

Back in the hall, Mark led Sean to the front room, and the two stood side by side, looking out at the ocean. 'Million-dollar views,' his father would have said, though they were worth far more than that.

'There's a handbag on the arm of the couch,' Sean said. 'It could be hers.'

'Could be.' Mark noted the neatly placed pink bag, the little latch on it closed.

From here, you could see the whole expanse of the bay, right out to where the ocean met the sky. If you looked directly down, to the bottom of the deck, you'd see Cherie's garden, the dark shrubs and low moonah like people curled up, crouching low. After that, the path, the bay road, then the water. To the right the land edged upward as the hill to the top of the cape began. No buildings on that side. It was all coastal shrubbery, banksia, saltbush, correa and spiky grass.

'Who's *that*?' Sean spoke in horror, pointing with a shaking finger to a darkened corner of the room, where a woman stood perfectly still, her features partly hidden in the shadows.

'Christ!' Mark took a step back in fright.

'It's a mannequin.'

'I know that now.' Mark's heart had not slowed. 'But I swear, that gave me the shock of my life.'

'Yeah, I nearly shat my pants,' Sean breathed. 'What's it doing there?'

It was a good question. The mannequin was wearing a long, flowing blue dress with loose threads running from it. Over the top, an oversized orange cardigan with missing buttons. No shoes. The men stared in bewilderment.

Mark took photos, noted the long blonde wig and the cracked veneer of the waxy face.

'What sort of outfit is *that*?' Sean said, wiping sweat from his brow. 'I don't get it. I don't get it.' The young cop was breathing heavily, short, high-pitched sounds coming from his mouth like a tiny bird in distress. He was at risk of going into shock.

Mark advised him to sit down while he examined the rest of the room. Couches, a small television, a side table laden with vases, little statues of cats and wooden inspirational quotes – 'Be Me!' – and a red velvet chair, which gave off a pretentious, salon-type air. The mannequin was facing the window, with an illuminated floor lamp just behind it. From where he stood, Mark couldn't see its features clearly, but if you happened to be standing on the street, or in Cherie's front yard at night, the mannequin would be perfectly lit.

On first glance, and without a close study, it would appear real.

CHAPTER 14

Broken Bay hadn't had so many cops in it since the disappearance of Eloise Sinclair, twenty years ago. And now, a woman murdered in the home where Eloise had once lived.

Mark met the investigative team at the station, just up from the church. A neat little brick building, clean but dusty from lack of use. No bickies in the kitchen or milk in the fridge. Someone went out for coffees, came back saying there were none. Why would there be coffees at this hour, after 6 pm? It was Broken Bay, not Carlton.

The room bristled with purpose. A whiteboard was set up. Subheadings in neat black texta. Two crime scenes now: the Doyle sinkhole and Cherie's house on Bay Road. Mark gave everyone a rundown of what he knew so far, what he'd seen. He didn't mention the ooze seeping out from Eloise's mask, or the little flies around Cherie's head. Didn't mention that.

He'd waited beside Cherie for two hours, and although he'd tried to set up a police cordon with tape and sat on the other side of it, her body felt too close. Her bashed head, the tiny ants . . . A creeping heat emanating from the undergrowth had unsettled him further. Surely it was not coming from her corpse? The minutes had ticked over slowly, so slowly.

It was a great relief when Investigations finally arrived, professional with their forensic equipment and determined expressions. There were five other officers on the team: Senior Sergeant Jane Southern from Water Operations and Forensics; Sergeant Chiara Rossi, another Forensics member he'd only just met; Sergeant Jagdeep Kaur, in training with Investigations; Constable Sean Cleary, the young policeman who'd accompanied him to Cherie's house; and Inspector Michael Richardson, head of Investigations.

It cheered Mark to see Jagdeep sitting in a seat before him, taking notes. Her no-nonsense features and competent stance never failed to rally him. In the few moments they'd had before the meeting was called, she'd explained that she'd been training as a specialist investigator under Richardson for almost three weeks.

Jagdeep would be just right for such a team. Super smart, ambitious, logical. In her role, she'd investigate major crimes, drug activity, organised crime, sex offences and fraud. Homicide too, of course. That would be her bread and butter, she'd devour it – but hopefully not before it would devour her. In her early thirties, she was still young.

Chiara, Jagdeep quickly told Mark, was ambitious and very good at trivia. 'Ask her what the capital of any country is, and she'll know,' Jag said. 'But she has no tact whatsoever, so don't take offence if she says she hates your shoes.'

'What's wrong with my shoes?' Mark looked down at his worn RMs.

Jagdeep held up her hands. 'That's not for me to say.'

'Right.'

'What's Sean like?'

'Young,' Mark said cautiously. 'He's learning.'

'Sergeant Ariti, you can take over the unidentified diver case for now,' Richardson, sitting on a table, was saying. 'In all likelihood, the body recovered will be Eloise Sinclair's, but we cannot make that assumption just yet. I'm expecting a formal ID any time now. There'll be more police arriving in a few days, but if you could manage the situation for now, Mark, we'd be grateful.'

All eyes turned to him. He sighed deeply. Nodded. 'Last night at the pub, Cherie told me that for the past couple of months, she was being watched. She agreed she'd come tomorrow to talk with me about it, here, in the station.'

'How'd she seem to you then?' Jagdeep asked, pen held aloft.

'Nervous,' Mark admitted.

'The barman, Barry Coffey, also said she'd complained about a stalker,' Sean added. 'He had cameras installed, said he'd gone over them, nothing to report.'

'When are you going to interview him formally?' Richardson asked. 'Tomorrow morning?'

Sean nodded.

Chiara was typing something into a computer. 'Says here the victim reported someone following or watching her at least twice in the last six weeks. "Someone watching her from her front yard", "Someone watching her in the pub", "Footsteps behind her when she was out walking the cape".'

Mark thought of the moonah trees, their bent shapes and erratic shadows. Anyone could hide among them. 'The victim's name was Cherie,' he said, cranky.

'We need to go over the CCTV footage,' Jagdeep said. 'I'm happy to do that if you like.'

Richardson told her to go ahead. 'Anything else to add, Mark?'

'Cherie was formerly an actor and a costume designer. The costume on the mannequin was a strange one, hardly fashionable

I would think. The scene itself, with the mannequin facing the window, the lamp behind it – it all looked kind of . . .'

'Staged?' Jagdeep asked.

'Yeah. There was something overly dramatic about it all.'

The police officers fell silent.

'Keep that detail strictly confidential,' Richardson said. 'We don't know why the mannequin was dressed like that, or who put it there.' Another pause. Did Mark imagine it, or was there a collective shiver among the group?

Richardson stood up and rubbed the back of his neck. 'Show us the images of the letters in blood, will you?'

Mark had sent Jagdeep all his photos. Everyone in the room was aware they were preliminary; the Investigations team would pore over the official photos, would examine blood spatter formation and conduct testing of Cherie's clothing and the surrounding soil. These were merely a start, to get an idea of what they were working with.

Jagdeep connected her laptop to the whiteboard and Cherie's pale neck appeared, her congealed hair, the dripping red scrawl. Mark's stomach churned.

Richardson didn't look affected. Talk among the force was that he'd seen some serious shit in his time. It was Richardson who'd discovered the four McCarthy siblings, all under ten, chained like dogs to a downpipe. Word got around that despite the scene and what he'd uncovered, the man didn't take a single day off. And now, five years on, he was as resolute as ever.

The letters came into view as Jagdeep clicked through: 81EU, 8LFU or 8LFV.

'Looks like it starts with a B . . .' Jane said. She was right. Now that the letters were enlarged, Mark saw that the 8 was in fact a B.

'Blfu', Sean said slowly. 'Doesn't mean anything.'

'Could be a tag,' Chiara suggested. 'We can ask around.'

There was silence in the room while the officers tried to digest the meaning.

'Bleu,' Jagdeep suggested at last.

Something dark unfurled itself in Mark's chest.

Sean snorted. 'Still means nothing.'

'Bleu,' Richardson said. 'It's French for "blue", isn't it?'

'The Sinclairs are half French,' Mark said. 'Their mother, Juliette, came from Paris. People around here call them Froggie.'

'Where's she now?' Chiara asked. 'Juliette, I mean.'

'Files say she killed herself. Her family used to own Cherie's house. Juliette really loved the place, but they moved away after she died.'

Sean waved his arms and made the comic sound of a ghost.

'I'm not suggesting there's any sort of supernatural crap going on in that house.' Mark felt irritated. 'What I mean is, the house where Cherie was killed was formerly owned by the Sinclair family, who have a French connection. Juliette Sinclair died either by suicide or accidentally falling from the cape.'

'So, don't call the Ghostbusters?' Chiara sounded disappointed.

'It is interesting, but nothing to get excited about,' Richardson said, ignoring her. 'Even so, Ariti, check it out. If it was something in French, maybe the Sinclairs will know more.'

Chiara turned now to Cherie's fingertips. Aside from the finger she'd used to write in blood, they were largely unscathed. 'No defensive wounds by the looks of it,' Chiara said. 'And the main gouge is at the side and back of her head. That's consistent with someone following her and then knocking her down.'

'Maybe Cherie saw something she wasn't meant to,' Sean suggested. 'She could have confronted someone, and they knocked her down hard. The injuries to her head are substantial.'

Sean at the station was different to Sean at the crime scene, shaky hands, sweating. Now, he was trying hard to mask his earlier anxiety with a matter-of-factness that wasn't quite convincing.

'A burglary gone wrong,' Jane mused. 'That house does look as if it's the best one in town. Maybe someone thought they'd rob it and got caught.'

Chiara nodded slowly. 'And the face is unharmed. No defensive injuries – perhaps Cherie knew her killer.'

Jane, Jagdeep, Sean and Chiara continued to talk theories, while Mark listened in.

'All speculation,' Richardson said finally, his eyes on the whiteboard. 'It's evidence we need and nothing more.' He stifled a yawn. 'Why don't you all knock off? Meet you here first thing – and I mean sparrows.'

Richardson's yawn was contagious. Jagdeep yawned, and soon they were a pack of old cats ready for a lie-down.

'What about we get some dinner?' Sean said, looking at Chiara hopefully.

Mark wanted to catch up with Jagdeep. 'We could get a souva,' he said to the group. 'There's a good spot in town.'

Jane said she had phone calls to make and reports to write. Chiara wrinkled her nose: 'I'm vegetarian. Might get a salad at the pub if they're still serving food.' Sean said he'd tag along.

Richardson had turned back to the whiteboard and was studying it. 'Bring me back a lamb and garlic, can you? No rush. I'll be here for a bit longer.'

Mark heard Sean ask Jagdeep in a low whisper what 'sparrows' was.

'It's early,' his friend said. 'Like, as soon as the sun comes up. I'd say be here at six-thirty am.'

'Why didn't he just say "come early" then?'

'He did,' Jagdeep told the young officer with the hint of a smile. 'He said "sparrows".'

How we speak, what we call things, Mark reflected as he followed the others out the door, *every single thing we say or write is open to interpretation.*

The police officers said goodnight. Sean said, 'Au revoir,' and Chiara said, 'Bonne nuit.' Mark wondered briefly if the two of them would get together.

Inside the King of Souva was aglow in light. The drinks fridge, with its jarring soft drink colours and screaming logos, gave off a headachy vibe.

Now they had time, Jagdeep explained to him how she'd started studying again. There were career options in Investigations, she said. She needed to build her qualifications. She was here on this case as part of her training and she aimed to do well. You never knew when openings became available – but if they did, she needed to be in the right place at the right time.

The right place at the right time.

Energy drinks shouted at him from the fridge, a Coke Zero sneered. All his life, he'd been in the right place at the right time. Opportunities landed in his lap: police college after school, jobs, invitations to fancy events, offers to introduce him to people in high places. When he and Kelly broke up, he'd had so many offers of places to stay that he chose the local Travelodge out of fear of offending someone. His sister Prue teased him about his good fortune, and not always in a friendly way. When she'd first gone for a job at the local supermarket aged fourteen and nine months exactly, she'd worn her best clothes, typed up and printed out a well-drafted CV and placed it carefully in a plastic binder. She'd practised standard responses – 'My main weakness is that I work too hard' – and broke out in a nervous rash before the interview.

In contrast, when Mark was that age, the same store manager shouted at him from across the meat section: 'Oi, Reets, you play in the Seniors on the weekend?'

'Yeah,' he'd shouted back.

'Getting to be a big bugger, aren't you? You fifteen yet? Wanna job, mate?'

Did he want a job? His sister had one. His friends had jobs. 'Yeah,' he shouted back over the thrum of the freezer. 'Wouldn't mind.'

'Start Mundee after school?'

'Yeah, Mundee. Thanks.'

And that was it. That transcript, Mark thought now, was basically a template for how he'd got everything in life. Being a big bugger helped. Being free and able to start on Mundee helped.

'That's good, Jag,' he said. 'And how's the family?'

Jagdeep adjusted her turban, smoothing it at the edges. 'Adi's fine. He's working hard, trying not to be away so much, and Tanvir is great. He's a good boy, nearly one!' She showed him a photo of her son. Cute and round, a cheeky look. Mark made the appropriate sounds.

'Don't worry,' Jag said, putting her phone away. 'I'm not going to rave on and on about how gifted he is or anything.'

'Thank God.'

'But he is *very* smart.'

'Kill me now, Jag. Leave me to die here while you go on and on for eternity about your progeny.'

Jagdeep laughed quietly, then looked out the glass windows to the black sea beyond. 'There's something really sad about this case, isn't there? Cherie in her big old house on her own. What's your take on it?'

'I think she was hit very hard in the side of the head with a rock, twice possibly,' Mark answered, flat. 'And as she lay dying, she wrote something on her arm to identify the person.'

'We know that.' Jagdeep pursed her lips in thought. 'But the other details: the mannequin, the lamp, the odd outfit – as you say, it smacks of the theatrical.'

'Cherie was an actor.'

'Her final act was her most grand, that's for sure. Everyone will know about it soon.'

They would. The media would love it. They'd find old footage of Cherie in films, singing and dancing for the crowds in the theatres. Right now, some journo would be sniffing for evidence of her supposed former lovers Gibson and Jackman. God, they'd love that. And the writing in blood! Once that got out, every cheap hack from Bunbury to Mossman would be onto it, every wannabe podcaster, every crank with a connection to the other world. They'd all come to Broken Bay for her.

In death, Cherie Swinson was finally a star.

'And the bodies in the sinkhole on that Doyle farm.' Jag shook her head. 'It's a nightmare.'

The two fell silent.

'Would you ever do it?' Mark asked. 'Cave dive?'

Jagdeep tilted her head for a moment, screwed up her nose. 'Me? No, I can barely swim.'

'I can swim quite well, and I'd never do it – those passages, the darkness.'

'And when you think about it, cave diving flies against every human instinct, doesn't it?' Jagdeep grimaced. 'Unnatural breathing, underwater, you're mute, you're wearing an extra skin, a mask, the tanks . . .'

'And if you get scared, you can't just swim straight up to the surface – you have to wait, decompress so you don't get the bends.'

That was one thing that Mark really didn't like, the thought of waiting to decompress. He'd read of frightened divers who had to spend five, even six hours underwater after their dives to the bottom, waiting for the nitrogen levels in their blood to go down.

'But even so,' Jag spoke slowly, 'if I could swim, if I'd been trained in it – I think I would give it a go. I mean, imagine!'

That 'imagine!' again. Mark couldn't imagine.

'I remember reading about this cave diver in Florida. The way they described the caverns and chambers: it was magic, like nothing else on earth. The crystal-clear water, the stalactites and the underwater plants – viridian shades and golden beams of light. It sounded exquisite.'

Mark didn't believe in magic. Rabbits weren't pulled out of hats from nowhere, they were always there, in a hidden compartment. 'What's viridian mean?' he asked.

'It's like a blue-green shade.'

Feeling dull and stupid, Mark stood up and stretched. The souvas were almost ready; he could see the man wrapping them up.

'Kali orexi,' the old man said.

Mark didn't know what that meant. He said thanks and moved towards the register.

Jagdeep asked him about Rose and the boys and he told her briefly about his sons, ending with Rose's plan to move to Tanzania for a year.

'What will you do?'

'Can't do much,' Mark answered blithely as he paid for the food. 'She's made up her mind.'

'You can't go for a visit, or holidays or . . . ?'

'We've been through all that. At my age, I don't want a long-term, half-in half-out thing – and Rose isn't convinced either. She's asked me to go with her.'

'And will you?'

The question amazed him. 'Course not, I've got the boys.'

'You can't take them with you?'

'For a year?'

His friend shrugged, and they made their way outside. 'I'd love to take Tan to India for twelve months.'

'You've got family there, Jag, you speak the language. Plus, you and Adi are together. You aren't ripping your son away from the other parent.'

'It'd hardly be a kidnapping, Mark.'

'It'd be a bit like one. Kelly would never agree anyway. The boys are starting at a new school next year and they can't wait.'

In Jagdeep's car, she pulled out of the car park, then turned right along the main road, rather than back to the station.

'Oi, it's the other way, and I've got this remember?' He held up Richardson's souvlaki.

'I just want to see what the house looks like again, at night, with no police lights or loads of people around.'

Mark knew what she meant. He fell quiet as they drove slowly along the main street. He wound down his window, sniffed the sharp saltiness, heard the lapping of the water, the light crashing of the waves.

Margery's house, nestled low next to Cherie's and almost hidden in a forest of moonah, was dark. Perhaps she'd gone to stay with a friend after the day's events.

Cherie's house rose like a king above it. The bottom storey was covered, so the top floor gave the impression that it was suspended, floating above the trees and the town itself. The house was completely dark. It would be locked now, cordoned off and photographed by other police officers, ready for finger-printing in the morning.

The window where Cherie had placed the mannequin was visible to anyone walking by, or even out in the bay. Murray Sinclair had bought the house for his new wife, the beautiful Juliette. Was it so that she could see her husband on his journey back from the ocean, so that he could see her in the window, waiting? There was something romantic about it, the old sea captain and his lass waiting on the shore.

'Cherie wanted that mannequin to be seen – she had the lamp trained right on it,' Jagdeep mumbled, half to herself. 'Perhaps she was trying to fool someone that the figure was her.'

Mark considered the idea. In the trick of light, the big hair, the alabaster skin: it would look real. Her yard was pitch black. Easy enough to hide there, wait till she appeared. He massaged his neck. There was a slyness to Cherie's set-up too, the faded mannequin in the tired old dress and shabby cardigan. Where was the clapping audience? She may have been thinking about entertainment, but Cherie was making a statement too.

'So, she wanted someone to think the mannequin was her, while she, what?'

'While she waited down here to find out who it was. You said she'd suspected someone had been watching her, remember?'

'Brave of her, a woman in her sixties, to do that. I don't know about that.'

'Maybe she had an idea of who it was, didn't think that after all this time of watching her they were likely to do anything bad.'

Mark was dubious. 'She was nervous, I saw that at the pub. She sensed that someone was following her.'

'Or maybe she was delusional.' Jagdeep waved towards the window. 'Life isn't the stage. People really do get murdered, attacked in real life and sometime for no reason. It's not all fighting with song and dance like *West Side Story.*'

The two detectives sat silent. A sea breeze rattled the she-oaks, making them sigh.

'I hate those trees,' Jagdeep said. 'They sound so sad.'

Mark was surprised. He liked the soft whispering between ocean, tree and wind. 'We should get some rest,' he said. 'Besides, I've got to get this food to Richardson. It's getting cold.'

Jagdeep nodded and they drove the dark streets to the police station, where a single light in the front room was on.

'Want me to come in with you?' Jagdeep offered.

'Why? I'm not in trouble. You're not my mum.'

'Want me to wait and give you a lift to your motel then?' The Adelaide police were staying at a Travelodge just out of town.

'Nah, I'll walk.' Mark got out of the car, bent down to talk through the window. 'See you in the morning.'

'Sparrows,' Jag reminded him before giving a wave and pulling slowly away from the kerb.

Inside the station, Richardson was deep into the files. He looked up as Mark entered the room.

'Souva,' Mark said, handing his boss the lukewarm package.

'Thanks.' Richardson returned to his notes.

Mark wondered whether to stay or go.

'I've been reading up about the divers they retrieved from the sinkhole,' Richardson said. 'It seems that both women were tangled up in lines. Can you explain what they mean by guide-lines and sidelines?'

Mark leaned against the doorframe. 'I'm no expert, not at all, but from what I've learned the guideline is like an umbilical cord. It's your safety line to the surface. Usually they're tied a bit below the surface of the entrance, under the water, to prevent thrillseekers.'

Richardson nodded.

'So, the diver usually holds the guideline as they dive down and through the cave systems. If there's silt, if there's a strong water current, if there's a blockage with other divers coming back, the guideline is always there so they can find their way out.'

'And the sideline?'

'When a diver wants to deviate from the guideline – or they've come to the end of it and want to go further – they tie a sideline near the guideline and then continue. It extends their route. They're mostly a different colour to the guideline. Sometimes, in the really popular caves, there are small arrows placed along the side ropes too, showing the way back to the guideline.'

'And in this instance, how many lines were found with Mya Rennik and the other, as yet unidentified, victim?'

Richardson, like Jane Southern, was still refusing to name the victim as Eloise Sinclair. Procedures, protocol, evidence. A big brother's emotive declaration and the town's opinion held little sway in court.

'Well, here's the thing: Eloi . . . the unidentified victim had a long, thick orange rope wrapped about her upper body as well as the thin blue rope Mya used as a sideline. Mya was also tied up in the ropes, and her torch was stuck in one of them. Theory is, her torch got tangled up in her blue sideline, she decided to leave, but got caught in the thick orange line. Eventually, she got trapped in both ropes and tried to cut herself out, becoming exhausted in the process and then drowning.'

'I see.' Richardson nodded again. 'And Mya used her own white rope as the initial guideline, then she used the blue as a sideline to go through that skinny tunnel, the squeeze. So where did the thicker orange line come from?'

Mark shrugged. 'The first diver's guideline?'

'But it wasn't tied to anything at the top of the sinkhole. From the photos Jane sent us, it seems as if it had been pulled in with her. Eloise – the victim – had the whole length of it with her.'

The two men were silent.

'Maybe she tried to tie a guideline and it became undone,' Mark offered.

Richardson unwrapped the souva and took a bite.

'Or maybe she was diving with someone else, there was an accident and the guideline came loose.'

Another nod from the Inspector, another bite.

'Or maybe, someone cut the guideline and she couldn't find her way back.'

Richardson finished chewing, swallowed, looked at the remaining souva as if it were an oracle.

'I've seen ropes like it before, the orange one,' Mark added. 'They were on the Sinclair fishing boat.'

'The French connection again. *Bleu*.'

'Yeah.'

'Check that out. Check it all out, Mark. I know you'll do a good job.'

'I'll try.'

'Angelo Conti says very good things about you.' Richardson looked at him over his glasses like an owl. 'I've heard about your last few cases, finding the missing cop.'

'Angelo is a friend.'

'Friend or not, Conti wouldn't put someone's name up for promotion unless he didn't think they were capable.'

Promotion?

'Ever thought about Investigative Homicide? We could do with some more good people here.'

'I don't know. I haven't thought . . .'

'Well, mull it over and talk to me before we go. There's some openings we could discuss.'

'I will.' Despite the day's events, Mark felt a warm glow spread through his chest. The power of a compliment, what it can do. It can change lives, make you turn direction, give purpose. In the right moment, it can make a man go to war. Mark saw himself propelled into the future, fronting a television camera, gravely addressing the nation about crimes of national importance. There were no ums in his speech, he didn't scratch his nose or widen his eyes. He was bigger, fitter, more presentable. *More.*

'I will think about it,' Mark repeated.

Richardson turned his attention back to the whiteboard and, without looking at the souva, raised it to his mouth and took another massive bite. No garlic sauce ran down his chin. Mark looked at the whiteboard too. *Bleu.* The word in an ugly brownish red, barely legible. It was a statement, a last screaming cry of defiance. *Bleu.*

'You can go now, Sergeant, it's been a big day. Get some rest, back here early.' Mark was being dismissed. Richardson looked at the board again. 'It's a Gordian knot,' he mumbled, half to himself before raising his head again. 'See you tomorrow, Ariti.'

'Goodnight, sir.'

Mark left the station and wandered back to the Hibernian. All was quiet in Broken Bay, save the intermittent cawing of a gull. The call could be for a number of reasons, Mark knew. It could be celebrating its chicks learning to fly, or protecting them from carnivorous neighbours. Either way, the high-pitched cry in the night sounded hollow and strange. He walked on, his footsteps steady on the unlit path, only a thin sliver of moon giving him light.

Richardson, he knew, would be at the station for hours. He was a man dedicated to the job, like Angelo Conti. He'd set aside his private life for the cases he was working on – a kid's twenty-first would come second to a breakthrough, relationships would falter but still, Richardson and Conti would go the extra mile.

Mark realised he had forgotten his own souvlaki. Removing it from his coat pocket, he took one bite, chewed. Took another bite, chewed some more. He passed a bin, threw the remainder in. He thought about the wound on Cherie's head, the blood-trickle down to her ear. He thought about her smiling face, fading into the crowd as he searched for Jane at the Royal.

When he got to his room, Mark took off his shoes and lay on his bed. He googled cave diving on his phone and read with equal parts fascination and horror about the sport. The restrictions, the danger caused by silt, the depths they went to, the deaths. Sleep, when it came, was thick in dreams of being trapped underwater, his father carrying Juliette's lifeless body to shore, of his mother and father shouting while he was trapped in an underwater cave.

He woke in a claustrophobic panic. 'Get me out!' he tried to cry. 'Air!'

In his nightmare, he was one of the Franklin Three. He was scratching on the walls, tearing at his throat, and all the while, his father was with him in the depths, carrying the young woman home.

CHAPTER 15

Mark woke to song. High pitched and pleasant, it was one of the newer tunes he kept hearing on the radio. His boys liked whoever it was: Katy whatshername? Ariana somebody?

The time was way past sparrows. At 8 am, the sparrows were having afternoon tea, putting their slippers on and watching the evening news. Mark had a shower in a time parents would approve of, got dressed, put on his shoes, grabbed his wallet and headed out the door.

'Hi!' A smiling woman was washing the windows of the room beside his. With her swept-up grey hair, small nose and green eyes, she looked like an inquisitive bird.

That 'Hi!'. A friendly greeting; there was power to it. 'Are you the policeman Dad was talking about?'

Ian's daughter. The one who once went out with Brett.

'Yep.'

'I'm Liz. Got to warn you, the town's agog with the news about Cherie Swinson. It's so sad! I mean, why attack an older lady like that?'

Why attack anyone like that.

171

'Did you know her?'

'Yes, I knew her, but not well.'

Mark knew what she meant. It was a mistake commonly made by city people and those who wrote about country towns that everyone knew each other well. Like anywhere, rural people relocated, had kids who then left town. Names changed, property prices went up, people with no prior connection moved in. In small towns, it was usually only the old families who really knew each other. The Doyles and the Sinclairs: they went back, they'd have some things to say.

'She'd been coming to the library recently, was interested in local history. I work there, so I used to try to help her out. Cherie was a really nice woman.'

'Yeah?' Mark asked. 'What was she interested in?'

'Oh, the usual stuff – local history, old photographs of people and places.'

Nice to think Cherie had hobbies, Mark thought.

'She also liked reading about farms in the area, buying and selling – that sort of thing.'

Mark made an interested sound.

'Sometimes, she'd get me to help her with her notes. Cherie was dyslexic, and she was terribly embarrassed about her spelling.' Liz gave a sad smile. 'We'll miss her in the library.'

'I'm sure you will. It seems like she had lots of friends.'

'Is there anything I can do to help?' Liz asked. 'Dad said you're getting your car fixed. I could drive you somewhere.'

'Well, that would be perfect, Liz, thank you.' He looked at his watch. 'I need to get to the station pronto.'

'Sure!' Ian's daughter looked excited at the prospect of assisting the force.

Mark watched as the woman ran to the admin office and came back out brandishing keys. Had she also put lipstick on?

Once in her car, Mark introduced himself. 'I already know who you are though,' she said. 'I remember reading about you when that policewoman went missing in Stone Town a year or so ago.'

People brought it up. The investigation occurred near his home town. Stone Town had never seen anything like it. The crowds, the press, the amateur sleuths. The same would happen here, in Broken Bay.

Mark changed the subject. 'Your dad mentioned that you knew Brett Twymann?'

Liz gave a snort. 'If you were a half-decent-looking female in your late teens in this town, you knew Brett Twymann, believe me.'

'Bit of a ladies man, eh?' God, Mark hated how he sounded. Was he eighty years old? *Nudge, nudge, wink, wink, say no more.*

'Yeah, he really was. Very good-looking, very much into himself.' She laughed. 'I was with him for a short span of time during one of the many breaks he was having with Eloise Sinclair.'

This was new. Mark pulled his shoulders back, felt in his pocket for his notepad and pencil. 'So, Eloise and Brett weren't overly serious then?'

'Oh, don't get me wrong, I think he loved her. They'd been together for years. But they were young, tempestuous. You know what it's like.' Liz looked at him knowingly.

Did he know what it was like? His late teens were decades ago. He could recall girlfriends and break-ups, but it was like a movie in his head. The only thing that was real about it now was the euphoria and the hurt. It was as if all his memories were in his gut and not his head. The stakes were lower in most teenage relationships – no kids, no marriage contract, no shared mortgage or pets. But, and now he remembered being dumped at twenty-three, the hurt was real, it cut deep.

'Brett had this act,' Liz was saying. 'All the girls used to laugh about it. He would take the ones he liked into his bedroom and show us photo albums of himself surfing and diving. It was hilarious really – we all knew that it was a precursor to kissing and whatnot. He used to look at that album all the time . . . the ego! Once, I went around there and he wasn't home, but he'd left it on the bed for me to look at. Inside, there was this note for me: *"Liz, I'm surfing, sorry. Come and watch if you like. Also, I can't stop thinking about you. Love B."* What a joke! He did the same for us all. The shit I used to put up with. I mean, *come and watch if you like?'*

'How long were you with him?' They pulled up outside the police station.

'I don't know – two weeks?'

'The joys of youth.' Mark unbuckled his seatbelt. 'Thanks, Liz, you've been a great help.'

'Are you in town for much longer?' Liz looked at herself in the rear-vision mirror. 'If you're bored, I could show you around. We've got some real hidden gems here.'

Mark thought for a moment. 'Do you know where the sink-holes are? I'd like to take a look at them, especially that one where those kids died years ago, the Tomb.'

Liz wrinkled her nose. 'I was more thinking a nice beach – there're some good picnic places around.'

An awkward pause followed.

'Ah,' Mark said. 'Well, I'm working, you see.'

Liz rushed in. 'It was just an idea. I'm only here a few more days anyway, and come to think of it, I really should spend time with Dad.'

'He seems a bit . . . preoccupied.'

'Dad's addicted to online betting. Between that and fighting with his ex-wife, there's not much time for anything else.'

'Oh.'

'Well, if you're at a loose end . . .' Her words dangled.

Mark gave a vague wave goodbye and watched as Liz drove off, at speed.

Inside the station, Chiara shot him an accusing stare as he snuck in and took a seat at the back near Jagdeep. Sean gave him a small wave, which he returned. Jane was out the front, detailing the successful retrieval of Mya Rennik from the cave. It was officially accepted that she had drowned in the underground chamber after becoming trapped in her own and the other diver's lines. David Furneaux's retrieval operation in the cave to collect his friend had been without incident. The sinkhole would be closed till further notice, much to the chagrin of Frank Doyle.

Jane sat down and Richardson took over, addressing the investigation into Cherie Swinson's death. Their boss turned to the whiteboard, where a floorplan of Cherie's house had been printed and taped up. He pointed out the layout of the house and the front yard where Cherie was found. They'd have to wait for the coroner, but blunt trauma to the head was the most likely cause of death. A viable footprint had been recovered from the scene; the suspect had been wearing boots, size eleven. The indentation of the print indicated it was possible the suspect had been standing there for some time, or that it was a heavy person. A short, black wig was discovered near Cherie's body and had been sent off for fingerprinting. Cherie's head had two injuries; a small bruise and swelling on her forehead, and a more serious wound behind her right temple. Along with bone fragments, small pieces of limestone were present in that wound, suggesting that Cherie had been hit hard with a rock. Limestone rock could be found anywhere in Broken Bay – Richardson had been for a walk this morning and seen numerous stones of various sizes.

Richardson suspected that the rock in question had been thrown into the ocean shortly after the attack, in which case they had no chance of finding it. Nevertheless, they would keep working. There was the footprint, and testing would be done on it that very morning.

Mark was impressed. Richardson had not stopped working. And not only that, he didn't look tired. Mark estimated Richardson to be in his late fifties. With his white hair and tall thin frame in neat collar and tie, he reminded Mark of a salt shaker from a posh hotel.

'But why the bruise?' Jagdeep asked and all heads turned towards her. 'Was Cherie hit twice in the head with a rock, once more hard than the other?'

'Why hit her twice?' Sean said. 'I mean, it's not as if she was a large woman, and she was in her sixties at least.'

'Sixty-eight,' Richardson said, looking at his notes. 'Cherie turned sixty-eight a week ago.'

'Around the bruise and swelling, the skin is barely broken,' Jane said, reading from her notes. 'To me that doesn't look as if that injury came from a rock. Maybe she was pushed first and then the person hit her.'

Richardson turned to an enlarged photo of Cherie on the board and they all followed his gaze. In this image Cherie was sitting at a table, Barry at her side, glasses held high in cheers. She was caught mid-laugh, her slightly yellowing teeth blurred with lipstick, hair was a wild mix of grey and brown, wiry and unkempt. The deep cracks at the sides of her lips spoke of a lifetime of smoking and her gaunt cheeks were thick with rouge.

'Cherie had blonde hair when I saw her last,' Mark said. 'But in most of her photos, she's got brown hair. She must have dyed it fairly recently.'

He watched as the police officers wrote the detail down. Details, details: that's how an investigation was built. Small moments, evidence, every bit joining together to form a solid case.

'The black wig's interesting,' Jagdeep said. 'A long blonde wig on the mannequin, a short black wig in the yard, dying her own hair from brown to blonde – what's Cherie's deal with hair?'

Mark remembered the young man in plaid. 'There's a kid who works at the local cafe – his parents own it. He was friends with Cherie, used to work with her on plays and costumes. He said he needed to collect a wig from Cherie.'

'Get onto him, Jagdeep,' Richardson directed. 'Could be nothing, but good to rule it out.'

'Only,' Mark recalled, 'he'll be on his way to New York. He flew out last night.'

Chiara and Sean groaned.

'I'll contact his parents and try to message him to call me when he gets in . . . that'll be tomorrow, I guess.' Jagdeep said.

The police turned to the nature of Cherie's injuries, the bruise and the gaping wound.

'The person who attacked Cherie was frustrated,' Chiara surmised. 'And angry when they were caught spying, or attempting to rob the place.'

Richardson took off his glasses and polished them with the edge of his navy jumper. 'All options are open. But given the fact that our initial searches indicated no sign of disturbance in the house and, from what we know, all valuable items remain in place, a robbery looks unlikely. Her handbag was on the arm of the couch. Cherie must have gone inside when she got home, and then back outside again. We have to find out why.' Richardson paused. 'The outfit on the mannequin does seem at odds with her usual, more flamboyant costumes. It's something we'll be looking into further. Hopefully the young bloke from the cafe can help us.'

The discussion depressed Mark. He was meant to be taking Cherie's statement today, hearing her thoughts and her account of the person watching her.

'Jagdeep, you'll go over the Royal's CCTV today,' Richardson said. 'And find out all you can about the victim. Mark, I want you working on the Eloise Sinclair file – go out to the site, learn as much as you can. Find out about those ropes. Talk to the ex-boyfriend, the brothers. But if you've got time, you can sit in with Jagdeep when she interviews the publican later.'

Mark told them all about Liz's revelation that Cherie Swinson was dyslexic.

'My brother's dyslexic,' Chiara said. 'He misspells words all the time. It's really difficult for him.'

They bought up the letters on the screen again: 81EU, BLFU or BLEV.

'It really does look like "Bleu",' Jagdeep said. So, given that Cherie was dyslexic, she may have been trying to write . . .'

They all read the letters again, mumbled them aloud.

'Blue,' Chiara said. 'Maybe Cherie was trying to write "blue".'

Mark nodded. The more they looked at the bloody letters, the clearer they became: Bleu. It could mean 'Blue'.

'Well, that hardly helps,' Sean said. 'This town is surrounded by blue.'

'It doesn't mean she definitely misspelt it,' Chiara warned. 'There are lots of different types of dyslexia.'

So: Blue, or Bleu. It wasn't much.

Richardson advised them to keep that detail quiet for now. Holding back certain information was vital in identifying genuine suspects and witnesses in any case.

Their boss told them to get to work, gave the others jobs. Chiara was working on fingerprints at Cherie's house, Sean was manning the phones and front desk for any locals who may have information, and Jane was going back to Adelaide later in the day to compile the forensics report, but for now, she'd accompany Mark to the Doyles' farm and the sinkhole.

With their roles neatly set out, they went their separate ways.

After telling Jagdeep about the rest of his conversation with Liz – in particular Cherie's interest in local history, Mark joined Jane in the police Hilux. He sat in the warm car as she drove, content for the moment to watch the land pass by.

Out of town the landscape was completely flat. No gentle undulation, no rises. It would flood easily, and for the houses lining the road, a rogue wave would be perilous. Before the settlers came with their axes and then their sheep and then their cows, there had been forests, wetlands and swamps. Now, almost everything on the surface was completely cleared and farmed. Only the subterranean world was a mystery.

Humans are inquisitive beings, Mark thought. *And curiosity propels us further, makes us build rockets and space telescopes and go into caves deep below the Earth's surface. It drives the human race, but it kills us too.*

'The bitter end' is what cave divers call it when they have to make their final tie-off before they head back to the surface via the guidelines. Mark knew this from his brief research into the sport. Despite the progress they've made, the potential for new and more beautiful sites, the human condition means they have to backtrack. Oxygen levels, risk of the bends, decompression time, temperature all had to be factored in. And yet, even at the point when they realise the extent of their human capabilities, cave divers want to push on further into the unknown.

Jane asked Mark if he was okay. He knew that she'd be referring to him finding Cherie. The shock of seeing dead bodies – even for cops, for first responders – it never went away. Mark once met a bloke, a retired ambo, who said that while on holidays he went over all the dead and mangled bodies he'd ever found. He named them, felt their presence as he swam, played with his kids and drank cocktails with his wife. It was only when he was on duty, sirens roaring and driving at speed to the next accident, that he didn't see their faces.

'I'm okay,' he answered.

Jane nodded; she understood. They slipped into a more general conversation – how thorough Richardson was, the strangeness of three tragedies occurring decades apart in the town, how green the grass was.

Something was happening between them. A loosening of a string that had previously bound them taut. He was no longer acutely aware of her perfume, the way her lips moved when she spoke. Her body would always be a marvel to him, but it came as a relief that he and Jane seemed to be slipping into something like friendship.

They pulled into the backyard of the Doyle house just as a ute was driving out. They slowed to talk over lowered windows.

'Need to look around again?' James asked.

'Yeah, that all right?' Mark knew it was all right. They had permission to check the whole farm, but still it was good to ask.

'Go for it.' James's face was pale in the morning light, his thinning red hair covered sensibly in a broad-brimmed hat. 'I'll be back later, got some business in Franklin.'

An idea struck Mark. 'You wouldn't have time to show me some sinkholes at some stage, would you? The one where the Franklin Three died, or just any I could have a good look at? I'd like to check them out.' He didn't add that he'd also like the opportunity to talk to James about his and his sister's whereabouts on the day Eloise went missing.

'I'll be busy with farm stuff today.' James hesitated. 'Maybe tomorrow?'

'Tomorrow's fine.'

With a nod, James continued up the drive. Jane drove slowly past him, each of them courteous in their careful manoeuvres. As they passed one another, Mark glanced into the open ute tray. There was the typical farming detritus: bits of wood, wire, some feed, a drum. And plenty of rope. The orange kind he'd seen on the lobster boat, and in the photograph of Eloise's retrieved body, the sharp twine used for all manner of purposes. A common rope for these parts, but even so, Mark felt a shiver as he held up his phone and took a discreet snap.

Rope. He thought about the word. It had a sinister feel to it. 'She roped him in', 'Give him enough rope to hang himself', 'Wouldn't throw a rope to a drowning man', 'I'm at the end of my rope.' When Mark thought of the word, he thought of 'bind', he thought of 'lash'.

Frank Doyle wasn't at home when they knocked. There was an old Mercedes in the carport, a tractor in a shed further down, but no sign of Doyle Senior. An ill-kept lawn at the back of the house had a structure in the deep corner, fenced in fading iron. Mark guessed it was an old swimming pool. It gave him pause for thought: there were loads of rules about pool fences, heavy fines for shoddy ones, permits refused because of gates without a child lock. Had Frank gone to the council to get his application for a pool approved? The sunken area was now more of a junk heap.

Mark wandered right around the perimeter of the house, while Jane took a phone call. The Doyle residence was a typical three-bedroom, two-bathroom weatherboard farmhouse, with a sloping verandah. No frills. Like most working farms, the money would all go into the land rather than the home. Mark could see through the closest window, a bedroom furnished with a single bed and a wooden dressing table with an oval mirror: Prue had one like it in her bedroom when they were kids. This would, in all likelihood, have been Geraldine Doyle's bedroom until she moved out.

Mark stood with his back to her windows, facing the paddocks. Sitting at her dressing table, Gerri would have been able to see the flat expanse of land that was her family farm. Green now, from all the rain, she would have seen it in all its hues, an orange yellow as summer bore down, brown and parched in drought with thin black-and-white Holstein cows making their way to the dairy.

Best of all, Geraldine would have been able to see where her property intersected with her best friend Eloise's farm and, if she left her room and moved alongside the west of the house, to where Brett Twymann lived.

'Show you the sinkhole site again?' Jane appeared, already turning to the paddock gate. 'We can walk, it's not even ten minutes from here.'

'Sure,' Mark said. 'I'm a walker.'

Jane opened an iron gate along the fence line and closed it again after they stepped through, fastening the iron chain loop over the bolt. 'It should be in the Ten Commandments, *Leave the farm gate as you found it*,' she said.

Before or after 'Thou shalt not commit adultery', he could have added, but wisely did not.

Jane strode along, lost in thought. 'When I grew up – not far from here,' she said, 'I used to be jealous of kids on farms, all that quiet time, big open spaces.'

'I was the opposite,' Mark said, quickening his pace, taking care to skirt over fresh cow pats. 'I felt sorry for them – all by themselves, no one to play with.'

'Different here,' Jane mused, her hands in her pockets. 'Eloise had her three brothers, and two friends on the neighbouring farm.'

'Plus her boyfriend, Brett, didn't live too far away, just a couple of k's to the west in Moyne Lane. She could easily have skipped across the paddocks to either of their houses.'

'All those boys!' Jane said. She was right, it was boy city in these parts. The three handsome Sinclair boys and the playboy Brett. And James. There was James too.

'And Scott Boxhall lived in town,' Mark recalled. 'Gerri's boyfriend and the father of her son.'

Police tape still surrounded the sinkhole, but all other evidence of the retrieval operation was gone. Mark peered into the hole. It would be so easy to miss; you'd only find it if you stumbled into or across it. Blue water shimmered, contrasting sharply with the grass around it. 'How did they find this place?' he asked in wonder.

'Frank said he'd been clearing the paddocks, heard a cow mooing in distress. It looked like it was stuck in the grass. When he got there, he saw that its front leg had fallen into a hole. Got the cow out of the way, cleared the grass and found this.'

'It's amazing down there,' Jane said, kneeling. 'You can't believe it – a whole cavern – and so beautiful. The visibility is almost perfect. In the ocean you're excited with ten metres, but under here, you can see for at least forty.'

Mark knelt beside her, the two of them bent like worshippers, gazing at the water. The reflection of clouds bobbed in the surface, and his own image shimmered in the peacock blue. He had a sudden urge to dive right in. It was easy to see how people might take a chance in a place like this, secret and wonderful.

'Poke your head under,' Jane said, and after a brief pause he did. Leaning low, bum to the sky, he lowered his face into the cool water.

Breathtaking. Water so clear, almost no difference above and below the surface of the pond: jewel colours, greens and blues, waving green fronds, tiny blue fish and no end to it. No end – Mark could not make out the bottom. 'God!' he said, coming up for air and wiping his face on his sleeve. 'That's unbelievable. How deep is it?'

'That cavern? Fairly shallow as underwater caves go, about forty to fifty metres.'

'And how wide?'

Jane grinned. 'Put it this way, Port Adelaide could play a whole game down there.'

Mark shook his head. This whole other world was just below them. Every day, and so few people knew. 'It's a wonder the cow didn't fall right in.'

'In that case, it's a wonder we all don't.' Jane pointed to the dirt track. 'Look at how we've driven over this land. All those vehicles here the other day. New sinkholes appear all the time. We might be standing on one about to open up now.'

You can eat all the veggies you want, you can count your steps, you can drink your eight glasses of water a day – but no one mentions you also need luck in order to not fall down a hole. 'Was that an old swimming pool back at the Doyles?' Mark asked, still staring at the glistening pool.

'Yeah, I think so – why?' Jane was also looking at the water. She ran her fingers over the surface and they both stood transfixed, watching gentle ripples across the blue.

'Nothing really,' Mark answered, but an idea, barely formed, was growing in the back of his mind.

'What I can't work out,' Jane said, 'is where Eloise got her equipment from. The tank and the guideline.'

'The Sinclairs and the Doyles both own rope like the one in your photo.'

Jane raised her eyebrows. 'Interesting – but that doesn't mean much.'

Mark nodded. He told Jane about Eloise's full wetsuit and mask, how Phil notified police they were missing a few days after they'd reported Eloise's absence. It was the same gear she was found in. She'd taken it with her wherever she'd gone.

'So, she went for an illicit cave dive then.' Jane shrugged. 'It's probably not uncommon.'

Sneak dives, they were called – when people dived without the landowner's permission or knowledge. It was what the Franklin Three were doing at the Tomb. Mark had once snuck into the Booralama swimming pool after dark with his friends. It seemed daring at the time.

'But she didn't take a tank from her house,' Mark said.

'That is a sticking point,' Jane conceded. 'We have to find out where she got it from.'

Mark was reminded about his query on oxygen tanks. 'I texted you about the tanks found on both bodies. Were you able to find out anything about them?'

'Ahh, yes,' Jane said. 'I meant to text you that both the old and the new oxygen tank recovered from the sinkhole were made out of steel – that's usual for cold water diving. It's more robust than aluminium.'

'Right.'

'But it got me interested in the tanks again. We'd already looked up the serial numbers for both and found nothing of interest. They are regular, mass-produced tank types – but the dates of the hydro test, now that's interesting.'

'The hydro what?' Mark asked, looking again at the surface of the pool. Honestly, it could distract you bigtime, that water. His reflection shimmered and shifted.

'If you've had a tank for over twelve months, you are required to have it hydro tested – to see if the pressure is okay and if it is still safe to use. Each time it's hydro tested, the date is stamped into the shoulder of the cylinder.'

Mark looked up from the water.

'And on Mya's tank, there was no stamp. That means it was fairly new, so no need to have it tested. But on the older oxygen tank . . .'

'Yes?'

'There was a stamp. Dated five months before Eloise Sinclair went missing.'

'Any way of finding out where the stamp was done?' Mark's chest rose in hope.

'Probably not. Every dive shop worth its money has testing facilities.'

'Damn.' Mark exhaled.

'But we'll try.' Jane gave him a smile. 'We'll start around here, see if the dive shops in the area kept receipts.'

'From twenty years ago? I doubt it.'

'Miracles happen.' Jane looked at her phone. 'You never know.'

'You're right, this could be like a movie, where some old bloke says, "As a matter of fact, I have them right here, in a box. I was going to get rid of them today, but something told me not to. The DNA on the receipts should be intact too, because I always wore gloves when I made a transaction."'

Jane typed a message into her phone. 'Shut up, Mark,' she said good-naturedly.

'Are you texting your boyfriend?' Mark asked. 'Because you are in a very good mood.'

Jane shook her head at him and put her phone away.

'Anyway,' Mark said, 'you're forgetting the biggest factor that goes against the sneak dive theory – Eloise couldn't scuba dive, as far as we know. She could snorkel, they all could, but scuba dive with an oxygen tank? No.'

The two fell quiet.

'Aside from all that,' Mark added, 'the Doyles have only known about this sinkhole for weeks, not years.'

Jane gave him a look.

'What?'

'That's what they *say*. Maybe some knew about it and others didn't.'

'Frank has only just opened it up to tourism. I'd hazard a guess he really didn't know there was a sinkhole on his property before now. But yes, sure, maybe others did.'

Mark scrolled through his phone, looking for the information Reynolds had sent him. The police interviews, the article in the paper, photos of Eloise – and there it was, the footage taken from the news helicopter of the Doyle and Sinclair properties during the search. He played it again, sound down and pressed pause when an image of a cows' drinking trough came into view. Mark showed his screen to Jane. 'This image was taken in

2003 during the search for Eloise. Think this is the spot we're in now?'

Jane cast a scrutinising gaze over the paddocks and then looked at his phone again. The proximity of the trough to the fence, the direction of the house, the nearby dam, the trough to the sinkhole. 'Yes,' she said.

They stood for a moment, studying the image. This footage had been shown around the world and all that time she lay there, underground, submerged in water. Mark remembered other reports of missing people in the bush, helicopter footage of the area, thick with woodland and hidden gullies. So many times when the body was found, it was close to the walking track, metres from help. In one tragic instance, after a national search and weeks of looking in the nearby state forest, the body of a missing man had been found underneath his family home. *Look close by* was the maxim in searches, in domestic violence cases, in murder investigations: the answer is mostly close.

His phone rang. Jagdeep.

'Your friends the Sinclairs are not popular.'

'Hi, Jagdeep.'

'Hi. Your friends the Sinclairs are not popular.'

Mark grinned. *Good old Jag.* 'What makes you say that?'

'Had three phone calls – two locals telling me that the younger Sinclairs were always nasty pieces of work, and another to say it's all linked to the failed submarine deal with Macron. There was a letter sent to the paper, the journo rang us – it won't be printed – saying that this murder is the reason we shouldn't provide foreign backpackers with working visas. Who knew a town could become Francophobic overnight?'

'It wasn't when the Sinclairs were winning their grand finals.'

'And Barry must have blabbed about the letters on Cherie's

arm. He didn't make any of them out, but that hasn't stopped half the town getting hyped, turning on their own.'

'What're the other half saying?'

'It was a stranger. An outsider. But people always say that.'

They did. They'd said that when Eloise went missing. Easier to blame someone else, less scary than thinking a killer is one of you. 'Okay, so what are you doing then?'

'Naturally, we've rounded up everyone of French descent,' Jag answered, deadpan. 'But more importantly, we've also put the call out for additional information, anyone who saw Cherie leave the pub and walk home and so on.'

'That's good.'

'And, Mark, before we interview Barry, there's some video footage I'd like you to take a look at.'

'Be there soon.'

'Right you are.'

Jagdeep occasionally put those old-fashioned expressions into her speech. 'Right you are,' like something from a seventies British sitcom. She liked languages, could speak four. He could speak two: English and South Australian. *There is a power pole. There is a stobie pole.*

Mark put his phone away and studied the sinkhole again. The water was right up to the surface, but it wouldn't have been then, not with the drought. Bushfires had raged across Victoria for fifty-nine days, burning over three million acres and the nation's capital, Canberra, almost went up in flames. It was horrible, those days of looking up each morning at the menacing blue sky, no clouds in sight. He remembered becoming obsessed with the weather reports, anxious for each update. A secret worry in the back of his head that it would never rain again. Twenty years ago, there wouldn't have been as much grass to cover the entrance, and the water in this sinkhole would have been lower. By how much? He'd need an expert for that.

There was a rumbling sound from a distance, and Mark looked up to see a tractor slowly making its way towards them across the paddocks. Cows parted in its wake, fans for a celebrity. And as far as tractors went, this one was Top of the Pops: a new model Fendt. It must have set the Doyle men back at least a quarter of a mill. Not too bad for a dairy farmer. Mark looked around, corrected himself. Landowner. All this fertile land, so close to the ocean, good rainfall and a wealth of opportunity under the grass. Come all ye city folk fed up with lockdowns and traffic! Come all ye lost, ye weary, ye dreaming of opening B&Bs and boutique breweries! Come all ye—

'When will you be gone?' It was Frank Doyle, beside them now, his boiled-ham face looking down at them from his throne in the cabin. 'I've got divers from all over the country wanting to book in here.'

'Two women were pulled from a sinkhole on your property, Mr Doyle,' Jane said, sharp. 'We'll do what we need to do to investigate.'

Frank's grey hair stuck up like a child's drawing. 'It's not my fault!' he said, hands in the air in a gesture of helplessness. 'I know everyone's mourning Juliette, but really, it's about time this town moved on.'

A beat followed.

'You mean Juliette's daughter, Eloise.'

'Yes, yes of course.' Frank's face, realising his error, settled into a deep scowl. He revved the engine again. Mark held up a hand for him to stop and the man sighed, turned it completely off. 'What now?'

'Nice tractor,' Mark commented. 'New, is it?'

'Yeah, it's new.' Frank flushed with pride, or was it high blood pressure? 'First good tractor I've ever had. This one's got guts, the others were shopping trolleys.'

Mark and Frank gazed at the machine in something like a hushed silence. 'Can you tell us again,' Mark made his voice pleasant, 'when you found the sinkhole?'

'I've been through this!' The man glowered.

'Even so . . .'

'About six or seven weeks ago, I was clearing up the paddock and found a cow half down it. There it was, a hole. My first thought was to push the cow down and then throw the bung Kelvinator into it, but the entrance was too small. So, I thought how I could make the most of it. Cave diving's big in Franklin, so why not let the right people know and see if we can't get it started up down this area? They have all the procedures and the right stuff. It's a lot safer now.'

'Not for divers on your land,' Mark said.

'I can't help it if they don't know what they're doing! I dunno what that Sinclair girl was up to, but the other one, the diver, she should have been prepared! When I know it's going to rain, I put a raincoat on, don't I?'

Jane looked sideways at Mark. 'Where were you the day Eloise Sinclair went missing, Mr Doyle?' she asked.

The man shook his head, thumped one hand on the steering wheel. 'You know where I was. In Adelaide with Bernadette, getting my teeth put in. See?' He pointed to his mouth. 'That's when I got these.'

Mark saw the man Frank would have been, in his early fifties when Eloise went missing. 'So who would have been here that weekend?' he asked.

'You know that too. Geraldine and James, of course. Who else? Ernest Hemingway?'

Frank Doyle would admire someone like Hemingway, Mark thought. He'd probably like to see himself as that handsome, macho, gun-toting, womaniser type. 'Are you a fan of Hemingway, Mr Doyle?' Mark asked, curious.

'No, I am bloody not!' The man roared his Fendt into life and bumped off down the paddock.

Jane burst out laughing. 'Why would you ask him *that*?'

'Why would you ask him where he was when Eloise went missing? We know that he was getting his falsies put in. You've read the files.'

'I wanted to see if he was the angry type, and he is. Those kind of men – they're so ugly and dangerous.'

'Hemingway was the angry, dangerous type. Women loved him.'

'Did they now? Who told you that?'

Jane and Mark walked back over the paddocks to their car. Before they left, Mark glanced at the old pool site again, now derelict; it looked like a scene from a horror movie. Stephen King would put a clown in there, hiding in the dark corner of the deep end, peeping out from rotted wood.

Once again, Jane drove while he sat back and watched the paddocks meet the sea. Kids growing up around this area would be able to see the ocean every day. It must have been a kind of calling – that sound of it, a clean rushing, the horizon tantalisingly close.

At the station, Jagdeep was leaning on the counter, filing a report for a young woman who'd had her purse stolen. It wasn't Jagdeep's job, but when the word's out that a country station is open and someone rings that bell on the counter, they expect a cop to answer. Jag had drawn the short straw. The woman was giving a detailed description of the item; cream, *not* leather – but it looked like real leather – a small gold shoulder chain and a gold tag on it, Gucci – again *not* real but you'd never know. From Seminyak, *not* Kuta. Inside it, fifty dollars, a pink lipstick and her licence.

'We'll do everything we can to get it back to you,' Jagdeep said. 'But as it was stolen or lost two weeks ago, I'm afraid there's not much we can do.'

We can do zip, Mark felt like saying as he sailed past them and into the office out the back, where Sean was typing purposefully. 'Aren't you meant to be on the front desk?' Mark asked.

Sean didn't answer. The headphones strapped to his ears made him immune to any criticism. From the back, he looked like a shy little alien.

He looked up as Mark entered his peripheral vision. 'Someone called in earlier, said your car will be ready to go tomorrow,' he said. 'They'll be in to drop off the paperwork in the morning. You have to sign something for insurance.'

'Was the name Stabber?'

Sean looked at him curiously. 'No, a Champ or Chump or something.'

Mark nodded. Booralama beckoned. He had gutters to clean, a garden to take care of and a couch to watch Westerns from. But even so, Mark was surprised to feel a conflicted twinge: this case, this landscape, the people – he felt it all, drawing him in.

Opening the photos on his phone, Mark studied the image of the rope in the back of James's ute. After a moment's thought, he rang Judy Sinclair. She answered on the second ring. Once past the usual niceties, Mark asked her what type of rope they used on the boats – it was a matter for the investigation, he said at her concerned tone, just getting all the details he could.

'We always used the ropes from the Boxhall Dive Shop, but it's been closed for years. Excellent rope for water and land. I know that all the fishing boats around here used it.'

Boxhall. The name rang a bell.

'Would this Boxhall be a relation of Scott Boxhall, the friend of Eloise's who died in a car accident?'

'It was his father who owned and ran the shop. Greg Boxhall – or Chomp as he is known. He still lives locally.'

'Oh! He's dropping off my car tomorrow!' Mark exclaimed, pleased to make the connection.

'That'd be right, the man can't retire. Once the dive shop was sold, he moved onto all sorts of odd jobs.'

'And this rope of his,' Mark circled back to the main topic, 'do you think farmers would use it too?'

'I can't see why not. For a start, it's marine grade, so it doesn't rot. Good for wet paddocks and whatnot.'

Mark said his thanks, went to hang up, then had a thought. 'Judy, do you know when the Doyles put their pool in?'

If she was confused at his line of questioning, Judy didn't show it. 'I can't be sure of the year, but I do know that Eloise and the boys used to swim there in their teens. Not Phil – he was older – but Nic and Mat used to live in that pool. So yes, it's been there for a long time. Twenty-four years, maybe?'

Mark thought about swimming pools – the building of them and the nuisance of maintenance. He and Kelly had had an in-ground pool at the house they bought together in Adelaide. It was an oval shape, with a glass fence around it. For two months of the year, Mark forgot about the pain of cleaning the thing, the clogged skimmer basket and green water; for two months he was the poster child for happy pool blokes, showing his sons the best bombs and telling them not to run around the sides. Then for ten months it was back to reading manuals on jammed filters and plumbing leaks.

He rang Broken Bay Council, was put on hold, then onto the planning team where no one answered. He left a message. Then he googled the offices on his phone and typed an email to the planning department to reinforce his request. He signed off with all his police credentials and, after a moment's thought, removed the 'Kind' from 'Kind regards'. *That'd show them.*

Jagdeep walked back into the room and to her computer. 'It's weird,' she said. 'This town has a lot of burglaries for a small place. So many cars broken into. Just in the last month there's been reports of Garmin watches, necklaces, phones – and the purse from Seminyak, of course.'

'Was that woman's car unlocked?'

'Yep.'

A general sigh from the officers. Not quite *She was asking for it* but close.

'Anyway, it's interesting after what I've found on the CCTV footage from the Royal.'

'You think the person was trying to steal something from my car? It was definitely locked.'

'I don't know.' Jagdeep sounded doubtful. 'Car burglaries don't usually involve smashing windscreens. But you never know. I've copied the videos from the pub: I'll show you.'

'Let me get a cuppa,' Mark said. 'I always like a cuppa when I watch a good movie.'

Jagdeep nodded, clicked into her laptop. Mark found a tea bag in the kitchen, made himself a cuppa. The fact that he called it a cuppa didn't make it taste any better. He read the label on the bag: Earl Grey. God, he should have just swallowed a mouthful of Chanel No. 5. He tipped it out, made himself a Nescafé. Nasty, but no pretence.

Back beside his colleague Mark looked at the screen. It was the Saturday just gone, 6 pm.

Vehicles started pulling into the car park. People got out, mingled, moved towards the pub. The camera from the side of the building showed the Bay Road view, and at around 6.15 pm Cherie Swinson walked into frame, pausing to let a woman with a small dog go past and then stepping through the doors of the pub. Mark recognised other patrons: Ian from the Hibernian, and Mat and Nic Sinclair all entered the car park around 8 pm. The pub was busy, full of patrons walking in and out, talking in the car park, pissing in the bushes. He saw himself, Jane and David Furneaux enter and leave. No surprises.

But it was Cherie they were primarily interested in. At around 9.30 pm, the door of the pub opened, and Cherie stood on the threshold of the building, as if wondering whether or not to leave. They couldn't see her face. After a short moment she took a long stride out of view.

They kept watching until the tape registered midnight, when the lights went off in the hotel. 'I wish we could see inside the pub,' Mark said. 'But at least we know for certain that Cherie was alive at nine-thirty pm on Saturday. It would take around ten minutes to walk to her place, so time of death is anywhere from nine-forty onwards.'

'Yeah. It also gives us a good look at who was in the pub that night.' Jagdeep adjusted her turban, then picked up her pen and paper and began making notes. 'We'll have to go over that again, plus all the regos of the cars in the car park and question everyone we can identify.'

'Better you than me,' Mark said. 'Richardson put me on the Eloise Sinclair file, remember?'

Jagdeep rewound the tape to Friday night. 'There's something here I wanted to show you from the day before Cherie was killed – take a look.'

Mark settled in. He saw his car pull into the car park just after 6 pm. This was after he'd been on the boat with Phil and Judy. In grainy black and white, Mark watched himself get out of the car, lock it and then walk out the side gate towards the front of the pub. It was eerie looking at his other self: like a crime show where he was the murder victim. Jagdeep played the tape at double speed. Later in the night, various people came and went, a few showing clear signs of drunkenness got into their cars and drove off. The tape whizzed on. Someone else vomited into a corner, a few pissed behind their cars. Mark paused the tape, looking at one of the urinators: 'That's Ian, the owner of the hotel I'm staying at!' he said, rewinding it a little to make sure. Ian was in bad shape, stumbling about. He looked at his can, studied it intently before throwing it into the bushes. Ian then took a piss, and stumbled back to the path and out of view.

At 11.30 pm a tall man walked straight into the pub wall, then turned and left.

At midnight, a black cat stalked the area before sliding under a garage door.

After 1 am, nothing.

'Did you see anything related to Cherie's death here, Jagdeep?'

'Be patient. I wanted to show you what a typical weekend at the Royal looks like.'

'Wait till they win the grand final, then you'll see something.' *Double the pissers, vomiters and wall starers. Triple the fights. It'll be* Funniest Home Videos *for lovers of shame and dickheads.*

'Watch,' Jagdeep said, leaning in. 'Now it's Saturday morning.'

His car was still there – and intact. Fast forward, cars came and went: people using the space as a convenient spot while they went for a walk or did some shopping. Nothing interesting. Mark yawned, looked at his watch.

Fast forward. Around 10.35 am someone walked into the car park, a hood covering their face, slouching. Mark sat up, focused. The person on the screen looked side to side, calculated. They stood for a moment, studying Mark's car, then, in one quick movement, picked up a piece of broken brick and threw it hard at the windscreen.

For a second, the hoodie fell back. Mark saw the face.

The windscreen didn't smash. The vandal picked up the brick again and moved to a closer distance, aimed again and threw, this time shattering glass.

'She wasn't strong enough to smash it completely the first time, probably thought it would shatter instantly like in the movies. She had to do it a second time.' Mark was talking to himself.

'You know who it is?' Jagdeep asked.

'I do. It's Georgia Sinclair.'

CHAPTER 16

Teenage vandalism was nothing new, but such a deliberate act in broad daylight was rarely undertaken by kids on their own. Mark thought of Georgia's scowling face at the Sinclairs' house and her delight in all things murder.

'I'll go around there,' he said. 'Sort it out.'

'This can't go unpunished,' Jagdeep warned. 'No favours because you like the family.'

'I know that.'

It gave Mark no joy to think that Georgia Sinclair, daughter of good people, would soon have her name added to the list of juvenile law-breakers in the state. Her record would be expunged once she reached eighteen, but police files were easily accessible.

A ring came from the front door of the station and this time Mark went out. Barry stood there, pale-faced and anxious, ready for his interview with Jagdeep. The confident air he'd given off on the drive to the Sinclair house was completely gone. Here was a man at a loss.

'How're you feeling, Barry?' Mark asked, slightly shocked at the publican's appearance.

'All right,' Barry answered, sounding anything but. 'Margery took me to the clinic, wasn't feeling too well. The nurse gave me the thumbs up, so I'm here.'

Before Mark could say anything, more words came tumbling out of Barry's mouth. 'I still can't believe it. Cherie! The life and soul. Place won't be the same without her.'

Mark guided him to a small room designed for interviews and went to fetch Jagdeep.

When they both returned to the room, Barry's hands were over his face. Mark, worried the man would start crying, snatched up some tissues and passed a handful to him.

'Barry,' Jagdeep said in her pleasant, low voice, 'we're going to be asking you about your relationship with Cherie Swinson and how you came to find her. We'd like to tape the conversation. Are you okay with that?'

Barry mumbled that he was fine with it and, after further questioning, said that no, he didn't require a lawyer, yes, he knew he could request one, and no, he didn't want a cup of tea or coffee. Once the preliminaries were over, the interview began.

JK: Barry, would you mind telling us about your relationship to Cherie Swinson? In your own time.

BC: Ahh, yes, well, Cherie and I were friends. We've known each other for, what, eighteen years? She was friends first with my ex-wife and then when Suzie up and left, she became more my friend.

JK: Suzie is your ex?

BC: Yeah, she's in Newcastle now. Married to a car salesman.

JK: How often would you see Cherie?

BC: Well, at least two nights a week, when she came into the pub. And, yes, well, on Sundays too, when she'd sometimes come in and help me clean.

JK: And were the two of you close?

BC: We were friends, yes. She could sometimes be a bit over the top, a little dramatic, I guess. But yes, Cherie was my . . . my . . . friend.

JK: Tissue?

BC: Thanks.

JK: When did you last see Cherie?

BC: Saturday night, at the pub.

JK: Can you tell us a bit about the night?

BC: It was busy, because, well . . . Broken's footy and netball teams made it to the finals. All the players came in after their games, and there were the usuals too. Lots of people for dinner, singing, that sort of thing.

JK: What time did Cherie get there?

BC: Not sure. She usually gets there around 6 pm, mostly stays till closing and then she walks home. Some nights, if I've finished up a bit early, I walk her back. But it was too busy Saturday. I didn't even see her leave. I should have . . . I wish I had . . .

JK: Do you want to take a break, Barry?

BC: No. I'm right.

JK: Did you talk to Cherie that night?

BC: Yeah, just to say hello. Nothing much. I felt a bit bad, because I'd told her off at one stage the night before, on the Friday.

JK: You had to tell her off, how? What for?

BC: She was, well, taking photos of people, getting in their faces. People were complaining. I said, 'Give it a rest, Cherie' and she laughed.

JK: Did you see her take photos of anyone?

BC: No.

MA: Actually, Cherie took a photo of me and her together on Friday evening at the bar. A selfie.

JK: Right.

BC: *Pretty sure it was Ian Bickon, from the Hibernian, who asked me to say something. He was getting riled up about it, said she'd taken photos without his consent and that I should do something.*

JK: *What did you say when he told you that?*

BC: *I said something like, 'Calm down, Ian' and then I told Cherie to give it a rest.*

JK: *How did she take it?*

BC: *She laughed and put her phone away. Cherie's not the angry type.*

JK: *What do you mean by that?*

BC: *She's a good sort. She's always up for a laugh and a drink and, I don't know. Maybe she drank too much sometimes. But she was always smart and a bloody good actor. She used to know all the top ones – you know, that bloke from* Mad Max, *for instance.*

JK: *Cherie's got a very nice house, yet she seems to have stopped professional acting over twenty years ago. Did she have a job?*

BC: *She cleaned for me. At the pub on most Sundays.*

JK: *Yes, we saw that. $40 per hour. That's quite generous of you, Barry.*

BC: *She was a good cleaner.*

MA: *So, basically, she had made enough money from her former acting career to live as she liked.*

BC: *Yes. She had lots of interests, mainly in theatre and in costumes. Plus, there were the Sunday Soirees – they were free. People donated small amounts to help pay for the tea and coffee afterward, but aside from that, she didn't charge.*

MA: *Tell us about those soirees. What were they exactly?*

BC: *Cherie would put on shows, usually extracts from musicals. They were bloody good too. She'd have all the costumes just right – you know she was into make-up and costume, don't you? She was always looking for the right material, looking for the best way to dress so that she was in character. She said that costume and make-up illuminate*

*the playwright's intention. Buggered if I know what that means, but
she did it all right.*

MA: And did many people attend the soirees?

*BC: At the start, there would have been at least thirty people there.
That was when she did* Chicago. *Her Helen Keller was less popular,
but I still liked it.*

JK: You sound as if you were a really good friend to Cherie.

BC: Not enough, clearly.

JK: Was Cherie a sex worker?

BC: What? No! No.

*JK: We have to ask, Barry – it's all those outfits in her cupboard. The
black lacy lingerie, the sexy nurse, the burlesque feathers and so forth.*

*BC: I told you, they're for her acting. She has all types of costumes.
I mean, have you seen* Chicago? *Or* Moulin Rouge?

MA: You've seen them, Barry?

BC: Thanks to Cherie, I have.

MA: On to Saturday night at the bar. Did you notice Cherie leave?

*BC: No, because it was so busy – but it must have been earlier than
usual, because she's often the last one in the bar. We have a little chat,
sometimes I walk her home. But she wasn't there at the end of the
night. It was only Sunday when I noticed she hadn't come around to
do the cleaning and when she wasn't answering her phone.*

*MA: Cherie told me on the Saturday night that she'd lost her phone the
night before, or had it stolen.*

*BC: Yes. That's right. Come to think of it, she did tell me that, but I was
so busy I barely registered it. She lost it sometime on the Friday night,
did you say?*

MA: Yes.

*BC: That would have really annoyed her. She'd discovered the notes
app on her phone. Said it was better than all the bits of paper she
usually wrote her ideas on and was then constantly losing.*

JK: What ideas would they be, Barry?

BC: Ideas for new plays. She wanted to write an original one, one that really resonated with the local community, that's what she told me. She was a good sort, wouldn't hurt anyone. Then someone goes and . . . goes and . . .

MA: Want a drink, Barry?

BC: I'm right.

JK: What ideas did she have, do you know?

BC: She had ideas on everything from Kubla Khan to bloody Bruce Springsteen. I don't know. She used to do a bit of research at the library, I know that. She'd been updating her play, she said. Always adding new stuff when things came to light. That's Cherie for you, always busy as a bee.

JK: Barry, do you know anyone who may have wanted to harm Cherie?

BC: No! Not at all. Not Cherie, she was one in a million. Everyone liked her. Can we turn this thing off? Can you turn it off? I'm feeling . . . my heart . . .

JK: Interview suspended.

Mark and Jagdeep looked at each other. Barry was panting, both hands on the table, head down.

'I'll call an ambulance.' Jagdeep stood, moving towards the door.

Barry held his hand up, shook his head. 'I'm okay,' he said. 'It's just been a helluva shock. I keep thinking of what she looked like when I first saw her. And that writing on her arm! Was it writing? What's it all mean?'

The police officers waited.

'I'm okay,' the older man repeated as his breathing slowed. He took a sip of water and then blew loudly into a hanky.

'Barry,' Mark asked, 'does the colour or word "Blue" mean anything to you?'

'What?' Barry looked startled. 'What do you mean?'

'It's just a question.'

'Not to me, no. If it's got anything to do with Cherie, well, I suppose she liked bright colours. She wore pink a lot, I know that. Not really blue.'

Outside, a plastic bag flew past the window wildly, ghostlike in its oval shape.

'Cherie wasn't a sex worker,' Barry said firmly. The man was obviously still upset at the idea.

'We have to cover all options.' Mark looked at his watch. 'I'm sure you understand.'

'Yeah, I know.'

Mark had to stop himself from patting the man's hand, or worse, giving him a hug. Barry was shrunken in grief, for Cherie, maybe even for his ex-wife. All the men in this town, they were broken. Old machines gone rusty, trying and failing to keep up. It wasn't a stretch, Mark thought – no, it really wasn't – to propel himself into the future and see his own body as wreckage on a mounting scrapheap of pathetic blokes.

Barry got to his feet, and both detectives rose too. 'You'll find the bastard who did this, won't you?'

'We're doing our very best,' Jagdeep answered.

Barry muttered something to himself, tucked in his checked shirt and passed through the door Mark held open for him.

'I didn't even speak to Cherie properly on Saturday night. That's my regret,' Barry said mournfully, shaking his head. 'I was a bit cranky with her on Friday, so I wasn't all that nice to her. I could've said all these things. The worst thing is, of course, that I ignored her after she said that thing about the Sinclairs.'

A brief pause followed. 'What was that, Barry?' Jagdeep asked. 'What did she say about them?'

'I was so busy that night, you were there, you saw!' He looked at Mark, pleading. 'I didn't have time to talk to her!'

'It was busy.'

Jagdeep cleared her throat. 'What did Cherie say about the Sinclairs?'

The old man looked up the hallway, keen to get out. Mark couldn't blame him.

'She whispered in my ear. It was a weird thing to say and that's why I remember it.' Barry cleared his throat. 'Cherie said, "Something is rotten in the state of Sinclair."'

CHAPTER 17

'*Hamlet*,' Jagdeep said after Barry had gone. 'Something is rotten in the state of Denmark.'

Mark remembered a little about the play, having studied it at school. 'Corruption, wasn't it?'

'Yeah. Interesting.'

Mark tried to recall it. He liked *Henry V* and *Macbeth*, found the comedies twee – but *Hamlet* he had trouble remembering. The death of the father, and the son exacting revenge?

'A family turning on itself,' Jagdeep said. 'Brothers fighting, sons pretending madness. A beautiful woman either drowning or committing suicide.'

'Pirates,' Mark added. 'People putting on a play.'

Jagdeep shook her head. 'It might not mean any of those things. And definitely not pirates.'

Mark pictured Phil Sinclair as he had first seen him, on the fishing boat on Friday afternoon. A veritable man of the sea, big and burly, confident in his terrain. No skull and crossbones on his flag, but Phil was a man who made his living largely by the ocean. 'Even so,' Mark added. 'It's strange.'

'Uncanny.'

Mark's mind was reeling. The Doyles, the Sinclairs and Cherie. Like Richardson had said, they were all tied together in a Gordian knot, solvable but overwhelming to the naked eye. 'I think we should be working together, Jag.'

'Exactly what I was thinking.' Jagdeep took a swig of water from her bottle. 'I'll drive you to the Sinclairs now, make some notes while you talk to Georgia.'

Pleased, Mark called out to Sean to let them know where they were going.

The younger man, still steadily typing on his computer, raised his head. 'When I was out on the counter this morning, a woman came in to say that the police should to talk to her because she had, and I quote, "something to say".' Sean raised his fingers in quotation marks. 'I told her we'd get back to her, but she just stomped out of the station. Total Karen.'

'What?' Jagdeep turned around. 'What did you call her?'

Sean faltered. 'A Karen, you know – demanding stuff.'

'Did you get this lady's name? Offer to call her back?'

'We were really busy here and we've had so many calls and people coming in about the body and we've . . .'

'Show some respect. That woman was probably your mother's age.'

'Well, more my grandmother's . . . but yeah, the way she was demanding—'

'*Was* she demanding though? This is a murder case. That woman could have had something really important to say.'

Sean looked shamefaced. 'Her name should be at the front desk.'

Mark looked for it. 'Margery Donald' was written in a neat hand.

Jagdeep marched in front of him, took the number off the desk and walked out the front door to the car. 'You've spoken to this lady before, haven't you? We should go see her again,' she said. 'Honestly, these young officers. Yesterday, he was telling me how he wants to rise up in the ranks, join Homicide eventually. Doesn't he know the work you have to put in to even get a look in?'

Angelo had put Mark's name up for promotion in Homicide, Mark remembered. He hadn't even asked for it. The story of his life; a boat on a favourable current, never needing to hoist the sails.

'This vandalism of your car has got me thinking,' Jagdeep said, changing course. 'It took two throws for Georgia to smash your windscreen, she wasn't strong enough to do it in one.'

'Yeah,' Mark said slowly, trying to catch up.

'Cherie's killer hit her twice. Maybe the suspect isn't a large person. They could have even been smaller than her.'

'The footprint was size eleven.'

'So, someone tall then, but not strong.'

'Or small, with big feet.'

The two fell into a comradely silence. Mark opened the glovebox for no reason, saw a packet of Minties. He held one up for Jagdeep in a question. She shook her head.

The image of the mannequin came into his head. Long blonde hair, the tattered clothes. Barry had said Cherie was always updating her plays, adding new things as they came to light.

'Perhaps the mannequin was meant to be Eloise,' he said, thinking aloud. 'She had long blonde hair, liked op shopping.'

Jagdeep screwed up her nose. 'Maybe. Although that would have to be very up to date, considering Eloise was only recovered on the morning before Cherie was killed.'

Mark took a Mintie, started tearing the wrapper carefully; as thin as possible, along the sides in a rectangle, trying to make a long Mintie rope.

A Gordian knot, he'd learned after waking at 3 am, is an intractable problem. Richardson had been thinking of the Greek tale, where Alexander the Great, on his march through Asia, reached the city of Gordian and was shown a magnificent chariot, tied to a pole in an intricate knot. The legend was that whoever was able to untie the knot would be the future conqueror of the whole of Asia.

Mark didn't like knots. His mother used to try to get him to untangle wool when she went on one of her frequent knitting frenzies. It never ended well.

All the ropes in this case . . . the fishing ropes, the farming ropes, the ropes tangled up in the bodies of Eloise and Mya. When Mark closed his eyes he saw them snarled and moving, like snakes hunting one another.

Barking dogs greeted them at the Sinclairs', farm dogs, friendly but socially unsure. They leaped up, sniffing crotches and planting big paws on the police officers' thighs. Mark laughed, but Jagdeep looked embarrassed as she fobbed off the keenest among them and wiped down her pants. 'I'm not a fan of pets.'

'Don't let these dogs hear you saying that. "Pets" is a dirty word to them.'

'But that one's quite cute.' She pointed to an old Blue Heeler, face low in the dirt.

Mark held up a flat hand. 'Save that kind of talk for pugs.'

The house, or series of ramshackle buildings, was quiet apart from the now sporadic barks. An old ute was parked out the front, dirty windows and 'clean me' scrawled in dust on the side tray. Empty casserole dishes and clean containers sat in a box at the front door. Important to give them back to the owners. Some might be Tupperware.

Mark knocked and the door swung open by itself. 'Hello?'

Judy entered the hall from the kitchen, tea towel slung across her shoulders and a harried look on her face. 'Oh,' she said on seeing Mark, 'is something wrong? Is there any news?'

Mark shook his head before introducing Jagdeep. 'Is Georgia here? We need to ask her a few questions.'

Judy looked at him in confusion before turning back into the hallway. She called out for her daughter and husband, while beckoning Jagdeep and Mark to another room. Georgia was reading while lying on a couch with her head near the ground and her legs up over the back of the seat. Phil was snoozing, glasses askew, a whiskey tumbler by his side.

'Sit up, Georgia! Phil!'

Father and daughter snapped to attention and Georgia, turning herself right-side up, could not hide the guilty look on her face.

In a firm tone, Mark told them what he'd seen on the CCTV. 'I'm sure you know that it was the wrong thing to do, Georgia, but what we're most interested in is why?'

Both parents looked shocked. 'She'll pay for the repairs,' Phil said quickly while shaking his head at his daughter. 'She'll make it up to you. I'm sorry, Mark, I just don't know . . .'

'Georgia!' Judy seemed to suddenly snap out of a stupor of incomprehension. 'That's why you asked to be dropped off in town after the sinkhole, wasn't it? Well, come on, why would you do such a thing?'

The young girl stared at a shoe near the fireplace. Everyone waited.

'Georgia!' Phil's voice had an edge. A high keening, the sound of a boiling kettle came from the other room. 'You answer them. What's gotten into you?'

The kettle was now screaming. Mark fought the urge to shout at someone to turn it off.

'It's because we need to find out what happened with Auntie Eloise,' Georgia finally said. In the background the kettle abruptly stopped. 'She wouldn't just go down there and not tell anyone, and how did she even know the hole was there?'

Phil leaned against the fireplace. 'What's that got to do with smashing the detective's car?' he asked, exasperated.

'I've read about him.' Georgia gave a quick glance up at Mark before looking back at the carpet again. 'He's solved crimes, he found that lady last year and there's been other ones . . . I heard him say he wasn't going to stick around in town, but I thought he should stay here and work out what happened.'

'It's Mark, not "he",' Judy said automatically.

'So, you thought you'd smash a police officer's windscreen to keep him in town a little longer,' Jagdeep said, and the room grew silent.

'I'm sorry.'

Mark wasn't sympathetic. There were other things she could have done. *Ask*, for example. 'Have you been involved in stuff like this before? Breaking stuff? Stealing from vehicles?'

Georgia's voice took on a panicked tone. 'No, no, I haven't, really I haven't.'

A door slammed. Heavy footsteps up the hallway.

Mat Sinclair appeared at the door. 'Where are you all? I wanted to get—' He looked stunned for a second before he rearranged his face into relaxed charm. 'What's going on?'

'Georgia is in trouble,' Phil answered his younger brother bitterly, 'for breaking Mark's windscreen.'

'What? Georgia!' Mat shook his head. 'Why would you do something so stupid? Jesus – and this week of all weeks.'

The young girl's face went from dismay to quick excitement. 'Uncle Mat's car got broken into last week, didn't it?'

Her uncle nodded, reluctant. All heads turned towards the tall blond man.

'And Uncle Mat punched him! Didn't you?'

'Steady on, Georgia. I *almost* punched him. Yanked him out of my ute so hard the bloke practically shat himself.'

'Did you know who it was?' Mark asked.

'You didn't mention this to the police?' Jagdeep spoke at the same time. 'I've just read over the reports of recent car burglaries and didn't see your name.'

'Well,' Mat said after a pause, 'what were you going to do about it? Nothing was taken.'

'It's break and enter.'

Mat sounded bemused. 'But my car was unlocked.'

Mark felt Jagdeep's frustration. So many times these minor incidents led to breakthroughs! It was the culmination of minor events, tidbits of information, a past sighting, a word. People didn't report for so many reasons. They couldn't be bothered, they didn't think it would be any use, they questioned what they'd seen, they'd rationalised things in their own head.

Mark caught sight of the watch on Mat's wrist. It was a nice watch, black with the kind of features that take a decade to learn. Yes, one of those watches that athletes and budding runners use. A Garmin. 'Who was this person?'

'Name's Vincent. Not sure of his surname.'

'Oh, yes!' Judy broke in. 'Vincent Stabley. He recently started up a towing business.'

It was common sense, of the criminal kind. Smash windscreens, steal stuff. Tow car, sell stuff.

'We call him Stabber.'

Mark eyed the watch again, and Mat caught him eyeing it. He spun the face around his wrist, fiddled with the dial, spun it again. Sometimes, people didn't report crimes because . . . they benefited from them.

'You friends with Stabber, Mat?'

'Wouldn't say friends. Know him from around the place.'

A quiet beat followed. Jagdeep tapped into her phone, oblivious.

'You ever buy anything from Vincent Stabley?'

A pause. Uncomfortable. 'Sometimes. Once, maybe twice.'

'Does anyone have a picture of this man?'

'Hang on, I might – there was an ad for his new business in the paper. I'm sure his picture was in it.' Judy rushed out of the room, Georgia taking flight behind her.

'I don't believe this, Mat,' Phil said. 'You buy stuff from a thief? Georgia's smashing windscreens? What's going on in our family?'

The question lingered, unanswered. Judy returned, waving the advertisement. 'I had it on the fridge – you never know with all the potholes and loose stones on these roads. I thought we might need it.'

'Looks like . . . wait . . .' Jagdeep's face was lit with intensity as she read from her phone.

Judy showed the ad to Mark. He studied it, and looked up at Jag just as she was putting her phone away.

'Vincent Stabley is currently on parole for bludgeoning a man eight years ago outside his home in Port Augusta,' Jag announced.

'Says here that he hit the victim in the head with a rock. He's got charges for theft going back years.'

Mark swore inwardly. Stabber was a small man, thickly built. In the advertisement he wore a bright blue shirt with 'Broken Towing & Repairs' on the front. The grinning man held a thumbs up for the photo, seemingly relaxed, with one large boot resting on the bumper of a car.

A small man with large feet. Previous conviction for striking someone outside their house, burglaries in the region. A bright blue shirt. *Blue.*

Mark jabbed Richardson's number into his phone while he nodded goodbye to the Sinclairs, who stood open-mouthed and confused.

'What now?' Phil asked, and Jagdeep explained they'd be in contact, before hurrying out the front door alongside Mark and into the Hilux.

'We'll get back to you soon, Phil,' Mark shouted out the window, but his words were lost as Jagdeep sped up the drive.

CHAPTER 18

Vincent Stabley's address was listed as Colindale Heights, on the outskirts of Broken Bay. Richardson gave them the go-ahead to question him while he arranged the warrant to search his house, vehicles and place of business. At the end of the call, their boss added that early DNA testing had confirmed what they all knew to be true: the body pulled from the Doyle sinkhole was definitely Eloise Sinclair.

No surprises there.

Mark read aloud Stabley's criminal background while Jagdeep drove. His rap sheet ran long: a decade ago, at the age of twenty-three, he was charged for a series of car thefts in Port Augusta, receiving a non-custodial sentence with community service. At twenty-five he was charged with breaking and entering, receiving another non-custodial, and then a year after he'd completed community service with excellent reports, he bludgeoned a man in the head, causing serious injury. For that he received jail time, sentenced to eight years and now, after seven, Stabley was out on parole starting a new life with his towing business. Mark tried calling the number Ian had given him for Stabber: no answer. He left a message to call back and hung up.

The ocean to Mark's left was a brilliant blue. The town was drab in comparison, a sullen grandfather, attractive years past it, fleeting remnants of arrogance in the bluestone and stained-glass windows.

Colindale Heights was situated to the north-west of the town on flat land. No rise, no sign of a hill. Ugly brick houses lined the one completed street in the area, little to distinguish one squat sibling from the other, save the occasional yukka planted squarely in the front yard. So different to his home in Booralama. The garden there, lovingly tended to by his mother, was a jungle of herbs and natives and cottage plants, alive with squawks and buzzing and the slithering of birds and creatures. He couldn't keep up with it; it was a life unto its own. And now, as they drove up New Street, he felt a real pang for the river redgum that lined the verge outside his home. One thing about this coastline, the settlers had done a thorough job of clearing it bare. Only on the dunes, or directly in front of the sea, did the old foliage remain, thick with coastal scrub and knotted moonah.

Vincent Stabley was recorded as living with his girlfriend at 16 New Street. The house was cheaply constructed; one strong southerly and it would blow over in an instant. No neighbours on either side of the house, just empty homes with For Sale signs out the front.

Jagdeep knocked on the door. Footsteps up the hall, and in the distorted pattern on the glass, Mark could see a short figure walking towards them. A woman answered, peroxide blonde hair, puffed lips and long talons painted in sparkly colours, like something done on a manicure session for witches.

'Yeah?' She held a cigarette between her fingers.

'Does a Vincent Stabley live here?'

'Vinnie's away for a few days.'

'He didn't mention that when he said he'd be repairing my windscreen,' Mark said. 'Do you know where he is?'

The woman shrugged and a bit of ash fell onto the wooden boards.

'Would you have a phone number we can call him on? We've called his business number, but he's not answering.'

In the background, the television was on. A movie, lots of shouting, a dramatic score.

'One of his new cards has two numbers on it I think, wait – I'll get it for you.' She turned and began walking up the hall. Without waiting for an invitation, the detectives stepped inside and followed her. The walls were white and bare. Mark caught a glimpse of a room to the left, nothing in it, no bed, no clothes. In a kitchen at the end of the hall, she turned to them, surprised. 'Oh, geez! You snuck up, didn't you?'

Behind her, a television took up almost a third of the wall. On the screen, a young Glenn Close was hiding in a car park while Michael Douglas strode towards his car, swinging his briefcase.

'Good movie,' Mark said, nodding towards the television while taking out his notepad. '*Basic Instinct*?'

'Nah, *Fatal Attraction*.' She mimed a stabbing motion with her hand. 'Bunny boiler.'

Jagdeep and Mark nodded. The adulterous affair, the reprisals, the rabbit in the pot.

'Are you writing that down?' The woman looked at him curiously.

Mark had written 'FATAL ATTRACTION' in his notepad.

'We leave no stone unturned,' he said, a pink tinge to his cheeks. 'And can we get your name, please?' he asked, pen at the ready.

'Celine Rooks, as in the singer, and the bird.'

Mark wrote it down. Jagdeep asked Celine to turn down the volume of the show and she did so, reluctantly. 'We need to question Vincent about his whereabouts on Saturday night.'

Celine rolled her eyes. 'He was with me, watching *Prisoner*,' she said before adding to Mark, 'You should write that one down too, it's good.'

'A serious crime was committed in Broken Bay on Saturday night and we'd like to have a chat with Vincent about it.'

Celine's eyes turned longingly towards the television, where Glenn Close was now crying hysterically, shoulders shaking, curly blonde hair all askew. 'People used to say Glenn Close looked like me,' she said, more to Mark than Jagdeep. 'Like, from a distance, you couldn't tell the difference between us.'

Mark narrowed his eyes at the screen, where Michael Douglas was now running, his stalker behind. 'Uncanny,' he said. 'Where's Vincent?'

Celine looked at her nails, screwed up her eyes at one of them. 'I pay them seventy dollars for a full set of French, and they still manage to muck it up. Last time I go to those bitches.'

Jagdeep looked at her watch. 'Do you know the exact whereabouts of Vincent Stabley?'

'He went to Adelaide for a few days, business.'

Celine's skin was orange; she'd spent ten hours too long in a solarium. Her arms were covered in gold and silver bracelets and around her neck was a chain with a purple love heart ringed in tiny diamonds.

Mark looked at Celine's nails again, her wrist, and felt a buzz in his head.

'You just moved in here, Celine?' Jagdeep asked. 'Looks pretty new.'

'Yeah. Been here two months, setting up the business.'

'Vincent must be doing well,' Jag continued. 'New house, new business . . . And only just out of jail.'

A nod from the woman, more cautious now.

'And nice jewellery,' Mark said. 'Where did you get it all?'

'Vinnie.'

One of the silver bands on her wrist had a charm on it. The thudding in Mark's chest was stronger now. 'What does that little trinket thing say?' He kept his voice as casual as possible.

Celine put down her cigarette, moved her forearm right up to his face, flicking the bracelet around. 'It's a letter J.'

A sickly sweet perfume mingled with nicotine breath overwhelmed him. It took all his strength not to turn away.

'There was another letter too, but Vinnie's taken it off. He's gunna reset it for me.'

'And,' Mark asked, holding his breath, 'what's that letter?'

Celine rolled her eyes towards the ceiling again. 'Why do you wanna know?'

'It's part of our investigation.'

Celine sniffed. 'It's an E. When you put them together, Vinnie says they're for *Just Everything*. But Vinnie's gunna change it to an F so it can be *Just Forever*.'

Glenn Close let out a bloodcurdling scream.

'When did Vincent give it to you?' Mark's brain raced over the decades, guessing at ages. Eloise went missing nearly twenty years earlier, and her bracelet hadn't been seen since.

'Yesterday.' Celine's voice turned cold. 'I think you should go now.'

The acoustics in the room were really terrible. Michael Douglas's wife was crying and hitting him. Jagdeep reached for the remote and muted the television. 'Why do you want it on so loud, Celine?'

The contrast from loud to sudden silence gave clarity to the senses. Mark thought he heard a scratching in the walls.

'No reason.' Celine's eyes flickered to the left, then back again.

'Mind if we take a look around?'

Celine lit up another smoke and Mark noted her hands were slightly shaky now. He squared his shoulders, felt for his phone in his pocket.

Jagdeep began opening and shutting cupboards, while Mark walked around the other rooms. The bathroom was clear, save for that lingering smell of smoke. In the background, he could hear Jagdeep asking questions, teasing out Vincent's movements over the past few weeks. Nothing in the main bedroom or the wardrobe. He checked under the bed and in the side drawers. The backyard was empty – there was a shed, locked. He went inside again, joined the others.

'Look, I've got to go out,' Celine said. 'How long will you be?'

Jagdeep gave Mark a look. 'We're going soon, Celine. Maybe you could call Vincent, see where he is?'

'Got a key for the back shed?' Mark asked.

Celine looked frightened now. She began opening kitchen drawers, muttering, while in between fiddling with her phone, saying something about lost numbers and not having batteries. Mark and Jagdeep waited in the kitchen doorway.

The fridge didn't fit into the cavity designed for it. This cavity wanted a fridge with numbers and dials and shopping remind-ers. Not this skinny white fridge with a large gap beside it.

A large gap.

Celine caught Mark eyeing the refrigerator. She dragged a chair across to the cupboards and stood on it, saying loudly that the keys to the shed were definitely in one of the top ones. If she couldn't reach, maybe Mark could help? On the television, Mark saw Glenn Close's deranged eyes, knife held aloft.

'Need to get a new fridge, Celine,' Mark said, before looking at Jagdeep.

Small black scuff marks dotted the space where the machine had been jostled and moved about. Mark stood in front of it, poked his head in the cavity. Jagdeep stood by the kitchen door, alert.

Nothing was in the cavity. Resting his face on the fridge door, he waved his hand up and down the empty space, curled his fingers around the back.

His fingers touched something. Cloth? He snapped his hand back, took a long look at Celine. 'Is somebody behind the fridge?'

Celine's hand raced to her mouth.

Mark faced the cavity again. 'Are you there, Vincent?'

A slight movement, sensed rather than heard.

'It's the police. We need you to reveal yourself.'

Mark couldn't get into position to move the fridge out further; only a smaller person could wriggle into the space without having to jostle it first. He needed a hand trolley. After a moment's thought, Mark began pushing the fridge back towards the wall behind it. 'Remember that scene in *Star Wars*?' he said. 'This'll be like that.'

'Hey!' Celine shouted. 'Stop!'

A shuffling sound, a sharp intake of breath.

Mark shoved the fridge closer to the wall. Felt resistance from the other side. Pushed a little harder. Jag joined in, gave it her all.

'Okay!' A muffled voice. 'All right!'

The officers took a step back as a small man crept out from behind the fridge, red-faced and defiant.

'Are you Vincent Stabley, registered tenant of this address?'

'I am,' he said. 'And from now on, I won't say a fuckin' word.'

CHAPTER 19

Hours later and Vincent Stabley was resolute in his determination: *no comment.*

A bleak atmosphere settled over the station. Jagdeep was tight-lipped after an argument with her husband, Adi, who was complaining she was never at home, and Mark was too hungry to think. Richardson had assured them that they were right to bring Stabley in for questioning. As a parolee with prior charges for bludgeoning, it was only natural he should be questioned. Except, their boss had pointed out, Stabley hadn't *technically* violated his parole – had Mark and Jagdeep actually identified themselves as police when they called for him to come out of hiding? On that note Jagdeep and Mark were quiet and, in any case, after three hours of questioning and cajoling, Stabley wasn't saying a thing. A veteran of the legal and criminal system, the man was well versed in his rights. A lawyer would travel down to see him in the morning, and until then they had around twelve hours to hold him. His house and belongings had been secured and would be searched by Jagdeep and Chiara in the morning.

It was 4 pm by the time Jagdeep dropped Mark off at the King of Souva, where he bought one garlic and lamb, chips and a potato cake. God, he was ravenous. He could eat someone's hat, he could eat the arse out of a low-flying duck. The old man wasn't there – a young girl was serving, sullen and bored. When he asked her for more garlic sauce, she looked at him with utter contempt.

Mark walked along Bay Road towards Margery's house as he ate. Jagdeep had already called ahead, asking to see Margery regarding her visit to the station that morning. She'd gone straight there after leaving Mark to sate his hunger.

The ocean was at high tide, lapping at the sea walls, the sound a threat or a comfort, depending on your mood. Nothing was certain in this place: the ocean's restlessness was making him a wreck. He wanted solid ground, not this thin veneer of lime-stone, where underneath was filled with dotted caves and tunnels. The night before Mark had dreamed of the purple, mottled arm of a woman being pulled from the sea. Was her forefinger pointing towards him? The languid, drooping finger must surely be fiction, but the bloated arm, dotted with blue webs, seemed so vivid in his mind that Mark could almost see it now, rising out of the waves.

He sat down on a bench facing the sea to wait for Jagdeep. Two women in lycra walked past at a fast pace. 'Don't tell me you did it, Teena,' one of them was pleading in mock dismay. 'Don't tell me!'

Mark strained to hear Teena's reply. But all he saw was a triumphant flick of hair and a pair of dangly dog-shaped earrings glinting in the sun. Mark guessed that Teena *had* done it and the thought gave him cheer. *Good on you, Teena, you did it, you really did.*

Jagdeep walked up the path towards him. 'Got any chips left?'

'Sorry, no.' He couldn't even remember eating them.

Jagdeep sat on the rock wall opposite his bench and dangled her feet over the other side. Mark moved to sit beside her and for a moment they were just two friends looking out to sea.

'Margery's devastated about Cherie. It must be really frightening for her.'

'Does she have family to go and stay with?'

'No, I don't think she'd want to – her house was full of people though. Cath Sinclair, Nic's wife, was there.'

Mark nodded. They'd been together at the pub too.

'Cath said that Cherie had been asking her about Juliette.'

A seagull perched metres from Jagdeep's side. Mark gave it a look. The gull looked right back, black eyes impenetrable. It reminded Mark of the girl who'd just sold him his food. Perhaps the two were in cahoots. Maybe everyone was in cahoots.

'And Margery said that as she got up to go to the toilet, she heard Cherie's front flyscreen door slam twice, only minutes apart on Saturday evening, before ten. I went and tested it out – that one is never locked – and it's true, Margery could have heard it from her house.'

Mark rubbed his eyes. God, he was tired.

'She didn't hear anything after that, because unfortunately, she put in her earplugs to sleep.'

'Helps to narrow down the time of death though,' Mark said, yawning. 'And also explain why Cherie's handbag was upstairs on the couch.'

They spent a few minutes swapping theories on Cherie's death: Cherie gets home from the pub, goes upstairs and puts her bag down, hears something – or sees something – in the front yard. Goes back downstairs, slamming the door again. Vincent pushes her, then hits her in the head with a rock in a robbery gone wrong, then leaves in a panic. She writes 'bleu' or 'blue' to identify his blue shirt.

'But it was dark,' Mark mused. 'How could she tell it was blue?'

'So, she really does write "bleu", because it's something to do with the French Sinclair family.'

Mark shook his head. It didn't make sense. 'She might have been dyslexic, but apparently it didn't affect her reading. The woman who works at the library, Liz, she told me Cherie was into studying local areas of interest. We should check what books she was borrowing if she was there so much. You never know . . .'

'And why the mannequin?' Jagdeep asked, more to herself. 'No one else reported seeing it, even though a group of bike riders rode past in the afternoon and stopped at the bay in front of her house – Sean took their message after we put the call out for information. Cherie must have set it up just before she went to the pub on Saturday night, and then was killed on her return. And there's that black wig too we found near her body. We should have fingerprinting analysis on that soon.'

'And you'll be hearing from the waiter from the cafe too, won't you?'

'Yeah. His parents said Corey – that's his name – went to visit Cherie on Saturday afternoon to talk about theatre. They've sent him messages. He should contact us as soon as he lands.'

'Good.'

Mark's phone rang, jolting him from his thoughts: it was Richardson, updating them on Stabley. He'd question the man again tomorrow morning, put the pressure on, and in the meantime Jagdeep could get started on analysing the forensics, questioning people close to Cherie, find out who she knew – what this 'bleu' or 'blue' meant. Mark should stick to the Eloise Sinclair file, look at the family situation. Both of them should check the crime scenes again: Locard's exchange principle and all that, every criminal leaves a trace. Find out more about the cave diving sites – who knew about them, were there others, the geography of the place, et cetera et cetera.

'I'll need to be getting home at some stage,' Mark said. 'Depending on which way the venetians are pulled, I'm sleeping in a room that's either *The Shining* or *Flipper*.'

'Two more nights, Mark,' Richardson said, 'then we'll have more of a team organised down here.'

Mark raised his eyebrows, doubtful.

After the call, Mark and Jagdeep fell back into silence, the sound of the waves lapping on the shore.

'So, you talk to Rose yet?' Jagdeep asked.

'Yeah.'

Did he want to follow Rose to Africa or not? A holiday seemed half-arsed, a relationship in limbo. Did he want to follow her down paths unknown? They could be dark tunnels with no clear light, or bright chambers sparkling with possibility. Follow her and leave the boys for the bulk of a year, save school holidays. Stay in Australia, spend a couple of weeks a year with Rose, miss her the rest.

'You're on earth in this form for a short time,' Jagdeep said. 'Make it mean something.'

The sky was a deep purple by the time Mark returned to his hotel room. An envelope containing an A4 yellow folder had been slipped under his door. A note on the front from Ian let him know it'd been dropped off by a 'woman from council'.

Planning had come through, and this quick! A miracle. Everyone who ever dealt with Planning knew how long they took to respond. In those departments, days were months, months were years.

Mark lay on his bed, barely able to keep his eyes open. The horizontal strips of light coming through the blinds gave the impression he was in a shimmery prison. He closed his eyes again, tried not to think about the mannequin.

After a few minutes, unable to fully relax, Mark fetched his reading glasses and wiped them with his T-shirt. A number of papers and diagrams were neatly placed in a plastic pocket within the A4 folder. *Sinkholes of the Limestone Coast* was the heading.

Broken Bay Council had commissioned a university in South Australia to write a report on the geological history of the Limestone Coast. Mark skipped over the part about Gondwanaland breaking up, the separation of the Antarctic and Australian continents and got to the section on sinkholes, or 'cenotes' as they were properly known:

> The extensive subterranean network of cenotes located in the south-eastern corner of South Australia lay hidden deep underground for many thousands of years. It took the gradual collapse of cave roofs to expose their existence, revealing places of startling beauty.
>
> In the Franklin and Limestone Coast area there are over fifty known cenotes containing water, one of the Earth's largest concentrations. The cenotes have been formed from the area's long-term exposure to the ocean and waves that have created large caves, blocked off by erosion. When the ceiling of the cave collapses, a new sinkhole is formed.
>
> Sinkholes are often situated near one another, as once the shared ceiling of a cave begins to form cracks and collapse through rainfall and heavy ocean swells, other areas of the ceiling weaken.

Turning on his side, Mark took off his glasses, closed his eyes and rested his head on the pillow. Immediately, three images came into his head: Glenn Close and the knife, Cherie's battered face and Eloise's mask, yellow brain matter oozing out of her wetsuit. What had Jane said? The body became a soap-like composition. He quickly flicked on his bedside light, sat up and put his glasses back on.

The second lot of council papers consisted of maps and photos of the Broken Bay shire from over twenty years ago. It was during this time – one of the worst droughts in history – that people started building inground pools. Every household had to have one; what was once the domain of the rich now became an object of desire for every middle-class family. Public pools lost out big time and all the fundraising barbecues in the world could not save the majority. It was goodbye to the five-metre diving boards, it was goodbye to spectacular bombs, witnessed by admiring crowds.

But more particular to Mark's interest was the fact that every in-ground household pool needed a secure fence, which the councils were responsible for signing off. After a spate of child drownings, Australian councils took it upon themselves to undertake a massive overhead mapping project, designed to hunt out the illegal pools. In Booralama, some households were fined thousands for not having an approved fence with secure locking. A deck did not suffice. Glass doors leading off a patio did not suffice. A sturdy hedge did not suffice.

Mark now had the aerial imagery taken by the council-commissioned plane of the whole local area in the year 2002. His eyes narrowed, his head drooped. The photos had been overlaid with maps and there were so many; so much of the shire to identify and sort through. Bare paddocks stretched out like cardboard, with rooftops here and there, a lighter colour for an empty dam. Some dams with murky green water. A cluster of cows, small towns with houses huddled together and all alongside the mighty ocean.

He was half-asleep when he found it: the paddocks that connected the Sinclair, Doyle and Twymann farms. Before he drifted into deep sleep, he managed to take a pen out of his pocket and carefully circle an area as wide as a coin.

CHAPTER 20

A casuarina tree outside his bathroom window was alive with fire-tails. Mark lay in bed and listened to the birds squabble. In the reflection of the glazed window, he could see flashes of their red tails and beaks darting in and around the grey-green leaves. He'd read that male and female finches shared the incubation of their eggs and caring for their young. What were they saying? The high-pitched reeling could either be a love song or avian abuse.

Mark picked up the paper he had circled last night and considered it for a long time. He was about to call Jagdeep when there was a loud honking from outside. He got out of bed, flicked the blinds open and saw his own car parked out the front, windscreen fixed, exterior nice and shiny. At the wheel was an old man with a walnut face and teeth as white as snow. Chomp presumably.

Mark opened the door and the man gave him a cheery good morning.

'No doubt you'll be aware that Stabber isn't working today.' Chomp grinned. 'He got me to do the tidying up while he's, well, otherwise occupied.'

Mark gave him a grin back.

'Windscreen's all fixed,' the man said. 'Paperwork's in the glovebox. Can you give me a lift down to my boat? I've got my ute parked there.'

Mark nodded and backed into his room, where he scrambled about for something to wear. He needed a laundromat. Did Broken Bay even have one? *Booralama does.*

Outside, he went to shake hands with the man, but was greeted instead with a rounded stump. The wiry fellow chuckled. 'Have to swap hands, sorry. Name's Greg, but most people call me Chomp in honour of the bugger that got me.'

Mark paused. 'Are you the man from the photo at the pub? The shark attack?' He cringed at the excited way he asked the question, then gestured for Chomp to hop into the passenger seat.

'That's me.' Chomp didn't seem to mind. 'Great white when I was out spearfishing at a local spot, the salmon holes.'

Mark drove slowly out of the hotel car park and headed towards the bay. It was good to be driving his own car; he felt a renewed sense of purpose as he wound down the window and put an elbow on the sill.

'And that was . . .'

'Almost fifty years ago now.'

'I've never met anyone who's been bitten by a shark. You must be a hit everywhere you go.'

'It's not a bad story. People like hearing it.'

'I'm all ears, mate.'

Chomp launched in, well-practised after five decades of people leaning in, agog. 'Last dive of the day. Perfect conditions, sea as calm as you like, water crystal clear. We'd caught lobsters, rock cod and salmon. Almost ready to go, and I just said one more dive, it was that good – I just wanted to get down there again.

Days like that, mate, you've gotta grab 'em. Dived in, visibility near perfect – was at about twelve metres down and, bam! It hit me like a train. Got me by the leg in his teeth, waved me around like wild dog with its prey.'

Mark could see raised red scars on Chomp's thigh. Angry lines, stretching all round his leg.

'No pain in it, just that thrashing body and shock. He let me go. I think it was the spear rod that made him spit me out – the spear was alongside of me, so he would have got it in his mouth.'

Mark's eyes widened.

'But then he came back for more.'

'What!'

'They say the shark that will eat you is the one that comes out of nowhere, and it's true – I'd seen sharks before, we all had – curious ones. Scare the shit out of you with their slow circling, tailgating the boat, coming to check you out when you're in the surf. But this one was different, it had purpose.'

'It came back for you?'

'Yeah.' Chomp grinned. His face was weather-beaten, haggard, cast in dubious freckles and crusty moles. But his smile was one to warm you.

'Jesus,' Mark breathed. 'What did you do?'

'When he let go of my leg, I took shelter near a reef wall. I wasn't game to make a run to the surface, what with the blood streaming out and twelve metres above of no man's land. I waited, trying not to breathe.'

'Did that work?'

'Shit no. Bastard comes at me again. I get my spear into it, try to stab the thing, but it barely touches the sides and then, next second, I feel a chomp and it's clamped down on my arm, takes the thing clean off.'

They came to the crossroads of Bay Road. Chomp indicated for Mark to turn left.

'With my arm half-out its mouth like a bloody kid's dolly or something, the shark comes back again, and its nose barges into the reef wall behind me. Didn't like that, because next, it just sailed over me and away. Like a road train going overhead, it was that big. Took my chance, shot up to the surface and my friends took it from there.'

Mark whistled through his teeth.

'Its eye was so close to mine that I could see this thin membrane close over it the moment the bastard bit into my flesh.'

Chomp's eyes were shut, his chin up, feeling the sun on his face through the windscreen. He didn't look traumatised; it seemed there were worse things than having half your arm bitten off by a great white.

'You're Scott Boxhall's father, aren't you?' Mark asked after a pause.

'I am.' The man was faintly smiling. 'And I always talk about him as if he's still alive. He's been dead for nigh on twenty years, but he's still here inside me, all around.'

The car accident his son died in had been a mere two weeks after Eloise went missing. Mark itched to ask him about it, but wouldn't. Couldn't. The way Chomp smiled into the light at the thought of his son, now wasn't the time.

They pulled in at the wharf, boats lined up like girls at a dance. It was shaping up to be a fine day.

'You used to own the shop that sold ropes around here, didn't you?'

'Yup. Ropes, life vests, fishing tackle, tanks, repairs – you name it.'

'So you sold oxygen tanks – for scuba diving or spearfishing or whatever?'

'Yep.'

'You might've heard that Eloise was found with an oxygen tank? It had a hydro stamp date for five months before she went missing. Could the tank have been tested at your shop?'

Chomp gave a short laugh. 'It could be, but I tell you what – you're in for a task. Almost everyone around here who dives would have their own tanks and get them tested. It's cheaper in the long run than renting, and much more convenient.'

'So, the Sinclairs would have had tanks tested through you?'

'Of course. I was the only dive shop in town. They were always coming in and out – along with at least a hundred others. All the ones you would have heard of: the Doyles, the Twymanns, Scottie and me, the Bickons – that's the bloke who owns the hotel you're staying at – all of them. The Sinclairs were some of my best customers, of course. Addicted to the sea, all of them.'

'Phil said in early reports that no tank was missing from his property.'

Chomp looked thoughtful. 'The Sinclairs had tanks, all right. I know because they bought them from me and had them tested here. There was a time when they had many. But after they lost their dough, they sold off a few, didn't need so many with only their family diving. So Phil could be right in that. Tanks are expensive – you want to know where they are and how many you've got to take out each trip.'

'No chance you kept the receipts for all the tanks you sold and tested?' Mark knew it was a long shot, clung to the miracle Jane said sometimes happens.

'Not a chance, mate. Got rid of it all when I sold the shop.'

'Worth a try.'

'It was a good shop. I enjoyed working there for the most part.' Chomp pointed to the old hi-vis jacket he was wearing. 'See here? My initials, GB. I used to sew initials on all the vests myself. It's good for fishing fleets. Everyone on a trawler becomes particular about their own gear. They don't do it nowadays.'

Police were protective about their own gear too. It was illegal for cops to give away official uniforms for fear of dodgy types impersonating officers to conduct crime.

'At one point, Scott and his mate Brett had plans to start their own business, repairing boats.' Chomp continued talking, almost to himself. 'Broken Bay Fishing Repairs, BBFR. They were best friends, you know, had been since they were knee high to a grasshopper. I stitched their initials into the vests along with BBFR for their business. Took me forever to sew that,' he said sadly. 'Scott was wearing his when he died. All of his ribs were broken, but you couldn't tell, because the vest held everything in so well. I would have liked to keep it, but well . . . they had to cut it off.' Chomp scratched at something on his neck, looked out to the sea.

Mark pictured the man bent over an industrial sewing machine, the energy and care taken in the stitching. The hours he spent doing it, each letter an act of hope and love.

'Course the BBFR business idea was never going to work. Scott was always headed out of here soon as he could, and Brett's family didn't want him to stay either, even though at one point they were going to buy the shop off me. I should have known it was a dumb idea. Not many of the young people hang around.'

The Sinclair brothers had. And Gerri and James Doyle.

'It sounds as if they were all such a good group,' Mark said, pulling up and cutting the engine. 'Can't imagine what it must have been like for them after Eloise went missing and your son died.'

Chomp gave a brief laugh. 'Nah – no matter what anyone tells you, it wasn't always happy families. That group of kids was fraying long before Eloise. It's fine when they're all little – families camping together and whatnot – but when they get old enough to bitch and scheme, that's when the problems start.'

Interesting. Mark fought the urge to get out his pen and paper. 'Who was fighting with who?'

Another chuckle, and Chomp unbuckled his belt and got out of the car. After a moment's hesitation, Mark followed. Chomp walked to the jetty, came to a small boat named *Scottie*, knelt and began untying the thick rope that held his boat to the pier.

'Mate, they were all fighting! A couple of weeks before Eloise went missing, Mat and Brett had a blue outside the pub, punches thrown. I told Scott to stay out of it. Nic and Brett didn't see eye to eye either, all protective over Eloise and a good bit of jealousy too. Brett was a good-looking bloke, they all were, but Brett had a way with the girls. You know the type. I liked the kid, but he was a bit of a root rat. No doubt about it.'

'Ahh.' Mark knew the type. The root rats, the slayers, the ladies' men, the players. Come their twenty-year school reunions and most of them were deadshits, still asking their mums for money and refusing to pay child support.

'Scottie was going out with Gerri Doyle, and look, she's the mother of my grandson and he's the best kid in the world, but it didn't take a genius to recognise that before he died, their relationship was on the rocks too. As I said, Scott always had his eye on the horizon. He was a year older than the rest of them and I could tell he wanted to spread his wings. He asked me about the financial state of the dive shop a few weeks before he died – we went out to the salmon holes for the day – and I said, "Scott, it's no worry of yours." Brett's dad had offered to buy it and it was a good deal. If Brett and Scott weren't going to get into the dive business, I was happy to sell. "You do what you want," I said to Scott, "the world's a big place." I didn't want him to feel tied to Broken Bay.'

Those ties that bind. They're restricting. They're a comfort.

'It was a good day out, just Scott, Brett and me. I've told Teddy about it. Caught enough salmon to last me months. Beautiful weather, and no fucking great whites.'

Mark nodded. No fucking great whites makes every day a good one.

'Next day, young Eloise went missing. Town went spare looking. All I could think of was her mother, Juliette. Her death is what ended Murray. It was like history repeating. I looked in the bay for days, expecting to find her body floating on the waves.'

As he untied the ropes, Chomp talked about Murray and Juliette, and how happy they'd been as a couple. The big burly fisherman and this little beauty from France, who looked like Brigitte Bardot, only better! And a good sort too. First time he saw her standing on this bay, Chomp said, his blue eyes misted over, Juliette just looked like a mermaid. Well, he added, she ended up in the sea too. Another fisherman pulled her out. He missed her, he missed them all.

The knot was untied. It lay on the jetty, a rope freely untangled. Mark felt as if a magic trick had just been performed on him. The knot had been thick and complex. Now, minutes later, it was gone.

'Have you been in Broken Bay since you were a kid, Chomp?' Mark asked. 'It sounds like you and the Sinclairs go way back.'

'Yep, me and Murray grew up together, learned to dive, fish, swim – you name it. Marriages, kids, the lot. One time, we retrieved bodies out of a cave, passed drowned kids one by one to the other, gave them back to their families. That's the sort of thing that binds you to someone.'

A beat followed. Mark recalled the newspaper article he'd read.

'You were with Murray for the retrieval of the Franklin Three, weren't you? You were the other diver.'

Chomp nodded. 'I was.' The genial smile was gone. 'The gouge marks on the ceiling of that cave have never left me. The shark's eye, the teeth clamping down and the speed of it – they're nothing compared to what I felt when I saw those marks after Murray brought the last dead boy up.' He held up his one hand, making frantic scratching gestures. 'Those kids were metres away from the tunnel that led to the surface, but it was panic that got them. That's the horror of it. There was nothing anyone could have done.'

A long beat followed as Mark tried to digest the words. 'At least now we know where most of the sinkholes are,' he said, thinking of the council papers he'd read the night before. 'And they're regulated now.'

Chomp jumped into his boat, moved to the steering wheel and started the engine. 'What a load of bull!' he called over the chugging. 'There's loads of sinkholes around here, most of 'em used for dumping grounds. Farmers won't let on for fear of the EPA, either that or they don't want inexperienced dickheads dying on their lands. Every farm around here has a sinkhole, secret or not. No matter how we tried to warn the young ones off, no matter the stories, they keep finding them, going into them. They're risking lives and breaking hearts – but, mate, they're having the time of their lives. We were the same at their age. Nothing changes.'

Chomp raised his half-arm in goodbye, the other steady on the motor as it turned around and chugged into the bay.

Mark sat in his car for a moment, watching the little boat leave. There was something momentous about a ship leaving a port. He supposed it had to do with history, and romance, risk and adventure. There were all sorts of dangers in the ocean. Great whites were just one. He closed his eyes for a few seconds, felt the warmth of the sun through the windows. Chomp mentioned that Juliette looked like a mermaid when he saw her – they were dangerous too. Seductive creatures who lured men to their deaths with feminine guile. And that thought brought him back to the Greeks.

Were mermaids the same as sirens, the mysterious women in the myth of Odysseus whose song called out to men, causing them to shipwreck? Juliette, Eloise and Cherie: they'd all been described as stunners by people who knew them. He called women stunners too, Jane Southern for one. It was a funny way to describe women, Mark thought. To stun someone is to render them immobile, knock them out. All these dangerous terms given to good-looking women, it was hardly fair. Not as if they could help it.

Mark peered forward and narrowed his eyes. Chomp's boat was no longer visible; the ocean had swallowed it up. Mark turned on the ignition, and headed out of town.

CHAPTER 21

The ocean is lapis lazuli, smooth as polished marble. It's like a giant's tablecloth, James thinks, as he rubs zinc onto his legs and behind his neck. Ten years ago, he might have made the observation aloud, but he doesn't now. The girls are lying on their towels at the front of the boat, their heads almost touching, feet upturned like curled shells. He watches for bubbles in the water, the thin stream that tells him where the divers are below. He's supposed to be in charge here, in case anything goes wrong – but really, what can happen on a day like this?

God, it's so hot and still.

Gerri and Eloise sit up, sweaty and red, their hair sticking to their foreheads, sunburn already appearing across their stomachs.

'Has Brett ever told you he loves you?' Gerri asks Eloise, and James tries not to listen. He turns back to the sea.

Eloise shrugs, reaches for a hat and pulls it low over her white-blonde hair.

'Because, you two have been together forever and you're like an old married couple.'

'No, we're not.'

James is surprised at how cold Eloise's reply is.

'You'll probably end up buying a house in Broken, living next door to the school.' Gerri is teasing, but James can tell Eloise doesn't like it.

It's funny, he thinks, as he peers again for the bubbles, how people don't know when to stop. Gerri can be so annoying.

'Boo.' It's Eloise, suddenly behind him. But she didn't yell it, and he's not scared.

They both rest awhile on the deck of the boat, scanning the ocean's surface. There could be anything out there. There could be nothing.

'You going to Roti too?' Eloise asks, then falters when she sees he doesn't know what she's talking about. 'The bastards,' she says softly. 'Don't worry, I didn't get asked either.'

It shouldn't hurt, but it does. He already knows who'll have been asked: Mat Sinclair, Scott Boxhall, Eloise's boyfriend, Brett Twymann, and Gerri. Nic will have organised it. Typical.

In the deep blue, on this side of the boat, they see no fish, no bubbles. It's like the sky has been turned upside down. They could leap into it, it's like they could breathe in it.

'Let's jump in,' Eloise said. 'Come on.'

'I'm supposed to be in charge up here — you know what Phil's like.' Phil, Eloise's oldest brother, was notoriously strict and safety-conscious.

'Who cares? I'll take the blame.' And before he can protest any further, Eloise is sailing out into the air.

'What?!' Gerri comes screeching up the deck. 'Was that El?'

James doesn't answer, because he's now climbing onto the side too and jumping and then coiling up and diving spearheaded into the sea.

Eloise is beside him, laughing, her hair in strands across her face, her mouth wide open.

'You two are idiots.' Gerri is looking down at them, smiling.

'Come in!' Eloise says. 'Don't be boring!'

'What if Phil finds out the deck's not manned?'

'Who cares!' And they're shouting out, the both of them, 'Come in! Come in!'

Then Gerri's jumping and there's a massive splash and they're screaming about sharks and they're diving underwater and pulling each other's legs. And even though the others could surface any second, that the consequences will be severe – in that moment, with just the three of them in the water, none of it really matters.

CHAPTER 22

Sean rang: they'd finally spoken to a jet-lagged Corey Burns from New York City. With the sounds of traffic in the background, the young actor told them of his brief afternoon visit to Cherie Swinson. 'I taped the conversation with Corey,' Sean said. 'It's pretty clear. Can play the main bit to you now, if you like.'

'That'd be great,' Mark said, turning up the volume in his car.

Corey's voice came through, at first crackling and then clearer as Sean adjusted the sound. 'I know. I can't believe it. I'm just . . . it's really sad. It's mad, she was murdered? But yeah, so I went there at around four on Saturday afternoon and we talked about her play. I'd lent her a short black wig ages before and was going to get it, but I ended up forgetting and we just talked. She said she'd nearly finished her play and she was looking forward to showing it to everyone. I didn't see the script, but Cherie said it was based on two old families in town and, yeah, she'd found out some amazing stuff that audiences would really be excited about. She showed me one of the costumes that she had on the mannequin, it was for one of the main characters. Totally naturalistic, you know? Old dress, cardigan and a blonde wig – a lot like Cherie's hair actually! I said to her, "So is that meant to be you?" and she just laughed and said no, it was meant to be a much younger person. Anyway, I forgot to get the wig. But it doesn't matter. I'm here now, and Cherie's gone.'

Sean's voice came back on the phone. 'Interesting, isn't it?'

'Yeah.' Poor Corey, probably in a state of shock at the new city, at the country and dealing with the news of Cherie. It was a lot for the kid from Broken Bay. And from what he had said, it looked as if Cherie had set up the mannequin for no reason other than to prepare for her new play.

'Well, what we're thinking is that Cherie went home after the pub, went inside, put her purse down and then saw someone in her front yard. She probably thought it was Corey come to get the wig back, so she ran downstairs to give it to him and dropped it when she was attacked.'

'Right.'

'I asked Corey if the word or name "blue" or "bleu" meant anything to him, and he said no.'

'Could Corey have killed her?' Mark mused aloud. 'Handy of him to be in New York right now.'

'Corey's got an airtight alibi, being on a plane.'

The young constable was showing him up. Mark straightened in his seat. 'Good work, Sean. Really good work.'

'Well, thanks. It was Chiara too.'

Before he hung up, Mark asked if Sean had time to look into another matter. 'A car accident from around here in 2003, Scott Boxhall. Can you hunt up the report on it, let me know what you find?'

'Too easy.' Sean sounded pleased to be tasked with another job related to the cases. Mark didn't want to spoil Sean's confident mood by telling the constable that nothing was too easy, least of all looking into a car accident of a man not much younger than him.

Ten minutes later, Mark was walking through Doyle's paddocks once again, a sheath of council documents in his hand. Richardson had told him to return to the scene of the crime. And so he was here, in the place where she'd been found. Mark sorted through his papers till he located the photo he most wanted. Holding the rest under one arm, he smoothed it over the top of a pine fence post and looked at it, then at his surroundings, then the photo again, checking the scale marked on it. He was sure of it – on the aerial footage taken of the Sinclair and Doyle farms in the search for Eloise, the trough he was now standing beside was at least five metres from the fence. But in the council imagery, taken before Eloise went missing, it was about ten to thirteen metres from the fence. The circle he'd outlined on the map was just about right.

The location where Eloise went missing looked the same as it did in 2003, save for the green grass and the full dam. The fences were the same too. Only one thing had changed: the oval water trough had been moved.

Mark studied the photo again and then paced it out. Yes, about five metres in Mark's estimation. Nowadays, troughs were made of plastic and silicone. This one was cement, the old type, sturdy and long lasting, green on the inside from algae. So why had the cumbersome tank been moved?

With a growing unease, Mark took photos of the scene before pacing to the sinkhole from which Eloise and Mya were retrieved. The police tape had been removed and, aside from a discarded takeaway coffee lid and indentations where the vehicles had been, the place looked serene. The deep blue pool hidden among the grass was as compelling as ever and, once again, Mark felt like plunging in. He could see how people would be enchanted by such clear water, the rippling cerulean depths, the unknown world beneath. He reached his hand in, felt a biting cold.

All about him was quiet. No Doyles on tractors, no mob of cows eyeing him off. He stood by the sturdy pine fence of the Sinclair property that linked with the Doyles, the sinkhole and the trough. In the near distance was the Doyle house. He couldn't see the Sinclairs' ramshackle place or Brett Twymann's childhood home, but they were close by too. Near enough to walk. Mark scanned the area again, felt an increasing nervousness.

Straightening, he shook his head, collected his papers and set off back to his car. Just before he reached it, he saw something flutter out the corner of his eye. He turned; a large crow was sitting on the fence, watching him.

'What do you want?' Mark asked it, forcefully.

The crow bent its small head forward and gave a long, drawn-out cry.

Mark had no answer to that. *God*, he thought. *This place gives me the creeps.*

As he drove back into town, a ute passed him and slowed. It was Mat and Nic, with Gerri in the middle. They'd just come in from fishing, they called through the window, had seen Chomp, who'd told them Mark might be here.

'Heard you want to look at some of the caves round here,' Nic said. 'Still keen? Could do it now, if you like.'

Mark hesitated. It was a good opportunity, but he really should get back to the station.

'There're some great spots they could show you.' Gerri leaned over Mat to speak. 'And on a day like this! Be a nice break.'

She was right. Too blue and warm to be stuck indoors, head in files, and once more he reminded himself of Richardson telling him to check out the lay of the land. Plus, he needed to shake off that creepy feeling from the Doyle farm.

'Sounds good.' Mark didn't want to mention the trough right now. He needed to assemble his thoughts, discuss them with Jagdeep.

Gerri declared she had stuff to do at her old home. She wanted to collect a few things before she moved from the area, she couldn't trust her brother or her father not to throw them out. She started walking down the Doyle drive, giving them a wave. Mark parked and took her spot in the ute.

There was breezy, beachy music playing on the radio and the Sinclair ute smelled pleasantly of Mars bars. The brothers bickered amicably, and once again Mark was drawn into the warmth of the Sinclair family, their closeness. Of these two, Mat was the more gregarious, Nic quieter, more like Phil perhaps.

'You two not working today?' Mark asked, elbow out the window, cool wind rushing by.

'Day off,' Mat said. 'Nic's helping me move house.'

'Yeah?'

'Me and April are breaking up,' he explained. 'Got a flat in town.'

'Sorry, mate,' Mark said.

'*I'm* not sorry, should have done it a while back. Like the day after we met.'

'He's staying with me and Cath for a week or so,' Nic told Mark before turning to his brother. 'Cath says you're cooking Tuesdays and Thursdays.'

'Shit – she's vegetarian, isn't she?'

'Pescatarian.'

'What in the hell is that?'

'She eats fish.'

'She better,' Mat said, grinning at Mark. 'Can't marry into the family if you don't eat pescs.'

Mark felt a pang of envy. He and Prue were close, he supposed. They spoke every couple of weeks, remembered birthdays. But she was in Canada, and he'd never visited. What did that say about them? It was so easy to slip into laziness where siblings were concerned.

Nic pulled into a rocky car park. A rusted sign leading to the beach alerted them to the fact they were now in a protected area: no dogs, no camping, no fires, no climbing over the fence.

Mark hesitated a moment, then followed Nic and Mat as they vaulted over the forbidden fence and began walking along a thin trail bordered by low saltbush and succulents.

'The place we're taking you to – it's a cave, the entrance is just up here,' Mat said. 'It's so cool, we used to play here as kids.'

'There're caves dotted all over here,' Nic continued. 'Some are really old. There were Aboriginal paintings in one of them, when Dad was a kid.'

'Collapsed now,' Mat added. 'They do that, after a big swell.'

Soon they reached a rocky outcrop where they had to scramble down a small cliff. At the bottom, two walls of limestone rose up with a thin, oval-shaped cave entrance between them.

Mark was surprised to see Mat light a cigarette. They stood around, waiting for Mat to finish it. There was a slight awkwardness to their interaction now; Mark didn't know why. It was as if Mat was doing something embarrassing, like taking too long in the toilet at a dinner party.

'Heard you been talking to Chomp,' Nic said. 'Good man.'

'He's good, yeah.' Momentarily thrown, Mark's mind whirred.

'Chomp seems to think Brett'll come down for a few days.'

'Yeah?'

'Doubt he will. Brett hasn't returned for over fifteen years.'

'Dunno why he'd want to.' Mat finished his smoke and flicked the butt into the bushes. 'Not many'd lay out the welcome rug.'

The day was growing warmer. Mark pulled his jumper over his head and tied it around his waist. It was 10 am. 'I can't be too long, got to get back to the station.'

'Let's go then,' Nic said. 'You been in caves before?'

'No, not really.'

'Stick close.'

They stepped inside the oval crack and darkness immediately fell. The space was the size of a lounge room, with large, slick black rocks jutting out. A steady dripping from the smooth walls was the only sound. Mark needed to put his jumper on again.

Nic walked to the end of the cave, where a darker space hinted at a tunnel. 'It's like a maze in here,' he said. 'We can show you the first bit if you like.'

Mark hesitated again. In the blackness, the tunnel appeared. 'Okay,' he said, a slight fear in him. 'Just the first bit.'

Nic bent low, hunching his shoulders, and entered the tunnel. Mark followed, Mat behind him. They walked this way for a short while, and just when Mark's back started really aching, they came to another opening.

'Here we are,' Nic announced.

Mark looked around, astounded. They were in a deep cavern, but above their heads, far above it seemed, he could see a line of sky. The light spearing down from that opening made a thin wall of golden light appear in the middle of the space. He put his hand through it – it was like a sci-fi movie, a portal to another world. He did it again, feeling the warmth and watching the dust particles sparkle in the curtain of gold. All up the walls of the cave, green ferns and hanging vines sprung from the dark rock and just below them, down a slope, was a small pool of dazzling blue water.

'Is that a sinkhole?' he asked in wonder.

'It is.'

'How'd you find this place?' Mark was still staring at the pool. *That feeling again, I could dive right in.*

'It's the Limestone Coast, mate,' Mat said, grinning. 'Spots like this are everywhere.'

When Mark looked back where they'd come from, it was difficult to distinguish the entrance to the tunnel among the sleek black rocks. He gazed up at the cave walls and all their greenery, wondered if he'd be able to climb up to get back to the surface. There were rock holds here and there, but you'd need a lot of core strength to be able to reach them.

'You could do it.' Nic was looking at the cave walls too. 'But it's not easy. Gerri can't, the first rock holds are too high for her to reach.'

The drip-drip of the persistent water. A faint rushing sound – the sea? He strained his ears. Yes, it was the ocean. Still a way off, but each pull of the tide was audible in the rush and fizz of the waves.

'This would be a good place to get rid of someone,' Mat said suddenly. 'Break a kneecap, then leave you here.'

A stab of confusion. Mark turned to the younger brother, who was leaning on a rock, his face an inscrutable calm.

Nic clapped his hands for action and Mark jolted.

'One more we can show you, it's the best one yet. Want to come? It's also a quick way back to the surface – just follow closely.' Without waiting for an answer, Nic turned to the rock wall behind him and bent lower this time – on his hands and knees – to enter another dark tunnel.

'We have to crawl?' Mark didn't like this; he didn't like it *at all.*

'Just for a bit.' Mat's voice behind him was pleasant. 'You won't believe the cave on the other side, it's like something from a dream.'

Nic disappeared into the hole and, nervously, Mark bent down and followed. It was pitch black. The ground was hard beneath his knees and the rocks dug into his hands. With mounting anxiety, Mark could sense the closeness of the walls, the thick darkness and, all the time, the maddening dripping sound. *God,* he thought in sudden despair, *I've got to get out!*

'Hey.' He aimed for a level tone. 'Are we nearly there?'

Nic said something Mark couldn't hear, and the tunnel took a sharp turn right and downward.

'Not long!' Mat said, close behind. 'It gets a bit tight here.'

No, Mark thought. *I can't do it.* He stopped, felt Mat edge up against his feet. In front, he could just see Nic now shuffling commando-style on his stomach.

'Come on!' Mat said, his voice muffled. 'Not a good spot to have a rest, it's dead air here.'

Dead air? With a groan, Mark started again, almost horizontal now, his forearms moving him along. The sides of the cave were so close there was barely an inch either side. Mark had a sudden panic: if there was a cave-in, they'd be stuck here, the whole of the Limestone Coast above and no one would know. He wanted out, but with Nic in front and Mat behind, he couldn't turn around even if he wanted to. The earth hemmed in.

Eventually, another space, this time large enough to sit up alongside each other. Mark put his head in between his knees and breathed.

'You okay?' Mat asked.

'I wouldn't have come if I knew it was like this,' Mark said. 'Where in the hell are you taking me?'

'Two more minutes, I swear,' Nic said. 'Come on.'

'I'll follow, move ahead,' Mark answered, none too friendly.

Mat edged past, and Mark heard a low, indecipherable comment directed to Nic but aimed at him. The brothers pushed on.

Christ, Mark thought. *How did I end up here?* He reached out, felt the earth on both sides and just above his head. It was a tomb. The thought frightened him anew and, once more, he moved from sitting to crawling, inching his way along the tunnel. Five metres ahead, and no sign of the Sinclairs.

'Mat!' he called, but not too loud, afraid of what noise would do in this space. 'Nic!' No answer. He was moving slightly downwards, and this made Mark hesitate. Perhaps he'd missed a turn-off? He wondered whether to crawl backwards to the place where he'd come from, and check. 'Mat!' he called again. 'Nic!'

Nothing. He kept moving.

Two metres ahead, and there was a slight change in visibility – a hint of light towards the right. Mark held out one hand and ran it along the side of the wall. There it was, an indentation. He used both hands to feel either side of the new space – yes! There was an opening there, and a dim, grey light beyond.

'Hello!' he called into it, and after a moment's pause he entered. He was right, it was lighter. He crawled on and was relieved to feel the space widen. After a few moments he was able to walk hunched over and in a few more he could stand. It was dark still, but he felt that he was in a large room. When he swung his arms about, he could feel no wall. *Those bloody Sinclairs*, he thought. *I've changed my tune about them.*

But where were they? Where was he?

'Hello!' A rustle to his left. He strained his ears, strained everything to listen. 'Hello?' He sounded ridiculous, like a posh Englishman being overly polite in a rough pub. He tried to remember which way he'd come. From the left? Breathe. It was to the right, but no – when he edged back through that way, he recognised nothing, only a dark tunnel again, and another leading off it. Had he gone through the wrong one to begin with? His heart hammered. Darkness. Suffocating metres of rock on top, and then the earth on top of that.

'Hello?' The tunnel led downward – he didn't remember this on the way in just now. Or did he? *God, God, God.* He really couldn't remember! At least he could walk now. *Move!* Taking a brisk step forward, he lurched sickeningly into an empty space and felt a crunch as his ankle gave way.

He rolled onto the stone floor. 'Help!' he called now, in agony, his whole lower leg shrieking in pain. '*Help!*'

The cold earth, smooth walls around him, and a dripping, dripping. He was, he realised, at the edge of a pool of water – black and unmoving, a slick membrane of something unknown.

The pain in his ankle screamed. *Fuck*, he thought in a sudden moment of clarity, *I'm not going to get out.*

Holding his knee, he looked wildly about. He recognised nothing, could see nothing. Only the oil-like pool was visible, a glistening black. *Think!* He tried to calm himself. There's always a way.

Drip. Drip.

'Hello?'

At first, Mark thought it was his own voice, but then he recognised it. 'Yes!' he called. 'Over here!'

A torchlight bore hard into his face, and he covered his eyes with his arm. The light did not waver.

'Can you put that down?' Mark asked. 'You're blinding me.'

The torchlight remained fixed.

'I said . . .' Mark felt fear – was it just the situation? 'Can you please . . .'

The torchlight switched off, and for a few seconds there was complete darkness, unlike any Mark had ever known.

Someone cleared their throat. 'Sorry, just trying to fix this torch.'

James Doyle.

CHAPTER 23

James's silhouette became apparent as the light beam was turned towards the ground, like a police-drawn outline of a murder victim. The cave walls dripped with freezing water.

'How do we get out of here?' Mark asked, his voice loud. 'I'm lost.'

'I can show you,' James said. 'You've come quite a fair way in the system.'

'I was following the Sinclairs. They left me.'

'It's hard if you get lost down here,' James said. 'So cold, and of course no phone reception.'

The trickle of water continued. *Drip, drip.*

'I've sprained my ankle,' Mark said. 'Is there any other way out?'

A pause, then, 'There is, but you won't like it.'

Mark's ankle throbbed, rhythmic and harsh. 'Tell me.'

'In there.' James's torchlight pointed to the body of inky black water, its membrane cover unmoving. 'If you go into the pool, you can swim under an arch and come up the other side, where it's shallow again. The pool on that side leads directly to the surface – you can see light from it. From there it's an easy walk to the outside.'

No! Mark's brain screamed. *Underwater? In this?* But his ankle, and that walk back through those tunnels . . . 'You've done it before?'

'Many times,' James said. 'Although usually I'm in a wetsuit. Having said that – the water's not too cold here, you'd be surprised.'

Mark bent down and felt the edge of the pond. James was right, it wasn't freezing. Cold, but not unbearable. 'How far is it to swim?'

'Ten or so strokes to the other side, and then you have to go down, underwater. You'll be under for five seconds max, as we go under the arch – then it's up again, to the other side. From there, it's easy.'

'How will I know where to go? I don't have a torch on me.'

'This is an underwater torch. I'll go first and guide you. You'll swim just behind me, hold onto me. You can't let go.'

It felt reckless. Wrong. But his ankle throbbed. It was so painful. Why had he come here? Who knew he was here?

'You're sure it will only be five seconds underwater?' Mark asked. 'If it's any longer, I might panic.'

James counted to five aloud: 'One thousand, two thousand, three thousand . . . yes, five seconds max.'

'Okay.' The seconds stretched out: they were hours, they were days.

'Take off your shoes and socks, jumper and jeans. I'll be doing the same. I'll come back and get them later.'

Mark did as he was told, putting his phone and keys inside his shoes, and wincing as he removed his left boot – God, his whole foot was swollen and hot to touch. Broken maybe.

Sitting down, he removed the rest of his clothes and folded them neatly. Undressed, he felt vulnerable, as if some other skin had been peeled off him. He was a worm down here, blind and soft.

'Ready?' James leaned down and helped him up. 'Stick by me, you'll be right.'

Though his ankle was soothed by the cold water, Mark baulked at the prospect of going fully under. James, the torch in his mouth, held Mark's wrist tightly as they waded out deeper into the pool. Yellow beams of light raced jagged against the ancient cave walls and the constant drip-drip became maddening the more Mark focused on it.

They were up to their waists, up to their chests, up to their necks.

'Ready?' James asked. 'You'll need to hold onto me, but remember, the main thing is to stay calm.'

Ignoring his words and in sudden panic, Mark grabbed James by the arm. 'Don't leave me!' His voice was childlike, insistent – he didn't care. 'I can't see a thing!'

'Keep your eyes open underwater. It gets a bit lighter once we reach the other side of the arch.'

Mark closed his eyes. Opened them again. Nothing had changed: he was still there, it wasn't a bad dream.

'You ready?' James pulled him closer so that the two were inches apart. 'One, two, three . . .'

Underwater, Mark saw nothing and immediately felt the need to breathe in. In his initial fear, he'd forgotten to take a breath. He'd never wanted oxygen more. The desire to return to the original tunnel became overwhelming.

James tugged at his arm and Mark was pulled down further. Five seconds, James had said, but it was more than that. His whole body ached.

Mark *needed* to breathe, and they were pushing out now, their bodies horizontal. James was swimming in front of him, flitting in and out, a strange creature pushing on ahead. Mark grabbed at him below a moving knee, and the two were plunged further under.

It was taking too long. Mark's mouth opened in a silent, breathless scream. He felt himself grow distant and he punched out at the space in front of him, clawing for something, anything. He couldn't help it, his lungs screamed open, and he took in the water.

Lighter now – light – and, and they were moving up and James was pulling him and then they were standing, and Mark was coughing and spewing water and then, and then . . . he could breathe.

He took in great gulps of air, hungry for it, marvelling at it. Snot poured out of his nose. 'That was longer than five seconds,' Mark spluttered.

James was walking into the shallows. 'Only a bit,' he said. 'You were too hesitant at the start.'

James's demeanour had changed underground. He was more confident, cocky even. In the subterranean world, he showed initiative, while on the surface he was awkward, shy. Mark saw for the first time how strong James was. Though not tall, he was sturdy, with broad shoulders and big upper arms.

Mark sat down on the rocky ground, wet and cold. *Get me out of this place*, he thought. *Get me anywhere but here.*

It was a slow, ten-minute limp to the cave entrance. When he saw the blue sky and coastal trees, Mark felt like kneeling down and giving praise. Instead, he lay on the warm sand.

'I'll run back to the other entrance, get your clothes and bring my car around.'

'Sure,' Mark mumbled, exhausted.

'I'll be thirty minutes max.'

A plane flew overhead, and Mark lay back, trying to get warm.

I'm never going underground again. Mark wanted, above everything else, to just go home. To get out of this place with all its small town fighting and tragedy. He wanted to be in Booralama.

He watched as the plane kept moving, high, so high. Rose would be on one of those flights in two days. Virgin? Or was it Qantas? He couldn't remember. At this point, he didn't care. Already his fear was becoming distant, something he'd talk about at parties in the future, but they'd never know, and he wouldn't ever be able to fully articulate it.

The sun was warm, he could have a little nap. He might for a few minutes. Mark's mind wandered. A pilot friend once told him that Branson picked the name Virgin Blue to be purposefully Australian, even though the planes were painted red . . .

Virgin Blue.

Mark sat up abruptly just as James arrived in his ute. He got out and strode towards him, thinning hair still damp and clinging to his head, darkened, but red even so.

Richard Branson named his red planes Virgin Blue, because in Australia, the entrepreneur had learned, it was an old tradition to call redheads *Blue.*

A phone was buzzing. Mark turned his gaze to the small bulky figure before him.

'It's your phone,' James said, curious. He handed it over.

As he took it, Mark saw Nic and Mat were pulling up in their ute. He pressed the answer button.

Jagdeep. 'Vincent's talking.'

'Yeah?' Mark watched James move towards the brothers.

'We know where he got the bracelet from.'

'And?'

The three men stood in a triangle. Mark's ankle throbbed in a steady thud, growing faster.

'Vincent stole Eloise's bracelet from Mat Sinclair's car.'

CHAPTER 24

After getting dressed, Mark hobbled to James's ute, asking for a lift to his own car. He figured he'd be able to drive, since it was his left ankle that was injured. It hurt. It really hurt. Sweat poured down his forehead and he groaned when he lifted his foot inside the passenger seat of the vehicle.

James opened the driver's door and got in. 'You okay?'

'Yeah,' he said. 'Thanks for getting me out, even though I hated every second.' *And it wasn't five seconds.*

'You did well.'

'How did you know we were here?' Mark asked. 'And where I was in that tunnel?'

'Gerri told me. I came along, and when the others couldn't find you, I just backtracked. I know this area pretty well.'

The Sinclair brothers leaned into the window, apologising to Mark for losing him in the caves. They shouldn't have gone so fast, they should have checked on him, they forgot other people weren't as comfortable as them underground.

Mark cut them short. 'Mat, we want you to drop by the station. Head there now – my colleague will meet you.'

Did he imagine it, or was there a subtle look between the brothers?

'Is something wrong?' Mat ran a hand through his blond hair.

Mark simply restated that he should head to the station. That he could bring someone if he liked.

'By someone, do you mean a lawyer?' Nic frowned.

'Just be there soon,' Mark said. 'I need to get my foot sorted. Where's the clinic?'

James started the vehicle, and Nic rapped on the bonnet, the gesture more absentminded than anything else. In the rear-vision mirror, Mark watched their figures recede, two dark blobs in the light of the paddock, the sea a brilliant background.

Hot stabs of pain shot through his foot and up his leg as James drove him back into town. The dark tunnels and underwater swim seemed an age ago, and in his memory the voices of the Sinclair brothers in the tight space took on a thin and reedy tone.

'You've been in those caves before, have you?' he asked James.

'Lots of times when we were kids,' James answered, eyes on the road.

Mark's whole body ached. God, he felt like spewing. 'Anyone ever called you Blue?'

The man looked at him as if he was mad. 'Blue? No, why would they?'

Mark shrugged.

'Sometimes people call me Doyley, or Doyles, or Jimmy, but that's usually about it.'

'Anyone else around here called that?'

James frowned. 'No. No one.'

They pulled up at Mark's car and he got out, vaguely listening as James shouted directions for the clinic. Getting in the driver's seat was agony. There was a T-shirt on the seat beside him and he rubbed it over his head, drying his hair.

He pulled out onto Bay Road. A P-plater overtook him, the car skirting dangerously into the uneven sides of the road before righting itself and speeding off. Young people's brains aren't fully developed; they value reward over risk. When he first had his licence, he used to drive out of town with mates, do burnouts. There'd been cans involved, he was sure, probably smoking.

But sneak diving? Would he have done that? The kids around here were on another level.

He pulled right in front of the medical centre and parked in the five-minute bay. He was in too much pain to be a good citizen. Inside, the line stretched to the horizon and back again. Old ladies coughing, a kid with an arm at a weird angle, and three old men who all looked perfectly fine. A cluster of toddlers with snotty noses, a mother with an eye patch, a tradie holding his ear.

Mark rang Jagdeep, letting her know where he was, and that Mat should be with her soon.

She texted back: *Mat's just arrived with his two brothers.*

All three Sinclair boys, interesting.

A nurse came up to him and took a brief look at his foot before helping him into another waiting room.

'I'm a policeman investigating the Sinclair and Swinson cases,' he said. 'Any chance we can hurry this up?'

The nurse felt around his ankle. He grimaced.

'Could be broken,' she said. 'You'll need X-rays. I'll see what I can do about getting you looked at earlier.' She handed him some paracetamol, a glass of water and an ice pack.

'I knew Eloise Sinclair when I was in high school,' she said as she was raising his foot onto a stool. 'Not well, but well enough.

She was really smart and so attractive. It would have been very easy to hate her, but you couldn't, because she was so bloody nice. We were both trying to get into a Rotary youth exchange program. She wanted to go to France, and I remember thinking that was kind of sad, because, you know, her mother was French, and she'd died when Eloise was little.'

The sitting down, the water, the leg raising: Mark was already beginning to feel better. 'Did she end up going?'

'I heard her application was successful but she wasn't allowed to go in the end. Her older brothers wouldn't let her do anything, so bloody overprotective. There was this surfing holiday they all went on, to Indonesia I think, and they didn't even ask her.'

'Really?'

'Yeah, she was pissed off. But I remember the French exchange, because Eloise said she'd go anyway, later. I know that she'd already applied for her passport – we sent off the forms together. When she went missing, that's what I thought she'd done – finally left Broken Bay. I was actually pleased for her.'

Mark jotted down some notes while the nurse popped her head out the door to talk to another medic. When she returned, he asked her what she thought happened to Eloise.

The nurse looked at her watch and shrugged. 'I think she found a sinkhole and checked it out. It's not uncommon. She couldn't tell her family, because they were so careful about her – especially after her father was involved in the recovery of the Franklin Three.'

'But Eloise couldn't dive.'

'Apparently.' The nurse made a dismissive sound. 'Who knows?'

Mark nodded. He'd thought about this. But still, something nagged. 'Did you know much about her boyfriend Brett?'

'Only that he was the best-looking boy around,' the nurse said, grinning. 'But also, the worst of boyfriends. He had octopus arms, if you know what I mean.' She waved her hands about, mimicked hugging a shapely figure.

'Why didn't she get rid of him?'

A man walked past the cubicle, groaning and holding his stomach. 'Who knows?' The nurse waved as she walked out. 'Maybe she didn't really care.'

Hours later, X-rays completed, a badly sprained ankle confirmed and strapped, Mark was able to go back to his hotel. The nurse practitioner said that he was technically allowed to drive his automatic car, but it wasn't the best idea. Mark listened carefully and then drove to the Hibernian, where Ian looked on in confusion as Mark clambered out of the car with two crutches.

The next thing Mark remembered was being woken up by knocking on the door. It was Jagdeep plus fish and chips. He could have kissed her.

Jagdeep, admiration in her voice, explained how they had got Vincent Stabley to talk. Richardson had quietly and patiently begun listing what the police would do if Stabley failed to speak. One: they'd let the word out he was a longstanding thief in the Broken Bay area. Two: they'd tell Celine where the bracelet came from, maybe show her photos of the day Juliette Sinclair was found wearing it after she'd drowned in the bay, her swollen, mottled arm. Three: they reminded him of his time in jail, let him know who else might be in the cell beside him when he got put back in for violating parole, including one of the blokes who'd bashed a young man to death with a fence post. They'd do it all, Stabley, Richardson said. Or, he could talk.

Stabley talked. Admitted he'd been stealing from people in town since he got here, call it habit. Just small things from unlocked cars – designer bags, wallets and laptops. He'd taken the bracelet and a few other rings from Mat's car for the simple reason that Mat had ripped him off on a sale. Mat had bought a necklace from Vincent for thirty dollars, only Vincent later found out it was from Tiffany's. He knew this because Celine told him, and Celine knew her Tiffany's. Mat owed him.

Mark was impressed. At Richardson, and Celine.

'Stabley said that Mat's a drug addict,' Jagdeep went on. 'Low grade, but needs to steal to keep his habit up. No proof, of course, but it is interesting. And the reason Stabley was hiding behind the fridge when we found him? Mat called to warn him, even though he hated him – he told Stabley he didn't want word getting out about the drugs.'

Jagdeep ate potato cakes and picked at the chips while Mark drank a beer and ate everything else. His foot throbbed, but he was enjoying himself. The paracetamol and beer helped. Mat a drug addict: he wrote it in his notepad.

Jagdeep and Richardson had then spent two hours inter-viewing Mat, and, separately and with less intensity, his brothers Nic and Phil.

Mat was insisting that Vincent had planted Eloise's bracelet in his car, and that he and his brothers had no idea how it got there. In all honesty, Mat said, he couldn't be sure it was the bracelet that had been his mother's and then his sister's. He'd forgotten what it looked like. It had been a long time since both of them were around. In a quiet moment, after a general chuckle about the state of the coffee in the station, Richardson had presented the scenario that Mat, fuelled by drugs, had killed Eloise in a fit of rage, then pushed her body down the sinkhole and left her to drown. Mat had scoffed and asked Richardson how could he do that, if he didn't even know where the sinkhole entrance was. And why would he do that to his little sister, who everyone knew was a much-loved member of the family? And wasn't she found in a full wetsuit and mask? How would he wrangle that?

All in all, Jag said, the three brothers appeared genuinely confused as to why and how the bracelet had turned up in one of their cars. 'I just don't understand,' Phil kept saying. 'I don't get it.'

Mark was tired. He cracked open another beer. 'I don't understand it either. But today I saw a different side to those Sinclair boys, a not altogether charitable one.'

Were they laughing, he wondered, when he went down the wrong tunnel in the cave? Were they pressed up against the sides, whispering to each other about how stupid he seemed? Though they were men in their late thirties, early forties, there was something schoolboyish about it. Cruelty overlaid with cheap humour.

'There's something else,' Jagdeep said. 'Jane rang with an initial report about forensics from Cherie's place. The size eleven footprint? They did a botanic analysis on it. All consistent with Cherie's front yard, but for one thing.'

'What's that?'

'Fibres of cow manure.'

Mark whistled. The dairy-farming Doyle family seemed to hold all the answers. Redheads. Small, stocky people. Size eleven feet. Knowledgeable about caves. A body found on their land. Nothing solid to charge anyone with yet. But questions to ask.

'And get this,' Jagdeep added. 'I checked out what books and files Cherie was interested in at the library.' Here, Jagdeep gave him a knowing smile. 'Your friend Liz seemed very sad it was me and not you who was investigating.'

'Me and Liz, we're getting married.' Mark made a heart sign with his hands.

'Cherie was mainly interested in local history and, perhaps more importantly, the section of land now owned by Phil and Judy Sinclair.'

'So, what's your theory? Sounds like boring reading, to be honest.'

'Not entirely sure, but I know that Frank Doyle sold some land to Murray Sinclair when he went bust in the lobster industry. That was right after Juliette committed suicide. Soon after, they moved out to where they currently are now. What's weird is the Doyles' land has, on balance, and especially now, done well. The Sinclairs' land never has.'

The two detectives fell quiet. Mark remembered the ramshackle Sinclair house, the geraniums haphazardly thrown into a pot by the door, the collection of family photographs. The whole place had a sense of hopelessness about it. He didn't remember many trees on the property but what he did remember, which was odd, was the sturdy fence that bordered the Doyles' land. Mark remembered fencing, that hard, hot work. On his friend Stitcher's property, he'd had one of the worst days of his life, the holy trinity of hell: a forty-degree day, a hangover and fencing.

'Good work, Jag,' Mark said finally, looking in admiration at his friend. 'Meanwhile, I was getting lost in a cave.'

Outside, the sky was turning from orange to dark grey. A family of four walked past, each with a suitcase on wheels. 'Mum,' the young boy said, 'when you're dead, are you still you?'

Mark strained to hear the answer, but the clattering of the luggage drowned it out.

'So, what's happening with the Eloise Sinclair file?' Jag kicked off her shoes and contemplated her socked feet.

Mark told her about the maps and his theory that the cattle trough had been moved after Eloise's disappearance. Jagdeep nodded slowly, taking it in.

'Also,' Mark said, 'Blue was used as a nickname for redheads. I should have known that straight away – one of my mother's friends was called Bluey. Thing is, they've all got grey hair now, so you can't tell they were once gingers.'

The two friends sat on the beds eating their chips. Despite their weariness, and the events of the day, it felt collegial, easy.

'I'm going to Rose's going away party tomorrow, just one night. Then I'm hoping to come back here, hand over to whoever the new team is and head home.'

'You could talk to Brett Twymann while you're in Adelaide.' Jagdeep offered. 'He's back from overseas now, flew in last night. He called the station while you were having your cave adventure.'

She gave him Brett's details and he jotted them down.

When she left, the room felt smaller somehow.

CHAPTER 25

Before he left for Adelaide, Mark made two phone calls: one to diver David Furneaux and one to Margery. In the first call, David gave Mark a brief description of the main chamber the sinkhole led to, and the entrance itself. Mark asked, among other things, whether or not the sinkhole entrance was an old one. David wrote down Mark's questions, said he'd get back to him after reviewing the initial notes made by Mya's team before she went down. She had always been thorough in that regard, he said: her studies in geology were what got her interested in cave diving in the first place. In the second call, Margery was more direct. Before he could speak, she told him that she couldn't talk. The ladies from book club were around and they were doing Helen Garner. She would speak to him later.

He should have known that *nothing* pips Garner in the book club world.

It was just after 9 am, another cerulean day and Mark's foot throbbed like a boom box. He took three paracetamol and drank a Berocca. Prue thought they worked; Mark wasn't so sure, but he did quite like the tangy taste.

On his way out of the motel, he told Ian he'd be back the following night, and could Ian hold his room for him? The owner nodded, took two angry bites of an apple, and pointed to a form that indicated Mark needed to pay for three beers and a small whiskey from the mini bar.

Mark paid, regretting his party for one. *You open Pandora's box, you pay the price.*

'Haven't left the room in a mess, have you?' Ian asked, grumpy. 'Hard to get cleaners and now that Cherie's . . .' He trailed off.

Looking at the man with new eyes, Mark shook his head. 'Were you about to say, "Now that Cherie's dead?"'

'I don't have time to clean up after pissheads,' Ian said. 'Cigarette butts, beds unmade, cans chucked everywhere.'

'Yeah? You're pretty fond of chucking cans around yourself.' Mark shook his head. 'Saw you on tape, off your tree throwing a can into the bushes outside the pub on Friday night.'

'Couldn't have been me then. I don't drink cans,' Ian said and reddened, realising his mistake too late.

'What's that?' Mark's mind raced. Ian complaining about Cherie to Barry, the grainy video of him throwing something the size of a can or smaller into the bushes.

'Wait, you took Cherie's phone!' Mark said, incredulous. 'After she annoyed you with all those photos, you tried to get rid of it. She told me she thought someone stole it.'

Ian didn't deny it. Red-faced and blustering, he fussed about with a stack of brochures.

'You've hidden important evidence, Ian.'

There was a jangling of the door and a woman walked in, her musky perfume enough to nuke a whole city.

'Don't leave town,' Mark said, not bothering to shield Ian from embarrassment. 'The police will need to see you this morning.'

'I . . .' Ian stammered, looking at the woman who was now frozen in place, mouth open.

'You've hampered a murder investigation.' Mark stomped out the door.

After ringing the station to tell them what he'd discovered, Mark drove to the Royal and searched for Cherie's phone. *Bloody hell*, he thought as he sifted through the bushes, wearing latex gloves, and trying to keep his sore ankle still, *why don't they hand out awards for this?* There was dried vomit, used condoms, cigarette butts and a dead rat. There were plastic bags, beer cans and a bottle of Bundy. There was a burned log, a woman's black top and a *Women's Weekly*. And there, among some hardy westringias and nestled between a Jim Beam can and an old hairbrush, was a cracked iPhone.

Chiara arrived and Mark handed it to her, telling her to get it to IT straight away.

'I'm not stupid,' Chiara said. 'I know to do that.'

'Sorry.' Mark paused. 'It was a dumb thing to say.'

Chiara looked at him, and gave a small nod before turning away.

Mark, wishing he had some soap, washed his hands under a tap at the side of the pub.

'Hey, Chiara!' he called to her. 'What's the capital of South Africa? I'll give you five bucks if you can name it.'

Chiara's head poked back from behind her car. 'There's more than one. I'll give you fifty bucks if you can name them.'

He couldn't.

CHAPTER 26

Heading out of Broken Bay, west to Adelaide, Mark listened to Ed Kuepper. It made him nostalgic, as it always did, and with his pressed shirt hanging up in the back, he was reminded of his younger days, when he, Dennis, Stitcher and Squirrel would drive to Adelaide for a Saturday night out. His ironed shirt was bigger now – size L – and a modest navy blue, but in the early nineties it was more likely to have been a hideous salmon pink. Four shirts hanging in the car, arms dangling, collars still clean, hoping for a night out to remember. He would have been driving, Squirrel and Stitcher in the back, and Dennis in the front passenger seat, elbow resting out the window, his luxurious hair blowing in the wind. They had been so hopeful then.

Mark tapped his finger on the steering wheel. He slowed down for a sign indicating a children's crossing, but he could see no children or schools. He sped up again, past the ghost children, and returned to his earlier thoughts. It was the small things he and his friends had wished for then: a girl to kiss that night, drinks with mates, laughs and the city lights. It was about the possible.

Now, what was possible? He'd been married once, couldn't see it happening again, not the big show anyway. His kids were doing well, his job was secure. How could he dredge up that sense of possibility now?

Mark was almost in Unley, waiting at traffic lights, when a sign for the Fullarton Home for the Aged caught his eye. With a jolt of surprise, he recognised it as the place where Bernadette Doyle now lived. He weighed up the options in his mind: he could go, on the off-chance of learning something, or he could get to Rose's family home earlier and catch her just before the party started. The traffic lights turned green and, at the last moment, he indicated right and followed the sign.

The residential village wasn't difficult to find, thanks to a billboard in muted tones showing two elderly people smiling benevolently, urging him to 'Come and live the good life'. Mark parked near reception. Clipped hedges of rosemary lined the wraparound porch, a large camellia bloomed hot pink in a pot beside the door. The sliding doors opened without a sound to a neat reception desk, where a woman was working, her back towards him.

'Hello?' Mark asked, when she didn't turn. 'I'm wondering if I could visit Be—'

'Oh sorry!' The woman swung round, a sheaf of papers in her hand. 'I'm new here and I'm just getting the hang of it. Barbara will be back this evening.'

'I'm here to see Bernadette Doyle,' Mark said, polite. 'Would you be able to tell me what room she's in?'

'Oh, sorry again! Visiting hours are over and Barbara said that we shouldn't let anyone in past them, as the residents need their rest.'

Mark's shoulders slumped. 'I see,' he said. 'That's a shame.'

'Have you driven far?' The receptionist's voice rose in concern. 'I'm sorry!'

'From Broken Bay,' Mark said, a little sadly. 'Four hours' drive from here.' He was pulling the country card. The long drive, the innocent ignorance of city administration.

'Four hours!' She looked as if she was going to start crying. 'And are you family?'

Mark looked at her, then inward at himself. 'Yes,' he said, after a pause. 'I'm her son.'

'Her son! And you've driven four hours? Oh my god!'

Is she about to flay herself?

'Yes.' He made his face as solemn as he could and stared down at his crutches.

'Go on through,' she said, shaking her head. 'I swear, no matter what Barbara says, it's wrong if a son can't visit his poor mother after a four-hour drive from the country.'

'You're a good person'—Mark looked at her name tag—'Destiny.'

'Thank you,' she said softly, eyes demure. 'I appreciate that.'

The reception smelled like flowers, but beyond the doors, the hallway reeked of old skin and Dettol. Mark's crutches and his one shoe made a sticky sound on the floor, and with the white walls and cheap prints of valleys and cows and thatched country houses along the wall, he felt older with every step. His mother would have hated such a place. 'Put a pillow across my face when I can't look after myself!' she'd regularly said. 'Or shoot me in the head! I don't care.' So many people said that, but really, who would be tasked with such a job? Hard to press down the pillow on a struggling face, point a loaded gun at a loved one's head.

Bernadette Doyle's room was 103. When he knocked on it, there was no answer. Mark knocked again, unsure of the protocol. A nurse came hurrying past.

'It's out of hours. Have you signed in?'

'Yes,' he said. 'I came to see Bernadette Doyle, but I'm not sure if I should just go in. She might be sleeping.'

'Oh, there's a high chance of that,' the nurse said and gently opened the door for him. 'Mrs Doyle!' he said in a soft voice. 'Someone to see you!' The nurse turned to him. 'What's your name?'

A beat followed.

'Mark Ariti.' He couldn't lie straight up again, he just couldn't.

'Mark Ariti's here to see you, Mrs Doyle,' the nurse said, waving for him to enter the room, then closing the door after him.

A single bed lay in the middle of the room, made up in a pink bedspread and white sheets. On it lay a tiny sleeping figure, propped up with pillows, mouth agape, no teeth.

'Hello?' Mark stepped into the room. A whiff of urine and something masking it – Domestos – filled his nostrils. He refrained from covering his lower face.

He hobbled towards the bed and looked at Bernadette. If she was the same age as her husband, she was around seventy-five years old. Here in this bed, she looked ninety-five. 'Mrs Doyle?'

Her dark eyes flickered open and fixed him with a dull gaze. 'James?' she asked.

'No, my name's Mark.'

Mrs Doyle sighed heavily and sunk back into her pillow. 'Geraldine needs to collect the eggs.'

Mark agreed she did.

The old lady raised a feeble hand and coughed before the hand made it to her mouth. Spittle ran in a thin stream from the side of her lips. Mark shifted on his feet, unsure of what to do.

'And tell James that there's a bloated lamb in the paddock near the house. It needs to go in the pit. There's flies everywhere and Frank won't do it.'

'I'll tell him.' He found a tissue on the bed and dabbed at her mouth with it.

'Good boy. You were always such a good boy.'

Bernadette's hand stretched out and after a moment's hesitation he took it, feeling the paper-thin skin and bony fingers. He'd been holding one of his mother's hands when she died, Prue holding the other.

'You've got no hope with her.'

Mark paused. 'With who?'

Bernadette muttered something and he leaned in close. Nothing. He couldn't make out what she said.

'A drink, Mrs Doyle?'

The old lady nodded, or maybe she'd fallen asleep again, but even so, he found a cup of water on the bedside table.

'Drink?'

She blinked, and her head bent forward obediently as he lifted the cup to her lips. She took one, two small sips before falling back onto the pillow.

The old woman's eyes closed again. Mark put the cup down and saw a black-and-white wedding photo of Bernadette and Frank on the table. The bride, pretty in her Little Bo Peep dress, stood almost half a head taller than her stern-looking groom. In another frame was a Catholic prayer, the 'Act of Contrition'.

Jesus, Mark thought. *A perfect pair.*

'You're a bad person.'

Mark turned, but Mrs Doyle's eyes were closed and her mouth had fallen open. He felt a deep chill in his bones.

Quiet snoring came from the bed: she was asleep. A tree outside her window bent and swayed in the wind, clouds scuttled across the sky. At least she had a view. Mark stared at the tree, the limbs stark against the blue sky.

He took one last look at Bernadette Doyle, her frail shape in the bed, and left as quietly as he could out her door. Like a thief, he stole back down the hallway, past the empty reception desk and was slowly making his way down the front steps when a voice called him back. It was Destiny, flying towards him despite holding a box under one arm and carrying a bag in the other.

'It's James, isn't it? You may as well take these now. I know Barbara was waiting for one of you to collect the rest of Mrs Doyle's things after the move to the smaller room. Here's the last of it! We just cleared that cupboard to save you some time. Your sister said she was coming up during the week, but we all get busy, don't we? So here it is! You don't mind, do you?'

There wasn't much he could do. Mark thanked Destiny and with her help packed the two items into the boot of his car. He would have to drop them off somehow, come clean to Gerri and send them to her.

On the drive out, he thought about the crimes he'd just committed – giving a false identity, entering a care home by deception, taking goods willingly and without declaring who he really was. And that didn't count the fact that he was now planning to examine the items, take careful notes. Mark remembered with a snort one of the many sayings he'd read on Cherie Swinson's wall: *Destiny gives you the tools, you make the decisions.*

Houses flashed past him, hidden by lush gardens and high fences. *No one knows what other people know*, Mark mused, and the thought gave him no pleasure.

The visit to Bernadette had made Mark late, and he arrived at Rose's at the same time as a large group of relatives and noisy friends. Other than a quick chat with Rose and pleasantries with her parents, he barely had time to collect himself and check his ankle before dinner began.

Mark was disappointed to find himself seated between an aunt and a cousin. There were too many people at the table; they all had to move along and squish in, everyone's arms pinned to their sides like in *Riverdance*. Over the din of cutlery and chatter, Mark turned to the aunt, introduced himself and listened to her as she spoke for fifteen minutes about her trip up the Rhine on a boat. It was for her seventieth birthday. She'd been to Germany once before, but not for thirty years. That time, she'd travelled mainly to Berlin. It was incredible for the history, but dirty – and honestly that Spree was worse than the Yarra. Couldn't the council there clean it up?

'The Yarra or the Spree?' Mark asked.

'Oh, both!'

Out came the roast lamb and tiny potatoes. Cologne was the aunt's favourite part of the most recent trip. The Cathedral, the old town, and the Hohenzollern Bridge. Honestly, she could have gazed at it for hours! Wasn't it just marvellous?

Oh yes, Mark agreed, his mouth full of meat. There's nothing like the Hohenzollern Bridge.

After five minutes more, Mark turned his head to the cousin. He hadn't been back to Adelaide for years, practically a Melbournian now. The rooftop bars! The graffiti alleyways (artful) and the music scene. Coffee! Just last week, he'd seen an all-girl synth-pop band in a hidden Fitzroy bar. Everyone was dressed in steampunk and the place *went off*. He wasn't dressed in steampunk, he had his chinos and RMs on and my God he felt like a dick. But the music was just wonderful. What's not to like about eclectic style?

Nothing, Mark said. Absolutely nothing. But how dirty did he find the Yarra?

The cousin stared at him, blank. 'What?'

Mark's head swivelled back to the aunt, who told him that she had irritable bowel syndrome, so wouldn't be eating the bread. She'd hated Perth ever since she went to Rottnest Island and was bitten by a quokka. The aunt held the back of her hand up to his face to show him the bite marks. Her mottled skin looked like pale vomit. Was she expecting a kiss?

He drank some wine.

Dessert was placed in front of him. He looked down at it; something wobbly – panna cotta?

His neck hurt.

Across the table and to the right, Dennis was sitting back in his chair, a group of people laughing at something he'd just said. His friend picked up a glass of red and took a gulp, winking at him from across the way. At the other end of the room, Donna and Squirrel were deep in discussion with Rose's parents. Everyone was having a good time.

'Mark!'

It was Rose, walking towards him like something from a movie. Aunts, cousins, waiters blurred in her wake. Was there a soundtrack to her approach? There was in his head. He stood to greet her, giving her a kiss, then hugging her like a life raft.

'Why are you sitting here? You should be up with the fun lot.'

'My place marker said here.'

'You should have swapped it! I would have. I'll kill my sister for putting you here – it would have been torture beside those two.'

'I've learned quite a bit.'

Rose was wearing bright red pants with a pink shirt, unbuttoned dangerously low. Her hair, a light caramel, was tied with a red clip to one side. She was, to Mark, the most beautiful thing he'd ever seen.

'Rose,' he said. 'Save me.'

She smiled and led him to a corner, helping him with his crutches. 'Are you liking the party?'

'I am now.'

Rose gave a great sigh and slumped down on a couch. He slumped beside her.

'Just my luck, I move to the country for a placement and meet the hottest dad in town. Now I'm leaving, and the hottest dad won't come with me.'

A shout from the corner of the room and a woman in a slinky green dress got up to dance to Depeche Mode, beckoning Dennis to join her.

'Actually, does Dennis have kids?' Rose asked, after a moment.

'Yes, a son.'

'Well, you're the hottest *cop* in town then.'

'I'm the only cop,' he said, smiling.

'I know.' She smiled back at him. They were grinning at each other, unable to stop. He'd mentioned it to Donna one time, how Rose made him grin like an idiot.

'If you meet someone who makes you smile like that, don't let them go,' she'd said. 'Squirrel may be a fuckwit, but he makes me grin every single day and I'm better because of it.'

'There's an English teaching program connected to the clinic I'm going to be working at.' Rose was brushing something off his shoulder. 'You could do that – teach while I'm at work.'

He nodded vaguely, looked around the room.

'Have you said hello to Grandma yet?' A coolness entered Rose's tone. It was probably to do with his lack of interest in her teaching proposal, but he couldn't find it in himself to dredge up any enthusiasm.

'No.' Mark hadn't said hello to Grandma. He felt tired of grandmas and cousins and aunts. But even so, as Rose left him to speak to a friend, Mark wandered over to her grandmother, who was sitting beside a girl with dyed grey hair. The two looked like twins, seventy years apart.

'Grandma, I'm sorry, but I *literally* have to pee.' The young girl looked up at her elder self in mock desperation and then left. Mark sat in her place. There was a short silence.

'*Literally*,' the old woman muttered derisively. She said something else before leaning over to Mark, saying loudly, 'Don't you hate people who say "literally" like that, and out of context?'

'Yes, I do,' he answered with fervour, before leaning over the table and pouring himself a large glass of wine.

Someone turned the music up and on cue the party guests relaxed their shoulders and wiggled their bums to the tune.

Mark considered Rose's grandmother for a moment. She wasn't quite eighty-five, so she'd have been a young woman in the sixties. This age group wasn't the silent generation anymore – it was the Beatles and the Rolling Stones and the Seekers. *We make the mistake*, Mark thought, *of thinking people older than us are ancient. We dismiss and disregard.*

Mrs Williams was tapping her feet. 'I love the Bee Gees, do you?'

'I don't mind them at all,' he said. 'My mother used to listen to them all the time.'

'My husband was more of a Robin than Barry, but he was just lovely even so.'

Mark nodded, smiling. 'You Should Be Dancin'' came on next. A few people started dancing, Donna and Rose among them.

'Is your mother still alive, Mark?'

Mrs Williams must have forgotten. 'Mum died last year,' he said.

'Oh, love.' She patted his hand. 'It's hard no matter how old you are.'

Mark blinked. It would catch him at odd times, the gulf his mother's death created.

Mrs Williams was doing a little jaunty move with her shoulders, the brooch of a harp shiny in the dimly lit room. Her husband had been dead for almost twenty years.

'Would you like to dance, Mrs Williams?'

'Heavens, yes! But you'll have to help me up.'

'You'll have to help *me* up.' He brandished his crutches.

Once standing, he held out a hand like a suitor and she took it, though she was quite steady on her feet. Leaning on one crutch and being creative with his upper waist, Mark found he could dance in a stilted sort of way. More people joined the small dancefloor. Barry Gibb launched into falsetto and little kids darted in and out of the moving group.

And then Dennis was doing the actual *Saturday Night Fever* moves and Squirrel had taken one of Mark's crutches and soon there was a limbo going on underneath it with Rose bending low. And as he and Mrs Williams did the twist, Mark thought that moments like these were the ones you remembered. Family and friends dancing: this was the stuff of life. In time, you would forget which rooftop bar in Melbourne you went to; you could mistake the Yarra for the Spree; but nights like these, he thought, as he grooved along with Rose's grandma, these were the ones to hark back to.

CHAPTER 27

The next morning, headache looming and ankle pounding, Mark searched around Rose's bathroom for Panadol. Finding some, he sat back on the bed and gulped them down with lukewarm water. Rose was still sleeping, her mouth open and face flushed. She always slept on her front, arms out to the sides like a starfish, legs taking up most of the space. Mark looked at her; silver threads ran through her caramel hair – he'd never noticed before. *Time*, he thought. *There is never enough.*

Mark's eyes fell to the box of Bernadette's papers lying on the floor. He'd brought it in from his car in case of a break-in – he didn't want any potential evidence going missing. He felt a pang of guilt, wondered how he'd explain his visit to James and Gerri. It wasn't hard to see that at some point in the near future, Destiny would come calling. But that did not prevent him from getting out of bed and rifling through the box. Lots of loose papers, letters to and from people, some photographs.

He didn't feel too good; he should give up drinking. He went to the bathroom and splashed cold water over his face.

Rose made a small groaning noise as if she was in pain: it was the tequila shots that did it.

Back to the papers. Shuffling through them, Mark came across a page filled with capital letters, all set out neatly. A child's writing practice? Mark examined it. The page had a series of the letter R, in capitals and lower case. RR and Rr and rr. He ran his eye down the page, puzzled.

A rustle in the bed as Rose yawned and stretched, gradually opening her bleary eyes.

He made them both cups of tea and they sat up in bed to drink them. She was hungover, but happily so, and her recounting of the night was peppered with things she still needed to do for her trip. Despite her proclamations of missing him, she clearly couldn't wait to go.

'Mum and Dad say they're coming over at Christmas to visit me. I'm taking them to the Serengeti.'

Mark made an interested sound.

'My sister is coming too, just for a two-week holiday in Feb.'

This was another conversation they'd had. Mark felt tired. He could bring the boys to Tanzania for a short break, of course he could. They'd have a good time, a great time even. And then what? He'd come home and wait another four months for a visit? Six months? There were only so many days he could take off work.

'Your sister doesn't have kids.' Mark didn't like the petulant tone that had crept into his voice. But they'd been over this.

Rose was silent.

He picked up the paper with the letters on it again, looking at it dispiritedly. Rose's cheek rested on his arm. Mark shut his eyes. He could fit in another hour's sleep before his trip back home.

'What's this? Where'd you get this?'

Mark's eyes flicked open. Rose was looking at the page in his hand. He gave a vague explanation, asked her if she knew what it was. She sat up, looking at the paper, her head cocked sideways, mouth in a thinking pout.

'Well?'

'This is a genetics chart.' Rose's voice was matter-of-fact. 'Looks to me like whoever did this was interested in red hair.'

'Yeah?'

'See here.' Rose's finger hovered over the page. 'Red hair carries on through . . . This person had red hair, this person had brown hair, this person had blond hair.'

Mark studied the charts again. 'Are these two different families then?'

'Seems so. Look, this family is predominantly blond; this one has a majority of red hair. Did the woman who wrote this have red hair?'

Margery had said she did. 'Yes, and her children do too.' He couldn't remember about Frank.

'Interesting. Redheads are rare, only one to two per cent of the population. And who are this other family, the blonds?'

Mark had a fair idea. 'Another family in Broken Bay – the Sinclairs.'

Now that he could study it properly, with some sort of recognition, Mark began to look at the figures and work out the people attached.

'Wow, who's this unicorn?'

'What?'

'That one,' Rose said, pointing to the person below those most likely to be Gerri and Scott.

'I think his name is Ted. His mother is Gerri Doyle – bright red hair. Why's he so interesting?'

'He's got red hair *and* blue eyes. See? The person who wrote this has made a special note of it. That's the rarest combination in the world. Less than one per cent have it.'

'What do you mean?' Mark's mind whirled.

'Well, if his dad has brown hair, as this chart suggests, and his mum red – then that's rare enough. But it's the blue eyes with the red that's interesting. What colour eyes did the parents have? I'm guessing blue?'

Images of Gerri flashed before him, her holding the plate of food, telling him about Eloise soaring through the cypress pines.

'The mother has brown eyes. Red hair and brown eyes.' He remembered Bernadette's dark eyes and the brown eyes of Frank Doyle as he stared down from his tractor. 'The grandparents on his mother's side have brown eyes too.'

Rose cocked her head to one side. 'Well, the father probably has blue – that would be the most likely combination. Anything else is less likely. Could happen, does happen, but less likely.'

Crimes were rarely solved with less likely. It was the likely cops looked for first.

Outside, it was already shaping up to be hot. Tiny white clouds sat high in the sky, and the still morning air clung like an unwelcome hug.

They went for breakfast, then wandered around the lush garden. Their last morning together. The conversation was pleasant enough, but Mark was aware of an edge to it all. Rose's dry hand in his was loose – she kept breaking free of him to show him something, or to shout to a friend across the lawn. It grew hot and Mark half-wished he could leave earlier. He went to tell a story about the Franklin Three and then stopped; Rose wasn't listening properly. He felt irritated and was relieved when one of her sisters called her to say she should come say goodbye to her nieces.

'This isn't going so well, is it?' she said, and he didn't disagree.

In the end, like most farewells, it was anticlimactic. Mark drove away, and then had to return because in his hungover state he'd forgotten his phone. When he said goodbye a second time, Rose patted him on the hand like a friend. Only out of town, once he'd escaped the snarl of the city, did Mark remonstrate himself for the things he should have said. He should have told her he loved her, how much she meant to him. Were his last words to her really going to be, 'Okay, then. Ta ta'?

Ta ta? Jesus, he wouldn't blame her if she shagged the pilot on the way over.

It was around midday when Mark, thirsty, sweaty and with a throbbing ankle, knocked on Brett Twymann's door. One block back from Henley Beach, Brett's house was an impressive double storey, all wood and glass. A four-wheel drive parked outside the garage had one of those stick-figure families on the back. Three kids, two adults and a dog. Mark wasn't a fan of those cartoon declarations of #happyfamilies. Where were the customised stick figures of single parents, gay parents or fat blokes on lilos eating chips and scrolling OnlyFans?

The door opened and there was Brett Twymann, former heart-throb of Broken Bay. Rangy and weather-beaten, a messy mop of blond hair, tanned skin and white teeth – Brett reminded Mark of one of those old movie stars, like Robert Redford in his heyday, or Steve McQueen. The men shook hands and Mark followed as Brett, in bare feet and jeans, led him down the hall. Children's drawings lined the walls, a hallstand displayed a massive bunch of flowers, and in the main room, there was a kind of luxurious messiness that suggested comfort and ease.

'Want a drink?' Brett ran a hand through his sandy hair.

Mark sucked in his guts. 'No, thanks.'

'We got in from the Philippines Monday night. Boracay. Have you been there?'

'No, I haven't.'

'Bloody nice. Stayed in some condo, but there's little beach shacks I wouldn't mind going back to. Water's warm, good fish, friendly locals. You should go there.'

Mark waited for the man to collect himself.

Brett took in a deep breath, held his hands up in disbelief. 'Gotta say, I'm freaking out here. Eloise found in a sinkhole!'

'It must have been a shock.'

'Like you wouldn't believe.' Brett paced around the room, picking up soft toys and a drink bottle.

'Sarah's taken the kids to her mum's place so we can talk. I can't wrap my head around it. El's body in a sinkhole, and through a squeeze? She couldn't dive! Man.' Brett collapsed into a chair and stared out the massive windows to a backyard filled with toys and an inflatable pool. He hugged a stuffed elephant to his chest. The bottle fell from his arms onto the floor.

'Thanks for agreeing to this,' Mark said. 'I just need to ask you a few questions.'

'Fire away, Mark. I'll do whatever I can to help.'

Mark felt himself drawn to the man. It was the way Brett used his first name and not the usual Sergeant, or Ariti, the dishevelled way he held himself, the toy elephant, its little trunk peeping over the man's long arm. 'Can you just talk to me about Eloise? The day she left, your relationship – whatever. Just talk.'

'About Eloise?' Brett's voice shook. 'I don't know. She was . . . she was . . .'

Mark paused, retracted. 'Tell me about the town then, Broken Bay. You get back there much?'

Brett gave a half-laugh and wiped something off his knee. 'Not much. My parents live here now. We moved after Eloise went missing and Scott died. It wasn't too nice being around after that. My dad was probably always going to move anyway – he's a bit of a wheel and dealer, rubbed a few people in town up the wrong way. But Mum and I, we loved it there. When we first moved to Adelaide and I started at uni, I used to drive back to Broken Bay every weekend for footy. Every weekend! It meant I couldn't go out with new friends here, and I missed out on a heap of twenty-firsts. I used to wonder why the hell I was doing it.' Brett spread one hand on the arm of his chair and looked at it. 'But then, after I got down to the oval and said hello to the boys, I'd remember *that's it, that's why*. It's the teammates, the ones I'd known since kinder, it's the place, the old grounds and the smell of the sea. It's even the wind, believe it or not. I went back to Broken Bay every single week for five years,' Brett said in a kind of wonder, 'and look how they all treated me.'

Brett's hurt was real. Mark got it. In part, it had been the same for him, driving home week after week for footy, half-angry, half-relieved he was doing it. The push and pull of the old country town. *It's like a guideline*, he thought. *Holding you secure, down all the highways and back roads and through the little towns you pass. It's forever linking you to your past.*

The whole country must be filled with these invisible guide-lines. Young kids gripping tight, travelling down into the unknown, then finding their way back home. If the line is cut, you have to ascend on your own or keep pushing on. The man across from him had had his line cut, irrevocably, and it still hurt.

Mark asked Brett about his relationship with Eloise, nothing specific. It was an easy question, designed to loosen the man up, get him talking. The answer was standard: Eloise was a great girl-friend, they were happy together, they had fun, they liked being outdoors, they liked the ocean.

Brett's easy charm was wearing off and Mark's head was starting to hurt. He wanted a sleep; he needed a drink of water. 'If Eloise liked the ocean so much, why didn't she go spearfishing or surfing with you all?'

'She never wanted to.'

'Did you ever ask her? I've heard that you used to ask girls to watch you surf, but did you ever say *let's go for a surf*? Women got the vote a long time ago, you know.'

Brett clutched at the elephant and frowned.

'Why didn't Eloise go to Roti?'

'She couldn't surf. And she wouldn't have been allowed anyway.'

'She was eighteen. She could do what she wanted.'

Brett drooped even further in his chair. 'Eloise wouldn't have had a passport.'

Mark raised his eyebrows. 'Actually, she had applied for one years before – for the French exchange she also wasn't allowed to go on.'

Brett stood up abruptly, the toy elephant sent flying. 'You don't understand!' he said, his words bursting out. 'Her brothers . . . Eloise loved them, especially Phil, and he worried about her so much. Phil was still young when their father died and although they had someone in to help, it was him who pretty much took over the reins. He was that obsessed about keeping them all safe. And, you know, Murray had always put the wind up him about the Franklin Three. We were all terrified of that story – I know I was. So anything risky, too extreme – Eloise wasn't allowed to do it.'

'But the boys were.'

'They were *boys*.' Brett shook his head. 'Murray had taught them to spearfish, surf, scuba dive. Eloise didn't do any of it except snorkel. I've got kids of my own now, two daughters and a son. My wife'd kill me if I treated the girls differently, but back then and in Broken Bay – I dunno. Boys, girls, it made a difference to how you were brought up.'

He wasn't wrong. In Booralama, Mark was out drinking by the river at all hours by the time he was seventeen. Prue was too, only she had to lie about it.

Mark's ankle was beginning to throb again. He rested it on top of his other foot and considered asking Brett for a Panadol. 'So, is there anything you can tell me about the day Eloise went missing? Or the day prior? Something you might have forgotten in the initial police interview.'

Brett screwed up his face, then shook his head. 'No. I mean, I saw El down the street that morning and told her I was going for a surf and then snorkelling . . . I said she could come along if she wanted, and you know, read, or watch or whatever.' He gave a guilty smile. 'And then I said I was going to a barbecue, and she could come to that. She said she wasn't feeling well and then she left.'

'How was Mat?'

Brett gave a humph. 'Mat was Mat. We'd had a fight about two weeks before that, and he still wasn't over it.'

'What was the fight about?'

'The two of us went through a stage when we were a bit wild. Nothing much, just breaking into cars, taking them for a ride.

We took some stuff too, I remember that. Wallets, a phone. There was a bit of drugs, mostly weed . . . Stupid kid stuff.'

'You didn't tell this to police twenty years ago.'

'No, I didn't. Scared I'd go to jail or something, and really, it had nothing to do with Eloise. But I'd said to Mat I didn't want to keep doing it, no way. I was semi-planning on starting a business with Scott Boxhall, and I wanted to be all straight and narrow. Reputations are everything in a small town.' Brett sniffed. 'Anyway, Mat was pissed off at me, but I didn't care. It had been a long time since I'd been intimidated by the Sinclair boys. He got all fired up, said I was bailing on him, that I was cheating on El. It got a bit heated – one or two punches thrown. I think he got into trouble with his work because of it – with all the stickybeaks in town, word got out pretty quickly.'

Mark wrote a few things down. 'What do you mean, "a long time since I'd been intimidated by the Sinclair boys"? You were all friends, weren't you?'

Brett gave a half-laugh. 'Yeah, we were friends, and neighbours. We grew up together. But it was Scottie I was mostly close to, and Eloise, of course. Phil's okay – I didn't know him as much. But Nic and Mat weren't always the best of blokes.'

'Yeah?'

'They liked to play stupid pranks on kids when we were younger, found it funny. Locking kids in the toilets, leaving them in the sea cave – that sort of thing. There was never any harm done. Not that I know of.'

Mark watched Brett carefully.

'And it was probably because I was going out with their sister, but they never did anything to me. I escaped that side of them.'

Mark paused. Jotted down some more things.

'Were you cheating on Eloise?'

Silence.

'Brett?'

Brett sighed. 'Look, I'm not proud of the way I was then. I didn't always behave the best towards women and, yeah, it was true, I did cheat on her. I'm sorry about that now.'

'Was it with anyone in particular?'

The atmosphere had taken on that of a confessional. *Yes, my child?*

Brett lowered his voice. 'Oh, I don't know,' he said miserably. 'There were a few. A local girl named Liz, someone else on holiday – not sure of her name. Then there was this girl in Margaret River one time – she was from Cape Town – and another one from the UK, but I don't remember her name either. There was one girl from Torquay – she was a professional surfer – and yeah, this older lady from Sydney, maybe a few others. So, yeah. It was bad.'

Yeah, it was bad. Australian cricketer bad.

'There was also Cath – she's married to Nic now – and well, I think he knew about it too. He wasn't happy at all, pretty much cold-shouldered me. And in Roti . . .'

Mark leaned in.

'Well, that's the one I feel most bad about. Gerri Doyle. 'Cause she was best friends with El and, even worse than that, Gerri's boyfriend was my closest mate – Scott.'

Mark looked at the man before him for a beat, then thought of the photo he'd seen at the pub of Scott and Brett together, the one where they'd stood with Gerri and Eloise: it had reminded him of *Neighbours*. He flicked through his phone, remembering that he'd taken a snap of the image. And there it was: Brett with sandy hair and blue eyes; bright blue, rockpool eyes you could dive into. Scott had brown hair and his eyes were a deep hazel, just like his father, Chomp.

The Twymanns all had blond hair.

'Brett, are you the father of Gerri's son?'

A car whizzed past, loud music. Then it was quiet again. Brett raked his hands over his thighs. 'I don't know,' he admitted. 'I did ask her once, but she said no.'

A pause. 'Brett, did you kill Eloise so that you could be with Gerri?'

Brett's head snapped up. 'Are you *serious*?'

'I am.'

Again, that raking of hands over his thighs. It was unsettling. Back and forth, back and forth, like nails scraping a chalkboard. 'No,' Brett said, his voice cracking. '*No*.'

Mark looked down at his feet as Brett Twymann began to cry. 'Eloise was my girlfriend. I cheated on her, but I loved her, I did. I was stupid, such an idiot – but I would never, ever have hurt El.'

There was no indignation, no protest.

'On that last day – the day before we found out El was missing – Scott told me down the pier that Gerri was at my house wanting to talk about university. Yeah, right – university! That was how we got around it, we were both going to go to Flinders Uni, so we were "meeting to discuss it". We'd already had three or four of those "university meetings".'

Brett gave a harsh laugh, wiped his face of tears. 'But on that day, I didn't go. I looked at Scott and I had this revelation. Betraying my best mate and my girlfriend – what the fuck was I doing? I'd known Scott since I was a kid, and Eloise was probably the best girl you could ever have. I really did love her. I'd already told Gerri that I was serious about El. So what the fuck was I doing? I didn't go back to my house to see Gerri. Instead, I hopped on the boat with Scott and his dad and headed out to sea. That was it, I thought, all that shitty stuff I've done in my life is over. All the cheating and the stupid stealing shit. It's all going to be a fresh start, all of it. That's what I thought.'

'And that was the day before Eloise was reported missing?'

'Yes.'

Mark wrote it down.

Brett and his family had left Broken Bay for Adelaide shortly after Scott's death; the cloud of suspicion and rumour following them like a swarm of wasps. The dive shop, bought by Brett's father, was managed by someone else and they rarely returned, just Brett driving back to see his mates. Had Brett found his fresh start? Mark wasn't sure. Fresh starts were better with clean breaks. The man in front of him was wretched.

Before he left the Twymann house, Mark asked Brett if he could remember anything else that was strange or different – not necessarily from those few days, but the weeks after, or before.

Brett took a few minutes. 'No, nothing really.'

Nothing really? Mark waited.

'Just that, well, a few strange things. My bike was missing. I only noticed it a week or so afterwards. I'd just turned nineteen and people were telling me happy birthday and I just wanted to get the hell out of the house, I couldn't stop thinking about El, thought I'd go for a ride, get away from everybody. But yeah, I couldn't find it. That was weird. I liked that bike, it was a Stumpjumper – remember them? I didn't tell anyone about it, what with all the searching for Eloise. It just seemed stupid. I probably got stoned or drunk and left it somewhere months before and I wouldn't even have known. Anyway,' he said, 'it didn't have anything to do with Eloise, so why would I report it?'

Mark didn't bother answering.

'And also . . .' Brett hesitated. 'This is going to sound ridiculous, but . . . My hi-vis vest was hanging on the front porch one day, near all the boots.'

'And?'

'And I never took it out of my room. Scott's dad had sewed my initials into it, as well as the initials of the company we were going to start up. I loved that stupid vest and always kept it hanging up in my room. But one day it was there on the porch.'

'How soon after Eloise went missing did you see it?'

'I don't know. A few weeks? It was just after Scott died. No joke, I thought it was him come back to play a prank on me.'

'You never lent it to anyone?' Mark asked, busy with his notepad and pen.

'No. The only other person who wore it was Eloise. She liked to put it on, sit on my bed and read and whatnot. She said it was really warm. Sometimes in the smaller pockets I'd find little rocks she'd put there, or poems she'd written. I never kept any of them.' Brett's face fell. 'But she always knew where to hang it back up, she knew how much I liked it. One day, she wore it on the trawler. I've got a photo of her somewhere . . .'

'Can I see it?'

Brett looked around him as if he'd never been in the room before. After a few seconds, he stood, wandered into another room, and came back with a box of photos labelled 'Broken Bay'.

'Sarah sorted out all the photos a while back,' he said. 'It'll be in here.' He shuffled through a pile, muttering to himself, then pulled one out and showed it to Mark. Eloise was sitting on a trawler, gazing out to sea. With a start, Mark recognised it as the same setting as in the one he'd seen in the Royal.

'There's one like this up at the pub. Who took it?'

'James, probably. He was the photographer, gave a lot to the pub when Barry asked, old shots, new ones.'

'Who else would have been around in this photo? Looks like no one else is on the boat.'

'We'd have all been underwater. James liked to stay up with Eloise and talk, whatever.'

Mark studied the photo again. 'You think James liked Eloise? Had a bit of a crush?'

'Oh, yeah, why not? She was always nice to him.'

From the casual way he said 'why not?' it was clear that Brett wasn't a man too bothered about love rivals. Especially not one as unassuming as James Doyle.

'You ever call James Doyle "Blue"?' Mark asked.

Brett gave him a curious look. 'No, I've never heard someone called that. Why?'

'Just wondered.'

'James was okay, but no one ever really knew him that well enough to give him a nickname. I called him Doyley sometimes.'

Nicknames were mostly bestowed with affection. First thing at a new footy training, the coach asks what the new boys' nicknames are, and if they don't have one, they're given one. *Nicknames create closeness. Mostly.*

Brett passed Mark the photo. Eloise was half-smiling, shielding her eyes from the sun. And the hi-vis she was wearing – Mark could see embroidered initials, BBFR. She held a book, the cover facing away. It must have been taken the same day as the one in the pub, or a day very much like it.

'Know what she was reading?' Mark asked.

Brett looked at him strangely and shook his head. 'She was always reading. Could be a book on lobsters for all I know.'

Mark doubted that. But if it was, what would that mean? She was a diligent member of the fishing clan, took an interest in the family business. Books could say so much about people. Mark David Chapman read *The Catcher in the Rye* before he shot John Lennon, Charles Manson enjoyed *How to Win Friends and Influence People*, Mark's friend Squirrel liked *The Barefoot Investor* and Rose read second-hand *Lonely Planet*s.

'How's the old town looking anyway?' Brett asked, wistful.

Mark put the photo down. 'It's okay. I'm not an ocean person, but I'll admit the bay's pretty nice.'

'Yeah.' Brett's voice took on a tone of longing. 'There's one spot, just below the top of the cape, where if you hold your fingers and look through them like this'—he made circles with his hands and joined them together in a telescope shape—'you can see the whole of the town and the bay in one little circle. I always used to do it. Yeah, I just used to make that shape and look through it.'

Both men were quiet now, lost in thought.

'You don't still have the jacket, do you, the one Chomp gave you?'

Brett looked at him curiously. 'I do actually. Could never throw it away, couldn't really bear to look at it either. Not after Scott died. But yeah, I still have it.'

An idea was forming in Mark's mind. Loose, jumbled, barely taking shape. The dynamics of the group twenty years ago, loyalty, jealousy and tangled relationships. 'Can I borrow it for a few days? I'll get it back to you safely, I promise.'

On the way back to Broken Bay, Mark stopped at the side of the road, unable to concentrate on anything but the image of Brett peering through his hands, and the hi-vis jacket given to him by Chomp Boxhall. Reaching over to the back seat, he took the vest, studying it for a moment before unzipping two pockets and feeling inside each one. Nothing. He put it down, stared out the windscreen at the long road in front of him, straight, no curves.

Images ran through his head, sorting themselves, becoming ever more plausible.

He picked up the jacket again, remembered when he was just out of Year Twelve and got work as a bricklayer for the summer. It was long days and the money not enough, but solid work, the sort that earned you a beer right on knock-off. In those days, he wore a hi-vis like the one he held now. The tradies he worked with had boats, big utes and expensive toolboxes. They kept their keys in little pockets at the hem, on the interior of the jacket. He turned Brett's hi-vis inside out, took a closer look. And yes! There it was, a small inside pocket. Mark took a deep breath, felt inside and saw then what it was.

After handing him the jacket, Brett had apologised for rambling, for not being able to add anything new to the investigation.

Now, Mark reflected on his time with Eloise's former boyfriend and marvelled at just how much he'd learned.

CHAPTER 28

Mid-morning, and the paddocks looked like old sandpaper, rough and dry. It was quiet, save the sniffs coming from Gerri. James stood beside her, close but ineffectual. He's like air, Nic thought suddenly, always present but you hardly ever notice him.

Nic cricked his neck and looked without pleasure at the results of his morning's work: new fence posts he'd put in on the property line bordering the Doyles and the Twymanns. The posts reminded him of toy soldiers, lining up for war. But who to fight? he thought vaguely, swiping flies from his face. Everywhere you looked there were people to do battle with. Time dragged, and where the hell was Scott? They'd been waiting almost half an hour.

Mat was muttering, kicking up dirt as he spoke. '. . . and I tell you if this happens one more time . . .'

'Calm down, Mat.' Nic looked at his younger brother. He couldn't blame him, he was angry too, but this ranting, what good did it do?

A dot appeared in the hazy distance and the group watched as Scott's motorbike revved dangerously up the dirt track towards them, little fishtails for fun or show. Hot dust flew in his wake and by the time he'd joined them, he was filthy.

'What's up?' he asked, smiling. Even his teeth were covered in dirt. They waited while he spat and then wiped a hand across his mouth. 'Why'd you call me?'

Jagdeep rang Mark. IT had accessed Cherie's phone records and she'd receive them shortly. She'd also had another chat to Barry, whose alibi checked out. 'I think,' Jag said, 'that Barry was a little bit in love with Cherie.'

Love: that old chestnut, Mark thought with a wry laugh. But then he remembered Barry's stricken face, his strident defence of Cherie, his insistence that she was a good person. Maybe Jag was right, maybe Barry Coffey did harbour a secret love for Cherie Swinson.

'So, did IT give you any hints about what's in the phone?' He was driving past the Coorong lagoon, two hours from Broken Bay. Tea-trees, currant bush and mallee grass lined the water, and on its smooth surface pelicans drifted, their scooped beaks low, bowed heads looking for fish.

'Nothing much by way of texts and calls, but as Barry said, Cherie kept ideas in her notes app. Few things to look into. I'll have more info by the time you get back.'

'Great.'

'Also, Sean said to say he checked out the fatal crash Scott Boxhall was in. It was a collision with a drunk driver. Scott died on impact, while the other driver broke a leg and did community service.'

The pelicans were taking off; big bodies, but they made it look easy, wings outstretched, flapping and then soaring off over the ocean. Scott had been trying to get out of town, didn't make it. Any lingering suspicion Mark had about his death, however minute, was gone. Poor old Chomp. Poor Gerri and her son, Teddy.

'And,' Jagdeep asked, 'what about your news?'

Mark filled her in on Mat and Nic's love of pranks, his interview with Brett, Gerri's pregnancy, Brett and Cath, Brett and Gerri, the infighting, Eloise's frustration with her family. He told her about Bernadette Doyle and her puzzling words, 'She's not right for you.'

'It's so . . .' Jagdeep said.

'Interesting.' They both said it at once.

'Jinx.' They spoke together again, and laughed.

'Got to go.' Jagdeep hung up.

An hour later, Mark stopped for a coffee at Kingston and read his emails standing by the Big Lobster. His name was Larry. Mark patted its big crustacean legs with fondness. *Good old Larry.* Out of all the world's giant fibreglass marine creatures, Larry was Mark's favourite.

David Furneaux had replied to Mark's email regarding the age of the sinkhole on the Doyle farm. According to Mya's notes, it was most likely a relatively new one. He wrote:

> *The opening itself shows signs of recent collapse and the roughness of the sides indicates little effects of weather. Sunlight has not overly bleached the limestone, so it is likely that with the recent rainfalls, the sinkhole had opened in the last four weeks.*
>
> *Although Mya did not specify this, I know that where there is one sinkhole, there is most likely another close by. We hope to get back to the Doyle farm for further mapping as soon as the current investigation is complete.*

David signed off, and then added a PS:

Mark, Mya was one of our very best cave divers. She was experienced and responsible. The other diver that was found there, who I believe you have identified as Eloise Sinclair, is to be commended for her intrepid attitude and success in negotiating a tight restriction. Although clearly inexperienced, it is divers like her who continue to inspire and teach us. We hope to name the chamber after both women if permitted.

There was justice in it, Mark supposed: the girl who flew across the cypress trees and longed to travel to France, and the other a world champion in her own right. But what was significantly more important for the case was the likelihood that the two women had entered the underwater chamber from different entrances.

He drove on. Ibis wandered the shoreline, poking around like frugal shoppers at an outdoor market. Bin chickens, some called them. What do you say at the pub when you want to pick up an ibis? *I bin chicken you out.*

Mark thought about all he'd learned on his trip to Adelaide. He rang Jagdeep back, left a message asking her to meet him at the Doyles'. Then he rang Chiara and asked her and Sean to come too. He let Richardson know what he was up to, where his ideas were headed.

Finally, he called Rose. Wanted to say, *Don't go.* Hung up before she could answer.

CHAPTER 29

The sky was a pale blue, clouds racing to the sea, when Mark pulled up at the Doyle farm. Jagdeep was already there, talking to an anxious-looking James.

Mark clambered out of his car painfully, crutches waving like a broken Ferris wheel till he managed to right himself. Jagdeep hurried over to help.

'What do you need?' James asked. 'I've just been saying to the, er, detective here, that we're busy with Gerri's move and we—'

'Is Gerri here?' Mark winced as his sore foot hit a rock and the crutches slipped. 'Can you bring her out?'

Though clearly wary, James nodded and walked inside.

'Chiara and Sean will be here shortly,' Jagdeep said. 'Richardson's got them on that cow manure sample and Cherie's IT stuff.'

While they waited, Mark showed her the genetic chart he'd taken from Bernadette.

'Did you open a private note from a dementia patient without consent, let alone a warrant?' Jagdeep was stern.

'Well, now.' Mark shifted on his good foot. 'That's a strong way of putting it.'

Jagdeep glared at him before snatching it and staring at the page.

Engrossed in the details of hair and eye colour, Mark and Jagdeep were startled by the sound of a screen door slamming shut. Gerri had joined her brother on the verandah. The two siblings gazed down at the police officers.

'What's this about?' Gerri had her glasses on. 'I hope you've got something to tell us about the investigation – it's just been so stressful not knowing.'

The porch door opened again, and Nic and Mat Sinclair walked out too.

'The investigation is continuing,' Jagdeep said, purpose in her voice. 'It's why we need to speak with you all.'

'We just . . .' Gerri's voice trembled.

'What, what is it?' Scott moved towards her, concerned. 'What's wrong?'

'Your mate has been up to his old tricks again.' Mat threw a rock out across the paddocks, then picked up another. He threw it hard at a fence post, where it smashed and ricocheted near their feet. Crows scattered.

Scott shrugged and looked back at his motorbike. 'Yeah? What this time?'

'Brett got caught with Cath near the boatsheds,' Nic said.

'So? She's not your girlfriend, is she?'

Nic straightened, his shoulders back. 'Not exactly, but we're—'

'It's not just that,' Mat exploded. 'He's our sister's boyfriend! Eloise loves the slimy bastard.'

'I don't know about—' James went to speak, but Gerri laid a firm hand on his arm.

'*Brett's not perfect, I know.*' Scott threw his arm loosely around Gerri's shoulders. '*But he's a mate and—*'

'*He's a mate whose father is just about to buy your dad's dive shop. D'you really reckon he's going to keep it as a place to buy tanks and rope? He'll knock it down for sure, build apartments or some shit. Brett said his dad thought it was a "real bargain". The rich get richer and all that.*'

No one spoke for an uncomfortable beat. The sound of dry wind and, far off, a fence banging.

'*Well,*' Scott broke the silence, '*Brett can't help it if his dad's a prick. We don't hold it against James and Gerri, do we?*' He gave a forced laugh. No one joined in.

'*Look, Brett's no saint,*' Scott tried again. '*But who is? We've known him forever and that's just how it is. You lot should get over it, stop bitching about him. Brett may have been stuffing around with Cath, but face it, Nic, she's not even your girlfriend and it's Eloise he's really keen on.*'

Mat shook his head in disgust.

'*He's cheated on her — yeah, we all know that,*' Scott continued. '*I mean, come on, even Eloise knows that. But when it comes down to it, she's the only girl Brett's serious about.*' Scott studied a graze on his hand. '*So why don't one of you finally tell me why the fuck I'm here?*'

Gerri plonked herself down on the porch with a great sigh. She took her glasses off, threw Jag and Mark a half-smile, before holding her face in her hands. 'The waiting,' she said, shaking her head. 'It's all so horrible. I just want to know what happened to El.'

Mark was struck by a sense of deja vu. Gerri taking off her glasses, lapsing into distress. She'd done that in the video he'd seen of her talk in Perth. The putting on and taking off. Far from being spontaneous, it was more like a calculating act to disarm.

'We need to see the sinkhole again – where Eloise and Mya were recovered. Can you come with us?'

The twins nodded reluctantly; the Sinclair brothers rolled their eyes.

It was difficult to walk across the paddock using crutches, so Mark gave up on them, and relied instead on Jagdeep's help, her shoulder steady under his arm. James and Gerri strode out in front of them, almost touching, the Sinclairs following behind.

Despite the size of the paddock and the open air, Mark felt boxed in.

The northerly picked up again, flinging hot dirt in its wake. Mat felt his blood churn . . . He wasn't just angry about Cath and Eloise. It was everything. Brett had everything. A mother and a father. Money. All the girls. He didn't have to live in some shithole farm. And that punch-up they'd had a few weeks ago? Brett had told him he was on the way to becoming a loser with all the weed he'd been smoking. Said it was time to give up the dope and the stealing. Fucking Brett, he was two years younger than him! And all the while, the scumbag was cheating on their sister.

'It's not only Cath he's been with,' Mat said. He was being cruel, he didn't care.

'What?'

'Brett's been fucking your girlfriend too. Tell him, Gerri. Tell him what you and Brett have been up to behind Scott's back.'

James flinched and turned to his sister. Gerri's face turned white, and she reached out to Scott. She shook her head. 'It was just a few times in Roti, and we were really drunk. You and I had a fight and I . . .'

'You slept with him?'

'Yes, but I didn't ever—'

'Brett's my best mate.'

'Yeah, I know and I'm so sorry, Scott, I'm so sorry . . .'

There was a pause. Scott looked at Gerri, hard. 'You slut,' he whispered.

There was a tightening in the atmosphere, a squeezing. James stepped back, while Nic and Mat moved in closer to Scott.

'It's not Gerri you should be angry at,' Nic said, hands up in a conciliatory gesture. 'It's Brett – it's always Brett.'

CHAPTER 30

They all gazed again into the translucent water of the sinkhole. 'It must be so tempting for you,' Mark said. 'It's a wonder you haven't all been diving in here since it was first discovered.'

Gerri cleared her throat. 'The Franklin Three stories made us so wary.'

'Not Eloise though, she wasn't wary.'

'Eloise couldn't dive.'

'Couldn't she?' Mark asked. 'She looked pretty well equipped when they pulled her out. And she was found in that second chamber after the restriction – hardly a spot for beginners.'

A cool breeze whipped around the group.

'But *where* did Eloise enter the underwater chamber?' Mark asked. 'Because this one here'—he pointed to the sinkhole—'is relatively recent, only months old.' Everyone was still. Impossibly still. 'And what I'd most like to know,' he said, looking at the crumbling limestone around the entrance of the pond, 'is why the cattle trough in this paddock was moved after Eloise disappeared.'

Gerri rallied. 'I don't know what you're talking about.'

'It was there in the council maps before the disappearance.' Mark pointed to a space metres away. 'And then here afterward. Why?'

When no one answered, Mark barked, 'Get the tractor, please. I'd like you to move it now.'

'But it's Dad's new one,' James protested. 'He'd never let us use it.'

'*We're* requesting you use it,' Jagdeep said. 'So use it, *now*.'

A flock of birds flew overhead. Starlings? No, plovers. Mark didn't like plovers. As a boy, he remembered cowering in paddocks as they swooped him, then racing like hell for the house. An image came to him of Prue in full protective mode, taking her jumper off and swinging it wildly about her head to distract them as she yelled, 'Run! Run!'

Finally, James slumped off towards the shed. As he did so, Mat and Nic moved away, talking low to each other.

'Gerri,' Mark asked in the quiet moment that followed, 'who is Ted's biological father?'

She turned slowly to face him, her freckled cheeks deathly pale. 'What? I mean, why do you ask?'

'I've been to see Brett.'

Brett's got blue eyes, Mark might have added. *Scott had hazel eyes like his dad. You've got brown eyes like your parents. What's most likely?*

'James knows,' Gerri said nodding, voice low. 'But no one else – at least I don't think they know. Maybe some suspect. There was no reason to tell anyone.'

'You could have told Brett,' Jagdeep said. 'Him being the father and all.'

'I wasn't sure whose it was,' Gerri said. 'So I let it be Scott's.'

The tractor was now chugging towards them, pick-up fork already raised.

'Plus,' Gerri added, 'Brett didn't want to be with me. He loved Eloise. And I didn't want to be accused of trapping him. And when Chomp – that's Scott's father – found out I was pregnant, it made him so happy to think that . . .'

He'd have a grandchild from his son.

The tractor stopped, engine still running.

Mark nodded, then called to James, 'Five metres.' He indicated the spot. 'Not even – three metres – just move it.'

James turned the tractor and lowered the lifting fork, edged it under the tank and pushed. The old concrete structure barely budged. James revved the engine, pushed some more.

Gerri and the Sinclairs stood back, while Jagdeep and Mark stepped forward. The tank was moving now, bits of concrete crumbling off it, slimy water heaving, the weight of it leaving gouge marks in the grass. Nothing there.

'A bit more,' Jagdeep called to James. 'I see something. Different coloured rocks.'

The tank moved another metre.

'That's enough!' Gerri snapped, waving her hands at her brother. 'You'll ruin the tractor.'

Half a metre.

'I see it!' Jagdeep breathed, and so did Mark.

A quarter of a metre.

The edge of a round pool appeared: about one-and-a-half metres in diameter. Deep blue water beneath a thin layer of concrete dust.

James killed the engine, took his time getting out. They all stared at what had been revealed.

'The water level would have been much lower twenty years ago,' Mark said. 'Drought.' He took a few steps, peered in. Around the sides of the small pool were stone cuttings, edging down and into the water.

'I've read about those.' Jagdeep pointed at them. 'Old cenotes in this area have steps like this – farmers in the late eighteen hundreds used to make them as ramps for stock to walk down and drink.'

An old sinkhole then.

'You reckon this is the place Eloise first entered the chamber?' Jagdeep turned to Mark.

'I can't be sure, but I think so. I looked at the aerial images the council took before Eloise's disappearance and matched them against the search footage taken afterwards. The trough was moved, so yeah – I think this is how she entered the underwater caves.'

'And then it was covered up.' Jagdeep nodded to herself, before addressing the others. 'But by who?'

Gerri and James shook their heads in unison. Nic held up his hands. 'We're as surprised to see this as you are,' he said.

'Who covered up the hole?' Jagdeep repeated. 'And why?'

Mark patted his side pocket for his phone. He'd expected Chiara and Sean to be here by now.

'I don't know what you're suggesting.' Gerri looked at them squarely. 'But there's no way we could have moved that tank. We didn't even have a good tractor then. You can check. Dad only bought this recently.'

Nic's response was sharper. 'Are you really saying that someone sent our sister, who couldn't scuba dive, down there, left her to die and then covered up the hole? This is pathetic. We're going.' He made to leave.

'Stay put!' Jagdeep snapped. '*All* of you.'

'No one would ever want to harm Eloise.' James's voice was soft, resolute. 'She was the best of us all.'

'You're right,' Jagdeep said slowly. 'No one would want to hurt Eloise. Everyone loved her. Her brothers, her friends, the people in the town.'

'But it wasn't Eloise you all were angry at, was it?' Mark added.

'We could teach him a lesson though,' Nic said after a pause. 'We could really knock the wind out of his FIGJAM sails.'

Fuck I'm Good, Just Ask Me. That's what people called Brett behind his back.

'Have you told anyone about the sinkhole?' Nic turned to Gerri.

'No. Not a chance. Dad would kill us if he knew about this, and Phil would absolutely murder you two.'

It was true. After the Franklin Three, any newly discovered holes would be shut down, covered up, filled in. When a new one cropped up, they had to be kept secret from the olds.

'What new sinkhole?' Scott asked.

'James found it, just near here,' Nic explained. 'It's unbelievable. When we got back from Roti, he showed us. It's been here all this time, covered in shitty grass, and we never knew!'

James blushed as all eyes turned towards him. 'I was bringing the cows in, and I almost fell through it. It's the best one I've ever dived in. One of those old ones, you know, with levels carved out on the side. Dad doesn't know about it. Us here now, we're the only ones who know.'

'It's like some fairytale down there,' Mat said, half to himself. 'First time we went down there, I couldn't believe it. It's a different world, like you never want to come up to the surface again.'

Scott's eyes glistened. 'Why didn't you tell me? When can I go down there?'

'Soon, soon.' Nic was pretending to think. 'But first – we could use it to really wind up Brett.'

Gerri nodded slowly. She was still so, so angry at what Brett had told her the night before – that it had all been a mistake and he should never have got with her. If he'd said anything to give her some sort of hope, he said, well, it was only because he'd been drunk. The anger burned. 'He'd kill to dive the sinkhole before anyone else. I could pretend I've only just found it. That I haven't told anyone but him.'

Brett liked doing things behind everyone's backs, Gerri thought bitterly.

'We could do it this afternoon,' she said. 'Eloise is sick, she'll be in bed all day and Mum and Dad are in Adelaide.'

Another pause, then the others started nodding.

'You'll have to help us, Scott,' Nic said. 'Get Brett to go out to Gerri's or something. Tell him she wants to see him.'

'No, he's not coming to my house,' Gerri snapped. 'But I could write him a note.'

'Tell him to go back to his house then,' Nic suggested. 'We'll leave him directions to the sinkhole in his room, that's easy enough.'

'We're about to go spearfishing with Dad,' Scott protested. 'Brett won't have any need to go back home.'

'It won't be your dad's business anytime soon, Scott,' Mat said. 'It'll all be Brett's.'

Scott looked at the horizon, didn't reply.

'Just tell him I'm at his house then.' Gerri spoke. 'Tell him I've got some info for uni.' She avoided Scott's eyes. 'That'll make him come.'

*

'You were all angry at Brett for one reason or another. Nic, because Brett had been seeing Cath; Mat because of the fight and the petty theft and drugs; and Gerri because Brett loved Eloise and not her. James, I'm not sure what gripe you had against him but . . .'

Gerri turned towards Mark in fury. 'What *is* this? Shouldn't we be in the station if you're going to interrogate us? I'm going back to the house to call a lawyer.'

'Maybe it was loyalty to Gerri, or something else, but I think you were involved too, James. I'm just not sure how . . .'

Jagdeep and Mark stood with their backs to the water, the others in a semicircle around them.

'I'm not having any of it,' Scott said, after Nic laid out the plan. 'It's a fucked-up idea and don't tell me you haven't discussed it before; it's so rehearsed it's embarrassing. I'm embarrassed for all of you. What are we, twelve?'

Scott wasn't as stupid as the others thought, James knew. He liked Scott.

'It's the prank to end all pranks,' Mat said. 'Remember how obsessed Brett is with the Franklin Three?'

'Well, why would he want to go in this one then?'

'Are you serious? This is Brett we're talking about! It's a sneak dive, he'd kill to do this. He'll be terrified because of the Franklin Three stories, but the opportunity to be the first, to go down a sinkhole no one's been in yet? He'll jump at the chance. We all would.'

Scott walked to his motorbike and sat on it. 'You're all messed in the head.'

'So, you'll do it?' Mat asked.

'Scott.' Gerri moved towards him, arms up in a pleading gesture. 'Scott . . .'

'We're done,' Scott said, dismissing her. 'Don't come near me again.' He revved the engine and was off in a cloud of dust.

'The thought of his dad's business being sold to Brett's family – it'll make Scott wild,' Nic said. 'He'll do what we ask.'

James wasn't so sure. Scott had been brought up by a man who'd survived a shark attack: unlike others, he wasn't intimidated by anything the Sinclair boys said or did.

'Well,' Mat said, looking around. 'It's just us then, the old crew.'

But it wasn't the old crew, James thought. If it was the old crew, Eloise would be there. And in truth, he reflected, he had never been in the crew. Only on the side of it. 'I'm with Scott,' he said, stepping away. 'It's mad.'

'Remember when Brett got you lost on purpose in the sea caves?' Nic called out. 'He meant to lose you in there, thought it was a real joke when you couldn't find your way out.'

James remembered – the fear of it, the darkness and the dank water, his voice a lonely echo calling out. 'We were thirteen,' he answered over his shoulder. 'And,' he said after a pause, 'you did that to me too, Nic, remember? You all did.'

Mat, Nic and Gerri were silent as he walked off, hands in his pockets, over the dry paddocks.

He paused at the fence, looking up. God, the sky is so blue, he thought. Kind of a brittle blue, like everything could shatter in a second.

Nic held up his hands. 'I'm not sure where you're going with this, detectives, but everyone knew James was in love with Eloise. He'd do anything for her.'

All eyes turned to James. 'No,' he stammered, red-faced. 'It wasn't like that.'

'It was,' Mat sneered. 'All that watching and the blushing whenever her name was mentioned. Like now – you're blushing now, Doyle. With your red hair and your red face, you look like a—'

'Shut up, Mat!' Gerri's voice was sharp. 'Shut the hell up for once in your life!'

'Eloise was never part of your plan, was she?' Mark continued. 'It was always Brett – but something went wrong. What was it?' Mark reached into his backpack for a drink of water, took a big slug while the others waited. Jagdeep checked her phone. 'Brett showed me a hi-vis jacket that Chomp initialled for him. Brett and Scott were planning on starting up a business together.'

Nic gave a nervous laugh. 'I remember that.'

'A month after Eloise went missing, the jacket was left on Brett's porch. He thought it was Scott trying to tell him something from the afterlife.'

Gerri gave a snort of derision.

'I brought it with me,' Mark said, half to himself. 'When Brett first told me about it, I thought it might give us a clue.' He pulled Brett's hi-vis out of his backpack. 'Can any of you tell me why this was found on his porch? Brett always kept it in his room, and he said that Eloise was the only other person who wore it.'

The group stared at the vest.

'Is this meant to be like an Agatha Christie moment or something?' Nic said. 'I have absolutely no idea where that jacket came from.'

'The thing is,' Mark continued, 'there's sometimes a small pocket on the inner lining near the hem. After I saw Brett I had a rummage through and'—he reached into his pocket and pulled out a piece of paper—'I found this.'

Everyone stared at the worn, folded piece of paper.

'It's a letter,' Mark added.

'No!' Gerri gasped.

Mark passed the paper to Jagdeep. 'You read it, Jag.'

His colleague shook his head in something close to admiration, then narrowed her eyes, brought the paper close. 'It's difficult,' she said. 'The words are faded – but I can make most of it out.' She read aloud:

> Brett, I know you don't love me. It sucks, but I kind of knew it anyway and I feel like shit for going behind El's back. It's over, I get it. Because I'm not a total bitch, and because it's your birthday next week, I'm going to let you know where a new sinkhole is. You can be the first one to dive it. Think of it as a goodbye gift and a birthday present. DO NOT TELL ANYONE ELSE. It's in the paddock directly west of our shed, near the cattle trough. I know how keen you'll be to see it, so I've left the ute there for you, with a line attached. You can go down it this afternoon – my parents are away. Don't be long. I'll need the ute when I come back from town.
>
> Gerri X

A long silence followed. Nic opened his mouth to speak, but no words came out.

'It was you.' Jagdeep looked at Gerri. 'You wanted Brett to go down the sinkhole, but Eloise went instead. She must have decided to go snorkelling with Brett after all, walked to his place, then found the note.'

'Eloise rode Brett's bike to the sinkhole.' Mark was thinking aloud. 'I bet that if we drained the pit on your farm we'd find the remnants of a Stumpjumper bike. It said that on the initial reports, didn't it? That an old bike was found there? No one thought that was very interesting, but it is now. If only Brett had reported his bike missing at the time.'

Mark nodded. 'We're bringing you in now, Gerri. In fact, you'll all have to come to the station for questioning.'

On the ride back into town and down to the bay, Scott admitted to himself: he'd never really loved Gerri. The fact was, he couldn't find it in himself to care about her cheating. Their relationship was a habit, convenient. And he knew Gerri's tears back there were more out of guilt than remorse. He revved the engine, went hard around the sharp corner into Bay Road. God, he couldn't wait to leave and be free of them all.

He arrived at the boat just as his dad and Brett were launching. He stood for a while, looking at his oldest friend. They'd known each other since before he could walk. Brett's dad could be a dickhead, but both Brett's parents helped look after him when his dad was busy with the boats or the shop, especially after his mum had racked off with a bloke from Portland. Brett was like a brother. They learned to surf together, they snuck out to parties, they did their first sneak dive down a cave near the Tomb, half-drunk, terrified and high on adrenaline. After his mother left, Scott had cried in Brett's lounge-room as his friend patted his back and fed him Cheezels. Now, as he looked at Brett, Scott tried to conjure up some emotion: anger or distress. But all he truly felt was tired.

'Hurry up, loser!' Brett was grinning, his sandy hair bright in the sun. 'You been doing the crossword or what?'

Scott held his hand above his eyes to see more clearly. In the sunshine, Brett was like some shimmering god. Everything came easy to him.

'You missed some good surf this morning,' Brett said. 'It was cranking, mate.'

Of course it had been. Scott couldn't go surfing because he'd had to work in the dive shop – the one he'd just learned would soon be owned by Brett's family.

The thought made him pause. He and Brett talked about going into business together, even had a logo. They both knew it would probably never happen, but it was good talking about it. Now, Brett's father was buying his family's business and Brett hadn't even bothered to tell him? Jesus! He felt a sudden, hot streak of anger and ran a hand through his hair. Plus, whether he cared or not, the bloke was rooting his girlfriend! Mates don't do that.

'Spoke to Gerri earlier.' It wouldn't hurt to dent Brett's ego by going along with the prank. 'She's going around to your joint just now. Said she had something for you.' The cheater deserved it.

Brett's face faltered. 'What is it?'

'I dunno.' Scott enjoyed his friend's discomfort. 'About the uni course, I think?'

Understanding spread over Brett's face. 'Yeah, that must be it. Look, I'll, I better go – maybe I'll meet you here later.'

Something hardened in Scott's chest. He jumped down to the boat as Brett was climbing out.

'What's this?' Scott's dad said. 'Musical fucking chairs?'

Scott watched as his friend slowly walked up the jetty.

His father pulled on the rope expertly with his one arm. 'You all right, son?'

'Yeah, let's go.' Scott started the engine, turned towards the bay. The chug-chug was either his heart or the motor, he couldn't tell.

'Hey!' his dad said. 'Hold up!'

Scott spun around to see Brett half-running back down the jetty towards them, and the relief was like a wave crashing over him.

Strangely, for the first time since his mother left, Scott felt like weeping.

'I'm coming with you,' Brett said, jumping into the boat, landing steady on his feet. 'Why the hell would I talk to Gerri about uni when I could be with you two sick buggers.'

CHAPTER 31

'What have you got on Gerri?' James asked quietly, more to the paddock fence than anyone in particular. 'A letter, and maybe some old bike in the pit?'

James was right; it wasn't enough. But he and Jagdeep were hardly going to admit it.

'Was it you, James, who put Brett's vest back in his hallway? Did you throw Brett's bike down the pit?'

'You were in love with Eloise,' Jagdeep added. 'Everyone seems to understand that. Maybe you hated Brett so much you—'

'It wasn't like that,' Gerri said. 'Leave James out of it.'

'But you had something to do with it,' Jagdeep continued. 'What was it, James?'

No one spoke. Was he imagining it, Mark thought, or did the semicircle of Sinclairs and Doyles feel even tighter around them?

'Come on then, Gerri,' he said, playing on the family loyalties, hoping one of them would bite. 'We'll need to speak with you first.'

James glanced at the Sinclairs, and then at his sister. 'It was me who taught Eloise to dive,' he said, flat. 'When the others were in Roti, I taught her.'

Nic looked as if he was about to explode. 'Fucking hell, James!'

'She was good at it. She loved it.' James spoke hesitantly at first and then in a rush. 'We went down the sinkhole almost every day when the others were overseas. She was so keen to go through that restriction – but I told her, none of us were ready, none of us. But in the end, she was the first out of anyone to do it, to go through.' James's voice was full of wonder. 'She was the most adventurous of us all.' He stared at Mat and Nic. 'I told you that.'

Jagdeep's phone rang, slicing through the still air. She answered, speaking low.

'You are so, so stupid,' Nic said slowly, shaking his head.

'James had nothing to do with her disappearance!' Gerri stood slightly in front of her twin. 'He's just trying to put the blame all on himself, but no part of this was his decision. Nothing! He'd never hurt El!'

'Well, tell us then.' Jagdeep shoved her phone back into her pocket. 'Who did?'

Back in her room, Gerri couldn't stop crying. Brett didn't love her, had never loved her, and what an idiot she'd been to think that he would. And now Scott had finished with her too. God! It had just been a holiday thing, it meant nothing. But she'd been stupid – Eloise was her best friend! How could she do it to her?

Gerri sniffed again, wiping her face. Brett had been a bastard to her, yes, but what about to his actual girlfriend Eloise? There'd been Cath and her, and who else that he'd cheated on behind El's back? Too many. God, Eloise was sick at home, probably in bed feeling like shit – and not even knowing what arseholes her boyfriend and best friend actually were. Gerri thought about calling her but couldn't bring herself to do it. What would she even say?

Letting out a long sigh, Gerri sat up in her bed and looked out the window.

Wait . . . was it? She rubbed her swollen eyes. There he was! Brett, riding his bike over the paddock towards the sinkhole and the ute that Nic had set up a couple of hours before. He'd clearly got her note.

She kneeled up and pressed her face to the window to see more clearly. Brett, in his orange hi-vis top, was getting off his bike and walking towards the ute. She saw him look around, move to the back of it, and come out again in a black wetsuit.

Gerri was giggling now. Ha! He looked like an ant, a weak little ant.

Next, Brett bent down and, in a few seconds, he disappeared down the skinny hole, using the rope Mat had tied to the ute for him. Gerri burst into action. Her role now was to play the final trick. Racing through the paddocks, a kind of wild joy in her, she reached the ute, undid the rope and threw it in the water. She bent down, poked her head into the hole: he'd get a fright soon enough when he felt the slackness of the line. Every fear about the Franklin Three would come racing back. Every story about losing your line. He'd be hauling it in to himself, wondering what the hell was going on, panic rising within.

She knew it would be easy enough for him to climb back out without the line – the carved stone steps were right there, and then roots from ancient she-oaks everywhere here, still thick and strong. He'd just have to work to pull himself up. James did it all the time.

But he'd be terrified for a few moments. And for that she was pleased.

'It was meant to be Brett who went down the sinkhole,' Gerri said in a monotone. 'I thought it was him. After I saw someone go down, I untied the rope, threw it in the water and moved the ute back to the shed. James was able to get out of the sinkhole all the time without a rope, although I always needed one to help me get back to the surface. It would have given Brett a fright all right, to feel the rope go slack. It's the stuff of nightmares for cave divers, and for anyone who's heard about sneak dives gone wrong. But he would have been okay. He'd have been able to get out.' She ran a hand over her face as if she was wiping it clean and repeated herself. 'I wasn't strong enough to get out of the sinkhole without a rope.'

And neither was Eloise.

'I drove off. Then the next day, Phil called, asking if I'd seen El. I didn't think anything too much, just thought she'd stayed at Brett's house. But Brett came around looking for her too . . . oh, that was just awful.' Gerri's voice broke off and she went pale at the memory.

What a horrible shock that must have been, Mark thought. A prank played and forgotten about, and then the ghastly realisation.

'I panicked. Without thinking I threw Brett's bike in the pit and shoved the vest in my cupboard. Then after Scott died, I put it back in Brett's house, on one of the coat hooks on the porch. It had that logo on it – the two of them were going to start some stupid business – so I knew how much it would mean for him to have it back. I didn't know he always kept it hanging up in his room. And I kept torturing myself thinking of that note – if Brett hadn't seen it, where the hell was it? At one point before I gave it back, I did look through the pockets in the vest, but not well enough, obviously.' Gerri ran her hands through her hair. 'I couldn't sleep, couldn't think properly. I kept imagining that maybe El had found an air pocket, that she was still alive down there. It was just horrible, such a stupid, stupid thing to do.'

'Why didn't you just come clean?' Mark asked. 'Would have saved a whole heap of trouble.' He looked over to Nic and Mat, who leaned forward now, silent and tense.

'Come clean? I was distraught, I couldn't think straight. Two weeks after, Scott was killed in a car accident. Then there was this whole other thing to deal with. You can't imagine it.'

'Let's move,' Jagdeep said. 'You too, James.'

'Not James,' Gerri's voice rose. 'I just told you, it was me. He doesn't need to come.'

'He does.' Mark, looking at James, remembered the man's confidence in the cave, the assured way he moved underground and in the water. 'Did you go down and check the sinkhole, James? Gerri was panicking about the air pockets and wondered if Eloise might still be alive. Did she ask you to go down there and check?'

The silence was electric.

'Or was it you, Gerri? Even when you were giving those talks and writing your book and volunteering with the families of missing persons, saying that you thought you saw her in Bali – you knew that Eloise was down this sinkhole the whole time, because you saw her go down there. So, was it you or James who, after you realised what must have happened, went down to check?'

James opened his mouth, but Gerri placed a hand on his arm. 'Don't, James. Don't say anything.'

There was a heavy clunking sound, and with a start Mark looked around to see that Mat had thrown a rock against the fence post. The youngest Sinclair picked up another, threw it again. 'Fucking Doyles,' he said. 'Eloise found dead on their land, James taught her to dive, Gerri so jealous of Eloise and Brett. Their whole lives, they've been obsessed with us. If it wasn't for her stupid prank, Eloise would be alive today!'

'*My* stupid prank?' Gerri gasped.

'You got the bracelet off her when you found her, didn't you?' Mat's words, directed at James, were full of quiet rage. 'It was *you* who put it in my ute, wasn't it? Jesus, how sick are you? What, you wanted to frame us or something?'

Mark saw menace written across the faces of the twins. There was a shift in the air, battlelines were being drawn across blood-lines. Maybe what Mat said was true, maybe it *was* all down to the Doyles. Everything they had on Eloise's disappearance was down to them. Maybe they *were* obsessed with their sporty, popular neighbours.

'It was *your* idea, Mat, *your* fucking prank!' Gerri spat out in a rage. 'You were furious at Brett after the fight. And you, Nic, you were so obsessed with Cath and so envious of how much she liked him. You Sinclairs just couldn't stand anyone to be better at everything than you. And look how you used to treat James! Bullies, the lot of you.' She turned to Mark and Jagdeep. 'Cruelty wrapped up as jokes was the Sinclair specialty. Real heroes, you bastards.' Her cheeks were scarlet with fury. 'They were in on it too!' She pointed to the brothers. 'Don't let them get away with it.'

'You took Eloise's bracelet?' Mark ignored Gerri's outburst and looked straight at James.

'I had no intention of framing Nic or Mat,' James said. 'I gave it back because I thought they should have it. Especially after Eloise was found. Georgia would've liked it and El was their sister, not mine. I got to have the bracelet for twenty years.' Tears sprang from his eyes and he swiped at them with his hand.

'Don't act the innocent,' Nic spat. 'You two are up to your necks in this.'

'Fuck you, Nic!' Gerri's voice was hard. 'I see what you're trying to do, pin it all on us.'

As Gerri and the Sinclairs began trading insults, James stood by, quiet.

All evidence pointed to a Doyle plan carried out. But there was something more, Mark thought. There was something more . . .

Like grim observers, four crows landed on the fence. On the other side of it was Sinclair land – a meagre fifty acres. It was a good fence, old-school, built with treated pine.

In the background, Mark saw Chiara and Sean walking fast across the paddocks. Jagdeep moved towards them, and the three officers began talking in low, urgent tones.

'Nic, you were doing fence work the day Eloise went missing, weren't you?' Mark said, looking at the crows.

The Sinclair brothers stared at him.

'Must have needed quite a few solid posts for that job.'

'What's that question for?' Nic asked disdainfully. 'I can't remember what I was doing.'

'In your original statement, you wrote that you were fencing.'

'So what?'

'It's bothered me how the cattle trough was moved,' Mark said thoughtfully. 'You didn't have a tractor, and the Doyles didn't have a good one at that time either. It couldn't have been just Gerri and James who covered up the sinkhole entrance. The trough is way too heavy.'

Chiara had walked over to James and was now talking with him. With his arms crossed and shoulders hunched, he could be mistaken for a little boy.

'Fuck's sake!' Mat exploded. 'Give it a rest – you've got your answers. Put the Doyles away and leave us to finally grieve for our sister!'

'James!' Mark called out. 'How did you move the trough?'

Without warning, Nic leapt at him, a fist knocking him to the ground. In shock, Mark went dizzy for a second, before rolling to the side as Mat joined in, trying to pin him down, throwing more punches. Mark held his arms up to cover his face and was vaguely aware of Sean trying to restrain Mat, and of Jagdeep sticking a knee with force into Nic's back. That gave Mark enough time to haul himself up.

Jagdeep drew her gun, as did Chiara.

'Not the smartest thing you've ever done, Nic,' Mark panted, wiping blood from the side of his mouth. He looked at the cattle trough, imagined the younger Mat, Nic, Gerri, James – and maybe even Scott? – lifting it up on one side and wedging something flat underneath it, then using the fence posts to roll the tank the short distance. That was smart.

'Whose idea was it?' he asked. It would have taken at least four strong young people.

No one said a word.

CHAPTER 32

Hours later, Mark lay back on his bed, listening to the endless crash of the waves. His room upstairs at the Royal had a small window where you could look out to sea, and before he'd spread out on the drooping double bed, he'd watched the ocean roar into shore. A high tide, he heard someone in the bar say when he'd had one beer before retiring. Waves are unruly, fish not biting. When the sea's like this, you don't even bother.

Earlier on, Richardson had offered Mark a full time job in Investigations. He'd declined. 'Give it to Jagdeep,' he'd said. 'She's better than me and she wants it more.'

Mark had no idea whether Richardson was affronted by the frank refusal. At this stage, he really didn't care. Everything hurt.

God, the sea was loud. The waves were like tsunamis. Broken Bay could enchant, but was equally capable of destruction, with its crumbling cliffs and underground caves.

When Angelo had called him earlier, as he was being patched up by Chiara at the station, he'd been confused at the direction the conversation had taken. 'Good work,' Angelo had begun with. 'Bloody good work, Mark. I've been following what you've been up to down there.'

'Thanks.'

'You finished for the night now, going home?' It was after 8 pm.

'Yeah, four in custody. Richardson and Jagdeep will take it from here, see what charges can be brought after so long. I've got some stuff to tie up tomorrow, then I'll be heading back to Booralama.'

Angelo made a sound of approval as Chiara gave Mark a thumbs up. She'd given him an icepack for his jaw, and put antiseptic on the cut on his lip. He'd had another Panadol and was resting with his ankle on a chair. Talk about the walking wounded.

'Angelo, what were you doing down here?' The question had been lingering in the back of his mind; why was Assistant Commissioner Angelo Conti so interested in the retrieval of Mya Rennik? 'Is there something going on in Broken Bay that I don't know about?'

There was a moment's hesitation before a female voice said something in the background.

'What's that?' Mark asked, straightening. 'Who was that?'

'Mark.' Jane Southern was on the phone, her tone brisk. 'It's me. I'm the reason he was at the retrieval site.'

'Oh, okay.' It took a moment for Mark to understand. 'Right.'

'And good work today at the sinkhole.' Jane was typically back to business. He could hear muffled whispering on the other end of the phone.

'Mark?' Angelo again. His old friend sounded uncharacteristically nervous. 'Yeah, me and Jane . . . You okay with it, mate? It's been a long time coming – six months of me putting on my best self and that's not easy, ha ha. So we're good? I'm sorry I didn't tell you earlier, just that with work and . . . your history and . . .'

What could he do? He congratulated them, said an awkward goodbye and hung up.

In his hotel room, which once promised bright comfort and now spoke of tired disregard, Mark texted Angelo back.

It's good, he wrote. *The two of you, it works.*

And it did, he thought. Angelo and Jane – both were married to their jobs, career-minded and lacking in any guile. They'd be lenient with working hours, go easy when the other had not much to say. Jane and Angelo.

He lay his head on the pillow, willing it to be morning.

At the station, just as they were putting the two Sinclairs and the two Doyles into the police cars to take them into custody in Franklin, Phil Sinclair had come roaring in, shouting questions in a state of confusion. His brothers knew *what*? They did *what*? He wanted to see them, hear them say it for themselves: that their sister's death was all because of a stupid practical joke. It couldn't possibly be true. *It couldn't.*

Judy had stood behind him, pleading, holding her husband back.

Mark looked out the window, saw mist or fog pass over it, making it impossible to see the stars. His mind felt clogged. Juliette would have been looking at a brilliant constellation when she slipped, freefalling into the night. Her daughter Eloise could fly in a way too – although only James was aware of that. *Unclip the ties that bind*, he thought. *Unravel. Untie.*

His eyes drooped; sleep was coming. The waves outside seemed gentler now, and his breath rose and fell in time. Someone from the bar below called, 'Last drinks,' and Mark, exhausted, drifted into sleep.

CHAPTER 33

The next morning was spent in paperwork, endless paper-work. There were reports to write, debriefs to be had with Adelaide colleagues, a call to be made to Mark's counterpart in Booralama with assurances that he'd be back on deck the following morning.

It was busy, but despite the team's industriousness, a strange hush had taken over the station, inspired in part by the mist that was enveloping the whole town.

Mark was dog-tired.

Gerri, James, Nic and Mat were being questioned again. Separate rooms – no secret looks or nods between siblings. No matter how they tried to spin it, the accidental death and the subsequent cover-up, it would all come out.

During his lunchbreak, Mark took a slow walk along the bay, looking at the boats through the white, soupy air. Eating a cheese sandwich he couldn't care less about, he ended up at the jetty, where he saw the ghostly figure of Chomp walking towards his boat. Without knowing why, Mark called out to him, and the man responded, waving his arm in the air.

'Heard about what happened yesterday,' the wiry man said. 'And I wanted you to know, Scott never went back out to the Doyles' or the Sinclairs' after our day on the boat. He never told me about this stupid prank, but whatever happened, I don't think he ever connected it with Eloise's disappearance. My guess is, he was just sick to death of them all by then.'

Mark was not so sure. It was likely that when Scott sped away from Broken Bay, he knew in his heart what had happened.

The two men peered into the fog and listened to the gentle clacking of the boat as it rocked back and forth. Mark thought about how the two sets of siblings had sided with their own families. Years ago, and from the outside, this group of young people must have looked effortlessly happy: youth and beauty on their side, a whole future to look forward to. Now two were dead and four were in custody. But what had Rose's aunt said? She went to Rottnest and got bitten by a quokka. Things that beguile often bite.

'You going out?' Mark nodded at the water.

'No chance. I come here sometimes to sit in the boat, just breathe in the air. It's good for you.'

'Well, enjoy.'

The men shook hands, and Mark walked back to the police station slowly, calmed somehow by Chomp Boxhall, a man who'd seen it all and more.

At the station, Jagdeep was deep in reading papers that Liz from the library had just dropped off.

'She hung around for ages,' Sean said, his headphones around his ears. 'Wanted to know when you'd be back. We said you might be gone for a while.' The young officer smiled knowingly, and for the first time Mark felt an inkling of fondness for him. He had no desire to explain to Liz why he had chosen to stay at the Royal last night rather than the Hibernian. Or why her father would no doubt be jumping with nerves every time the phone rang, expecting to be called in to explain what he'd done with Cherie's phone.

Mark sat across from Jagdeep and asked what the papers were about.

She held up a hand in a signal to wait and then slowly put down the photocopy. 'It's a report on land titles, old housing permits, records of sale,' Jagdeep explained. 'What Cherie had been looking up at the library. Here, take a look.'

Mark scanned through – something on titles and caveats, building permits. He could lay down here, right on the floor, and sleep a bit more. And then, an old report buried under articles on land sales and highlighted in red by Jagdeep:

Doyle family sells fifty acres to local Broken Bay family for less than what the land is worth. In an act of generosity, the Doyles sold acreage along Bay Road to a family recently struggling with financial difficulties and bereavement. The land includes a house, two dams and a shed.

'That doesn't sound like the Frank we know,' Mark said, putting the paper down. 'Who knew he was an old softy?'

'Maybe not in all regards. Read this: another of Cherie's discoveries.'

Farmer Frank Doyle from Bay Road, Broken Bay, was fined $3000 for burying sheep and farm dogs in a shallow pit on his farm. Up to eighty animals were disposed of in this way, with less than one metre of soil covering them. Doyle appealed the decision, stating the severe drought and financial difficulties. However, the law is firm on the matter of correctly disposing of carcasses to prevent soil *contamination, pollutants leaching into groundwater, and the spread of disease. The land parcel on which the pit is situated is deemed not fit for resale or building until a subsequent professional soil examination has taken place.*

A map of the land in question was provided in the report. Mark studied the Doyle house, the Twymann property bordering Moyne Lane. The Doyle house again, the fence lines.

'Do you see it?' Jagdeep asked.

'Yeah,' he breathed, excitement building. 'I do.'

'Doyle sold the Sinclairs that land dirt cheap after they'd fallen on hard times. Made himself look good doing so.'

'And part of the land was contaminated soil. No doubt the groundwater was dodgy too. The Sinclairs have been struggling ever since,' Mark said. 'What an old bastard! No wonder they hate him.'

'"Something is rotten in the state of Sinclair,"' Jagdeep said aloud.

'Cherie meant the *land*, not the family.'

'I'm not sure the Sinclairs know the reason why their land is so bad,' Jagdeep said. 'They might have suspected, but they'd never been farmers before, and fishing was still half their work.'

Mark thought about it. It wasn't difficult to see how farmers would compare a farm's productivity against the history of the land. Perhaps Murray kept quiet because he was grateful for an affordable place to live; perhaps he was so grief-stricken about Juliette that he didn't even care. Now, Phil and Judy seemed more invested in sea than land.

'Wait, there's more,' Jagdeep said. 'Liz told us that Cherie was interested in the Franklin Three. She gave us the old newspapers that reported on the incident, and guess who is mentioned in one of the very early pieces as someone who helped in the recovery of the bodies?'

'No,' Mark breathed. 'Frank Doyle?'

'The very same. He didn't dive down like the other two – that was Greg Boxhall and Murray Sinclair – but he was at the top on ground level, providing assistance. Perhaps that's why he didn't get the same attention. That's what Cherie found out when she was researching the Franklin Three.'

'Cherie was writing a play about it,' Sean said. 'It's all there in her notes. She was researching the Franklin Three and found out about Frank Doyle being present at the retrieval, and then she must have gone down a rabbit hole to find out about the dodgy sale of land. The dates of her research all add up.'

'Great work,' Mark said, and Sean beamed.

'Wait up,' Jagdeep was nosing through various papers, 'I haven't told you the best bit yet.'

'You're killing me, Jag.' Mark shook his head.

'IT managed to get into the notes app on Cherie's phone. There were loads: shopping lists, reminders to buy presents and to get her car serviced, and obscure notes, with costumes and accents and ideas for plays. But I've printed the ones of interest. Tell me what you think.' She passed him the page.

1 Aug: New idea for play! Tot original, local content.

8 Aug: Research at library. Franklin Three. V int.

9 Aug: CB and BD at the Tomb with MS!

12 Aug: 3 rescuers Potential titles: The Tomb, Families at War, Sink

15 Aug: MS broke after bad fishing season. BD land sales. Contamination.

19 Aug: Visit BDD in home, v ill. Keeps saying BD obsessed w J. 'Won't leave her alone. Always watching.'

1 Sept: Costume practice with Corey. Says I look like mannequin?

'I like "Sink" best,' Sean declared. 'It's clever.' Then added, looking at the others, 'I'm talking about the titles she was coming up with.'

Jagdeep considered him for a moment. 'We know what you meant.'

Sean held his hands up in a 'what can I do?' gesture.

'Okay, so Corey is Corey Burns, now in New York. MS is presumably Murray Sinclair, at the Tomb. But who are BD, CB and BDD?' Jagdeep asked. 'All these Bs!'

'It says there that BDD is ill. That could be Bernadette Doyle,' Sean suggested.

Mark nodded slowly. 'Visit BDD in home,' he said, an unpleasant thought dawning. Without speaking, he punched in the number for Bernadette Doyle's residential care home. A man answered, surly. Mark could hear a television in the background.

'Senior Sergeant Mark Ariti here. Could you please give me the list of people who visited Mrs Bernadette Doyle on August nineteenth this year?'

'We don't give out the names of visitors. It's private information.'

'What's *your* name?'

'Riley Hay.' Riley was chewing gum as he spoke.

'Well, Riley Hay'—Mark rolled his eyes at Jagdeep—'it's against the law to hinder a police investigation. You could be in for up to six months if you fail to assist in providing evidence.'

Jagdeep mouthed 'Liar' at him.

'For real?' The television in the background snapped off.

'For. Real.'

Mark waited while Riley put the phone down and sifted through a computer. After a moment, he came back on, his tone considerably more polite.

'We digitise all visitor names after they sign in,' he said and then paused, waiting for Mark to comment. Mark didn't. 'So yeah, we have all guest names in the visitor book and on the computer here at the desk.'

'Riley, who visited on that date?'

'Yes,' Riley said in a hurry; he'd also got rid of the gum. 'There was only one on that day. Mrs Doyle's sister, Roxie Hart. There's a note next to the visit from the nursing staff – says Mrs Doyle was highly agitated after the visit.'

'Thanks, Riley.'

'So, we're okay?'

'We're okay, Riley.'

'Cheers.'

Mark hung up and looked at Jagdeep. 'I doubt that Bernadette Doyle has a sister called Roxie Hart.'

'That's the lead character in *Chicago*!' Sean said, leaning back in his chair. 'My mum loves all that shit. Geez, imagine that, sneaking into an old folks' home just to get information.'

'Yeah,' Jagdeep said, looking hard at Mark. 'What kind of monster does that?'

Mark widened his eyes. 'Someone truly evil.'

'Does this old lady we're talking about have serious Alzheimer's?' Sean asked. 'Because my grandmother has it, and it's sad, but honestly, you cannot believe the stuff that comes out of her mouth. She thinks my brother and I are literally Mormons who plan to steal all her money and set fire to her KitchenAid.'

Jag continued studying the list. 'So, who are CB and BD?'

'CB is probably Chomp Boxhall, he was definitely at the Tomb with Murray. Everyone calls him Chomp, although his real name is Greg.'

'Okay,' Jag said slowly, 'so who is BD then?'

'Yes,' Mark echoed, 'who is BD?'

There were any number of Bs in town but none with the right combination of letters: Ian Bickon, Barry Coffey, or someone to do with Blue/Bleu.

'Could BD refer to Frank Doyle?' Sean asked, shrugging. 'We know Cherie found out he was at the Tomb, so why not? She might call him something else, she calls Greg, Chomp. Plus, she's written "BD land sales. Contamination" – that's got to be Doyle, right?'

Mark stared at him for a second, then: 'You're a genius, mate! You've just sawn the Gordian knot in half.'

'What?'

'Yes.' Jag's voice rose in excitement. 'And J is Juliette. BD was obsessed with Juliette.'

'But what's the B for, if it's Frank?' Sean asked.

They all paused in thought.

'Could *he*,' the young policeman was on a roll, 'be Bleu?'

'Or Blue,' Jagdeep said, looking at Mark.

The elderly citizens in town would be the ones to ask, the ones who'd known all the family dramas, who'd seen the kids grow up and leave, who'd be aware of old quirks and habits. Nicknames bestowed and why. Heart thumping, Mark got out his phone and rang Margery's number. She answered on the first ring.

'Hello, Margery, Mark Ariti here. The last time he rang her, Margery's book club had held him up. It wouldn't now.

'Hello, Mark, any news on Mat and Nic? I've got Cath here with me. She's in a real mess with Nic and all these revelations and—'

'Margery,' Mark cut her short. 'Is there any particular name you used to have for Frank Doyle in the old days?'

'Well, yes,' Margery said. 'We knew him as Bluey when we were young. He had the reddest of hair. Bernadette did too, of course, and the twins.' There was a long pause. 'I don't think many people call Frank "Bluey" anymore. Most people now call him Frank – even I do.'

Jagdeep indicated for Mark to turn on the speaker and she leaned over the phone, speaking into it: 'Margery, was Frank in love with Juliette?'

'In love! Oh, that's a stretch, I think. Lots of men liked Juliette, you know. But now that you say it, Gordon and I used to laugh at how much Bluey doted on her. She knew who he was, but not well – we didn't mix in the same circles at all. Even so, Bluey would just hover nearby and send her all these dewy looks.'

Jagdeep was now bringing up an image on her laptop, one of the photos Mark had taken when he first entered Cherie's house after her death. Mark kept his eye on it as Margery's voice rang loud in the room.

'We thought nothing of it – he was harmless! But you know, now I'm remembering, she did mention him once waiting with her when her car broke down. She said he stood so close to her. It's funny I've remembered that just now.'

The image on the screen was of the mannequin, dressed up in the blonde wig, the old cardigan and long dress. Mark swore. It did resemble Cherie – but someone else too. A beautiful young mother of four children who loved buying ugly paintings and clothes, a mother who'd supposedly thrown herself in depression off the cliffs of Broken Bay.

'Is this something to do with Cherie?' Margery was sharp. Because sometimes you could be forgiven for thinking she was Juliette, especially with her blonde hair. Up close, of course, they were very different, but lately when Cherie stood in her living room looking out – like Juliette used to – in a certain light, well, they did look similar.

'Margery,' Jagdeep's voice broke through again. 'When did Cherie dye her hair from brown to blonde?'

'Cherie goes to my hairdresser in Franklin . . . It would have been just before her birthday and she gets it done every six to eight weeks, so yes – around two months ago.'

'Thanks, Margery, thanks so much.' Jagdeep hung up and sat back, shaking her head.

'Holy shit,' Sean breathed, looking at the screen. 'The mannequin is Juliette – and Cherie looked like the mannequin, especially since her hair was dyed blonde. She was just beginning to understand that it was probably . . .' He shook his head. 'I mean, holy shit!'

'Cherie first reported someone following her around two months ago, the same time she dyed her hair. She looked more like Juliette than ever before,' Jagdeep said. 'And you're right, she was probably just making the connection – especially when Corey mentioned to her how much the mannequin looked like her.'

So, Frank Doyle had been obsessed with Juliette. He was known as Bluey. A size eleven footprint had been found at the scene of the crime, cow manure samples present. Cherie knew things about Frank that would not make him popular. She resembled Juliette from a distance. Bernadette Doyle had told her that he was 'always watching'.

Frank Doyle, *Bluey.*

CHAPTER 34

'Juliette,' he says, and she turns, frowning slightly. 'I know you're sad, Juliette – I can tell. I've been watching you.'

Juliette knows this, of course. She's a woman men watch. But she's kind to this odd man, this small Australian farmer with dirt in his fingernails and the smell of cow on his clothes.

'Yes, I'm sad.' She's sad for many things: she misses her sister and her friends and Paris. Long dinners at restaurants around candlelit tables, talking about books and ideas and film. She misses bouilla-baisse and wine in the afternoon. But mainly, she wants to rest: lie down and sleep for hours without children fighting and needing her. She'd like to be free too, from the financial strife bearing down on their business, which makes her husband mad with worry. Things are so much harder now, than her first days here when everything was bright with possibility. Her carefree life in France seems a world away.

But here, here the ocean is so stunning, and this country is natural and bare and wild. And her three boys and little girl, Eloise, she aches with love for them. Only, she needed this – this time to herself on the cliff top. Its magnificence – the falling constellations, the sound of the ocean below.

Time to go back to her family. Murray will have the fire on, and he'll be cooking something for dinner – a stew? He always overcooks it, she thinks fondly, but he does try to do it the French way. She must go now.

And what is this man doing? Bluey – Frank. She wishes he would go away.

'*And lonely too, I bet you're lonely.*'

She turns to look at him better, sees him clearly for the first time. He's the man who lingers around the park where she takes the boys to play, the man who was there when her car broke down a few months ago. He waited with her for almost an hour on the side of the road, only leaving when Murray's headlights appeared in the distance. He'd stood so close.

'*No,*' *Juliette says now, more firmly than she means to.* '*I've got my three sons and baby daughter. I'm never lonely.*'

The man starts. Cocks his head to one side, confused. '*Murray can't be much of a husband to you, always away – out to sea. He shouldn't leave you alone, not someone like you.*'

The wind whips up the cliff face and smacks into their faces. Far out on the horizon, a ship's light moves slowly in and out of sight.

CHAPTER 35

'I've had an email from Corey in New York,' Sean said, eyes on his phone. 'Says that he's just checked his, and Cherie sent him her play to read.'

'Forward the email to me,' Jagdeep said.

'Done.'

Jagdeep tapped into her laptop. Mark tried to call Frank Doyle. No answer.

'Corey wrote that he forwarded the play to Phil and Judy Sinclair because he thinks it might cheer them up about Eloise – it's mainly about Murray Sinclair being a hero at the Tomb,' Sean said, then added after a pause, 'Corey probably shouldn't have done that.'

Understatement of the year.

'We need to head out to the Doyles',' Mark said. 'Pay Frank a visit.'

'I'm just printing the play. Hang on.'

The photocopier started spilling out pages before coming to a sickening halt. 'Paper jam,' Sean said. 'I'll sort it.'

Mark and Jagdeep groaned.

'Really?' Jagdeep said, watching Sean open and shut compartments. 'Now?'

'It's just a . . . Maybe this one . . . It says here to . . . Now, let's see . . .'

They all stared at the machine, willing it to work. Paper began churning out again and they gave a cheer.

Mark grabbed the papers and brought them over to the table. What exactly did Cherie know?

`Sink, by Cherie Swinson`

'Yes!' Sean muttered. 'I told you that was the best name.'

```
List of characters:
(Names will be changed prior to rehearsals)
Murray Sinclair: Young man, tall, strong and
handsome. The sad hero of this tale.
Chomp Boxhall: Murray's closest friend, loyal
and true.
Frank 'Bluey' Doyle: Short, red hair, devious.
Obsessed with Juliette, jealous of Murray.
Juliette Sinclair: Beautiful French woman, wife
of Murray, tragic love interest. (To be played
by Cherie Swinson.)
```

'I'll read it to you in the car,' Mark said. 'Let's go, Jagdeep.'

As they headed out the door, Jagdeep gave instructions to Sean to stay put until Chiara returned, and then come to meet them at the Doyle farm. She told him to call Richardson, let the boss know what was going on. Sean nodded, face flushed in excitement.

With Jagdeep's help, Mark put his crutches in the back seat and they pulled out of the drive. Jagdeep turned on the headlights to negotiate the foggy air.

'Read it to me,' Jagdeep said, tense.

```
Act 1: Scene 1
Voiceover: The Franklin Three. Three bodies in
a sinkhole, their watery grave metres below the
earth, in dark caverns barely traversed by man.
Three men are tasked with their recovery, and
are each affected in starkly different ways ...
Meet Murray Sinclair, Greg 'Chomp' Boxhall and
Frank 'Bluey' Doyle. *Names will be changed*
(As narrator talks, each man comes on stage and
performs an action typical of their lifestyle.
Murray fishes, Chomp checks scuba gear and
equipment, Bluey tallies up accounts of his
dairy farm. The three men on stage do not
acknowledge each other.)
Blackout, then blueish light.
MS: Hey there, Chomp, how's about a fish in the
salmon holes? It's a fine day for it.
CB: As long as there's no great whites, I'm up
for it!
```

'I don't think Cherie was going to win awards for her play-writing,' Jagdeep said as she sped out of town towards the Doyles' place.

Mark agreed, began flicking through the scenes.

```
Act 2: Scene 1
BD: Anyone seen Juliette?
CB: Oh, hello, Bluey — she's out on the boat
with Murray.
BD: With Murray? What, is she learning to dive
or something?
CB: (laughing) Something like that, mate.
```

```
BD: Do you know when they'll be back? I might
ask Juliette if she wants to . . .
CB: Mate, don't you get it? Juliette's mad about
Murray — he's mad about her.
BD: (frowning) No, that can't be right.
CB: Bluey, forget her.

Act 2: Scene 2
Bluey is looking in a mirror, muttering to
himself.
BD: Juliette and Murray? That can't be. Juliette
and Murray? Why? Because of what he did at the
Tomb? (Bluey adjusts his expression, makes his
voice mild) Hello, Juliette! Thought you might
be here. How are you? Would you like to get
a drink? I was just about to . . . (his face
droops) I was just about to . . . !
```

'Get to the end,' Jagdeep said. 'What's the last thing she wrote?'

Mark flicked over the pages.

```
Act 2: Scene 5
BD: It's a good night, isn't it? The stars are
incredible!
JS: Ahh, yes. I was just looking at them — but I
might go in now, Murray and the children . . .
BD: Juliette, I have to talk with you . . .
JS: (in a rush) I know what you are going to
say, Bluey, but no. Thank you, but no — I'm
happy where I am and . . .
BD: But I love you!
```

```
JS: Leave me alone, please — I . . .
BD: Juliette, I . . .
JS: Leave me alone!
```

'I hope Cherie had a good lawyer,' Mark said. 'I know she was planning on changing the names, but geez. This Sunday Soiree would have blown some minds all right.'

'Is there any more?' Jagdeep asked.

'Not much. There's another blackout, and then they are all devastated, then Frank sells Murray some cheap land — but it's cheap for a reason.' Mark was reading quickly, scanning down the page.

'That's it?'

'It's not finished, but then here in the margins on the last page, the bit about the land, she's handwritten and underlined, "Bluey obsessed with blondes".'

Jagdeep made a whistling sound and shook her head. They were along Bay Road, the fog so dense now that she had to slow right down. A rabbit ran across in front of them, ghostly in the low-lying cloud.

His phone rang: Judy.

'Mark!' Her panicked voice rang out loud in the car. 'Phil's been reading a play that Cherie wrote before she died. It got sent to him by—'

'We know about the play, Judy,' Mark said. 'What's Phil doing?'

'He's gone crazy, saying that Frank was obsessed with Juliette. He's jumped to all sorts of conclusions about his mother's death and Cherie — and now he's taken the ute and driven to Frank's. We're so worried that he could hurt somebody, or himself!'

'Thanks, Judy. We'll go out there and take a look.'

'Find him, Mark,' she said. 'Please. He's drunk and out of his mind.'

Darkness had fallen and the car's headlights were eerie in the white mist. Country roads are so lonely, the deep shadows beyond. Once more the moonah took on malevolent shapes. To the right, the ocean was an inky creature, restless and huge.

The Doyles' home was shrouded in crepuscular stillness, and the first thing the two detectives heard as they turned into the driveway was a high cry for help. 'Over here! Get here!'

Jagdeep jumped out and ran ahead, Mark following as best as he could on his crutches. At the back of the main building, Frank was cowering in what remained of the derelict pool beside some old wood and tarp. 'Help!' he cried. 'He's going to kill me!'

Phil Sinclair stood above him, a spear gun in his hand.

'Phil,' Mark said calmly. 'Give me the gun.'

'Did you read the play?' Phil's voice was thick with emotion and booze. 'This man was obsessed with my mother. He killed Cherie too. Did you read it? Cherie knew all about Frank and that's why he killed her.'

'Let's talk about it.'

'Admit it, Doyle. You killed that poor woman,' Phil spat. 'What did Cherie ever do to you?'

Frank was a shaking, whimpering mess, 'I didn't . . . I . . .'

Phil placed the spear gun against his chest and pulled the rubber band towards him, loading it into the notch above the trigger.

'Phil, Phil, mate. Steady on. Don't stuff it all up.' Mark's words were ignored as the big man, previously unsteady and now dangerously still, aimed the gun at his neighbour.

'I'll shoot you, Frank. I'll aim straight for your fucking face.'

'No, no, no!'

'You've got three seconds. One . . . two . . .'

Phil moved forward and Frank fell to his knees, in a begging pose. 'I thought she was Juliette. I really did, just for a second.' His voice came in high-pitched bursts and then in low moans. 'There was this mannequin in the window, dressed up like Juliette, and just for a second, I thought it was her. It gave me one hell of a fright. I used to watch Cherie sometimes, when she had the blonde hair; she looked a bit like your mother. Nothing in it, I just liked to watch her. But that night, when I saw the mannequin lit up in the window, it was like a . . . like a flashback! Then Cherie startled me – I called her Juliette and she, she . . .'

'She what?' Phil had not moved in his stance. The spear gun was still trained on Frank. 'She what?'

'She kept accusing me of . . . polluting, and of stalking even! I was saying, no, no, but then she turned away from me and she tripped on those stone steps and I went to help her up and – how she looked at me! Like I was some sort of . . . Like I was a . . .' Frank paused, looked up at them pleadingly. 'She said I killed Juliette. I never did. I loved your mother! There was a rock in my hand, and it went down. It's a blur, Phil, I didn't mean to.'

Jagdeep looked at Mark, tilted her head in the car's direction and took a step back. In deadly precision, Phil turned the gun on her. 'Don't go anywhere, officer. Not yet. We're not finished.'

Mark realised in a kind of horror how easy it was for a happy family man, loved in the community, to descend into despair and violence.

'He'll shoot me!' Frank gasped.

'Give me the spear gun, Phil,' Mark repeated, firm. He took two steps closer to the big man.

'*What* did Cherie accuse you of, Frank?'

'Things, stupid things . . . That I knew the land I sold to Murray was contaminated and . . . that I was obsessed with Juliette all this time and that Bernadette knew it. She said she knew now that it was me who'd been watching her. It's all a blur, Phil, it's like a . . .'

Phil took a step towards the pool. 'You fucking mongrel. You—' He angled the spear gun more pointedly at the cowering man.

'Stop now!' Mark was sweating with anxiety.

Phil ignored him. 'And what about our mother? What did you do? Push her when she rejected you? Was that it, Frank?'

'Do something!' Frank called to Jagdeep and Mark. 'He's mad!'

'You're the one that's mad,' Phil spat out, still training the deadly spear on him. 'Did you really think my mother would leave my father for *you*? What have you ever done, Frank, besides be a corrupt, petty little leech?'

'I didn't push her! I swear, I talked to her at the cape, that's all. She stumbled and fell. I didn't push her!'

'*No, it's not like that. Murray's a wonderful husband. We're very happy.*'

'*What do you mean?*' *Frank's mind feels cluttered. He looks at his hands as though puzzled at what they are. When he closes his eyes, strange, jagged lines dart across the dark. All the times he's spent thinking about her, how he can help rescue her from Murray and that big, messy family.*

Juliette moves to go. Her face is frozen in a half-smile and he can't stand it, the way she looks, as if she's desperate to get away.

'Wait,' he says. 'Please wait.'

But she's pushing on ahead and his arm reaches out and stops her.

She steps back, surprised, and something else. Frightened. He moves one step closer, and it's just to reassure her, it's just to tell her to be careful. His arm moves out and she stumbles. He didn't mean it but – that look on her face – like he's something hideous. And then, in one instant, she's falling, falling into the dark, conspiring waves.

CHAPTER 36

'You sick bastard.' Phil swung the gun around wildly, his face flushed.

A car sped up the driveway. *Let it be cops*, Mark prayed. *Please let it be backup.*

It wasn't cops. It was Chomp.

'Phil, mate!'

No one yelled in reply. They waited for the fisherman to find them.

'Phil!'

As he rounded the corner, Chomp spun his head about, gauged the situation. He peered briefly in the pool at the diminished figure of Frank, and walked past the police officers towards his old mate's son. 'Phil. What's this shit? Judy rang me, she's mad with worry.'

'Leave me, Chomp. I know what I'm doing.'

'Like hell you do. Give me the gun.'

Mark took another step forward. He was less than three metres from Phil, Chomp closer still.

Noting their progress towards his aggressor, Frank stood up.

'He killed my mother,' Phil said. 'Dad was broken after she died. He killed him too.'

Chomp nodded sympathetically, his eyes on Phil. 'Murray was a good man, that's true. You're a lot like him, Phil.'

Phil lowered the gun slightly and gestured towards Frank. 'This scumbag was jealous of him. Because my father was a hero, and he had my mother.'

Eyes on the weapon, Mark advanced another step. 'You can do this, Phil. Drop it now.'

'Think about your family, Phil. They need you, and not like this.' Chomp said it with force.

Phil lowered the weapon.

'Murray wasn't the great man you thought he was,' Frank burst out, seemingly buoyed by Chomp's presence.

Mark wished Frank would shut the hell up, but a flicker of intrigue stopped him from stepping in.

Phil ran his hands through his wild hair. 'What the fuck do you mean?'

'At the Tomb. I was there, along with Chomp and Murray. We retrieved those kids.' Frank edged to the side of the pool where a rickety ladder hung.

Jagdeep held a hand up for him to wait.

'Chomp dived in and found the first dead kid – the one heading straight down instead of up. Murray, he went back for the siblings.'

'We know that. Dad got them out,' Phil said, stumbling. 'The family thanked him. Everyone knows that.'

'He did. But what no one ever talks about – what we never talk about – was how one of the kids was still alive when he found them.'

Phil frowned, shook his head. 'No.'

'When Murray went down to collect them, they'd found a small airspace at the top of a cavern, about two inches high. The sister was dead – drowned – but the brother was still conscious.'

'Shut the fuck up, Bluey,' Chomp said. 'Shut your fucking mouth or I'll shoot you myself.'

Another car was hurtling up the driveway.

'Just face it, Phil. Your father, the hero, left the boy down there to die.'

'That's not true!' Phil shook his head emphatically. 'That can't be true.'

Chomp looked at Phil, held both his hands up. 'The kid was at full panic. Murray tried to calm him, showed him they could share his regulator and take turns breathing from it, but the kid was having none of it. He kept trying to pull Murray's respirator from his mouth. Every time Murray went to help him, the kid went nuts – diving at him, attacking him. Murray stayed down there as long as he could, and more. He came up to the surface, got more air, went back down again. But by then it was too late. Your father did everything right.'

Frank laughed. 'If you think coming to the surface without the kid is "right".'

Mark could feel his own hatred for the man bubbling up. As Jagdeep kicked the pool ladder away to keep Frank trapped, Chiara and Sean arrived. Someone turned a light on.

'There was nothing Murray could do.' Chomp was talking softly to Phil. 'We weren't equipped for prolonged rescues. The three of us – me, Murray *and Frank* – we decided that it was best for the families of the kids to never mention it again.'

Phil was leaning against the wall now, the gun dangling at his side. His brothers were in custody, his sister was dead because of them, his mother had possibly been pushed to her death. And now his father's story, false. 'God,' he said.

In one terrible moment, Phil pointed the gun at a terrified Frank, then flipped it down, so the spear was aimed at his own head.

And as Mark and Chomp dived towards him, a deafening shot – abrupt and awful – rang out.

CHAPTER 37

Mark couldn't remember if he blacked out for a moment, but after diving towards Phil Sinclair, his next memory was blood. Lots of it. Where did it all come from? he thought stupidly.

Jagdeep was beside him, examining the red mess that was his hand. A groaning Phil had been shot in the leg. Chomp was pressing down on the wound, all the time telling Phil that he was a bloody idiot, that Judy would have his guts for garters, that he was going to be okay.

Jagdeep to Mark was more blunt. 'You were shot with the spear gun,' she said. 'It's gone right through your hand.'

'Will I be able to play the violin?' Fuck, it hurt. 'Professionally?'

'Shut up, Ariti.'

'What happened?'

'Your mate shot Phil in the leg.' Chomp looked at Jagdeep in admiration. 'Just when he was about to top himself.'

Chiara was busy tearing open the package of a bandage Sean had collected from the police car. With Chomp's help, she began to wrap it around Phil's leg. He let out a cry of agony.

'You reckon he'll be okay?' Mark asked.

'He's been through worse,' Chomp said. 'It's his hangover I'm worried about.'

But Chomp looked worried. Mark had little more to say. Acting the brave Aussie took effort. His hand hurt. His ankle throbbed. In all honesty, he wanted to cry.

Chomp began talking to Phil in a low, sing-song voice. 'And you know, Phil, the girl who helped your dad get through it all was your mum. Frank and I were with him when we saw her for the first time, walking on the beach. We'd just come from the police station, giving a report on what happened at the Tomb days before. Juliette looked like a mermaid come out of the sea. I think the three of us fell a little bit in love with her that day. But your dad won out and, mate, it was a joy to see.'

'Murray and Juliette never told you the full story of the Franklin Three, and maybe one of us should have, but they didn't want to frighten you, and they didn't want to remember. We oldies don't talk much about stuff like that. It's too painful.'

Chomp was silent for a moment, and Mark guessed he was thinking about Scott.

'Only the old families know the whole story, and there's so many new people now, it seems pointless to bring it up.'

'Shit!' Sean was staring at the phone in his hand. 'There's been a car accident near the Vic border. Ambos say they won't get here for at least an hour and thirty. Franklin cops'll get here sooner.'

Chiara cursed too. 'He won't last till then. He's losing too much blood.'

'We'll have to transport him in your car.' Jagdeep looked at the other police officers. 'Sean, put the seats down and drive it right up close to here, then come back and help us lift him.'

'Use the board as a stretcher.' Mark pointed to an old fibre-glass surfboard in the pool near Frank and told the old farmer to throw it up to them.

There was a burst of activity. Sean moved the car and then he, Chiara, Jagdeep and Chomp lifted Phil as gently as they could onto the board. With supreme effort, they carried it towards the waiting car.

'Sean, go to the hospital with Chomp and Phil. Then, Chiara, go back to the station and get Richardson. We'll wait for someone to come back for us.'

Sensible, Mark thought, even as he sweated in pain. There was no way Jagdeep could drive both him and Frank right now: if the old farmer tried to escape or went mad there'd be little he could do to assist.

Phil lay on the back seat, quietly groaning. Chomp climbed in beside him, while Chiara clambered into the driver's seat with Sean beside her. Without a glance behind them, she reversed the car, and then drove out of sight.

All was quiet.

'Your father was a hero, Phil,' Mark remembered Chomp saying. 'Don't you let anyone tell you otherwise.'

Mark closed his eyes. Saw deep red patterns overlaid with jagged lines. *It's so easy*, he thought, *to pick and change parts of your life you like and don't.*

You meet your future wife days after you've retrieved two kids and left a panicky boy in a watery cave. You're traumatised, filled with guilt. Why not forget that, focus on the good part: love at first sight on the beach of Broken Bay. Why not? It's romantic, the kids will love it. You'll come to believe it yourself.

Every day, in small increments, we rewrite history.

Mark held his bloodied hand to his chest like a patriot and wondered how he'd retell this story in years to come.

Jagdeep and Mark waited fifteen more minutes, and still no sign of the cops. In the pool, a subdued Frank was muttering to himself.

'I didn't push Juliette.' His voice suddenly rang out clearly.

'Save it for the station, Doyle,' Jagdeep called back, tired.

Mark looked closely at his hand for the first time. With most of the blood wiped off, he could see that there was a thin, round metal spear protruding out of both sides of his left hand, in the fleshy part between his forefinger and thumb. The arrow tip, red with blood and flesh, weighed heavy, although it could not have been bigger than a paper clip. It looked like a torture instrument from the Middle Ages. He felt sorry for fish. He felt sorry for himself.

'If this was the old days, I'd pull it out myself,' he said.

'Ahh, the good old days,' Jagdeep said, looking into the sky. 'I'll pour whiskey over the wound and you scull the rest, grit your teeth and go for it.'

A hoarse voice came from the pool. 'Is there whiskey?'

Jagdeep and Mark ignored him.

'I just got a text from Chiara – police are arriving in five. They can take Frank to the station, and I'll drive you to the clinic.'

In his makeshift prison, Frank Doyle was sitting glumly on an old crate, staring at the walls. 'This fucking pool,' he said. 'I never wanted it.'

And even in his pain – his wounded hand roaring in bloody communion with his ankle – Mark could sympathise. *I hear you, Frank, I hear you.*

CHAPTER 38

When he'd had the time and energy to reflect on all that had happened in Broken Bay, Mark marvelled at how the whole episode had elements of a Greek myth. Weren't the young people in the story like half-gods, sons and daughters of Poseidon? And the setting itself, the idyllic ponds: on the surface mesmerising; below, a labyrinth of tunnels and dead ends.

But then again, Mark thought, as he stared at the ocean, there was something very ordinary about it too: young people drawn to beauty and peril.

There was James Doyle, diving into the sinkhole after the horror of realising it was Eloise and not Brett who'd gone down there. Then, with dread, seeing that the guideline had vanished and understanding that Eloise, a new cave diver, must have side-mounted her tank and swum through the restriction. Risking the squeeze himself, he'd found the object of his dreams, floating dead.

'She was like an angel,' he'd said in his police interview. 'Her hair was flowing all about and . . . caught in the rope. She was suspended above the ledge, so it looked as if she was some sort of queen, like she owned the cavern.'

It had been difficult for James to get the bracelet off her wrist, but he did it and had treasured it for almost twenty years. It was James, out of all of them, who knew Eloise's true, adventurous self and he did not try to quash it.

Piece by piece, the police had worked out the events as best as they could: Nic, Mat and Gerri, all angry at Brett, had conspired to play a trick on him – to lure him to a sinkhole and then petrify him by letting the guideline loose. For kids brought up on the stories of the Franklin Three, it was a terrifying prospect.

Only, Brett never saw Gerri's note. Eloise – maybe thinking that she would go snorkelling with him after all – had walked across the paddocks to Brett's house where she found the note. Who knew exactly what went through her mind as she read that her boyfriend and best friend were sleeping together? Perhaps she was devastated – or, as the nurse who tended Mark's foot said at the clinic, perhaps she didn't really care. Either way, this was the first chance for Eloise to go cave diving alone and she took it.

She put the note in the hidden pocket of the hi-vis, grabbed Brett's bike and one of his many oxygen tanks, and rode barefoot to the sinkhole . . .

And afterwards? When the group realised what had happened? Blind panic and devastating grief.

Gerri threw Brett's bike down the animal pit on her farm, but she had no idea what had happened to her note. Would it incriminate them? They were frightened and so young. Rather than coming clean, Nic made the call to move the cattle trough over the sinkhole. The bike, the trough, the note, the bracelet: no matter how they tried to swing it, each of them felt terrible guilt over Eloise's death.

So they covered it up.

And they waited.

No one asked them anything; no one suggested any foul play.

Scott, who could have given the game up, died in a car accident.

Days, months and years passed and none of them said anything about it, not even to one another. There was a false sighting of Eloise, and a small part of them believed it. *History*, Mark thought, *really is constructed in the present.* Gerri spoke publicly about her grief, wrote a book; she thought she saw her friend getting off a ferry in Bali and hoped that it was real. All of that was true.

Charges would be laid, on that Richardson was firm. For perverting the course of justice, at least – but involuntary manslaughter was a real possibility too.

Frank Doyle, meanwhile, had taken back his confession that he killed Cherie. It had been made with the threat of a spear in his face, and Mark could not argue that point. Without it, the police case was starting to look shaky.

That was until Mark was summoned to the front desk. A man and a woman he vaguely recognised were asking to speak to the detective investigating the Swinson case.

'We're terribly sorry we haven't come in earlier,' the man said. 'But we've just been holed up with a succession lawyer in Adelaide. Who gets the farm and all that, ha ha. Not all that fun really.'

'What did you have to report?' Mark asked, as pleasantly as he could.

'Oh! Hello, it's you! I didn't know you were a policeman. We loved the pub you recommended. There's nothing like country grub, is there? I had fish of the day, Daa had the steak. Bloody nice!'

'Right, yes.' Mark looked at his watch.

His wife cut in. 'We decided to take the long way home so we could take a look at the town again. On the way here, we heard again about the lady who was killed. I had read about it some-where a few days ago, but unfortunately "Woman bludgeoned to death outside her own home" doesn't really make you sit up anymore, does it?'

No, it didn't Mark thought. Not with it happening at least once a week. 'Celebrity loses battle with the bulge' got more attention.

'Anyway, I remembered something. On the Saturday night, I couldn't sleep—'

'It's the menopause,' her husband added. 'Daa doesn't sleep.'

'—and I saw a man rushing along beside the bay. He'd come out of the front yard of a large house at the end of the street. This was Saturday night, around ten-thirty pm. He seemed in a great hurry. I did think it was strange, of course, but why would I report something like that?'

'Did you see this man clearly?' Mark asked.

'Yes. When he passed one of the streetlights, I saw his face.'

'And you could identify him?' Did he dare hope . . . ?

'Of course!' Daa sniffed.

They asked her to describe the man. They showed some photos of people who lived in the town. Daa was firm. The man she had seen was Frank Doyle. Police rubbed their hands together: their case was getting stronger, evidence piling up.

Frank's involvement in Juliette's death was harder to prove. Perhaps she really did just slip. It happens. Clifftops are hazard-ous places, particularly at night. Better to think that way, Mark thought. Better to think that Juliette fell into a star-filled night, swept up by an ocean that gently brought her home to her family the next day. Better, too, to think that Eloise went down into the cavern full of fire and energy. Better to think that as she used the rope to lower herself, she was already relishing the chance to dive on her own. And once there, what did she see? Mark only had Mya Rennik's initial notes, sent by David, to go on: *A giant pool of sapphire blue, silver light refracting from limestone walls and a golden beam, spearing down. Visibility is near perfect. On the bottom eastern side, a crack in the limestone walls hints at kilometres of tunnels. Excellent potential for further exploration on this unique and impressive site.*

Yes, Mark thought. Best to think of all of that, and not of blinding clouds of silt and panic in the tangled dark. The other term for Nitrogen Narcosis was 'Rapture of the Deep', and that was how Mark preferred to think of Eloise and Mya, euphoric in the blue. No sense of a bitter end, only joy and a way back home.

He breathed in the ocean air. Ahead a young man was having a heated argument on the phone and gave Mark a suspicious look as he passed by. Mark couldn't blame him. With his bruised face, bandaged ankle, plaster across his jaw, and hand wrapped and immobile against his chest, he looked like a boxer who always came last.

The night before, he'd spoken to his sister. A friend from Booralama had contacted her after seeing Mark on the news. Doped up on painkillers, he'd told her his theory that he and his father had been in Broken Bay when Juliette was found.

'But when was that?' Prue asked.

'In June nineteen eighty-five. I was about sixteen.'

There was a pause. 'But that can't be right, Mark. That was the year we all travelled across to Perth in the caravan. Remember? We took the Christmas holidays and the first four weeks of term off.'

'Oh.' For some reason, Mark felt cheated.

'Dad took you to Broken Bay the year before that, because he and Mum were having some troubles. She needed a break. I went to our cousin's, but you wanted to go with Dad. From memory, you had a nice time, apart from when you almost fell out of the dinghy. Dad had to scoop you back into the boat like a fish. Don't you remember? You were apparently covered in seaweed.'

Mark tried hard to dredge up some memory, good or bad. From somewhere, vague in the back of his head, he remembered being handed a hot Milo, being cold and wet, asking for a bickie to dip into his mug. But who knows what was real and what wasn't? He'd tried to insert himself into a tragic event; now, he was imagining sweet drinks.

'Maybe you're remembering Mum and Dad fighting – it wasn't a very nice time. They yelled a *lot*. Then, the water, the boat and you being down in Broken Bay . . . Sounds like you've mixed up your memories.'

Mark thought briefly and in wonder how easy it was to blur the past, make it softer, make yourself the centre of events. So easy to believe untruths.

Every day, and in small increments, we rewrite history.

He snorted, kept chatting to Prue, letting her know that he was fine and would be back in their mother's old house the following night.

Light drizzle began to fall, the sea was rippling, tiny circles on it, a live painting. Mark listened to the gentle patter and thought about the *drip-drip* of the caves. The pranksters Nic and Mat would not be so full of bravado now. Were their vicious pranks, honed from a young age, all in the spirit of good fun as they said?

And those caves, those tunnels, Mark thought – they all led to the sea. Now, as he took in the whole of Broken Bay, and as the horizon became visible, the sea had never seemed so vast, and the world had never seemed so full of possibility. An ashen sea could turn cerulean in one break of the clouds.

He could choose this track, or this one, or this one, and each one would lead here, to the ocean. It could mean nothing, or everything.

His ride back to Booralama gave a toot of the horn.

'Come on!' Jagdeep called, poking her head out the window. 'Let's hit the frog and toad.'

Taking one last whiff of the salty air, Mark said goodbye to Broken Bay, and hobbled towards the car.

CHAPTER 39

Three months later

There's a grey light tinged with orange, when Mark passes through security and moves towards the exit.

He feels a shyness, mingled with quiet excitement. It's the newness, overlaid with an acceptance of a decision made and acted upon. He has crossed the ocean, far away from his home and country, and yet he's acutely aware that it is guidelines that have pulled him in this direction, at first tentative, and now insistent. *Without guidelines*, Mark thinks, touching the plaster across his nose, *we're freewheeling and untethered, and that's fine for some but not for most.* He checks his watch. Timing is good. He takes a deep breath.

The sliding doors open a crack and light floods in.

Welcome to Vancouver, reads the big red-and-white sign.

It's been more than a year since he's seen his sister, and five since he's shaken the hand of his brash brother-in-law and given his nephews a hug. He'll see them soon, any minute now.

Grabbing his children's hands, Mark almost glides straight through.

EPILOGUE

She enters an ethereal world. Silent. It's a wonderland of blue, and with the golden beam of sunlight spearing down, there's a majesty to the place which could leave her breathless. The cavern shimmers, she spins slow, slow. It's wonderful to be here alone, suspended in the crystalline space, no distractions and no one else to consider.

Loosely holding the line with one hand, she swims past emerald-coloured plants, down to the bottom, taking care not to touch the sides. Tiny silver fish dart by, their shadows flitting the sculptured limestone in lively patterns. She checks her watch – plenty of time, an easy depth of thirty metres. She's breathing well, oxygen levels good, and despite the euphoria she feels a queenly calm.

The line sways close to a crack in the rock – and she lightly places her hands on the top of its smooth surface to peer in. It's dark in there, but not impossibly so. A faint beam glimmers in the distance, hinting at further chambers. She shivers, feeling for the first time the real possibility of a future without limitations. The crack is not too wide; if she manoeuvres her tank to the side, she could do it, she really could.

Behind her, the beam of gold is a portal to the outside. She could leave now, climb up the rope, get back on Brett's bike and ride home before anyone knows she's gone.

Seconds pass. She feels the line, nice and taut. It's strong, steady. Like a friend.

She remembers her brother's words. The main rule of safety in cave diving is: don't go cave diving.

She grips the line. She should leave now.

She doesn't.

ACKNOWLEDGEMENTS

This book has taken me to the Limestone Coast, and for that I am grateful. It is an inspiring, beautiful area and every moment there has been a joy.

I'm grateful as always to Bev Cousins at Penguin Random House Australia for her support, expertise and encouragement. Kalhari Jayaweera has been with me since the start of Mark Ariti, and I thank her for her insightful editorial advice. Many thanks to Amanda Martin, Tanaya Lowden, Veronica Eze and Hannah Ludbrook for their combined efforts in helping to get this book into the world.

A big thank you too, to Archie Bee for his crucial input, and to Jo Canham for being such a champion of Australian writers.

There have been a number of tragic cave diving deaths in Australian sinkholes. I acknowledge the bravery of the retrieval divers involved, and the terrible toll these deaths must have taken on loved ones.

Finally, thank you as always to Bernie, aka Disco.

AUTHOR'S NOTE

This book was written on the lands of the Waywurru and Dhudhuroa peoples, whom I would like to acknowledge as the Traditional Custodians and Storytellers of their country. I pay my respects to their Elders past and present, and celebrate all the histories, traditions and living cultures of Aboriginal and Torres Strait Islander people.

Margaret Hickey is an award-winning author and playwright from North East Victoria. She has a PhD in Creative Writing and is deeply interested in rural lives and communities. She is also the author of *Cutters End* and *Stone Town*. *Cutters End* won the BAD Sydney Danger Prize and was shortlisted for the Ned Kelly Award for Best Debut.

Discover a
new favourite